THE DOM WITH A SAF[illegible]ORD

CW01590006

SORCHA BLACK, [illegible] [illegible]OOD,
LEIA SHAW

2ND EDITION

COPYRIGHT 2012, 2013

WC PRESS

All Rights Reserved. No part of this book may be reproduced in any except for the inclusion of brief quotations in review without written consent from the author.

To our husbands, who inspire us every day

Chapter 1

Sabrina

"This block is a hot bed of activity!" Sabrina declared. She sounded like a kid in a toy store even to her own ears. Q's eyes must be rolling out of her head. "It's gotta be one of these old houses. There's so much history here."

The pin on the EMF detector bounced from point three to point six every time she pointed due north. The mansion stood out from the other houses even without her equipment going berserk. At least one story higher than its neighbors, with old cracked windows and ivy crawling up the front roman style columns, it practically screamed *Haunted: enter at your own risk.*

Oh, she would enter all right. This could be the breakthrough she'd been waiting for. And it looked completely abandoned – unkempt and not a single light on inside or outside of the house.

She crept closer, ignoring the shudder that rocked her. Now was not the time to chicken out.

A song voice started humming the *Ghostbusters* theme song behind her.

"Shh!" Sabrina scolded, laughing. "For the millionth time, I'm not a ghostbuster!"

"Ghostbuster, ghost hunter…" Q drawled, pressing the button on the Trifield Meter hooked to Sabrina's belt. "Same thing."

She batted Q's hand away. "I'm a paranormal investigator." With an air of pride, she took out the badge she'd just received in the mail. It came with her online certification in investigating spectral disruptions to the real-world plane.

Q leaned in to take a closer look then arched a brow. "Where did you get that? Cheesy Gimmicks 'R Us?"

Sabrina scowled at her best friend. She was so getting revenge next time they went to a heavy metal concert. Maybe she'd buy the purple punk tutu she'd seen on the fetish store website Q had left open the other day. Her other one was black.

Q nudged her, jarring her from her diabolical thoughts. "Keep going. It's getting late and super creepy out here." She shivered and rubbed her arms.

Sabrina smirked. "Scared? Thought you didn't believe in ghosts."

"I don't. But I do believe in serial killers and rapists. And maybe zombies." She gave her a little shove forward. "Hurry up."

Sabrina pointed to the mansion, one house away. "It's leading us there."

To her amusement, Q stiffened then sighed. "Of course it is. It couldn't take us to a cute, friendly-looking cottage, could it?"

Sabrina summoned a saucy smile. "Don't worry Q. Lucky for you, Cheesy Gimmicks 'R Us sells zombie repellent." She held up a bottle of pepper spray.

"Smart ass."

She chuckled then turned toward the house and crept along, grateful for the frequent streetlights. The house grew more ominous the closer they got. When they stood, staring up at it, mouths wide open, even Sabrina wondered if this was a bad idea.

"This is a bad idea," Q whispered beside her.

She shook off the momentary lapse in courage. "Don't be silly. Supernatural spirits can't hurt us."

"You say that, but that's not how it works in the movies."

Ignoring her friend, she studied the fence surrounding the property. About ten feet high and black iron, it appeared to run the length of the yard. She pushed on the gate door in front of them. Locked.

She stared up at spikes lining the top of the gate and sighed, pushing back her trepidation. "We'll have to climb it." Careful not to jar anything, she began removing her equipment, setting each device carefully on the ground.

"What? You're insane!"

Possibly. "We'll be fine. Just mind the spikes." She placed one foot on the bottom rung and wrapped her hands around the bars.

Q stopped her with a hand on her arm. "Wait. There's got to be another way."

"There's not. The fence runs the whole property. That's how rich people protect their stupid stuff." Sabrina pulled herself up one step.

"Wait!" Q tugged her back down. "Let me look before you go on this suicide mission." Then she gave Sabrina that stubborn look she knew all too well. "Wait. Right here. No climbing."

Sabrina knew not to argue with her when she got like this. She rolled her eyes. "Alright. But hurry up. We don't want the cops to come this time."

Q disappeared into the dark and Sabrina resumed her climb. Q would tackle her to the ground before she'd let her do something dangerous. And she just had to get over this fence. Overprotective friend. She'd never known anybody who cared so deeply for her. They weren't a couple, but something more than friends. It was strange, she admitted when she thought about it too closely. So she didn't. We are what we are, she told herself countless times.

Sabrina made it to the top of one side then froze while she analyzed the iron spikes. If she could get one leg between the two spikes then she could straddle the fence without impaling her girly bits. She grimaced at the visual.

"What the fuck are you doing?" Q said from below.

"Shh! I'm trying to concentrate!" Her muscles ached from holding herself in the awkward position.

"Don't fall!"

She rolled her eyes. "Yes, thank you. Whatever would I do without your genius advi-ahhh!" The foot holding most of her body weight slipped and she tumbled to the ground.

She landed mostly on her ass, but it knocked the wind out of her.

"Are you alright?" Q asked frantically, helping her up.

Miffed at the setback, Sabrina grumbled. "I'm fine." A little soreness where she'd landed but it could've been worse.

Q sighed and turned her around, looking her over. "There's dirt all over you. I told you this was a bad idea," she scolded, brushing the dirt off her back and ass – a little too roughly. "What did you think was going to happen?"

"Ow! Not so hard!"

Q held her still with hands on her upper arms. "I found a broken rung. We can squeeze through. But if we do this, you have to promise, nothing else dangerous."

"Dangerous?" She smirked. "What could be dangerous about ghost hunting?"

Q gave her an exasperated look then released her. "Smartass."

"You already said that." Sabrina collected her equipment off the ground.

"You go through life in a perpetual state of smartassery."

Sabrina handed Q her photography gear, thankful her friend had experience and was willing, for the most part, to help her. "Only for you, sexy." She winked.

Grinning, Q shook her head. "What have I told you about flirting with bi chicks? One of these days you'll get more than you bargained for."

"I'm willing to chance it. Now show me where this broken rung is."

They slid through the gate with very little trouble, both being on the slender side. The half moon didn't provide much light and having moved away from the comfort of the street lights, Sabrina couldn't stop the rapid pitter patter of her heart. She grabbed the flashlight from one of the pockets on her cargo pants then shone it around them.

The ground was covered in dead, overgrown grass. A dilapidated shed sat behind and to the left of the house. Several garbage cans blocked the shed door and the quiet beeps of the equipment pointed straight toward it. A dark entrance in the creepiest part of the creepiest yard of the creepiest house. This was shaping up to be a great beginning for a horror movie. Was she the character who survives or the screamer who dies first?

The air temperature gauge, attached by Velcro around her upper arm, lit up bright red. She froze and Q bumped into her back.

"What the –"

"Shh!" Sabrina ripped off the meter and studied it. "There's something by the shed. Behind the garbage cans."

"Something?" she squeaked. "Fuck."

Something that scanned the body temperature of a person. But that couldn't be right. Ghosts didn't register the same temperature as humans. "Stay here if you want. I'm going closer."

Q grabbed her shirt sleeve. "I'm not letting you go alone."

They walked, slowly, Q holding onto Sabrina's shirt sleeve, toward the cluster of cans.

"Your weird beeping shit is going crazy," Q whispered.

"I know. I've never had this much activity before." Ever. And it scared the hell out of her. Almost as much as it thrilled her. Maybe if she had proof she could detect something otherworldly, she could actually charge people money to do this.

A few more feet to the garbage cans. Closer. Closer...

A dark figure leapt toward them from behind the cans and growled.

Sabrina's heart jumped to her throat and she screamed. Q's fingernails dug into her arm and she screamed too.

A human male chuckle rose up over their screams. She stopped. Human? She looked toward the tall figure but couldn't make out any details. Where was her flashlight? She must've dropped it in the chaos. She reached down, her fingers scrabbling frantically until she found it. Cold dancing up her spine, hands shaking, she clicked on the light then swung it in the direction of the laugh.

"Whoa!" a deep voice rumbled. "Get that out of my eyes."

A man. Young. Handsome – trim blond hair and high cheek bones. But now was not the time to remark on such things. The shit had scared the hell out of them. Her heart was still thudding like a stampede in her throat.

"Calm down," he said, gentler, shielding his eyes with his hands. "Put the light down."

Calm down? In a fit of anger, she chucked the flashlight at his head. "What the hell is wrong with you?" she yelled. A second later she was aghast at her move. She'd just assaulted a stranger?

He'd caught the flashlight – thank god – then he turned toward the shed and picked his way through the debris on the ground toward the door.

"Hey!" Sabrina called after him. "That's my flashlight!" He ignored her and she spun on Q. "What is he doing?"

"You shouldn't have thrown it at him. And *we're* the ones trespassing. Just apologize and let's get out of here."

A light above the shed flickered then turned on, illuminating the area where they stood. Heavy steps came from the side of the shed. The man who came out of the darkness wore a wife beater, a frown, and a set of biceps she could sink her teeth into.

He held out her flashlight.

She grabbed it rudely.

"Thank you," he said, ignoring her glare. "That was very helpful. Now, what are you doing sneaking around on my property?"

"We're very sorry," Q said. "We had no idea –"

"*Your* property?" Sabrina eyed him up and down. He didn't seem the type to own a run-down mansion. "How could anybody live here? There aren't even any lights on."

"I'm renting it for the summer and a fuse blew." He returned her stare. "Not that I need to explain anything to you. Just because it appears that nobody lives somewhere doesn't mean you can do what you want to the place."

"We weren't going to *do* anything to it –"

"We're sorry," Q jumped in. "We didn't mean any harm. Sabrina, apologize to the nice man so we can be on our way."

"Sabrina," he said evenly. "A pretty name. For a criminal."

"So sweet." She rolled her eyes. "And you are…"

"Still wondering what you're doing in my yard."

Maybe if she explained, he'd let her continue the investigation. She did have a way of convincing people to do what she wanted.

"I detected signs of paranormal activity. It happens frequently with these old houses. I just know there's something here. All I need is a few hours. This house is probably rich with history –"

"Oh, I know all about the history of this house," he said.

Her chest tightened with excitement and she took an involuntary step closer. "You do?"

He nodded.

"Then you'll let me come back and do a full invest –"

"No."

She stepped back, puzzled. "Why not?"

"Because I'm not interested." He crossed his arms and stared down at her, mimicking Q's stubborn expression.

"But…it won't take long." She gave him her best smile – the one that always worked on her father. "I won't even charge you."

His brows shot up. "Oh, you won't charge me? That changes everything."

"It does?"

"No." His voice grew stern. "Now go home before you get yourselves shot by someone who thinks you're a burglar."

Asshole! Sabrina had never been known for her mild temper. "It won't hurt you any, why are you being such a d – ow!" Something had pinched her ass. Q?

"I apologize for my friend," Q said with a sincere smile. "She's just very…"

"Persistent?"

"Passionate. About ghost hunting."

"Paranormal investigating!" Sabrina corrected.

"Not now, Sabrina," Q gritted between her teeth. "Sorry for any inconvenience. We'll be going now." She grabbed Sabrina's arm and tugged her through the yard, back the way they'd come.

Sabrina followed, reluctantly. Disappointment filled her and her shoulders sagged.

"Wait," he said.

They turned.

He rubbed his face and mumbled, "I can't believe I'm doing this. Do you have a card, little Miss Ghostbuster?"

Sabrina grinned. "Of course!" As a graphic artist, the first thing she'd made after becoming a paranormal investigator was a business card.

She yanked out of Q's grip, walked back to the stranger, and handed him the card with her name and phone number.

One brow arched as he looked it over. "Sabrina Romano. Paranormal detective, otherworld investigator, and spirit guide."

His gaze went to Q as if in question. She shrugged.

"What's your name?" he asked, gesturing to Q.

"Q."

"Just Q?"

"Yup."

Sabrina snorted. No way was this guy getting her real name from those tight lips. As far as she knew, she and Q's brothers were the only people alive who knew her real name. And Sabrina had been sworn to secrecy.

"Are you going to tell us your name?" Q asked.

He looked back and forth between them then gave a short laugh. "After being given a whole first letter? Sure. It's Jude."

Jude? He looked like a Jude. If it weren't for the wife beater and dirty jeans, he'd reek of money. Sabrina sidled closer with a wicked grin and batted her lashes. Then she broke out into one of her favorite Beatles songs, hoping he loved the song that shared his name as much as she did.

He rolled his eyes as she sang *Hey, Jude*. His lips twitched and he flicked his gaze to Q. "Is she always like this?"

"Pretty much." She took Sabrina's hand and squeezed it. "Come on, Lennon. Let's not torture the poor guy any longer."

Jude gestured to the front of the house. "I'll let you out the front. There's no need to slide through those broken rungs again."

They followed Jude to the front of the house. With a jiggle and a kick, he unlocked the front gate. Now why hadn't she thought of that?

"Here," he said, stooping to retrieve something on the ground. "You dropped your..."

Sabrina looked down at his outstretched hand as he fumbled for the right word. "EMF detector," she answered for him.

He nodded as she took it from his hand. "Right."

She had to admit, he was kinda cute. His lips were full and perfectly kissable. He smelled nice too – not cologne, just clean but still masculine. It had been a long time since she'd gotten any action. Except for that ass pinch. She glared at Q as they headed toward the street.

"Did you pinch my ass?" she whispered.

Q gave her a mysterious smirk. "You deserved it."

Chapter 2

Q

Q could feel Sabrina's gaze on her from across the living room. "What?" she growled.

Sabrina sidled up to her. With her hand on the back of Q's chair, she looked at the computer screen. "What's with the face?"

The casual pose Sabrina struck showed she had no idea of the clamor she'd created in Q's head. She deliberately did not lick the sensitive skin on the inside of Sabrina's elbow. Yet…it was right there.

"My ex, Nico. He just told me he can't make it to the Slipknot concert tonight. He's dropping his ticket off at lunch."

With a grimace, Sabrina grabbed Q's hands and tried to pull her toward the couch. She resisted. They had dubbed it The Couch of Sloth, because it sucked in victims and made them watch black-and-white movies until the wee hours of the morning. She had things to get done today.

"Why would you want to go to a concert with your ex, anyway? It's weird. And he was a total jerk to you."

Q grunted then pulled away and minimized the screen so Sabrina wouldn't see his newest request for a date. She couldn't decide if she could handle the roller coaster that was Nico, again. "He's not that bad. It was better than going alone."

"What? I'll go! I love concerts."

Could she be any more fucking adorable? Q could just eat her. She'd once thought Sabrina an airhead, but now she knew a lot of intelligence lurked behind her general enthusiasm for life. "You hate Slipknot, Sabrina. You're going to sit around bored and insist we leave early. You're also going to dress all cute. You can't dress like that," Q gestured to her current green sundress, "to go to one of my concerts. I saw what you were looking at on that fetish website the other day. A tutu? What are you, five?" she teased. It was a running joke between them. Granted, the tutu would have looked sweet on her – it just wasn't acceptable for a Slipknot concert.

Sabrina glared at her indignantly. "It was a *punk* tutu!"

"There's no such thing, girly. And there's no way you're coming unless I get to dress you. Why do you want to come anyway?"

"To check out the hot rocker guys with the long hair."

"Rocker guys? Seriously? You can't *still* use terms from the eighties. We were born in the eighties!" Q shut the lid to her laptop. "How did you manage to stay so innocent all these years, anyway? You're almost twenty-seven for fucksakes."

Sabrina grinned and started to dance, singing some song she didn't recognize. She was always doing that – like her life was a Broadway musical. Though Q was honored to get to play a bit part in it, even if that's all she ever was to Sabrina. The light that shone from Sabrina was dazzling, and sometimes she felt like an ugly moth that couldn't bear to be away from it.

Q rolled her eyes. "I should go alone."

Sabrina ended her solo number and frowned. "You can't go to a concert alone. That's creepy, even for you."

"I'm nothing if not creepy. Or so you always tell me. I don't want to take you to see Slipknot if you're going to act and dress like a doofus."

"I won't sing if I don't know the words and you can help me pick something to wear. But it has to be cute. I don't want to look like you."

"Oh? And how do I look?"

Taking a step back, Sabrina examined her, gesturing for her to turn. Q just crossed her arms and raised her brows. Sabrina huffed. "Like a scary, dyke, mentally-unbalanced goth chick who needs a makeover."

A laugh burst from Q's mouth. Sabrina was nothing if not blunt. "I'm not goth. But it's nice to feel the overwhelming love you have for me." Q stood and stretched, her back popping satisfactorily. It was a constant battle between them – Sabrina trying to make her over, while she steadfastly refused.

That description had been the best yet. There was still no damned way Sabrina was getting her into a dress. She had detested them since she was little – always getting in the way and needing to be careful you didn't flash people. So much trouble. Nico had insisted she wear dresses when they were dating – he'd said if he wanted to date a guy, he would have.

Sabrina slid her arms around Q's waist. "You know I love you, sexy. You're my best friend."

It was impossible for her not to hug Sabrina, even though having her close was such a temptation. *Leave it to me to fall in love with a straight girl.*

Q leaned her temple against her forehead. She wasn't a tall woman at five foot four, and Sabrina was only a couple inches shorter, but somehow she felt like an Amazon beside her. "If you want to go, I get to pick out your clothes. No negotiations. I have no problem going alone." It was a lie, but she'd rather go alone than go with Sabrina looking like she'd just come from an art gallery.

Sabrina smelled like bubblegum again. It always made Q want to lick her.

"Okay, okay," the smaller girl conceded. "But I want a skirt. And cute shoes."

***

The shop Q dragged Sabrina into was a sea of black with hints of red and lime green. The prospect of picking out clothes for the girl was an interesting one. Pulse racing, she thought of being alone in the changing room with her, helping her dress, running her hands over her smooth, tanned skin. She rolled her eyes. Sabrina had given her imagination a lot to play with today.

In the midst of the evil-looking displays, Sabrina resembled a virgin sacrifice. The little white sundress and shiny pink lip gloss marked her as prey. She had even tied her shoulder-length blonde hair back with a big white ribbon. It was Sabrina's idea of a joke, dressing like this to go to some of the edgier stores in town and it was keeping Q in a constant state of distraction. Visions of Sabrina bound and helpless flashed like an old film in her head.

Q avoided looking at her. Mouth-watering yet unavailable. The sexual tension tortured her. From the twinkle in her eye, Q could see this was the reaction Sabrina was hoping for.

She was so damned confusing. Sabrina swore she was straight, but she was such a tease. She obviously liked Q's attention, but rejected her on an intellectual level. However, physically she was starting to give Q mixed messages. It gave her reason to hope.

At that very moment, Sabrina was leaning over a glass jewelry display, the hem of her little sundress barely covering the bottom of her ass. Q caught a flash of the stylized purple butterfly tattoo Sabrina had gotten on her ankle a couple of years before. They'd gotten their tattoos at the same time though Q's covered almost the whole side of her torso.

Sabrina sent her a sassy smile over her shoulder and turned back to shopping.

The thickly-muscled, tattooed store owner cast an admiring glance over Sabrina's shapely legs and nodded at Q, giving her the thumbs-up. "Yours, Q?"

"I wish, Cross," she muttered back.

They browsed the racks fast, since they were short on time. Several armfuls of clothes later, Cross showed them to a big fitting room at the back. He threw Q a wolfish grin. "Don't make a mess in there."

Q rolled her eyes and ushered Sabrina in, dumping a pile of dark clothing onto the bench. She stepped back and tried to close the door, but Sabrina caught it before it swung shut.

"Come in and help me. I'm going to need you for the buckles and things. You know how to put them on right." She toyed with a lock of her hair, like she did when she was nervous. What was she up to?

Her grip on the door tightened, making the edge dig into her hand. "I don't think that's a good idea." All the images she'd ever had of Sabrina naked slipped back into her mind. She tugged at her bottom lip with her teeth.

"Oh please! You're not going to try to have your way with me in a dressing room, are you?" she asked with a flirty smile and naughty gleam in her eye. Sabrina knew damn well Q would love to do just that.

Heaving a sigh, Q walked in and shut the door behind her. She was making a big mistake. As she chanted in her head that she could control herself, she locked the door. Sabrina shucked off her dress, and Q averted her eyes. At times like this she wished Sabrina was a little shyer.

"What do you think?" she asked after a few moments.

Q looked up and swallowed hard. Sabrina was standing in front of her in a white lace bra and panty set. The wispy fabric left little to the imagination.

"I just got them yesterday. Are they cute?" She turned to show Q that the underwear were of the thong persuasion. The curve of her perfect ass beckoned.

Q balled her fists at her sides. There was no way even Sabrina was this naïve. What was she playing at? The feeling of her clit throbbing hard against the seam of her jeans made her lightheaded. "Very... uh... pretty," she gasped.

Sabrina smiled seductively. "Pretty? Is that all you have to say?"

With every second, her control was slipping away. "Put some clothes on before I make you regret it, little girl," she growled. Maybe spanking her ass – or biting it – would teach her to behave.

"Little girl? I'm older than you are."

"By six months. You're also lighter and shorter than I am. I could do all sorts of naughty things to you and you wouldn't be able to stop me."

"I dare you try."

This close, she could see Sabrina's breathing deepen and the faintest tremble take hold of her.

Q took two steps and glared down at her. "I don't take dares." Their gaze locked and there was a silent battle of wills. The pupils of Sabrina's eyes dilated and she blinked. Slowly, Q lowered her lips until they hovered just barely above hers. The other girl shifted her gaze to her mouth. Q brushed her lips softly against Sabrina's, then drew back.

Sabrina made a little mewling sound, frowned, then gave herself a shake. She turned fast and grabbed the topmost skirt and slipped it on as though nothing had happened. The rapid rise and fall of her chest suggested she wasn't as unaffected as she was trying to act. The matching purple PVC shirt she'd picked buckled up the front, and Sabrina fumbled with it for a few minutes before conceding defeat.

"Can you help?" she asked in a small voice.

Q sat in the pile of clothing on the bench and waved her over. Could a person faint from lust? Sabrina stopped in front of her, reddening. By the time Q got to the third buckle up, the soft swell of Sabrina's breasts became impossible to ignore. She brushed her fingers lightly over the tops of them. Her breath caught in her throat. The nerves in Q's fingertips felt like they were sizzling with electricity.

Sabrina's eyes closed and she thrust her chest out in a silent plea for more.

"You don't act like a straight girl."

"You don't make me feel like one," she breathed, looking down at Q.

"Unhook your bra."

"What?"

"Do it," Q commanded. She was often shocked at how easily she could get Sabrina to obey her. This was pushing things. Would she do it?

"Uh..."

"You can't wear a bra with this shirt. This one's got a hole in the back and the strap will show."

"Oh!" Sabrina gave a nervous giggle and turned away, unclasping it and slipping it off through the armholes. She tried to yank the edges of the top together to cover herself before turning back. By holding it in place, she just barely concealed her nipples. "I think it's too small."

"No, it's fine. It just needs to be tied. Let go."

"But..."

"Now, little girl."

Sabrina's fingers slowly let go and the sides of the shirt slid aside of their own accord. The shirt didn't cover anything important anymore, but held her breasts up like a bustier. She brought her hands up and covered her nipples. "Just buckle it already!"

"No. I want to look at you first. Drop your hands." If Sabrina did this, there was no more wondering about where things stood between them. Q waited, holding her breath and shifting to ease the seam of her jeans away from her clit.

Sabrina whined and flushed terribly red, but she obeyed.

Oh fuck. Q leaned back against the wall and let her gaze slide over her friend, from her conflicted eyes to her parted lips, and down to the luscious curves of her breasts. Her pretty pink nipples were hard and Q fought not to touch. Yet.

"Are you done now? Help me get this buckled. What do you want to look at me for, anyway? You ogle perfect models all day." Sabrina's words came out in a rush, like they were falling over themselves to leave her mouth.

"You're perfect. And as for the models, if I was into plastic, I'd buy myself a Barbie."

She grumbled and her brow creased. "Well just take a damn picture already. It'll last longer."

"I'd love to take pictures of you. Are you volunteering?" Q felt a little guilty for pushing her – Sabrina did think of herself as straight. This was a big step.

"Can we discuss this some other time? I need to find something for tonight so we can go home and get ready." And yet, despite her protests she didn't move.

Interesting.

"Can I touch you, Sabrina?"

A fresh flood of color rushed to her face, but after a pause she nodded, looking at her toes. She bit her pretty bottom lip endearingly.

Q squirmed in her seat, trying not to let on that her control was evaporating. *God, she makes me so crazy.*

The first touch of Sabrina's skin was like silk and she barely held back a groan. Part of her brain clamored for her to stop, but she couldn't will herself to do so. Possessed by her inner hedonist, her hands slid up to cup Sabrina's breasts. She rubbed her thumbs gently over her nipples.

The hiss of Sabrina's breath spurred Q on, and the girl thrust forward into her caress. "Please, Q! You're killing me."

"Shh! Cross is going to hear you. He'd probably come watch. And such a pretty show he'd get. It's a shame not to share it." She rolled both nipples between thumb and fingers.

"No, Q," she whimpered quietly.

"Do you want me to stop?"

"No! Just don't call your friend in here. I'd die."

"Okay then…quiet." Q leaned forward, the light scent of bubblegum on Sabrina's warm skin making her want more. Even the smell of her was intoxicating.

Her gaze met Sabrina's as she swept her tongue over the point of her nipple. It tightened, and Q kissed it lightly before sucking it into her mouth. She pressed Sabrina closer with a hand on her lower back, her other hand brushing from just behind her knee, upwards under the PVC schoolgirl skirt. As she sucked, flicking her tongue, Sabrina's little moans of pleasure encouraged her. Q traced her fingers under the skirt, along the globe of Sabrina's ass then drew them toward the front of her panties.

A loud knock made them both jump. "Yes?" Q managed to say, hoping she didn't sound too breathless.

"You two are taking awhile in there. You need a hand?" The bastard was laughing.

Q grinned up at Sabrina who still looked dazed. "Do we need help?"

Sabrina's eyes focused and she shook her head emphatically.

"No, Cross. We'll be out in a couple of minutes." Internally, she swore a blue streak. The interruption was welcome, in a way. She didn't know if she would have been able to stop without intervention, and Sabrina deserved better than to be with her first girl in a changing room. They were too old for that shit.

"Suit yourself, Q. If you change your mind just holler."

Sabrina covered her face with her hands. "Let's just take this and go. Can I wait for you in the car? Take my bank card."

"It looks like it will fit and it's hot on you. You okay?" Q stood, drawing her friend into her arms. Sabrina clung to her, which pleased her immensely. She kissed her forehead. "Don't worry about it. I'll go to the cashier. Here are my keys. I'll be there in a minute."

Sabrina changed back into her little white dress so fast Q didn't get a good look at anything. She bolted out of the fitting room for the car.

As she paid, Q wondered if Sabrina would ever let her touch her again, and hoped to hell she hadn't just fucked everything up.

Chapter 3

Jude

Jude leaned back in his chair. Fifth row back from the front row of the seats, with the mosh pit swarming in front of him – almost the best place at a Slipknot concert. He'd not dared the mosh pit itself. His father's words ran through his head whenever he considered it.

Think ahead, Jude. Keep your head on your shoulders, think ahead, and stay safe.

Well. Done that. Thought ahead. A surgeon didn't need broken fingers from some overweight wrecking ball bouncing off him in the pit. Though… He heaved out a sigh. This would be his last heavy metal concert.

He scrubbed his hands through his hair, feeling the short strands curling over his fingers. His surfer cut had gone too. He hadn't worn his guitar-playing Fuck-the-Empire Stormtrooper t-shirt in case somebody here decided that made him a pussy. In the future, that and the Dethklok shirt he'd bought in Germany would only see the light if he was mowing the lawn of his picket-fenced mansion.

What about his kink life? Would he have to give that up too? That was one thing he didn't think he could live without. A quarter of the kinksters at the local BDSM club seemed to be professionals, so maybe not. Tying up women, dominating them – since his early college days, he'd delved further and further into that fascinating world. Though he'd never checked out the BDSM community in Michigan, maybe it would be the same?

He looked down. Plain black buttoned shirt. Boring. Stable. Black and boring like his future. Years of pre-med, then diversion in Europe for a few years to "get his head straight" but now he was cornered. Even since he was a kid, his father had expected him to be a doctor. Planned it, labeled him, squashed him into a mold.

The music pulsed to life, ramming straight into his skull and clearing away all his good, doctor-like thoughts. The crowd screamed. The mosh pit surged inward.

"Fuck." He stood up, feeling the sheer energy from swearing course through him like a storm tide sweeping a beach clean.

Playing it safe and thinking ahead could wait another day. He edged along to the aisle and jogged down. The strobing lights flashed on something purple ahead of him. A woman? At least she was staying on the edge. Up on the tiptoes of her black boots, she strived to see past a shaggy-haired teenager. She jiggled about, teetering. Her curves invited appraisal, especially where the pert mounds of her ass showed beneath her short skirt, and he admired them as he walked closer. There must be a boyfriend, here, moshing.

Tendrils of her hair curled down to the neckline of the little purple outfit – the back of which was wide open and displayed a delicious amount of skin. The PVC schoolgirl skirt drew his eye to her beautiful legs. Fetish wear – he'd bet his life on it. As he drew closer, aiming to squeeze between her and a six-foot bruiser of a guy, her profile stopped him dead.

He knew that face. The right shade of blond hair too. The name snapped into place in his mind – Sabrina – the smart-mouthed crazy one who liked ghost hunting. How could he ever forget the two sexy girls who'd invaded his yard a few nights ago?

Fetish wear, though? His mind wandered down that kinky path for a second. But…so what? Some wore it just for fun. Didn't mean she liked getting tied up and dominated. Unfortunately.

Despite the drowning volume of the heavy music, he heard her scream.

"Q!"

Jude put a hand on her shoulder and saw instantly why she'd screamed. Her friend was down on the floor, arms flopped to the side. A circle of men had formed around her, stopping her from being trampled by others. By the time he got past the big guy, another had dragged her to her feet and propelled her toward him and the screaming, waving Sabrina.

Somehow he ended up taking one arm and supporting Q across the back while Sabrina helped on the other side. Together they made it outside past security on the doors. The sound muted as the doors shut behind them.

"Thanks," Sabrina panted then she cut short and scanned up and down Jude's face. "Hey. It's you!"

"Who?" Q turned to look, trying to wriggle loose from his arm. She seemed steady so reluctantly he let her go and stepped away. "Oh. I know you." She frowned, clearly trying to think of his name.

He brushed some of her raven black hair from her forehead and couldn't help noticing the cool flow of it across his fingers. A scratch on her forehead trickled blood down to her cheekbone. But her pretty eyes were focused. Her stance was solid. She blinked at him.

"You don't seem to have concussion." Jude lowered his hand, let a bit of the tension ebb away.

More security was approaching as if to check they were okay. The guard raised both eyebrows and spoke into his shoulder mic. When Jude shook his head, he backed off.

He turned back to the girls. "Yeah. It's me. You trespassed in my yard, remember? You two seem to like trouble. Come on, ghost hunters. Let's sit down."

Sabrina peered up at her friend while patting her shoulder. "Hmm. She's never this quiet. I agree. You should sit down."

"Look. I'm okay. Someone tripped me and I landed badly. I'm okay." Q put out her arms as if to push them away. "*Both* of you. I'm okay. Let's go back in, Sabrina."

"No."

The set tone and stern, if pouting, look from Sabrina seemed to startle Q but she recovered and said indignantly, "Excuse me, miss? I'm not your little –"

He took her arm again. "You've got blood on your elbow too. You should at least get cleaned up." These two had some interesting dynamic going. But now wasn't the time for figuring it out.

Sabrina smiled and mouthed, thank you, at him.

A few yards away, was the broad row of concrete steps leading down toward the parking lot. He pointed. "Over there."

Q shut her eyes. "Fine. Let's hurry up and get this over with."

The steps were cold even through his jeans but the floodlight above let Jude methodically go over Q to check for wounds. Elbow and forehead grazes were all he could find – the elbow one hard to find under her full-sleeve tattoo. Cybernetic enhancements inked in dark colors extended from the back of her hand up her arm and into her shirtsleeve. He rotated the hand he held to double-check her palm. "Nice tat. Your cyborg parts probably saved you from any real harm. Though," he looked into Q's eyes, "you might have injuries, bruising, elsewhere. Under your clothes."

"Well." Q pulled her slender hand away. A tingle ran across his fingers as her skin slipped over his. She straightened and seemed to gather her dignity. Her breasts jutted out. "Thanks for your… help, but you're not looking under my clothes."

"I never…" He couldn't help smiling. "I wasn't saying I would, Q."

"Idiot." Sabrina muttered. She leaned across Q. "Jude, you sure she's not concussed?"

Her sudden yelp and jump and Q's smug expression said it all. She'd been pinched.

Definitely an interesting relationship.

"Ladies…" He stood and dusted the back of his jeans with his hands. The girls rose to their feet. "I just had a thought. There should be a first aid room. How about we find it and clean off the blood. If you two want to go back in after that, okay, but no more mosh pit."

"Hey. Stop right there." Q set her mouth in a line. "If I want to go back, I will."

"Not if I tell security I think you have a concussion. By the time they figure that out, most of the concert will be over."

Or he prayed it would. He sure wasn't letting her go do that again. A mosh pit was no place for a beautiful woman…women. The two of them were enough to tempt him. They both stared back at him as if he'd sprouted horns. Glossy kissable mouths, and these women looked so good as a pair that he could just see them on their knees before him. He shook his head. Damn, if his dick wasn't thinking of rising to the occasion.

Q stirred. Her forehead creased. "You can't –"

"Can." His Dom side was coming out, but hell, he was going to let it. "I don't actually know for sure you aren't concussed. You were looking stunned there for a while." He inhaled, held it. The thought he'd just had was so good. Would they? "Tell you what. I'll let you come and check my house for ghosts, if you promise to stay out of the mosh pit. Deal?"

"Yes!" Sabrina's eyes lit up and she let out a squeal. "Deal."

Her grin made him grin back. "Good."

Q shook her head. "A Slipknot concert and we're out here arguing over ghosts." She sighed and smiled ruefully down at Sabrina. "Fine. For you."

"Thank you." Sabrina went up on her toes and kissed Q's cheek.

The softening of Q's expression gave Jude pause. So cute.

Maybe they were bi, but that didn't rule a man out. He could still hope. He let one side of his mouth twist up. Yep. He was sure doing that. If only his hopes weren't so kinky, and didn't involve rope and spankings, and the two of them begging permission from him to orgasm, he might have had a chance. As it stood, a snowball in Hell had a better chance.

Chapter 4

Sabrina

"Looks so much friendlier in the daylight, doesn't it?" Sabrina said, staring up at the decrepit mansion. Maybe the house was run-down but it had a certain charm – when the afternoon sun was bright and her equipment wasn't going off.

She looked at Q standing beside her. Her relaxed shoulders said she was at ease too. "Why can't we ghost hunt during the day again?" Q asked.

"Spirits are more active at night." So said her many books on the subject. "Three AM is the witching hour."

Q snorted. "Figures."

This meant, of course, they'd find nothing this afternoon. Her equipment bag felt more like a bowling bag. Why did she even bother to bring it? She sighed. "Talk a lot, Q, so he'll let us stay 'til dark."

She turned-on her with a shocked expression. "Me?"

"Yes. Go on about that crap you call music." She tried to hold back a smirk. Teasing Q about her taste in music and fashion was one of her favorite hobbies.

Q chuckled. "Brat."

They walked up the front porch stairs, stepping over a broken one, just as the door opened. Jude's built body took up the whole entryway. Had he always been that big? A bit daunting, but he was safe. She knew that on an instinctual level. She'd always been a good judge of character. Plus, he'd shown them the utmost respect and care at the concert last weekend.

"Hello again," he said from the doorway then held his hand out, motioning to Sabrina's bag.

"Um…" She looked down at his hand, her grip tightening on the handles.

"I'm just offering to carry it for you." He smiled a little. "The house is big and that looks heavy."

If she couldn't trust him to carry a bag… She handed it off. "Thanks."

"Q." He nodded to her. "How's your head?"

She tossed him a sly look. "I've never had any complaints."

Jude's eyes widened then he barked a laugh.

Sabrina rolled her eyes and mumbled, "Gross." Call her a germophobe but she didn't share her roommate's passion for giving head. Or sex in general. "Who doesn't like sex?" Q would say anytime the subject came up. Her, for one. At least not the few times she'd tried it.

Jude's masculine chuckle filled the front foyer as they stepped in.

"Someone who shares her adolescent sense of humor," Sabrina grumbled to herself. "Fantastic."

"It was funny," he said, his gaze glued to Q, a smile touching his lips. "A sense of humor is a great asset."

Q grinned stupidly. "Um, I don't think I said thank you. For the other night. It was kind of you to –"

"It was nothing," he cut in. "Just trying to be the gentleman my mother taught me to be." He winked.

Sabrina watched them. Was Q blushing? Oh, this was going to be good. After that last asshat of a boyfriend, Q needed someone sweet – someone who would treat her right. Even more importantly, she needed action. In the last six months they'd lived together, a pattern had emerged. When Q got needy, she also got a little handsy – not that Sabrina ever stopped her. The dressing room incident, she tried not to think about. A mistake, she chanted in her head. They had recovered. Everything had gone back to normal. Except for the enormous monster of guilt eating its way through her belly. But being Catholic – she wore guilt like a second skin.

She held back a sigh.

It wasn't fair what she was doing to Q. Her friend deserved someone with a better sense of self-identity, not some insecure, practically virginal germophobe. Someone who could love her the way a girl should be loved. Someone prettier who said the right things, who didn't put her foot in her mouth all the time. Someone...just...better.

So what was her excuse for flirting back when Q started it? Well, everybody wanted to be wanted, didn't they? Not to start a pity party but what man wanted someone like her – with her big mouth and too honest opinions?

Having been raised in a strict religious family, most of the guys she'd dated were carefully picked from the already slim selection of their Roman Catholic Church. Those little boys couldn't handle Sabrina's big personality. Sure, everybody liked a flirt in a skirt. Not everybody liked what came out of her mouth. "One woman shouldn't have so many opinions," her mother often said. Ironic because she was the most opinionated person Sabrina had ever known.

Q liked her short skirts, maybe too much, and she didn't mind her brash personality either. Q could handle her – laughed at her even. She always did attract the weirdoes. A smile tugged at her lips when she pictured telling Q she thought she was weird. She'd laugh and say, "You're surprised by this?"

She did love Q. As a close friend loves another friend. Didn't she? How the hell should she know? It wasn't like she had a whole lot of practice when it came to relationships. A whole three boyfriends. She should have figured this out in high school like normal people. But she was too busy memorizing Hail Mary's. Well where was Saint Mary now while she was stuck in freakin' sexual purgatory?

Q's booming laugh shook her from her thoughts. Jude was making her laugh already? A small fire started in her chest. *That's my job.* She gave her head a shake. No. She wouldn't be selfish with Q. Jude would be good for her.

She studied the first room they entered – a grand foyer. Or, what used to be grand. Now cracks ran the length of the walls and the beautiful picture window was stained and lined with chipped crown molding.

"Why would anyone rent a dump like this?" she said with a grimace.

"Sabrina!" Q scolded. "Be nice."

Jude raised his brows. "I only moved in a few weeks ago. Want to give me a little break, sweetheart?"

"Sorry," she murmured. She wasn't.

"She's not," Q stated bluntly.

Damn, Q knew her too well.

Jude chuckled then motioned through a set of double doors. "Come on. The living room is better."

"You said you knew the history of the house," Sabrina said, following close behind him. "I'm very interested to know. It might help with –"

A heavy metal riff sounded behind her. Q's ringtone. She yanked her phone from her back jeans pocket and looked at the number. "Shit. It's about work." Putting it up to her ear, she signaled them to keep going then stepped onto the front porch. "What do you mean you can't make it to the Johnson wedding?" Her harsh tone faded as Jude ushered Sabrina into the next room.

"Wow," she exclaimed, peering around the impressive space. Sun beamed in from the arched windows on the other side of the large room. The frames had been newly painted – she could tell from the sheen. The hardwood floors shined with polish. A TV hung on one warm brown wall. Next to it were two built-in bookshelves stacked with a few DVDs and video games, and a couple of empty beer cans. She *tsked* at Jude. "No books? For shame."

He grinned. "Just wait 'til we go upstairs."

"Is that how you lure girls to your bed?" she asked with a smirk. "Come upstairs and see my impressive book collection."

"Would it work?"

"Maybe," she answered with what she thought was a mysterious shrug.

"Noted. So what's the deal with you two?"

She looked toward the porch with a frown. "What do you me –" She stopped, realizing he'd picked up on their…complicated relationship. "Oh. Nothing. We're just friends." With what she thought was a perfectly passable expression of determination she looked him in the eye and said, "I'm straight."

He seemed to consider this then asked, "And she's…"

She eyed him a fraction of a second. Should she be saying this?

"Bi," Sabrina finished on a sigh. Why did people have to be bi anyway? They should stick to one or the other. Everyone in their box, compartmentalized neatly so they made sense and she could feel like she understood something in this fucking universe – like she understood Q. As a second thought, she rushed to add, "But she likes guys." She'd get her friend laid by this hottie if it was the last thing she did for her. "She *really* likes guys."

Ugh. She could have smacked herself. She just made her best friend sound like a slut!

"Um," she started, shaking her head. "What I mean is…" Protection for her friend overrode her embarrassment. Steeling herself, she raised her chin, stepped into him, and whispered in her best threatening voice, "Q is pretty and smart and funny, and if you hurt her, this Italian New Jersey Catholic schoolgirl will go all heels-off-drunken-chick-fight-in-a-bar on your ass."

She watched him, looking for signs of anger while maintaining the diva attitude she'd learned from her aunts.

His lips merely twitched then he took her hand, which she'd just noticed was clenched into a fist, and brought it to his lips. "You're awfully cute when you're threatening me, Jersey girl."

Her bones turned into a pile of mush when he ran his lips over her knuckles.

The porch door slammed, startling Sabrina into pulling from Jude's grip. Q walked in, eyeing them suspiciously. Shit. A chance at hooking Q up with someone decent and she'd ruined it in a moment of spineless lust. Her face heated. She'd win the worst friend of the year award, hands down.

Q put an arm around Sabrina possessively while giving Jude a glare that would scare the mafia. She should know. One of her cousins was mafia.

"What did I miss?" Her gaze stayed fastened on Jude like a soldier eyeing an unexploded bomb. Maybe Sabrina should have warned him about Q's protective streak.

"Nothing, Q," Sabrina said, returning the hug to ease her. "Jude was just going to tell me about the house."

"Let's sit down," he said, gesturing them toward the cozy, overstuffed furniture.

Q plopped down on one side of the sofa. Sabrina waited for Jude to take the seat next to her but he sat on the love seat instead, leaning back, one ankle crossed over his knee. Slightly disappointed he didn't seize the opportunity, she occupied the spot next to Q. She seemed pleased and scooted closer until their thighs touched.

"This is a big place for one man," Q said. "Or is there a wife and kids somewhere we should know about?"

"No wife or kids."

"Are you a flipper?" Sabrina asked.

His brow descended. "A what?"

"A person who buys an old house and fixes it up then sells it again. I saw it on TV. A house flipper."

"Ah" He nodded. "No. I'm renting this place for the summer. Actually the owner is letting me stay for free if I work on the interior. I happen to enjoy renovating old houses."

"Why just for the summer?" Q asked. "You have other plans after that?"

His face drooped a little. "Medical school."

"Aren't you a little old to be in school?"

"Sabrina!" Q elbowed her in the ribs.

"What?" she said, dumbfounded. It was a valid question.

Jude chuckled. "I'm twenty-eight, Jersey girl. But it's good to know I look old. Maybe I'll invest in some new skin cream."

"No," Q said, giving Sabrina a harsh look. "You don't look old at all. You look…" She trailed off, her face reddening.

"Distinguished," Sabrina finished for her.

"Distinguished?" Jude laughed. "That's the polite word for old."

"Pretty much," she agreed. Cause it was.

"Foot in your mouth," Q whispered under her breath. "So what kind of doctor do you want to be?

"A surgeon. Like my father was. And my brother." He waved his hand lazily. "And my father's father and so on."

She zoomed in on the one discrepancy. "Like your father *was*?"

His pained expression made her almost regret her nosiness.

"He's been sick for a while…years." He nodded a little and stared into space for a few seconds. "But, yeah, he was an orthopedic surgeon."

"You don't seem too thrilled about becoming one," Sabrina pointed out.

He shifted in his seat and shrugged. "Family tradition."

She assessed him, using what she'd dubbed her Bullshit Detector. And it was beeping like crazy. "Family tradition, huh?"

Q gave her knee a squeeze. "You should know all about family pressure," she whispered.

She dropped her gaze, fumbling with her hands. Damn her. Q always knew how to throw her off balance. Her family's disapproval was the number one reason she refused to act on her more serious flirtations with her. Q knew it too.

"Anyway," Jude started, stretching his arms overhead. The sleeves of his navy t-shirt slid up displaying his well-muscled biceps. "This summer is kind of my last hoorah before I'm forced to buckle down and grow up."

"Growing up is overrated," Q said.

"But necessary. Speaking of not growing up…" he said with a mischievous smirk at Sabrina, "how can I help with your ghost hunt?"

She narrowed her eyes. She'd ignore that little insult for now. "Anything you know about the former occupants of the house would help."

"Well," he leaned forward in his seat, "there was quite a scandal back in the eighteen hundreds."

"A scandal!" She could almost feel her eyes lighting up.

"A tragic romance, a love triangle, and a murder," he added in an exaggerated tone. "Some of it's in the town records. But I had to read between the lines to get the real story."

She clapped her hands excitedly. "Do tell!" If he was shitting her, she didn't care. She could always kick his ass later.

Jude told the story. It was eighteen-fifty-three. The mayor lived in the house with his wife, three kids – one an infant – and several servants. His wife had fallen ill after giving birth and one of the servant's young daughters came to help with the children. Her name was Naima and she caught the mayor's eye with her stunning beauty and grace. She was keen on him as well and, as was common in that time, they had a tryst. As his wife, Grace, recovered, she and Naima spent time together looking after the children. Grace suspected the affair and grew jealous of the pretty girl. But Naima admired her and begged the mayor to ask his wife to allow her into the bedroom. Grace was appalled at the request. Jealousy and bitterness grew and formed a poisonous knot in her heart. Finally, she couldn't look at the two exchange flirty glances any longer. She took the pistol from her husband's study and shot him first. After, she went to the nursery to find Naima. When she walked in, Naima was facing away, looking out the window. Grace raised the gun and shot her in the back. But when she fell to the ground, Grace's baby boy rolled out of Naima's arms, bleeding from the head. He too, died.

Grace lived the rest of her long life in a miserable sorrow.

"Former occupants have said they could hear a woman wailing from time to time, especially in the early morning," Jude finished.

"That's awful!" Q cried.

"Yes, but that was ages ago." Sabrina was practically bouncing out of her seat. A real haunted house! God, she must've looked like a hyper poodle that had to pee. But she couldn't stop her excitement.

Jude laughed when she squeaked in anticipation. "Alright, little ghostbuster. Get to it then," he said as he walked from the room.

She wasted no time unpacking her gear. It wasn't dark quite yet but maybe, with some luck, she'd find *something*. And it still gave her a chance to charm her way into his good graces so he'd let her come back.

After throwing on her fishing vest to help stow her gadgets – which she'd bedazzled to match her knock-off designer denim skirt – she turned to check on Q.

"Do you have your camera stuff?" she asked her.

She was crouched as she assembled some fancy lens. "Yes."

"You've got it on a fast shutter speed, right? I don't want to miss anything."

She gave her a tired look. "This isn't my first time, little girl."

"I know. Sorry."

She snorted. "No you're not."

Sabrina grinned. Right again. She tucked the final EMF detector into her back pocket then sucked in a deep breath. "Ready."

Q rose to her feet, her camera strapped around her neck. Jude returned and froze in place as ran his gaze over Sabrina, from head to toe.

Sabrina looked down, trying to see herself from his point of view. Lit up monitors and tape recording devices were stuffed into the vest pockets. A few gadgets hung from her utility belt, swinging into her bare thighs when she moved. A flashlight stuck out of one tight-fitting skirt pocket, her cell phone from the other.

She turned her head to peer at Q. She looked all photographer-like with her fitted black t-shirt and dark jeans. Her long straight black hair was perfectly styled to appear as if she'd just had a good tumble, which made her all the sexier. And here stood Sabrina, usually the fashionable of the two, looking like she'd dressed for some high-tech fishing-wear fashion show while tripping on acid.

Jude stared, his forehead creased, lips tight as if he were biting the inside of his cheek. Then he burst into laughter.

Sabrina put a hand on her hip and waited. "Go on. Get it out of your system."

Q bit her lip but, like a good friend, didn't laugh.

"I'm sorry," he managed between the roars. "I'm sorry. You just look so cute."

She stomped a foot. "Cute?"

He sobered and cleared his throat. "Sorry. You look very foreboding. I'm sure all the ghosts will take you very seriously."

"This is Sabrina," Q told him, matter-of-factly. "She's at the height of fashion even while hunting for ghosts."

Stomping past them with a scowl, she muttered, "Shut it, you two."

Jude walked them up the rickety old stairs. When she grabbed the banister for balance, it teetered and she pulled her hand away fast. This place was fraught with danger. She grinned. So fun.

Jude ushered them from room to room – most were in the same decrepit condition as the front foyer. No action on any of her equipment, sadly. The largest bedroom had already been renovated, like the living room below. Empty, it would've made a lovely room. Large windows, refreshing light blue paint, beautiful hardwood floors. But she couldn't ignore the laundry pile in one corner, the messy bed in the center of the room, and the cluttered dresser across from it. Definitely a bachelor pad.

"Sabrina," Jude said. "Come here. You'll be happy to see this."

He stood by a closet door, hand on the doorknob.

A boy's closet? She tossed him a skeptical look. "If it's a porn collection, I'm not going to be impressed."

"I will be," Q piped from behind.

Jude swung open the door and motioned them inside. A tiny alcove with racks of clothes, as well as shelves – this wasn't just a closet. Two walls were lined with floor-to-ceiling bookshelves. Her mouth dropped open. Not just that but filled with books. She flitted over the titles quickly to gauge the kind of reading material the man owned. Everything from *The Great Gatsby* to *The Hitchhiker's Guide to the Galaxy*.

"Be still my heart," she gushed. "Books and clothes in the same place!"

She heard two chuckles behind her then Jude scooted by and put his hand on the side of one of the shelves. "Check this out." He pushed and one of the shelves moved, opening to reveal a narrow passage.

"A secret passageway!" Sabrina bounced on her toes. "Where does it lead?"

Q stepped up with a sly smile. "To the dungeon where straight girls are defiled then pleasured until they scream."

Jude laughed.

Ignoring him, Sabrina turned to give Q a challenging glare. "In your dreams, sexy."

"Every night, beautiful."

A loud bang from downstairs interrupted their heated stare-down. Jude excused himself with an explanation of materials being delivered.

Sabrina broke eye contact and peered inside the passage. "Should we see where it leads?"

"You're not scared to be in a dark, abandoned tunnel with me?" she asked with a raised brow. "Especially after the dressing room?"

With a gulp, she pushed on the shelf and it slammed shut.

Q laughed. "I guess that answers that."

They continued on their tour while Jude was gone, staying in the same wing so they didn't get lost. Then, at last, her equipment came to life.

"This is it," Sabrina said with the seriousness of a funeral attendant. She stared at the blue door ominously.

"It is?" Q squinted as she stepped closer.

"Yes. Get your camera ready. I'm going to open it and you snap as many pictures as you can."

"But what if we catch some ghost in the middle of getting changed?" Q asked. "That would be awkward."

Sabrina glared at her friend. "Very funny. Just do your part, please."

"Yes, ma'am," she said with an exaggerated salute.

With a deep breath, Sabrina slowly pushed open the door. It creaked on the hinges as the dark interior lit up from the hallway light.

Q's shutter clicked several times in succession while Sabrina pushed the door open all the way.

"A *closet*, Sabrina?" Q sighed and perched a hand on her hip. "A haunted closet?"

Sabrina's heart sank. She frowned at Q and mumbled, "Sorry." This time she meant it.

Q's expression softened as she wrapped her arms around Sabrina and pulled her close. "Don't be sad." She kissed the top of her head. "We can always try again."

Q was kind to humor her, despite failure after failure. Maybe she should let her off the hook and start going alone. Or maybe she should just hang up her badge and give up for good. In a fit of discouragement, she tugged away from Q's embrace and pulled off all her gadgets, tossing them on the floor. Then she shucked her vest, lowering it more gently – she had spent time decorating it, after all.

When she looked up, Q was standing in the closet, holding Sabrina's flashlight. "Fuck."

She rushed to her side. "What?"

Q looked at her with a wicked grin. "Someone's got a kinky side." She fingered a long stick hanging on the back of the door.

Next to that stick was another, this one with tendrils of leather hanging down. Like an old-fashioned whip. No. She'd seen that on one of Q's websites. A flogger, she thought it was called.

On a shelf inside the closet sat neatly displayed items, all in pristine condition. Toys, looked like. Adult toys. She recognized the vibrators, she wasn't a complete idiot. Every girl had one. Hers was purple.

The rest of the toys were foreign. A few downright scary. She looked at Q then did a double take. Her eyes gleamed as she toyed with the flogger tendrils, her lips parted in a small smile. Holy shit. Q was turned on by this?

"You know what this stuff is?" she asked her. Q didn't move her gaze from the flogger. "Of course you do. Creepy as you are."

She snapped her head to Sabrina and raised a brow. "You're not so innocent. I've seen you browse that fetish site."

Her face heated. "To buy clothes!"

"Mm-hm."

Changing the subject, Sabrina grabbed a chain with two clips off the shelf and analyzed it. "What's this?"

"Nipple clamps."

She gulped. Her eyes must've looked like saucers because Q chuckled beside her. She tried to imagine the ends attached to each nipple, pinching it tight. A rush of warmth slid through her, tingling her most intimate parts. She threw the thing back on the shelf. She picked up a long, flexible stick with a leather tip instead. "And this?"

Q's gaze flicked from her face to the toy in her hand then she smiled. "Turn around and I'll show you."

Sabrina spun, putting her back to the wall so fast she slipped off her heel and toppled all the way into the closet. Her heart raced and her clit throbbed. What the hell? Why was she turned on by this?

Q laughed and took the crop from her hand. "No? You'd probably like it."

Yes. She squeezed her eyes shut. What? No! No, no, no. She was not a freak. Not like Q. A delirious giggle escaped her. She opened her eyes to see Q staring at her in question. "I just called you a freak in my head."

Q took a step toward her. "Don't count yourself out of that number so soon, little girl." She swung the crop twice, smiling when it whistled through the air then placed it back on the shelf.

What would that feel like against her skin? On her ass and thighs? She could almost feel the sting as it slapped against her flesh. She felt herself clench…down there. She was getting wet. Was this what had been missing from her sex life all this time?

"Here." Q placed a pair of leather cuffs in her hand. "What do you think of these?"

She turned them over. The leather was soft but strong. The silver buckles made them look industrial but still sexy. "Um." She cleared her throat. "They look very…well-made." She tried to hand them back but Q had turned away.

"See anything you like?" came a deep voice from the hallway.

Shit. She scrambled out of the closet with her hands behind her back, feeling like a toddler caught with her hand in the cookie jar.

Jude stood, arms crossed, in the hallway.

"It was her idea," Q said. "I tried to stop her."

Sabrina could've kicked her. "Traitor," she hissed with a glare.

He took several steps closer, a stern set to his jaw and a determined look in his eye. Now why did that fill her with dread at the same time as making her flush with excitement?

He put out his hand as he stared at Sabrina. "Bring them here."

Instinct had her moving toward him before logic kicked in. Why was she obeying him so easily? She did Q, most of the time, but that was because Q had proven she wouldn't take no for an answer. Apparently all Sabrina needed was to hear a stern tone and she turned into a puppet. How annoying.

He kept eye contact the entire long-ass journey from the closet to where he stood. When she gingerly placed the cuffs in his hand, he looked at Q. "Do you know how these work?"

Q looked a little less affected by his presence but still nodded obediently.

Gaze back on Sabrina, he said, "Would you like to see?"

The challenge in his voice had her stumbling for a reply. A simple *no* would do. But she waited too long. His mouth shifted the tiniest bit – like he'd assessed her and found something he liked.

The tension in the room cranked up a notch.

"Give me your wrists," he demanded.

She hesitated, looking to Q for help. Her eyes were locked on Jude. Sabrina's silent pleas went unanswered. Some friend. Where was that damn stick when she needed it?

His voice drew her back. "Afraid I'll trap you in my sex lair, Jersey girl?"

Hmph. Not one to back down from a challenge, she slapped her hand into his. With a smirk, he wrapped the first cuff around her wrist. He took his time fastening first one then the other securely, buckling it, searching for the right hole to slide the metal tongue into. His expression remained focused but every once in a while he looked in her eyes, as if checking her reaction.

Her heart thudded in her ears. Swallowing was suddenly difficult. Each touch seemed electric – sizzling across the sensitive skin on her wrist. Her eyes fluttered closed as she soaked in each feeling. Hard, uncompromising cuffs, callused but gentle hands. The sensations blended together and put her in some kind of mind-numbing haze.

She realized he'd stopped touching her and popped open her lids. Jude was there, his lips quirked up in an amused but sexy smile. She looked down at her bound wrists – one cuff on each, with two buckles fastened, and a length of leather hanging off each. She could tell the two could connect if he chose to buckle them together – or onto something, like a headboard or railing. An image came to mind – her tied, spread-eagle, to a bed, Q stalking around her like a lion assessing tasty prey. And damn if she didn't get wetter.

She gave her head a shake and twisted her wrists this way and that. Funny how her movement wasn't constricted yet they still made her feel trapped – in a deliciously exciting way.

"So…" she said, forcing herself to speak matter-of-factly and not betray her arousal. "You do this to women then?"

"I do. When they want me to. I don't lure young women who don't want it." He gave her an ironic grin. That deep male voice, right there and up close, did such nice things to her insides. "But you…" He traced a finger along her bottom lip. "You look like you need it."

Q appeared beside her. "If she says yes, you have to share."

Share? What?

"And you." He dropped his hand from Sabrina's mouth and fingered a piece of Q's silky hair. "What side of the crop do you fall on?"

"Both," she answered.

What the hell were they talking about? Some secret kink code? She needed to pay closer attention to those websites. Or, heaven forbid, read one of Q's dirty books.

Q looked Sabrina over with a calculating eye. That never boded well. She nodded to Jude as she backed away a little. "Fasten them behind her."

Sabrina gasped. "Q!"

Jude raised his brows. "Usually I'm the one giving orders, but I'm curious to see where this is going. However, she hasn't said yes. I need that."

Her tight breathing settled a bit. At last someone was making sense.

Then he focused on her and put a single finger under her chin then made her look up at him. "Willing to try this, little ghost hunter? I'm letting your friend call the shots here."

No almost spilled out, but, there was a *yes* too. Mouth half-open, ready to speak, she tried to think. Her mind spun to a halt.

It came out as a squeaky whisper. "Yes?"

Before she could say more, he turned her, gathered her wrists in a firm hold and fastened them together. If Q wasn't here she'd be bolting for the door but… She glared at her traitorous friend, vacillating between terror and a fucking annoying as hell desire to keep tumbling down this rabbit hole of debauchery – with Q at her side. Or standing over her with a wicked smile, stick thingy in hand.

Sabrina looked up at the ceiling and whimpered. Dear Jesus, where were these thoughts coming from?

"Can you hold her against you?" she heard Q ask.

Jude tugged her tight up against his chest, facing her forward, arms locked in his hands.

Q nodded in approval then stalked toward her. "Now you're in trouble."

Sabrina felt her breath go in and out in shaky waves. And were her knees trembling? She hadn't been this nervous since that first kiss when she was thirteen.

Q stepped in close and pushed her hair back from her face. Her eyes fluttered shut as she leaned into the touch. Was she so sex-starved?

"Relax, beautiful," Q said softly. "Just tell me you don't like it and I'll stop. Jude too. Okay? We'll let you go if you tell us to."

Her awareness centered on the loud beat of her heart, on Q waiting patiently.

She'd liked it in the dressing room alright, when Q had put her mouth on her. This wasn't any different, was it? Yes. It was. There was the almost stranger at her back, breathing so close she felt the warmth on her neck, in her hair. Tremors ran through her again. He gripped her arms so tightly.

She could always wiggle free, stomp on Jude's foot, kick Q in the –

What the hell was she thinking? Kick Q? She'd never in a million years hurt that girl. And now she was rambling in her head like a lunatic.

They'll let me go if I say. She clung to that thought as Q lowered her lips to hers.

"God forgive me," Sabrina whispered. Their lips touched.

Gentle. Giving. Cinnamon. Q tasted spicy like cinnamon. And familiar, though they'd never kissed. Soft lips pressed against hers, before they lifted away to press in again. Sabrina returned the kiss eagerly, and took some flesh, liking the feel of Q's bottom lip between her teeth.

When she nipped harder, Q pulled back and gave her a stern glare. "Behave, little girl."

Then she grabbed Sabrina's hair and held her place while she did exactly what she wished to Sabrina's mouth. There was no timidity now. Just a woman on a mission to prove exactly what kissing a girl was like.

Sabrina groaned quietly, inhaling the warmth of Q's breaths, dissolving into mush. Q kept on kissing and biting and licking. Between her legs turned liquid and hot. She squirmed and wanted so much to arch forward and grind herself on something…on someone.

The tug and small twinges at her scalp, the lack of freedom, the sheer control of her body by theirs, and the kissing that went on forever – she succumbed, and all her resistance fell away.

At last, slowly, eyes bright with passion, Q pulled away. Sabrina whispered breathlessly, "I'm so going to hell."

Q chuckled and loosened her fingers in Sabrina's hair. "Poor girl." Then she pressed more kisses in a soft trail down Sabrina's neck.

Goose bumps rose on her arms. The kisses crossed the vulnerable part of her throat and she gulped as a tide of arousal tingled to her breasts and southward. At the spot between her shoulder and neck, Q bit. Her teeth hung on for a long second, marking her. Sabrina yelped and squirmed against Jude.

His grip hardened. "I think she likes it," he said, amusement coloring his voice.

Q ignored him, seemingly lost in her own world of nibbles and licks. When her lips grazed behind Sabrina's ear, her breath tickled. Sabrina giggled and arched her back. Her breasts pressed against Q's, shocking her into a sharp awareness of what they did.

"That's enough," Jude said in a quiet rasp.

After the slightest hesitation, Q stopped. Her face was as flushed as Sabrina's must be. "Okay," she croaked. Her tongue curled across her lips one last time as if she were remembering Sabrina's taste.

Now look who's breathless. Sabrina twisted her lips in a crooked smile, pleased at the power she had over her friend.

Q returned the smirk as if reading her thoughts then she studied Sabrina. "Yes. Her wanting more is a good place to leave her."

Leave me? No! She rubbed her thighs together, trying to ease the pressure between them. Q watched her, looking like a cat that had a wriggling mouse before it. A whimper escaped Sabrina.

"Impatient thing," Q teased.

Jude uncuffed her, and let her step away.

Blindly, she found the wall with one hand and leaned her shoulder into it. Her thoughts spun like a whirlpool. Wanting reassurance, she eyed her friend, but going to Q for comfort right now was a bad idea. What just happened? Wasn't this wrong in some way? Two women, one man. If Jude hadn't said to let her go, what would she have let Q do to her?

For a millisecond, she shut her eyes. Had they all gone crazy? But then, this was something he'd done before. Q also, maybe. She'd have to remember to ask her later.

Jude looked a little shaken, himself. He let out a long breath then simply stood, watching them. He still held the cuffs. The leather ties of the cuffs trailed down and almost reached the floor.

What the hell were they supposed to do now? Her heart thudded through ten or twenty beats.

Unable to take the silence, she blurted, "Well, I guess there's no ghosts in the Closet O'Kink."

A few seconds later Q chuckled.

"That's a damn shame." Jude broke out a grin. "I thought for sure if I had ghosts, they'd be kinky ones."

Chapter 5

Q

The line in front of Q had stalled, and she wondered if she'd manage to get coffee before her break ended. She fiddled with her money, folded it, and stuffed it in her pocket. Her phone vibrated and she pulled it out of her back pocket and checked the message.

Coming home for supper? I'm cooking. Remember, real food equals big strong muscles. ;)

She rolled her eyes, imagining Sabrina's sarcastic tone. A warm feeling started in her chest. If it was just lust it wouldn't be so bad. But this was worse. Unrequited love was pathetic. She pressed her lips together. Well, even if she never got anywhere with the girl, at least she wouldn't die from malnutrition.

Q confirmed then shoved her phone back in her pocket and sighed. She considered going to the cafe down the street with their over-priced designer beverages.

"Bad day?" drawled a deep voice behind her. Sexy... and so close to her ear it made her shiver.

Q turned her head, her gaze meeting a broad t-shirt covered chest. She looked up into Jude's amused blue eyes. *Fuck, he's hot. Okay, Q, don't be a dork.*

"Oh... Hey, Jude." She winced. Real smooth, girl. "Sorry. And sorry for Sabrina teasing you about your name the other day, too."

He chuckled. "At least you didn't do it on purpose. That joke was already old by the time I turned three."

"I can imagine." She did her best to remember that big, blond and muscular wasn't her type. But her libido had other ideas, like him shoving her face down on a table and using her. She so needed to get laid. After the only six-month dry spell of her adult life she was getting a little crazy. When things had gone sour with Nico, taking a break had seemed like a good idea. She wasn't a slut by any stretch of the imagination, but sometimes she felt like an adolescent boy. Everything reminded her of sex – from the cream-filled éclairs to the barista's name, Virginia. Instead of seeing the world through rose-colored glasses, she wore sex goggles.

"With a name like Q, I'm sure you can imagine. What's Q really short for? Queenie?"

She grimaced. "Sorry. I'd tell you but then I'd have to erase your memory. We'd have to spoon feed you so you didn't starve to death. I just don't want that on my conscience." The line moved and they shuffled forward – sideways for Q.

"So, how would you erase my memory?" His sexy grin derailed her for a moment.

Fuck him until he couldn't remember his name? Nah, not subtle enough. "Shake you and hope your brain Etch-a-Sketches."

He laughed, flashing even white teeth. "You on a lunch break?"

"More or less. The models I work with don't eat lunch, so I tell them they need to relax so their expressions look more natural. That way I can grab a decent coffee, at least."

"That's a nefarious plan."

He was so close she could feel his body heat, smell him. Again, she imagined him holding her down and almost whimpered. "I've had worse."

"There are models around here? I would have figured they'd move to New York City." He ran a hand through his short blond hair and her fingers itched to do the same.

"There are a few. The ones I'm working with today are girls from the college looking for extra money. I'm doing a shoot for the new wedding boutique downtown. Lots of white."

"Are you running back now or do you have time to hang out?"

She contemplated calling in sick for the month. "That's the beautiful thing about being the photographer. They have to wait for me. Sneakiest coffee date ever, by the way."

"I'm an opportunist. It's a gift."

Q laughed just as she reached the counter. Jude ordered with her and insisted on paying. He grabbed a booth near the window.

"So did Sabrina freak out after you guys left the other day?"

"Not where I could see. She got a bit quiet for a couple of days, but she bounced back fast after that. We might have blown her mind a little... and mine. Every time I think of it I'm in danger of spontaneous combustion."

He choked on his coffee.

Q grinned mischievously and handed him a napkin. "Swallow, it makes less of a mess."

Jude shook with mirth. "You're bad."

"Yes," she admitted. "No one's managed to teach me any manners."

He eyed the silver chain around her neck and the pendant she generally kept tucked into her shirt. Q reached up and toyed with the trefoil, a little embarrassed by it when sitting with someone who knew what it was. The BDSM symbol wasn't recognized by most people. It wasn't her public collar, though. Nico had taken that back when he'd chosen Isabelle over her. She always wondered if he'd given the necklace to his new submissive – and that made her more upset than the rest of it.

"Maybe you just haven't met the right person. You seem pretty cozy with Sabrina – but as lovely as that is, I don't foresee her teaching you to behave." He smirked.

"We've been close for a few years, but we've only been roommates for six months. I wish we were cozier, but I'm not sure we're going there. She keeps telling me she's straight." Frustration crept into her voice, unbidden.

"You two looked pretty into each other when I was there. It was..." He looked enthusiastic but gestured vaguely, like he didn't have words to describe his thoughts.

Q realized that he'd barely taken a sip of his coffee since she'd made him choke on it. He'd ordered it black. Nasty. "I wanted to do a lot more, trust me. But thanks for stopping me when you did. I have trouble being rational where she's concerned."

She recalled the longing on Sabrina's face after she'd stopped the kiss. How could Sabrina think she was straight when she reacted like that? Q sighed, already knowing the answer. It was her family's expected reaction that held her back. Sabrina's mom and aunts had verbally crucified her cousin – right in front of Q – when he came out of the closet a few years ago.

"I don't know if I could have handled much more. I almost imploded, as it was." His exaggeratedly pained face made Q snort. "It's more than lust for you, though, isn't it?"

Q was impressed he'd noticed that in the short time he'd been around them. She got the feeling this would've come out eventually, but baring her soul to a virtual stranger was still difficult. "Yes, I'm in love with her. She knows I love her as a friend, but she's not ready to hear it's more serious than that and I don't want to mess up our friendship if she doesn't feel the same way, you know?"

He nodded and smiled kindly. "I won't tell her." Jude took a drink of his coffee, then set the cup down and eyed her a moment. "Quincy?"

"Don't I *wish*. My name was my mother's maiden name. Family reunions would be a blast if I had that kind of family. You'll never drag it out of me."

"Not close to your extended family?"

"No. My parents were victims of a drive-by when I was twelve. Wrong place at the wrong time." She fiddled with her cup.

"I'm sorry, Q. That's awful." He was trying to make eye contact, but she looked out the window instead.

She shrugged. It wasn't time for that. Nothing like being a downer on a first date. "It was a long time ago. Anyway, my older brothers raised me. They ran off all of our meddling aunties, so there aren't any family reunions for us." She shrugged. "It was fine by me. The last thing I would have wanted is lectures on the dangers of premarital sex."

"Your brothers didn't sit you down for that chat themselves?" He chuckled.

"Um, no. Not unless you're counting the times I borrowed their porn." Did she really just tell him that? Ugh. At least he looked amused. Maybe he thought she was joking.

"So… what methods have failed to teach you manners?"

She was relieved by the change in subject, but had no plans to give him ammunition. "Hmmm. Most. Brats are notoriously hard to teach." Q took a sip of her coffee, but watched him closely. Time to see if this one was up to the challenge or if he'd bolt.

His face lit up. "I have a soft spot for brats. So you're a brat switch?"

"Yes," she said, surprised. "A brat switch. A veritable social pariah in the fet world. You don't have a hate-on for girls like me?"

"Not a hate-on, no." He winked and Q got caught in the wave of a full on, hot-faced blush.

There was an awkward silence as she floundered for something to say that wasn't *tie me up and make me your bitch*. He smirked and waited, like toying with her was amusing. It made her submissive side go straight into overdrive.

She dropped her gaze and waited.

"I haven't seen you at the club before. I would have remembered you."

Q smiled at the thinly-veiled flattery. "I think I know pretty much everyone, except maybe some of the newer people. Small city with only one club."

"Do you know Fredrick? He's my landlord. He introduced me to a few Doms. One guy, Cross, is going to help with renovations. I think he owns a store downtown. Good guy."

"Yes. I was just at Cross's shop with Sabrina the other day. That's where we got the outfit she wore to the concert. I know Fred too. Do you know Ivy?" She'd forgotten how much she missed the club until he brought it up.

"I've met her. Nice girl." His eyes were warm, but it didn't look like Ivy had caught his fancy. "You haven't been going lately though. How come?"

"I've been avoiding someone," she hedged.

"A Dom?"

She nodded and drew a long breath while she chose her words carefully. "Yes. I've only had one. We broke up about six months ago. It was messy." In the *he-ripped-out-my-heart-and-kicked-the-shit-out-of-it* sense. She wasn't about to tell him that though. "He left me for a 24/7 service slave. I'm not into that level of submission. We were supposed to go to the concert together anyway, as friends, but he backed out at the last minute."

"Would it have been awkward to go with him?"

"Yeah." Especially since they might have run into Jude.

"So have you been into Slipknot for long? In my experience hot girls usually only go to concerts like that because of their boyfriends."

"Oh no! He's cute but sexist. What's a girl to do?" She batted her lashes sarcastically.

"I'm cute?"

"I'm sure you own a mirror, sunshine. As for Slipknot, I've been into them for about seven years. Their music is... it makes me want to..." She paused, weighing her options. She decided on the truth, even though it might make her seem crazy, sex-obsessed, or both. "You know how some music's described as the singer making love to you with his voice? The music I like is more like a good hard fuck."

Jude slapped a hand over his mouth like he was struggling not to spit out his mouthful of coffee. He finally managed to get it down then gave her an incredulous look. "You really don't mince words, do you?"

"Sorry. I swear a lot. It can be a bit shocking, I guess. I wanted you to understand that I don't just go for the mosh pits." It wasn't the first time Q wished that she was a little less crude, but better he got used to it now if this was going anywhere.

"Maybe not, but you seemed to be fighting pretty hard to go back in. What's the attraction?" He looked honestly interested.

"You've never been in a pit, have you?" Statement rather than question. If he had to ask, the answer was obvious. "The energy, the violence...what's not to like?"

"I've been in my fair share. But you...you're built like a little bird. Getting an elbow to the face, getting trampled. Those possibilities alone should be reason enough for you to stay out."

Q refused to rise to his baiting. She took a last drink of her coffee and sat back. "I can take more abuse than you seem to think. I like pain, and you don't get trampled if you stay on your feet. Besides, what's life without adrenaline?"

"I get most of my adrenaline from other sources."

"Like?"

"Torturing willing young damsels."

Q grinned saucily and leaned forward on her elbows – enough to give him an eyeful of cleavage. His gaze obligingly fell in. "You'd be out of luck with me then," she said huskily. "I don't play a very good damsel in distress."

"A challenge, huh? I like that."

She shook her long bangs down across one eye and inspected him like a piece of meat. "Oh, I'd have you lying down and taking it like a man in no time. I don't think you could dominate me. You're nowhere near mean enough."

"And I have no doubt I could teach you some manners."

Q arched a brow, trying to look blasé even though her pulse raced. Her gaze fell to his biceps, and she caught herself about to lick her lips. Despite her words, she was sure he could make her do all sorts of things. She shivered. "Be careful. I might hold you to your word."

"*You* should be careful. I'd be the one holding your leash."

"Isn't it a little early to be talking collars, sunshine?"

"If we played together, you'd wear what I told you to."

She bit her bottom lip and gave him a naughty look. "If we decided to look into this idea more seriously, how would you feel about Sabrina joining us? Do you think you could handle two?"

His blue eyes widened. "Hell, I'd be willing to die trying. Could you handle sharing Sabrina with me? Is she even into kink?"

Q considered the question for a minute, although she'd been thinking about it for days. She figured Sabrina would be more likely to get involved with her if there was a guy to fall back on. She seemed to have a need for a traditional relationship. If nothing else, Jude would be a good public cover. He was probably her best chance to get Sabrina to give her a shot. And easy access to cock would suit Q – she didn't believe in getting intimate with inanimate objects. If he was as nice as he seemed, and he knew how to Dom without being an ass, this could turn out to be pretty awesome.

"As far as kink goes, she's never tried it, but she's starting to get all submissive around me. Don't cut me out of things and I won't go bat-shit crazy. I haven't talked to her about this, though. You'd have to give us some time to discuss it."

"I wouldn't cut you out of it. I like both of you for different reasons. As a package deal you're pretty irresistible. I'm not a switch, though. I won't submit or bottom for you."

"That's fine. Sabrina is almost more sub than I can handle most days, and we're not even together. Yet."

"I've never played with a switch. The dynamic might take a bit of time to figure out. It would be... interesting."

Q could almost see scenarios running through his head. She wondered if they were similar to the ones running through her own. This idea made her damp enough that she might have to go home to change, even though she was wearing jeans. She swallowed. "Let me talk to Sabrina and we'll go from there."

He nodded, reaching out and tracing his index finger over her hand where it rested on the table beside her cup. Her lips parted as she absorbed the tickling sensation. He turned her hand over and traced designs on her palm and wrist. It was getting hard to keep her breathing even.

"Does she want to investigate the house some more?"

"Evil man," she laughed breathlessly. "Using a poor, innocent girl's pastimes against her. But yes, she's been going on about wanting to have a séance at your house."

"She has to know that if she comes over again, we're probably going to do more dastardly things to her. She's not that naive."

"No, but she's new to messing around with girls and she has no real knowledge of kink. She's only had a couple of boyfriends, for that matter. We'll have to be careful with her, if this is going to work."

"That works for me. It's a complicated situation, and I'll need time to adjust, myself."

She bit back a smile. "You need to adjust yourself? Need a hand with that?"

He chuckled and grinned wickedly, then leaned in. "Anytime."

The challenge in his eyes made her gaze drop to her hands. He was not going to be an easy one to shock. That pleased her.

They rose and walked to the door. "Would Friday night work for the séance?"

"That gives me a few days to talk to her. The séance she'll go for. As far as anything else is concerned, you might have to take my lead at first."

He smiled down at her. "Okay, little brat. Just don't get used to being in charge."

***

Sabrina handed Q a plate of stir-fry as she walked in the door. Q kicked off her shoes and followed her into the living room. "You've got this timing thing down to a science. Smells great!"

Her friend grinned and sat down on the other end of the couch after grabbing the remote. "At least I have you eating something other than popcorn for supper now."

"Unfair! Sometimes I had cereal." Q laughed.

"When you bothered eating at all," Sabrina grumbled, flipping through the channel guide. Q had the chance to watch her for awhile. Boxers and a t-shirt with no bra. So very almost naked. The worst part was knowing that Sabrina would probably let Q strip her, but that she'd act like an innocent victim.

Sabrina arched her back, her nipples visible under her t-shirt. She knew Q was watching – the little tease. Q forced herself to eat, but it wasn't food she was hungry for.

Soon Sabrina lost interest in their silent game and settled on watching a comedy movie she knew backward and forward. Every so often she would laugh and mumble a line of dialogue as they said it. She nibbled at her food, pushing a stray lock of hair behind her ear. Such tiny ears. Q sighed, wishing she could pull Sabrina into her lap and cuddle with her. She was a lost cause where this girl was concerned. They needed to talk.

"Guess who I ran into at lunch today?" She tried to keep her tone light.

Sabrina said the next line of the movie before the actor did then turned to Q, looking smug. "Who? Not Nico, I hope. He left a message for you to call him back. Why are you still talking to that jerk anyway?"

Second call from him in a week. Odd. "He just wants to be friends, Sabrina. It's the polite, adult thing to do after a break-up."

Sabrina rolled her eyes and put aside her plate. "Back in a sec." She padded barefoot into the kitchen and came back with a bottle of wine and two water glasses. "We really need to get wine glasses at some point."

"I hate wine." Q made a face. "You don't have to be fancy on my account."

She scoffed then poured two glasses anyway. "You will not be drinking whiskey with my stir-fry, young lady. Now be good and drink your wine."

After taking a sip, Q wrinkled her nose. The wine was sour and made her tongue feel funny. She chugged the whole glass and banged it on the coffee table, hoping she'd done her duty. To her bemusement, Sabrina refilled it. By the time they were done eating, Q had a mild buzz going.

"Oh, I forgot. Who did you see?" Sabrina asked.

"I saw Jude. We had coffee together." Q watched Sabrina's face in profile. Her mouth tightened for a fraction of a second, but then she smiled, turning to look at Q.

"That's good! I like him. You should totally date him."

The words hurt. She knew Sabrina didn't love her back, but she wished she'd be less eager to pawn her off sometimes. It was like Sabrina didn't care if she dated other people. But then, why would she? That made her heart sink. Q tossed back the rest of her wine. Best if it got past her tongue as quickly as possible.

Sabrina poured her another glass. Q stared at her incredulously. "You think I should have a third? These hold more than wine glasses, you know." She tapped the side of the tumbler with her fingernail. "You trying to get me drunk?"

"Maybe. Maybe I'll get you drunk and have my way with you." The words were glib, but there was an edge to them.

If only there was some way to get inside the girl's head. When Sabrina finished her third glass of wine, Q shut off the TV.

Sabrina's gaze snapped to her. "Hey! I was watching that!"

"You can recite it to yourself later, beautiful. We need to talk." This discussion was her idea, but it didn't mean that the butterflies in her chest would settle – although the wine was making her braver. "Come here."

Sabrina pouted. "I don't want to."

"Come here, little girl," Q commanded.

Her friend smiled a little and slid closer on the couch, stopping just out of reach. Brat.

"I said here, not there." Her tone was stern.

Sabrina bit her lip and complied.

Q got the impression she was amused. "Playing games with me is funny, is it?" She put her arm around Sabrina's waist and pulled her into the crook of her arm, then swatted her on a bare thigh.

"Ow!" Sabrina whined, rubbing her leg. "You could have talked to me when I was over there. Now you're going to do naughty things to me and I won't be able to concentrate on what you're saying."

"You wish, woman. We're just going to talk right now. If you want more later, you'll have to ask nice." The idea of Sabrina actually asking her to do things made her insides clench. She wasn't going to hold her breath though. Sabrina liked to pretend she was innocent in this whole thing, even though they both knew otherwise.

Sabrina predictably changed the subject. "So what did Jude say? Does he want to do you, or what?"

"He wants to *do* both of us, actually."

Sabrina pulled back. "That cocky bastard! He didn't really say that, did he? You can have him! He's too full of himself for me."

"Actually," Q whispered mischievously, "it was my idea."

"What! That's crazy. Why would you suggest that?" Sabrina looked completely mystified – and maybe intrigued.

The hint of curiosity was gone as fast as Q could blink. Did she imagine it?

"It would just be for the summer. Think about it. Freaky, uninhibited sex with no strings attached. With a hot guy. And me." She took a deep breath and plunged on. "If you don't like it we'll stop. No questions asked. And if you want to try on a temporary basis, we'll just make it until the end of the summer. Think of it as an experiment." Q held her breath, her heart beating hard. Though she tried to act calm, her world seemed to hang on this moment.

The way Sabrina sat staring in an unfocused way made Q realize she'd made a mess of it. Ugh! She should've prepared her for this more, somehow. If she'd doomed their relationship…if Sabrina walked out on her because of this…

At last Sabrina raised her head. "What if things didn't work out with us? Will you stop being friends with me?" Her brown eyes were soulful pools.

Q kissed the spot between her brows. "No worries. If you don't like it, I'll understand. You're straight. It would be very open-minded of you to even consider trying it. Sabrina... you know I love you. I also fantasize about having sex with you, but I can live with our relationship being platonic if that's what you want." Could she live with going back to being just friends with the woman she was in love with? It would be painful. But she could deal with it if that was Sabrina's decision. Q was already used to hiding her feelings. But she couldn't pass up the opportunity to try, even if getting hurt was almost inevitable.

"Would that make me your girlfriend?" Sabrina asked uncertainly.

Q's heart leapt into her throat. It sounded good to her, but she didn't want Sabrina overwhelmed with labels. "That would be up to you. Titles aren't that important for now."

Sabrina chewed her lip and frowned. She was quiet for awhile and Q had to stop herself from interrupting her thoughts with more persuasive arguments. She kicked herself for not being able to express this better.

"I don't know Q. I have doubts this will work. And I don't want people to know. Especially not my family."

"Okay, if that's what you want. But will you try? Just for the summer?"

She nodded then gave her a serious look. "You can't tell anyone about us or it's over. An experiment. That's all this is. Call me... Q Curious." Sabrina drew up her knees and hid her face behind them.

Excitement coursed through her, and she stroked Sabrina's silky hair. Hell yeah! Q felt like singing and dancing around the room.

"I can't stomach the idea of losing you *when* this doesn't work out. And I mean *when*...you have to promise you won't disappear on me. Please?" Tears welled in her eyes, and Q leaned in to kiss her nose.

"Yes, Sabrina. I promise."

Sabrina's brow creased. "And how is it going to work with Jude. Do you really think you can share him with me without getting jealous?"

Q tried hard not to grin like an idiot. "I don't think I'd mind sharing anything with you. You aren't going to use him all up and not leave any for me, are you?"

"No!" She laughed. "I don't even like sex that much. It's awkward and messy and embarrassing. Don't be surprised if this doesn't work for me. Okay?"

"Okay. But we'll work on fixing that." Q hugged her. She still couldn't understand how it was possible for anyone to not like sex. Though the thought was awful, what if Sabrina was right? Maybe she wouldn't like it no matter what they did. She'd try her damnedest "Will you mind sharing Jude with me?"

"No. I'm a little jealous about sharing you with Jude, though. But it will be better with him there, I think. It would take the responsibility off of me. I don't know if I could... uh... do things... uh... to you." She blushed and looked away.

"Don't worry about that. I can fix that myself if it's not something you want to do. We should come up with a list of things that we will and won't do, so that Jude will know ahead of time." Even the thought of making the list was turning her on. How was she going to get things done at work with her mind in her pants all summer? "Do you want to do more things like we did at his house with the cuffs?"

"That would be... interesting." Sabrina's blush deepened and she fumbled with her hands.

Q's eyes were drawn to Sabrina's bare legs. Her boxers had bunched up, making her legs look impossibly long. She forced away the thought of them wrapped around her head, her mouth making Sabrina cry out in pleasure.

"Yes, I thought you enjoyed that." Q smiled widely and ran her fingers up Sabrina's arm.

She shivered. "I didn't know you knew so much about those kinds of things. Did you learn it all online, or have you done this before?"

"It was something Nico was really into. He got me into it then left me for Isabelle because she was more serious about it than I was." Somehow that thought wasn't painful at that moment.

Sabrina's eyes were round. "Really? Did he hit you with whips, like in movies?"

"Not quite the same as you see in movies, no. He did use a flogger and a crop on me. But he was more interested in service. He trained me to do certain sexual things on command, plus take care of his things, cook for him, clean... that sort of thing. He wanted me to stay home and serve him 24/7, but I didn't want to give up my career. He didn't want me to have friends or much contact with my family, for that matter." Q downed the rest of her glassful of wine and poured Sabrina another. The room was getting fuzzy.

Sabrina grimaced then, seeming to come to some conclusion. She looked straight into Q's eyes. "I'm not going to be some sort of nineteen-fifties housewife for Jude for the summer. No way in hell. I'm not signing up for that. This is about sex, not him controlling my life."

Q nodded, starting to feel relaxed because of the wine. "He doesn't want that anyway, little girl. He just wants a chance with you, like I do. But he has to leave and I don't. Poor bastard. Oh, and he wants to do that séance at his house on Friday, if we can make it."

Sabrina squeaked and jumped on Q, straddling her legs and hugging her hard. "On Friday? But it's already Tuesday! I have to start getting things ready." She tried to get up again but Q held her in place.

"Where are you going, beautiful? I like you right here." Q held her by the hips and stared up into Sabrina's eyes. The feel of her body in her hands made Q squirm and warmth suffused her groin.

Sabrina sucked in a breath but rubbed herself against Q's jeans. The wine had apparently made off with some of her inhibitions.

"What do you want, girly?" Q's voice was thick with lust and the effects of the alcohol.

Her girl whined and wriggled on her lap, rocking her boxer-clad hips against Q.

Q slid her hands around to Sabrina's ass and squeezed, controlling her movements. "Kiss me or I'll leave you frustrated."

Sabrina's eyes widened. "I don't really know how to kiss. I'm terrible at it. I can let you kiss me, but I don't know how to do it right."

"Well now's the time to learn then. Put your lips on mine."

"No! You're going to make fun of me." Sabrina turned her head to the side and crossed her arms under her breasts, presenting them unintentionally to Q.

She leaned in and latched onto one of Sabrina's hardened nipples, nibbling on it through her t-shirt. Sabrina squealed. Q continued nipping and sucking until Sabrina ground her groin against her, lost in the sensations.

Sabrina grabbed her by the shoulders. "No more," she gasped.

The words hit home. She stopped immediately, despite the wine's effects on her better judgment.

Sabrina made a sound of frustration. "Why'd you stop?" she glared down at Q, looking about as scary as a grouchy kitten. It made Q want to kiss her silly.

"You told me to. Are you the kind of girl that says stop when you don't mean to?" Q asked, grinning up at her.

"I don't know!" Sabrina grumped.

Q wished she could spank her – just for fun. But it was too soon. "Then I guess we'd better talk about safewords. And we're also going to save this game for when we're a lot more sober."

Chapter 6

Sabrina

"Have you seen Jude's online chat picture?" Q asked, her gaze locked on the computer screen. So that's what she'd been up to. Chatting with Jude? Well, that explained the random giggling.

Sabrina shifted uncomfortably on the couch, for the millionth time since having started one of Q's kinky sex books.

"Uh-uh," she managed to choke out. Her face must've flamed bright red. It was amazing Q hadn't teased her yet. But she did catch quite a few amused smirks when Q snuck in peeks from the desk across the room.

Had Sabrina been hiding under a rock for most of her life? No, just in church. She couldn't believe some of the stuff authors wrote in these books. Graphic words and scenarios she'd never dreamed of. Whips and chains didn't often cross her mind, but that wasn't the majority of the book's content. Soft, silky ropes, leather-lined cuffs like she'd seen in Jude's closet, gentle dominance – not the laughing sadists whipping girls until they cried like she'd seen on crime TV shows. It was all so…fucking erotic. She squirmed again, embarrassed of the dampening in her pants. At this moment, the heroine was being brought to orgasm with a crop on her…lady parts.

"Sabrina?" Q's voice pulled her from the riveting scene.

She jerked her head up to meet Q's amused gaze. "Hm?"

"I said, how do you like the book?"

"It's…" *So hot that if the seam of my jeans rubs up against my clit one more time I might orgasm right here on the couch.* "Interesting."

Q nodded, looking like she might burst into laughter any moment. Sabrina glared. Bitch. Sexy bitch, but still evil. When she turned back to the computer, Sabrina watched her. She had the brightest blue eyes she'd ever seen. An exotic contrast to her dark hair and olive skin. Her full pouty lips made Sabrina think of the feel of them between her teeth. Damn sexy. And that was saying a lot for a straight girl.

She still didn't know what on earth had compelled her to agree to a summer fling with her best friend and some random – and granted hot – stranger who had a closet full of torture devices. For now, she'd blame the wine. And Q, of course.

She sighed. No. This mess was her own damned fault. She'd gotten Q drunk because she'd wanted to see how far she could push her – if she could get Q to act on her desires. It had backfired. Not only had she been left frustrated, but now she was stuck being bi! For a few months anyway. That's what she got for tugging on the lion's tail.

Q pushed away from the computer and looked at Sabrina. "I'm hopping in the shower."

If she kept reading this book, she'd need one herself. A cold one. She did her best to smile nonchalantly. "Okay."

Q disappeared down the hallway. Back in Constant Screwing Land, the heroine was having twenty screaming orgasms in a row. Sabrina threw down the book and went to check her email instead.

Just as she logged into Gmail, a ding signaled an online chat message. She clicked on the blinking window minimized on the bottom of the screen. Jude's handsome face greeted her.

"He does have a hot profile pic," she murmured to herself.

She almost clicked the logout button then stopped short when she saw her name in a few messages. They'd been talking about her? She scrolled up the screen.

Q

Sabrina agreed to experiment for the summer.

JUDE

That was fast.

Q

We were both pretty hammered when we talked. Lol.

JUDE

Funny. But you better double check to make sure she agrees sober too.

Q

She does. I've already mentioned it here and there. She seems nervous but I can tell she's interested.

JUDE

What kinds of things does she like?

Q

I don't know. We've never talked about kink before.

JUDE

I'd like you to find out before we go any further.

Q

Is that a command, oh Domly One?

JUDE

If you need it to be. *evil Dom eye*

Q

Oh no! Your evil Dom eye has me so intimidated I can barely type.

JUDE

Lol. Brat.

Q

You're surprised?

JUDE

Not in the least. Just preparing myself. Is Sabrina a brat too?

Q

Yes, but in a different way. She's easier to intimidate. Me, you'll have to beat. Her, the Dom eye may suffice. You man enough to handle both of us?

JUDE

I eat brats like you for breakfast.

Q

Is that a promise?

JUDE

Depends on your behavior. What time are you coming over?

Q

I have a photo shoot in the morning. Is 3pm okay?

JUDE

That's fine. Google BDSM checklist. I want you to fill one out with Sabrina.

Q

Homework, oh Domly one?

JUDE

Yes. It'll make things smoother. Trust me. And Q…

Q

Yes?

JUDE

One of these days I'll have you calling me Sir while you beg me to come.

Q

We'll see. Bye, Jude. See you Friday.

JUDE

Bye, brat.

Sabrina inhaled a deep breath. Wow. As if her nerves weren't frayed enough just dealing with Q's advances. Now Jude wanted to eat her for breakfast. She gulped but her clit warmed at the idea. She needed more information. Keeping a keen ear out for the sound of the shower, she typed a message to Jude.

Q

Are you still there?

JUDE

Yes.

Where to start. She thought for a moment, then typed again.

Q

I meant to ask you…what do you like?

JUDE

Hmm. Strawberry ice cream. A nice cold beer. Long walks on the beach ;)

Smart ass. She smiled.

Q

That's not what I meant and you know it.

JUDE

I have a wide range of interests but I stay away from extremes.

Q

Extremes? Like what?

JUDE

Inflicting severe pain. Blood and knife play. I have no love for costumes either. Lol. Except for sexy outfits on obedient subs.

She chuckled, picturing Jude wearing cowboy chaps and wielding a whip. But blood and knife play? There was nothing funny about that. Hesitantly, she typed another message.

Q

Have you tied up girls before?

JUDE

Lots.

Q

And they've never been injured or anything?

Flashes of limp limbs from lack of circulation needing amputation crossed her mind. She grimaced and fought not to call the whole thing off. Jude took longer to answer this time.

JUDE

I am very careful. I've never injured anyone in my five years of experience. But just in case, I keep a pair of scissors nearby and a first aid kit. Anything else, Sabrina?

Sabrina? No, he couldn't know. A door slammed shut behind her. She startled then swung around. Q stood behind her, wearing baggy cotton pajama pants and a white tank top. Wet hair swung in front of her face. She looked from Sabrina's face to the computer screen.

"What are you up to, trouble?" she asked suspiciously, walking toward her.

Shit. "Nothing. I was about to log into my online chat account is all." She tried to turn the swivel chair back around but Q caught it with her legs.

She looked down at Sabrina, her eyes narrowed, as if trying to read her thoughts. Sabrina did her best to look innocent, which seemed to only make Q more suspicious. Q broke eye contact and read the screen.

Embarrassed, she tried to get up. But Q straddled her, pinning her to the chair, Q facing the computer and Sabrina facing away.

"Q," she whined, trying to rise.

"Hush." She continued to read the screen, ignoring Sabrina's half-assed attempts to get free.

Sure, she could've fought more, but she kind of liked the feel of Q there, so close. She smelled good, like herbal shampoo. Her body felt warm and comforting. And she knew Q wouldn't let her up easily. The last thing she wanted after getting hot and bothered by that book was a wrestling match. Q's breasts were at eye level and she hadn't put on a bra yet. Her nipples stuck out like tempting little peaks. How easy it would be to nibble one while Q was distracted.

That thought caught her off guard. She sighed. *You're slipping, straight girl.*

"Hm," Q said, arching a brow. "I see you've been up to no good."

"Are you going to tell Jude?" she asked in a small voice. She did kind of feel guilty about deceiving him.

"I don't think I need to. Smart man. He already guessed." She started typing on the keyboard.

"What are you writing?" Sabrina tried to turn toward the computer but with Q sitting on top of her, and her feet pinning the chair in place, she couldn't move enough to see.

"That's none of your business, nosy. But since you're here, you can answer a few questions."

Why didn't she like the sound of that? She groaned.

Q looked down at her. "That's what you get for interfering." The printer came to life beside the desk, spitting out two pieces of paper. Finally Q stood. "Stay," she commanded when Sabrina tried to rise.

She flopped back down with a huff. Q grabbed the papers and two pens then set them on the coffee table. What the hell was she doing? Taking notes? She smiled devilishly at Sabrina then grabbed the arms of her chair and rolled her across the hardwood floor, stopping in front of the couch. Q sat down, tucking her legs under her body.

"Jude wants us to fill this out." She handed Sabrina a pen and paper.

Confused, she looked over the paper. *BDSM Interest Checklist.* Below the title were dozens of kinky activities with boxes marked yes, no, and maybe.

She shoved the paper back at Q. "I'm not filling this out."

"Why not?" Q asked, her brow creased.

"It's weird. I barely know him. What does he need to know all this private stuff for?"

Q sighed. "He wants to play with us. I know you barely know him, but he and I have been talking non-stop since we met."

"About what?" She couldn't help but feel a little left out.

She shrugged. "Everything. He comes from money, which is a little weird considering my background. But he's not like other rich people I've known. His whole family is doctors. I can tell he loves them very much. But," her forehead wrinkled, "I also get the impression there's something going on there. Something big. He changes the subject whenever it comes up." Her eyes brightened. "He's very well-travelled. You should hear some of his stories about hitchhiking in Europe."

Jealousy speared her. Why weren't they including her in these chats? Deep down inside, she knew the answer. She guarded herself too securely. Trust was hard earned when it came to her. Maybe she'd let Jude and Q seduce her physically this summer but she wouldn't give away her heart. Long-distance relationships didn't work. Temporary romance was for love-struck teenagers.

"Anyway, he's safe and experienced with BDSM," Q said. "I have a good feeling about him."

Unable to hold back the twinge of hurt – even though it was her own fault – she snapped, "Well excuse me if I don't let a stranger tie me up naked based on your good feeling. I don't even know what half this stuff is. Tell Jude I'll figure it out as I go."

"Fill it out for me then. I can get a good idea of what you like and make sure Jude doesn't go beyond that."

"Fill it out for you? Definitely not."

She frowned. "Why not?" She actually sounded hurt.

Sabrina winced. The last thing she wanted to do was hurt Q. But this…talking about sex by filling out a checklist….it was so clinical. Like a check-up for her sex life.

Q pulled herself together and smiled. "I bet I can guess a lot of what you like anyway. This will just be confirming what I already know."

"That's creepy!"

Q laughed. "We've known each other a long time, beautiful. It was bound to happen."

Sabrina's stomach fluttered with nerves. Could she really do this? She let out a long sigh. Q probably sensed her acquiescence. She caved too easily when it came to Q. It was like she held some strange power over her. Sabrina ached to please her, no matter the cost. But she could trust Q. She hadn't betrayed her in the five years they'd known each other. A bloody miracle as far as Sabrina was concerned.

"We'll do it together," Q declared brightly. "I don't know what all of it is either."

Sabrina looked at her, surprised. "You don't?"

She snorted. "Despite what you think of me, I'm not some porno-addicted sex fiend looking to get off with anything that has legs. I'm pretty tame compared to most kinksters."

Oh god. She shuddered to imagine in what world Q – her kinky, gender confused, bisexual friend – was tame.

"First section," Q started. "Role-playing."

Sabrina browsed the list. Family play, fantasy rape, doctor/nurse play – she grimaced at the thought of examination tables and speculums. Interrogations, prison scenes…

"Animal roles?" she blurted out loud, aghast.

Q smirked. "What? You don't want to be my little pussy?"

She felt her eyes widen then she burst out laughing. "That's crass, even for you."

"I know," she said between giggles. "But I couldn't resist."

"Crossing off role-playing." She made a big X over the section. "Next up, sexual play." Grimacing, she read down the list. No, no, no. Most of them she could guess by the titles and they triggered her gag reflex. Finally, she reached something familiar. "Vibrators!" She put a big check mark next to that one.

Q chuckled. "Figures."

"What?" She snapped her head up to look at Q.

"I know you own a vibrator, little girl." She winked. "But your secret is safe with me."

She fought back the wave of heat threatening to redden her cheeks and swallowed hard. Back to the list, she coached herself. So what if Q knew she had a vibrator? Didn't every girl own one?

"Skip down to the domination/submission section," Q said. "That's the stuff I need to know."

Heart thumping, she read on. Some words popped out immediately, causing a stir to start down below. How could a mere suggestion work better than her past three boyfriends? Begging. Following orders. Kneeling. Those words called to her, making her face flame with heat. When she looked up at Q, she noticed her eyes fixed on Sabrina.

"Be honest," she said. "Check off the ones making you blush."

Damn her. She scowled.

Q chuckled. "Don't be embarrassed. We're probably checking off some of the same things."

She looked down at the list again. "You're not making me stand in a corner," she told Q firmly, just to express her annoyance.

Q raised a brow. "You'll stand where I tell you to once we start playing."

Sabrina huffed. Sad fact was, she probably would. She checked off a few boxes, steering clear of ones like bathroom control and forced eating. Next section was the most daunting. Masochism. She was familiar with the word. It meant taking pleasure from pain. The crop in the closet had made her tingle. She'd itched to feel the flogger on her thighs and ass. But a masochist? Did she qualify?

If so, she was going straight to hell – do not pass go, do not collect two hundred dollars. She was pretty sure they didn't let freaks like her – like Q – into church.

Q studying the list, her brow creased, pen resting on her lips. Alluring lips. Sex was an expression of love. Why would God discriminate against different kinds of love?

Again, certain words jumped out, causing a stirring deep within her. The most surprising – over-the-knee spanking. Well shit. Did that mean she was into age play after all?

"What's got you so confused?" Q asked.

She'd been watching Sabrina again. "Nothing," she murmured, keeping her head down.

"Tell me. I might be able to help."

She shook her head, her pen hovering above the yes box.

"Tell me, little girl," she said more sternly.

Damn her again. She sighed. Why did she always cave when Q called her that? Like some involuntary reflex kicked into overdrive, making her submit to any dominant personality nearby. Worse with Q. "If I like…" Ugh. She couldn't even say it out loud. Quickly, she circled the word then thrust it at Q. "That one. Does that mean I'm into age play?"

Q looked at the paper and hissed in a breath. "Um. Not necessarily." Her voice shook and her eyes brightened with lust.

Sabrina almost laughed out loud. Well, well, well. Q wasn't quite as composed as she thought. She was getting turned on by the list too. Sabrina hid a grin as a devious plan came to mind.

She circled another word. "What do they mean by this?"

Q kept her gaze on the paper but she squirmed in her seat the same way Sabrina had been while reading the erotic book. After a moment, she rasped, "Being beaten with a belt."

"And single tail?" Oh this was too fun.

She snapped her gaze to Sabrina and narrowed her eyes. "Read your selections out loud."

Shaking her head adamantly, she pulled the paper back and looked down. "I'm not done. I still have to fill out the bondage part."

"Read what you have so far," she ordered.

"No thanks. But you can see it when I'm done."

"I don't want to see it," she said more firmly. "I want to hear you read each one."

Sabrina flicked her gaze to her friend, feeling her eyes widen. "But –"

"You wanna play games with me, little girl? You should know better. Read each selection out loud and let's see how you like being watched when you're aroused."

"You're so mean!"

"You started it. Now go."

Sabrina gulped then looked down at her list. "Um." Her voice squeaked and she cleared it. Come on, Sabrina. Man up. Or woman up, rather. "Okay. Well. Vibrators, begging, following orders, hair pulling, floggers, biting." She rushed through the list then stopped at the words over-the-knee spanking.

"Um. The other one I showed you."

"Say it."

"No."

Q studied her for a moment then sighed. "Alright. We'll work on that later. Keep going."

Grateful to be off the hook, for now, she read the last few things on the list. "Belts, punishment, flogging." She finished with an exhale. Torture. That was nothing short of torture. Maybe she should add that to Q's list. She built up the courage to look at her friend. Would she laugh at her?

Q's eyes glittered and her lips parted as her breaths came out shallow. "That was hot."

Sabrina laughed hard. "You're seriously disturbed, you know that?"

She gave her a sly smile. "And yet you're going to come over here and kiss me."

And suddenly, there wasn't anything else in the world she'd rather do. As if Q had strings attached to her body, Sabrina rose from the chair and walked to the couch. Q crooked a finger and Sabrina leaned over.

"Kiss me," Q ordered.

"You know I'm not good at this," Sabrina breathed, her gaze transfixed on Q's mouth.

She grabbed onto Sabrina's t-shirt and tugged her down. Their lips almost touched. Sabrina waited for it, but Q didn't make the first move. She kept Sabrina hovering with a firm grip on her shirt.

"Kiss me," she whispered again.

"I can't." But god did she want to. The urge to kiss was mixed up with that stupid feeling that it was somehow wrong.

Q narrowed her eyes. "I dare you."

Sabrina's resistance snapped. She sucked in a sharp breath and planted one knee on the couch at the same time as she lunged for Q's mouth. Self-preservation made her slow just before they touched. So soft and so light Q's lips seemed, that the air stopped still and jammed up in her chest.

Mmm. She didn't shut her eyes, though she always had before, with boys. She didn't because seeing Q's eyes there, right in front of her, all big and beautiful and watching…just did something awesome.

Then Sabrina overbalanced and fell, landing sideways on Q's lap. Their mouths crushed together. She groped for something to take the weight and found one hand on the armrest and the other on Q's breast. A giggle erupted, and she drew back an inch.

"Ouch," Q whispered.

"Sorry," she whispered back. "About my hand, I mean." Their voices sounded cozy, the moment turning even more intimate.

"Keep it there."

She hesitated then complied. "Okay."

"Now kiss me again."

Right. Girl Kiss, take two.

This time she started out gentle, pressing in and taking little holds of Q's lips with hers. But the stunned quietness radiating from Q made her pause. Not good. She remembered how the heroes did it in movies and books. No point in going at this half-assed. So she used her weight and crushed her lips harder onto Q's, then shoved her tongue in and out, turning her head for a better angle.

A hand slapped against her ass. Q pulled back, panting. "Not so rough!"

Sabrina sat back, a little dazed, staring at Q's red freshly kissed lips. "Sorry. I copied the books you gave me. I was plundering."

"Plundering?"

She nodded.

Q chuckled. "Be gentle, little girl. I'm not a conquest." She reached up and pecked her lips then smiled. "You already won me."

Disheartened, she asked timidly, "Let me try again?"

"Go for it, beautiful."

Another deep breath. Third go. The curve of Q's full lips were as tempting as any man's. More so, maybe. Being gentle was easy, wasn't it? Instead of crushing, she brought her mouth right up close until the first barest feather-soft sensation flowered into being. Then she moved along, sideways, breathing on Q, letting the skin on their lower lips slide. Again, Q seemed stunned or… maybe just rapt in what she was doing.

"Is this okay?" she asked quietly.

"Yes," Q murmured.

She smiled then teased Q with petite kisses. Kiss…and draw away. Nibble with teeth and lift away. Stick the tip of her tongue between Q's lips and lick slow as honey over that plump sweet curve…and kiss.

The contentment on Q's face vanished. She growled, and grabbed the back of Sabrina's head.

Sabrina's squeal was cut off as Q yanked her in right up front and center. This time they met with mouth on mouth and stayed that way, sighing and making little noises of appreciation, toying with each other's tongues, and tasting. Q was fresh and yummy and hot. Their breasts compressed together and Sabrina noticed the hard bead of Q's nipples near her own.

Their kissing fell into a rhythm that seemed to carry them both away. Heat rippled in waves through Sabrina.

Gasping, licking her lips, she raised her head. Uh-oh. She'd been grinding her crotch into Q's. She froze. Q's face went from shocked arousal to a more composed calm.

"Well." Q cleared her throat. "That was good. I didn't know you had it in you."

A wicked giggle escaped her. It felt good throwing Q off balance. It reminded her she wasn't entirely powerless in their dynamic.

Q pinched her thigh, giving her a stern look. "Don't get cocky. Remember your place."

Reckless with lust, she sassed, "And what's that, Miss Bossy Pants?"

In one move, Q dumped her off her lap and she landed on her ass on the floor. Sabrina grunted and moved to get up, but Q pointed to the ground by her feet and ordered, "Kneel."

A soft growl grew in Sabrina's chest as she fought with herself whether to obey.

"Did you check kneeling on your list?" Q asked, brows arched.

"Yes," she grumbled. But to Q? Like this? She stared at the floor.

"And between me and you, who did you picture doing the kneeling?"

She opened her mouth to tell her neither but that wasn't quite the truth. With a sigh, she answered honestly. "Me."

"So that makes you what in our relationship?"

"The sub," she answered with an eye roll. What kind of monster had she unleashed in her best friend?

Q ignored the attitude. "Then kneel."

With a glare, she obeyed, sitting up on her knees and waiting for approval.

"Good girl." Q nodded, maybe a little proud. "Now sit with me and we'll fill out the bondage part together."

Oh goody. She sighed but shimmied to the couch and climbed on next to Q. The list continued with a dozen types of bondage and restraint play. Most of them caused the same stirring as the damn spanking.

She chuckled at mummification. "Hey, Q. Want to mummify me? Then I can haunt you in your sleep." Opening her eyes wide, she put her arms out and rocked back and forth like a mummy. "Kinky best friend mummy…*raaaaa*…"

Q shook her head and mumbled, "No, but the gags are looking pretty enticing."

She snapped her mouth shut instinctively then cursed herself for the wussy reaction. Q chuckled beside her. With a pout, she went back to the list. Handcuffs, rope bondage, blindfolds…*mmmm*….

"Plastic wrap?" she said out loud with a face. "Ugh. Soooo unflattering."

Q laughed. "Leave it to you to think of fashion when it comes to bondage."

"I'm just stating the obvious. Cling wrap does nothing for your figure."

Q grinned.

"What?"

"I'm just imagining picking out a pretty collar for you." Q tucked a piece of hair behind Sabrina's ear. "Maybe purple."

A collar? Her heart fluttered in her chest. If it were anyone else, she'd have been insulted. But for Q…. A smile tugged at her lips. "But Q, I didn't mark collars on my list."

Q barked a laugh. "Smart ass." She took Sabrina's questionnaire from her hand and placed it with hers on the table. "Alright, missy. Time to apologize to Jude for deceiving him." She held her cell phone out to Sabrina.

Sabrina looked back and forth from the phone to Q's face. "Seriously?"

Q arched a brow in a look of stubborn determination.

"Fine." She rolled her eyes and took the phone from Q. "You already have his number programmed in your phone?" she asked. "How often do you guys talk anyway?"

"Often. And you should too. You're part of this."

"Not by choice," she mumbled under her breath.

Q plopped back on the couch and ran her fingers through Sabrina's hair lazily. "Still pretending to be the innocent victim?"

She kept her gaze down on the phone, scrolling to find Jude's name. "Shh! I'm following your orders, oh Domly one." She smothered a giggle.

Q swatted her thigh with her other hand, making Sabrina laugh. "Ow! Stop. You're distracting me."

"Oh, am I?" Her expression changed and she shifted her body to face Sabrina.

Uh-oh. What ideas had she just unintentionally put in Q's head? "Hey Jude, it's Sabrina," she said out loud as she typed a text. "Q is making me apolog –" She cut off with a yelp when Q's hand tightened in her hair.

A second later, Q's lips were at her ear. "Do it right, little girl," she growled then nipped her ear lobe, causing her to squeak in surprise.

"Okay," she whispered, unable to move with her hair pulled tight in Q's fist. The prickles on her scalp sent a wave of lust straight to her clit. Every time Q called her little girl her stomach dropped and a throb started between her legs.

"Good girl." Q released her hold and went back to combing through it gently with her fingers. Just having Q's hands on her did…something she couldn't explain. Like, the way she played with her hair now made her so relaxed she wanted to strip down and beg Q to touch her whole body. Then that thought led to more dangerous ones – images that questionnaire put in her mind.

"You done yet?" Q's voice startled her back to composing her message.

"I'm sorry I deceived you on online chat," she read out loud then clicked send. "There. Sent it." She tried to hand the phone back but the text alert beeped. She looked down. It was Jude.

"What did he say?" Q asked.

"'I forgive you. Next time just ask upfront if you have questions.'" Sabrina smiled. "He's sweet, isn't he?"

Q gave a mysterious chuckle. "I wouldn't be too sure about that."

She looked at her friend. "He's sweet to me cause I'm not a brat like you are."

"Oh, you're a brat," she replied, taking the phone back. "You just haven't paid for it yet." She began typing a message.

"What are you writing now?"

"I'm telling him that we filled out the questionnaires."

The phone rang, the familiar metal riff startling her.

"It's Jude," Q said then thrust the phone at her. "Answer it."

She leaned away. "You answer it! It's your phone."

"He wants to talk to you." Q shook it at her.

Sabrina sighed dramatically then took the phone. "Hello?"

"Who's this?" Jude's sexy voice chimed on the other end. "Brat one or brat two?"

"Uhh…*no hablo ingles*." A strangled laugh escaped her as a snort.

"Ah," Jude said. "Brat two then. Tell Q I said hi."

"He says hi," she said to Q.

She gave Sabrina a mysterious smile then gestured with her hands to keep talking.

"Uh…" She stammered, grasping for topics. "We filled out that questionnaire." She cringed as soon as the words left her mouth. Why on earth did she bring that up?

"Good," he said. "You can email them to me tonight."

Panic started in her chest and she blurted, "No."

A pause then, "Excuse me?"

The Dom voice. This was dangerous territory. "Um, safeword. That's a thing, right? Safeword to you seeing my answers," she said, forcing her voice to sound firm.

Another pause then he burst out laughing. "You're safewording a questionnaire?"

Q sighed. "I got a good idea of what she likes, Jude," she yelled at the phone. "I'll sum it up for you when I send mine."

Sabrina waited for Jude to protest. Would he push her despite her safewording?

"That works," he said and she exhaled a breath. "For now."

Q nudged her and whispered, "I'm getting a drink. You want anything?"

She pulled the phone away from her ear. "Uh, no. But what about him?" She pointed emphatically at the phone.

"Talk," Q answered with a grin. She got up and headed for the kitchen. "Get to know each other."

Talk? On the phone to a guy? It had been ages since she'd done something so simple. Why was she so nervous? Shit, even her palms were sweaty. This wasn't junior high school for christsake! "Um," she said into the phone. "So how are you?"

"Better now that I've heard your voice."

She rolled her eyes. "Oh my god. Do you ever turn it off?"

"Turn what off?" He sounded honestly confused.

"The smooth-talking arrogant male complex," she answered boldly. Thank goodness for his chuckle or she'd have worried she put her foot in her mouth again. "You don't have to compliment me to win me over. I prefer honesty."

"You want honesty? Alright." He exhaled into the receiver.

Was it so difficult for him to just be himself?

"I wish you would chat with me on online," he said, a hopeful lilt in his voice.

"I hate online chat."

"Text then. I feel like I know Q. I'd like to know you too. Obviously you're someone worth knowing if Q likes you so much."

She should set him straight – tell him Q was one of her only real friends for a reason. And they fit together only because of their shared oddness. If she were a good person, she'd warn him like she'd warned Q when they'd first become friends – though she'd ignored her and stuck around anyway. Sabrina wasn't worth getting to know. Not with her big mouth, confused sexuality, and quirky habits.

But today…today she just wasn't in the mood to play fair. This was temporary anyway, wasn't it? A summer fling to try out some wild, kinky sex. He wasn't sticking around so she'd let him think he liked her for a few months – at least enough for him to want to have sex with her. Her confidence could use it. Finally she cleared her throat and answered, "Q will sum up the questionnaire."

"I don't mean I want to know you in bed, Sabrina. Well, I do. But I also want to know *you*. As a person. What are your favorite things? What's your family like? What are your hopes and dreams?"

She chuckled nervously. "Well you get right down to it, don't you?"

"You wanted honesty," he answered.

Well now she'd screwed herself good. "I did. I mean, I do." She inhaled a breath then released it slowly. Okay, she could give him this. "Um, well, I'm addicted to diet cola. I love watching dance shows though I couldn't dance to save my life."

His soft chuckle made her smile.

"The way into my heart is through humor and chocolate," she said, shifting her body into a more comfortable position on the couch.

"Mental note," Jude said. "Buy giant box of chocolate."

She laughed then noticed Q standing just outside the living, watching her with a grin. Sabrina waved her over but she motioned she was going to bed. Sabrina blew her a kiss with a wink and Q walked away, smiling and shaking her head. She turned her attention to Jude.

For the next hour, they talked. About her big Italian family that made The Sopranos look sane, the best places in town to get seafood, their shared passion for cheesy B-movies on the sci-fi channel. She didn't get to her hopes and dreams before Jude had to go, but she felt as if she knew him – on a deeper level than just a sexy potential Dom. And for the first time in a long time, she had an inkling of hope for her love life.

Chapter 7

Sabrina

Sabrina ran her hands over her long, flowy black dress, smoothing out a few crinkles. The top swooped low and the straps tied on her shoulders – which she'd double knotted – but she was hoping the length would save her.

Tonight was séance night. She'd been waiting for it for days with an equal sense of excitement and foreboding. She could, potentially, reach a spirit tonight – one who she'd know the name and history for.

It was also just as likely she'd be ravished tonight. No, wait. More likely. Hence the long dress. When she wore sundresses and short skirts, she could practically see the wheels turning in Q's head. It would be so easy for her to reach a hand under the short fabric and…

She forced those thoughts away before she needed a date with her B.O.B. Again. Ever since that afternoon at Jude's house, she'd needed her purple friend far more than usual. The memory of her forced against Jude's body, wrists wrapped tight in the cuffs, Q's soft lips against her skin… She shivered.

And that closet. It both terrified and titillated. Some of Q's sexual habits must've rubbed off on her since living together. Q should have mentioned that before they signed the lease – not that it would have changed her mind.

Well, she'd get it all out of her system this summer. She only hoped Q could go back to being friends when it was over. Because it *would* end. There was no choice about it. She could picture her mother fainting then spending every evening in church, praying for her soul. Her entire extended family would find out within hours. She'd be ostracized at every family event, and even though nobody would say anything to her face, the whispers would be hard to ignore. It had happened to her cousin, Anthony, when he'd come out.

"Sabrina!" Q knocked on the bathroom door. "I'm sure you look gorgeous. It's time to go."

She tucked her hair behind her ears with a sigh then walked out of the bathroom.

Q ran her gaze over Sabrina's outfit, looking like she was holding back a smile.

"What?" Sabrina peered down at herself. "You don't like what I'm wearing?"

She bit her lip and her eyes gleamed with mischief. "No, the dress is fine." She walked closer and brushed Sabrina's hair off her shoulder then fingered the dress strap.

She shuddered. Q's recent habit of touching her often – running her fingers across her lower back when she walked by or touching her cheek when she told her she was beautiful – was driving her to distraction. To her shame, she had run the batteries out in her purple friend yesterday.

"You look beautiful," Q said as she tucked a lock of Sabrina's hair behind her ear.

Sabrina rolled her eyes. *There she goes again.* "You ready?"

"Yes."

She looked Q over and sighed. When was she going to get a new wardrobe? "Black shirt and jeans," she mumbled. "What a surprise."

Q arched a brow. "Jude doesn't seem to mind."

"He was probably picturing what was underneath."

She chuckled and held open the front door. When Sabrina went past her, Q swatted her ass. She threw an indignant look over her shoulder. She could almost feel Q's satisfied grin at her back all the way to the parked car.

"We'll take mine," Q said then pressed the unlock button on the key remote.

They drove in silence, Sabrina picking at her nails to relieve her nerves.

"What are you so nervous about, girly?" Q asked.

That you and Jude will convince me – by the unfair means of making me so horny I could probably come with one stroke – to let you do naughty things to my body. She gulped. "Nothing."

Q put a hand on her knee and she jerked. A chuckle came from beside her. "You're not scared, are you?"

Sabrina froze.

"Of the séance, of course," she added.

She exhaled a breath. "A little," she admitted, unsure whether she was answering about the séance or...other things. There was no doubt in her mind, Jude and Q had nefarious plans for her. Plans that made ghost hunting look like child's play.

Q gave her knee a squeeze. "I'll be with you. Through all of it."

Sabrina smiled. Yes. This was Q. Just her Q. They always looked out for each other. That hadn't changed. Not even after their drunken agreement to try being girlfriends for the summer.

They pulled up in front of Jude's house and parked the car. The front porch light was a relief to see on the dark moonless night. No blown fuses for the séance would make things more relaxed for all of them. Sabrina grabbed her bag from the back seat and they walked to the door.

Jude was there, holding it open. She looked him over, appreciating his muscular body again, covered in a fitted black t-shirt. That gave her pause. The last two times she'd seen Jude, he'd been wearing a black shirt and jeans. He was tall, kinky, and liked heavy metal. He even had blue eyes. Q and Jude were the perfect pair. Sabrina's heart sank. Yeah, maybe their little fling was only for the summer, but who wanted to be the third wheel? Maybe this wasn't going to work after all.

"You coming, Jersey girl?" Jude slung an arm around her petite shoulders.

Oddly, she felt cozy there in the crook of his arm. She bit her lip and tightened her grip on her bag. No going back now.

After he dragged her inside, she spotted Q texting on her phone, a frustrated look on her face. "Q!" She scooted out from under Jude's heavy arm, placed her equipment bag on the floor, and crossed the room. "Is that Nico again?" she demanded, peering over Q's shoulder.

"Calm down." She placed the phone back in her pocket. "I'm just clearing up a few things. Everything is fine."

Sabrina glared. Q grinned. It wasn't fair that Q was so difficult to intimidate.

"So what do we need for this séance?" Jude interrupted their stare-down. "Candles? Ouija board?" He smiled slyly. "Virgin sacrifice?"

"No, smartass. Just a round or oval table will do."

He nodded. "Dining room then."

They started through the living room then Q sighed and whipped out her phone. It was vibrating. Sabrina growled. Q had no sense when it came to her ex. She should've told him off a long time ago then changed her phone number.

"Ugh," Q grunted, staring at the screen. "He wants to stop by my photo shoot tomorrow. Hang on a sec. I just want to settle this before we start."

"Q..." Sabrina started, revving up for a fight.

"I promise I'll turn it off for the séance," Q said, her hands up in a peaceful gesture. "Just get everything ready and I'll be right back." She was already dialing as she walked through the living room and outside.

Sabrina continued to glare in her direction several seconds after she'd gone.

Jude's voice interrupted her soon-to-be violent thoughts. "I take it you don't like this Nico guy."

She watched Q's slender shape pace back and forth in front of the screen door. "I don't trust him for shit."

He stiffened beside her. "Is he harassing her?"

"No. But he wants to get back together. Major asshole." It was after they'd broken up that Q moved in with Sabrina. She'd seen first-hand the mess Nico had left behind. "Q is too nice to tell him to fuck off." And she wouldn't let Sabrina do it for her either.

"She doesn't seem like the type to take shit."

Sabrina turned on Jude, putting a little bite in her voice she told him, "Q is the nicest person I've ever met. She would never hurt somebody's feelings on purpose." She turned back to face the porch. "She's too nice. I tell her so all the time."

"And you're not?"

"I don't have those concerns when it comes to people I don't like."

He chuckled. "You made that quite clear with your little threat last week."

She looked up at him with narrowed eyes. "It's still true."

"I'm very intimidated," he said, not sounding the least bit intimidated. "But you don't have to worry about me hurting Q. I have no intentions of hurting either one of you. At least not in ways you don't want me to." A glint of humor hit his eyes.

"Huh?" Did he say hurt?

"You protect each other," he continued, ignoring her bewilderment. "It's sweet."

She shrugged. "She's one of my only friends. I don't want to lose her." She thought of their summer plan. Not many people could remain friends after trying something more. Was she doomed to lose her best friend?

No. Q had promised. They'd be friends, no matter what. "I won't let anything get in the way of our friendship," she muttered.

A strong hand came under her chin and lifted it. Warm blue eyes stared down at her. She sucked in a breath, letting his scent fill her. Masculine yet sweet. It made her want to wrap herself in it after a long day.

"You won't lose her, Sabrina," he said with a heart-stopping smile. "She's very attached to you."

Attached? That made her feel as warm and fuzzy as Jude stroking her cheek with his thumb did. Crushing on two people at the same time? She squeezed her eyes shut. It was too much to handle.

Jude let her go and she opened her eyes. He'd stepped back, as if sensing her confusion. "So how did you two meet?"

She inhaled a deep breath, pulling herself together. "An art class at college. We have the same silly sense of humor."

A wide smile crept onto her face when she remembered their very first conversation. They'd both ended up in the same PhotoShop class. Sabrina noticed Q swearing under her breath while learning how to make subtle changes to body parts. She had a knack for the program, which was how she turned out majoring in graphic design. So she offered Q some help. After looking at Q's project, she burst into a laughing fit that left her almost crying. Q had managed to make the model's nose look like a dick. When she insisted it had looked like that before she started the project, they both erupted into giggles and Sabrina knew she'd found a kindred spirit.

Sabrina cleared her head and looked up at Jude. "We clicked right away and have been inseparable ever since."

He nodded. "You make an interesting pair."

Pair? She opened her mouth to correct him but Q interrupted her.

"Sorry," she said with a remorseful expression then looked at Sabrina and smiled. "Don't pout, gorgeous. I'm done now."

Q turned her phone to show Sabrina she'd shut it off. It frustrated her that Q didn't even understand what Sabrina was upset about. She let Q protect her, fight her battles at times. Sabrina wanted to do the same for her once in a while. But she couldn't force Q to look after her own heart. Sabrina would just have to be there to put it back together when it broke again.

She sighed. "Let's just get started."

The dining room was in a sad state of affairs. Similar to the rest of the unrepaired rooms, cracks ran the length of the dank and stained walls. A long sturdy-looking table sat in the middle of the room, three mismatched chairs around it. It wasn't ideal, but it would do.

Sabrina pulled a sunny yellow table cloth from her bag and placed it on the table. It didn't quite fit, but it was better than nothing. She searched for the sage bundle and lighter next.

"What's with the florescent table cloth?" Q asked with a grimace.

She fumbled with the lighter before it lit, setting the sage aglow. "Spirits are attracted to bright colors."

Jude coughed as she waved the smoking bundle. "Good thing I didn't install smoke detectors yet."

"It'll protect us from any spirits who want to harm us," she explained. After burning half the bundle she blew it out and placed it back in her bag. "And these candles," she set three pink candles on the table, "will attract the good spirits because they like heat and light."

"Should we put out a lava lamp too?" Q said with a smirk. "Maybe we'd channel some hippie ghosts."

Jude laughed.

Sabrina bit back a chuckle in favor of a scowl. "I'll do this alone if you're not going to take this seriously."

"No," they both said in unison.

"Keep going," Q urged. "We're just being silly."

"Sorry." Jude cleared his throat, as if choking back another laugh. "We'll behave."

Q's gaze snapped to his face. "I never promised that."

He arched a brow. "Do you need a lesson in manners already?"

What the hell were they talking about? They stared each other down, Q's eyes gleaming and Jude returning her saucy glare. He shifted his body to stand straighter.

"You did say you could teach me," Q answered huskily.

He snorted. "I don't think you're ready to go there tonight, pet."

"I don't think you have any idea what I'm ready for," she sassed back.

Jude inhaled a sharp breath and –

"Stop!" Sabrina shouted. There was enough sexual tension in the room to choke any ghost that attempted to make contact. "Take your raging hormones elsewhere! You're messing with the energy of the room." She turned on Q. "Let him make you his pet in the Closet O'Kink if that's what you want. But leave so I can get started."

It took a few seconds for Q to take her eyes off of Jude. "No. I'm not leaving you to contact the dead alone."

Sabrina smirked. "Thought you didn't believe in ghosts."

"Doesn't matter," Jude answered for her. "We're doing this together." He took a seat at one end of the table. Q sat at the other end. They both looked at her expectantly.

Sparks of unbridled lust sizzled between them, even a table length apart. This was never going to work. "I'm serious," Sabrina told them. "I need your full cooperation or it won't work. Positive energy. Open-mindedness and....and...all that shit." She waved her hand vaguely in the air. Well, she was no expert.

"We're ready," Q said.

Sabrina gave her a skeptical look.

"Sit down, little girl," she said, sternly.

"Not until I know you're –"

"Sit. Down." Jude's voice had her butt in the chair in an instant.

Damn it! She really wished that would stop happening. With a sigh, she held out her hands, one toward Jude, one toward Q. "Hold hands. It will help channel our energy."

They each grasped a hand – Q's soft and familiar, Jude's rough and masculine. It felt...nice. It was too bad there wasn't a fourth to complete the circle. Though she was a Gemini – sign of the twins. Maybe that would help.

She closed her eyes and exhaled a deep breath. "Oh spirits of the...um...house of Jude," she winced at how amateur she sounded, "we humbly ask for your presence this evening."

She paused. Silence.

The Idiots Guide to Holding a Séance said she might feel movement in the room before hearing a voice – a sign that a spirit wanted to be reached. She waited, listening, feeling with all her senses. Nothing.

She tried again. "Benevolent spirits, if you are present, give us a sign." The book said to let the energy run through her body, fluid like water, with no expectations, no boundaries. So she thought of water – flowing streams of energy and love and peace and…other good stuff that would bring the spirits forth. But the only thing she could feel was the sudden urge to pee.

Discouraged, she sighed and opened her eyes. Q and Jude both had theirs shut, and to her surprise, seemed focused on the event. A devilish thought came to mind.

Pushing back a grin, she slipped on a mask of sincerity. "Huh. I'm not getting any – whoa!" She gasped and squeezed Q and Jude's hands.

Q's eyes popped open. "What?"

"Did you feel that?"

"Feel what?" Jude asked, brows raised.

She shook her head, doing her best to look confused. "I don't know. Energy or – shit!" She gasped and squeezed their hands tight.

"What!" Q shouted, sounding concerned.

"Shh!" Sabrina made her hands tremble against theirs, fighting hard not to giggle.

Q looked down at her hands. "Are you okay?"

"Oh my god! I can feel her." She shook harder and added a little panic to her voice. "It's Grace. I can't believe it worked. She's…." She crinkled her brow as if in concentration. "She's…wailing. So much guilt."

She peeked at her audience. Jude's forehead creased and his lips pursed, making his chin dimple. They were buying it. Damn she was good. Those acting classes were really paying off.

Then her mask slipped. A little smile tugged at her lips before she could stop it. Q caught it and narrowed her eyes. Shit.

"Sabrina Romano!" she said, pulling her hand out of Sabrina's grip. "Are you fucking with us?"

That was all Sabrina could take. A big burst of laughter came tumbling out of her mouth. Jude released her hand with a growl, but she couldn't stop laughing. It went on and on until tears streamed down her face and her sides ached. Q's disapproving frown slowed her down.

"I'm sorry," she panted. "I just couldn't resist. Did you see Jude's face?" The chuckles faded and she wiped her eyes. "It was so adorable."

Jude rubbed his hand over his mouth. Holding back a smile? Then he sat back in his chair, straight-faced again. Neither of them looked too pleased with her joke.

Q looked at Jude. "I think she deserves to be spanked."

"What?" Sabrina almost shrieked.

"At the very least," Jude agreed.

Somehow, none of it seemed funny anymore. She looked back and forth between the two. Q's expression, she recognized. She was about to get all "little girl this and little girl that" on her.

"You've been asking for this, little girl," she said.

Sabrina rolled her eyes. "You guys are joking, right? You're not really gonna…" She couldn't even say the words.

Q arched a brow. "Did you agree to try this for the summer, Sabrina?"

There was that. "Well, yeah, but…" She was trapped – and not just by some stupid drunken agreement. Jude sat on her left, looking much larger tonight than usual, and Q on her right, wearing her Bossy Pants face.

"Aw, hell." She jumped up from her chair and booked it.

About three steps into her rush for the door, she was caught. A few seconds later, she found herself pinned, face down, bent over the table, Jude's heavy body holding her down.

A harsh whisper tickled her ear. "Your safeword is 'ghost'. Say it and we stop. No other word will work. Say yes if you understand."

She blurted without thinking, "Yes."

"What do you say if you want us to stop?" Jude asked again.

"Ghost."

"Good girl."

The small praise made her heart leap. Was she really going to do this? Let Q and Jude dominate her? Q made sense, in a way. They'd had this strange dynamic for a while now. She looked up at Jude from the corner of her eye. His Bossy Pants face was worse than Q's. But at least Sabrina had known Q for more than five minutes.

She wiggled a little, testing his hold. Her arms were free and gripping the table cloth tight in her fists. One large male hand spanned her lower back, pressing down firmly but not painfully. The other hand was wrapped around the back of her neck. She could turn her head side to side, but couldn't lift up. Though all her limbs were free, it still felt pretty damn confining.

Ghost. She stamped the word into her memory. She could always say ghost and she knew without a doubt, Q would make sure she was okay.

Q. Sabrina looked for her. She turned her head to the left and watched her approach. She stalked, just like the lioness Sabrina had pictured only a week ago. Her smug smirk made Sabrina's insides clench in anticipation.

Q moved in behind her, out of Sabrina's line of sight. She stared at the cracked paint on the wall, waiting. The light touch on the back of her dress made her jump. Q chuckled. The zipper slid down, exposing her bare back.

"Wait!" She tensed then tried to pull up. Jude leaned harder. Though she wore a bra, pretty soon she was going to be half-naked – she'd chosen to wear a thong so panty lines wouldn't show. Stupid vanity. Half-naked? More like nine tenths. And Jude was watching.

If she shouted stop or ghost, would she upset Q? They'd barely begun and, in a way, she'd agreed to this. Wimping out so early seemed wrong.

"Wait, Q." Jude's terse order made Q falter then stop the slow descent of the zipper.

Relief filtered through Sabrina. She caught the tail end of a searching look Jude had sent her way.

Her heart thudded as they discussed her fate.

"Why? I thought I was in charge this time?"

"You are. But this isn't the start of a race. Slow down. Let's do it this way."

Jude lifted his hand from her lower back and the spot felt suddenly cold. She almost complained but caught herself. No way would she give any indication she enjoyed this. When his hand came down again, she could tell he was gathering handfuls of her dress. Inexorably, like the raising of the curtain on a stage, he was hauling it up.

Then the hand dragging up her dress switched from hard and heavy, to a lighter grasp. Q had taken over the task while Jude went back to holding her down at neck and lower back. Her dress was staying on. The threat of sudden, terrible nakedness was gone.

Yet that hold of Jude's on her – so firm, unrelenting, and male. His calluses rubbed her nape. He'd shown her such consideration without relinquishing a single bit of control. And without him speaking a word to her, she felt their connection sink in, from where his palm touched her skin, and spread through her flesh.

The hem of the dress reached her upper thighs. Trembling, she adjusted her grip on the tablecloth, and put her forehead to the cloth. If they looked, they'd see her thong was drenched.

A touch of cool night air hit her bared ass. So vulnerable.

Q came into her vision again. She looked down at Sabrina curiously.

Maybe she could appeal to her too-nice side.

"Q," she said in a small voice. "Just…just be nice."

Q smiled. A good sign, right? "I don't think you really want me to be nice."

Uh-oh. The thrilling meaning of those words quivered all the way to her bare toes. She clenched them into the cool timber floor, because squeezing her thighs together was too obvious.

"I've never seen you sexier than this. Waiting for me." Q seemed fascinated with looking at her body. Her fingers touched Sabrina through the dress fabric, just above where Jude pressed on the small of her back. Q stroked her, shifting lower, and Sabrina shut her eyes. Her hand must have travelled over Jude's then the touch returned on her naked flesh, stopping when Q reached the cleft of her ass. She drew little circles on Sabrina's skin.

Warmth spread like a small wave, rippling between her legs, making her throb. Imagining where Q was looking, knowing where she was touching, and what she intended to do…Sabrina groaned and wriggled. The edge of the table was just too high for her clit to grind against.

At that Jude leaned in and nuzzled her ear then nipped her. The sharp pain made her gasp. "Is she getting wet, Q?"

The grating rumble of his voice and the intimate question made everything so much hotter, sexier, and naughtier. She was ass up and pinned. She couldn't move, didn't want to. Limp, flattened onto the table, she heard her own harsh, wanting breaths. They might have weighed her down with stone.

"Let me check."

No. No. She tried to move her hips away from Q, but couldn't get far.

But Q's fingers slipped under the thong and along her slit, gliding up and down as slickly as a tongue along melting ice cream.

She choked back a whimper.

"Yes." Q stopped and Sabrina heard her swallow. "She's very wet."

"Good girl." This time he kissed her hair and breathed on her for a while as his big hand massaged her nape. "Now spank her. And if she's really good and doesn't make too much noise, we'll take off her underwear."

Oh fuck. Did she want this? Sabrina tongued her lip. Being silent had taken on a heavy significance. If she was quiet, they'd make her naked.

There was hesitation in the air. At the back of her mind Sabrina knew Q was tussling over saying she was in charge again, but the hand moved from between her legs, cupped one globe of her ass then lifted away.

The first smack alone reverberated deep down into her flesh, thrumming into her clit. Q hit her again and again. The slaps burned as they grew harder. Then Q paused and hit her in a different unexpected spot. Though she whimpered and tried to curve her back to the side, Q steadied her with a hand on her hip. And Jude held her down even harder.

Ghost. Ghost. She could use that if she wanted to.

More smacks, more force, more throbbing.

The burning heated her down there and merged, making her lower body one big molten ache.

"You can do it," Q murmured. "Stay quiet, and I'll take off your thong. Stay quiet and I'll put my mouth there. Three more."

Her mouth? Sabrina's eyes sprang open, and she saw Jude looking back at her. Oh god. Mouth meant tongue…lips.

He smiled the smallest amount, pressed his finger and thumb in on the sides of her neck. "I'm not letting you go." Now she was utterly surrounded by him, controlled. *And I love it.*

Smack. She gasped and her mouth stayed open…because he was watching her lips. Two more harder-than-hell smacks and she still lay there, trembling, breathing raggedly, and locked into Jude's gaze.

"Done. You're such a good pet." His thumb stroked at the angle of her jaw. "Take them off. I want to see her come."

There was no hesitation this time – Q hooked her fingers beneath Sabrina's thong and began to pull them down. Her weight made the thong gather between her skin and the table. "Lift up, Sabrina."

She blinked. Helping them undress her seemed wrong. When she waited a few seconds before raising herself only a tiny amount, Jude narrowed his eyes.

He glanced down. "More."

She frowned, sucked in her lip. Q was going to do things to her. Fantasy was one thing…

"More," Q growled, smacking her ass hard enough to make her squeak.

"Ow!" Instinctively she tried to edge away.

But Jude held her. His grip allowed zero movement, she could only squirm and rise up on tiptoe.

Then Q leaned on her too.

"Fuck," she whispered.

At that Q bit her left butt cheek. "Mine." She moved and bit again and stayed there with teeth fastened into her.

There were so many places they held her down, and made her theirs, and where Q bit was such an exquisite point of pain that it seemed to nail her down like…like…

"Ohhh," she groaned softly, relaxing every muscle. She was their plaything. Theirs.

When Q released her, she begged with her eyes even as Jude went back to caressing her with his thumb.

"You liked that." His blue eyes seemed as intense as a surgeon's might be while he decided precisely where to cut next.

The thong was at her ankles. Q grasped each ankle to make her lift her feet. It was whisked away. Naked.

Jude kissed her cheek. "You're teaching me. I'm learning what you like." He looked away. "Take off your t-shirt, Q, before you go down on her."

Both determination and challenge came through in Q's words. "No, sunshine. I'm not doing that. Not today."

Her friend must be kneeling between her legs. She'd spread her legs without thinking. Q would be looking at her, at her wetness. She'd never, ever, let her… Sabrina inhaled and tried to close her legs.

"No," Q snapped and her hands were on Sabrina's inner thighs stopping her. "I want to look at you."

She huffed, quivering, feeling her pussy clench inward, and all because the idea of Q looking at her there had sent her arousal soaring. She let Q hold her open, and closed her eyes. Heat seeped through her, and she became wetter with every passing moment. She held onto the tablecloth like it might save her from some awful fate. Maybe from being licked and sucked and orgasmed to death?

Fuck. She so wanted to come.

"Wait there." Jude said gruffly. "Don't move." He released her and walked away.

"Can't," she whispered belatedly, to no one, choking on the word. Lightning had hit. Q had touched her and now stroked her with a fingertip, lightly. Up, down, and each time she stroked, she spread Sabrina's lips the littlest amount more.

In the distance a drawer opened and shut. She heard the tread of Jude returning.

Q took away her finger. Gah! She curled her toes on the floor, wanting her back but not wanting to say.

"What are you doing?" Q asked.

"This." Jude was on the opposite side of the table. He took each of Sabrina's hands and wrapped the wrist cuffs about them, giving her little reassuring smiles now and then as she stared at what he did. "I'm tying you to the table. So I have my hands free to do other things. Don't worry. Q will be loose."

Dazed, she merely whispered, "Oh." And she tried to ignore Q, her friend and predator, who waited to do wicked things between her legs. She should be worried if he tied them both up, shouldn't she? She gulped, and let him clip her wrists together, let him attach a rope and pull it taut so her arms were dragged out straight above her head. He knotted the end of the rope to something below her vision, at the other side of the table.

Then he stalked back around to the other side where Q must be kneeling. She strained to see. He stood there in his sexy black jeans and shirt. He placed a hand on her ass, stroked her, stirring up yet more heat. She'd be so swollen down there. She wanted them to touch her, wanted…

She wiggled her butt, vying for their attention.

They ignored her.

"What did you tie that to?" Q asked.

"A metal ring. I have them here and there. I learned a long time ago to make sure my furniture has multiple uses."

"What a resourceful man," Q said in a dryly amused tone.

"Yes. I'm also a man who knows when a sub needs more."

What the hell were they doing? Discussing furniture? She was going to combust. She wriggled some more and moaned. Jude only planted his palm on her harder and fastened her butt to the table.

"More? More what?"

Uh-oh. Q seemed to be daring him.

She peeked out the corners of her eyes.

"Is this a designer shirt? A favorite?" He fingered the sleeve of Q's black shirt.

"No." She began to rise from her crouch.

He let her but slid his hand up into her hair and crunched a hold among her black locks that made her gasp.

Neck craned back by his tight grip, Q protested. "What the hell are you..."

His head angled, Jude hit her with a kiss so brutal, Sabrina gasped at the same time as Q did. Only Q's gasp was muffled by Jude's mouth. There were kisses and there were *kisses*, and this one would have rated as assault with a deadly weapon if reported to the police.

Wow. Mouth open and with her wrists still tied, Sabrina watched, feeling like a spectator to a force of nature ripping apart a house all the way down to its foundations.

When Q brought her hands up to his face, Jude snared one of them and took it behind her. With her wrist still grasped there, he dragged her up against him. Q clawed her fingers into his biceps and took what he gave her, while he kissed her and bit and tongued her mouth and neck.

Q groaned softly, "No, no, no," before she at last fell silent and sagged in his arms, as pliable as a rag doll. More bites, more owning kisses then he drew back. He panted and stared down at Q in a way that made Sabrina want to *be* her. If he could kiss like that…*oh my god.*

Q half-opened her eyes and waited, looking downward.

"Now." Jude bent his head to ear level and said in a harsh whisper, "Stand still. These don't rip easily but I don't fucking care if that happens." Then he let Q go and hauled her shirt off over her head. "If you sass me again, I'll put cuffs on you and make you go down on Sabrina without touching her with your hands. She might be yours, but while this arrangement stands –" He grabbed her and shook her a little as he spoke the next words "– you are mine. Got that, Q?"

Wow again. She'd never ever seen Q cowed. She swallowed before she spoke quietly. "Yes."

He paused, running his fingers up Q's cyborg sleeve, over the shoulder piece, to where it twined down the side of her ribs and waist. Sabrina could almost hear him wondering how far past the waistband of her jeans it went.

"Good. On your knees." He pushed her down and unzipped his jeans. He pushed the jeans down until his erection sprang free.

Jude caressed the top of her head until Q sighed and peered up at him. "Ready?"

"Yes." Q's voice shook.

Sabrina rolled her eyes and groaned. Maybe if she whimpered someone might do her? But as she opened her mouth and uttered a single syllable, Jude whacked her hard, again. She yelped and bit back a grumble.

"Quiet," he murmured.

With his fist wrapped in Q's hair he brought her to his cock and slid the tip, then another few inches, into her open mouth.

The way his shaft plunged between her lips, the little grunts Q made and the sheer dominance in the act was so erotic that Sabrina's clit swelled. She sighed and fought not to whimper.

After several more long thrusts that left Jude pink in the face but Q even redder and breathing hard, he stopped. He withdrew from her mouth and zipped himself up. The look of disappointment on Q's face made it hard not to smirk and giggle, but she managed. They'd left her alone a while but she was still tied down and helpless.

"Me now, pleeese," she said quietly and in her most begging voice. They both looked at her. "I'm so horny I could hump the table."

Jude grinned but shot her an evil glare. "Between the two of you brats I'm going to have my hands full."

This time the snicker escaped. "I'm the good one though."

"Are not." Q's mouth curved in a lopsided smile. "She's the –" Casually, Jude had reached out and grabbed her hair again without sparing Q more than a glance. Q's eyes fluttered closed.

"Shush. She's right. You're brattier." He tightened his hold a smidgeon. "Sabrina, you're going to behave, aren't you? I don't need to punish you? Though I can see you like spanking, I assure you I can make it Much. More. Painful." The grin faded and he cocked an eyebrow.

She gulped. She could hear her heart beating, could feel the stretch of the rope on the cuffs, and the coolness on her pussy. Before she could squeeze out a word, he placed his palm on top of her ass then wriggled his thumb in her moisture until it sat between her lower lips, and right over her entrance.

She exhaled and made a little sound of pleasure, praying he'd move that thumb even deeper. "I'll behave, Jude."

"I thought so. Keep your legs apart. Q is going to take off her jeans and then make you come. Now."

She shut her eyes and so could only listen to the sound of Q unzipping her jeans and slithering out of them. Without sight, the feel of his thumb was making her pussy beat in time with her heart. When he started to move the tip in and out, she opened her mouth and took some sharp breaths.

"Have you ever had a woman touch you down there, little one?" he asked.

"No." She put her forehead down and arched her back. "No…I haven't." Something softly wet and hot brushed across her clit and another hand pulled her lips wider as Jude took his away.

"Then I'll enjoy watching Q defile you."

"I…oh, god." That was Q's tongue dancing atop her clit, doing lovely long licks and dabs. "God…I don't…mmm..." The words tumbled out as she concentrated on what was happening below.

From the thump and slide of cloth on the table and the body warmth, Jude had perched himself beside her. His thigh shifted up against her body. She turned her head and found his hand at her lips. Q toyed with her – flicking her tongue across or sucking, then waiting while her hand held Sabrina's pussy as wide open as it would go. And then…then her tongue dipped inside there too. She wriggled and groaned, trying to somehow get that tongue in deeper, which only made Q chuckle. The cuffs stopped her from reaching back and pulling Q in closer. But she squirmed anyway. Q withdrew that teasing tongue and poised her fingers where tongue had been.

Then her whole mouth settled over Sabrina's clit and sucked the little nub inside right up against that evil tongue.

"Oh." She raised her head. "Ohhhh, fuck." The pressure inside her built and subsided in waves – cramming her full then lessening.

At the same time as Q worked her forge-hot tongue all around her clit and sucked and sucked, she coaxed two fingers up inside her and began to pump them slowly in and out.

"Oh my god!" Sabrina sobbed. Almost there…almost… She rocked her groin, tightened her thighs on Q, flexing.

And that was when Jude chose to V his hand over her neck and pull her to him for a deep kiss. Confusion, heat, and the glorious wet sucking made everything wrench together. Pleasure ruptured inwards. Eyes jammed shut, she strained with every muscle of her toes and legs, shuddering at Q's mouth and groaning into Jude's as the orgasm overtook her, shook her, and slowly wrung her dry.

Panting, she let Jude tuck her into his chest and arm, pat her head and murmur sweet words against her hair.

When they freed her from the cuffs, she only lay there on the hard table, curled up on the crumpled tablecloth. She filled her lungs with air then exhaled, while her eyelids flickered at the mind-blowing memories of her Q-induced orgasm. She didn't want to move.

"Come on, beautiful." Q leaned over her and kissed her, softly. "Come with me and Jude over to the couch. We're going to cuddle."

"Cuddle?" She blinked up at Q and frowned. "You okay?"

"Yes." She smiled big and wrapped a lock of Sabrina's hair around her finger then tugged. "Come on, or I'll have him all to myself."

Sabrina followed Q, a little wobbly on her feet. Jude wrapped his arm around her waist, steadying her. He sat down on the big couch in the living room, pulling Sabrina down with him then tucking her under his arm. Q sat stiff on the other side. Sabrina peered at her over his chest. She looked uncertain, uncomfortable. Did she regret what they just did?

She reached over Jude and grabbed Q's hand, pulling her toward him so their hands rested together on his stomach. Q gave her a small smile.

A contented sigh escaped Sabrina as she rested her head against Jude and enjoyed the warmth of Q's hand in hers. This was the most satisfied she'd felt in a long time.

Was that what it would take to get her to enjoy sex? An orgy? No, there weren't enough people to qualify. But whatever it was…it was amazing. Being pinned down, Q's mouth on her, an orgasm that left her limp and whimpering.

Q…God she could do amazing things with her mouth. She gazed up at her friend dreamily. Such beautiful lips. She licked her own, fighting back the urge to ask for a kiss.

Jude had certainly given Q one to remember. He'd kissed her like he owned her. A thought struck her and she huffed.

"Q," she whispered harshly. "You let *him* plunder your mouth but not me!"

She grinned and flicked her gaze to Jude before answering. "The Dom makes the rules, sweetheart."

Chapter 8

Q

As Q brushed her wet hair, she typed in her password one-handed. She logged into instant messenger, without sitting at the desk. No time for that – she had to find something crappy to wear so they could go help Jude paint. She wondered if he'd left her a message while she was in the shower. Anticipation rose as she waited for the program to initiate.

His last message had been sent about two minutes ago.

JUDE

You're still naked, aren't you?

She barked a laugh, blushing as she tried to think of a response. She typed.

Q

And wet.

JUDE

Hot, naked and wet. That's an ideal combination.

Q

Kind of cold, actually. Too bad Sabrina's not available to warm me up. Maybe I should jump in the shower with her.

JUDE

If you do, bring a camera.

Q

Perv.

JUDE

Oh come on, I've said worse to you in the past few days.

She shifted where she stood, thinking about all of the naughty IM-ing they'd done lately. He was sexy, clever, funny and perverted. Keeping him at arm's length because he was leaving at the end of August wasn't working. She was a little smitten.

Q

True, but you should still make an effort to be a gentleman.

JUDE

Sure, but don't expect me to be a gentle man.

She grinned at the screen and shook her head.

Q

Now quit bugging me so I can find something to wear to your house. We'll be there in 45 minutes, unless you keep talking.

JUDE

sigh Fine, I'll go get things ready. It's not my fault you keep talking to me. You could just ignore me.

Q

You're a hard man to ignore.

JUDE

Good. Then my work with you has been successful.

Q

Bye, sunshine.

JUDE

Remind me again why I shouldn't spank you for calling me that?

She changed her settings so she appeared offline to him. It was either that or they'd keep chatting all day. It had happened before. Hopefully he'd see it for the bratting it was and punish her for it later.

Another conversation popped up.

NICO

You there, Q?

She thought of ignoring him, but he could see she was online. Why hadn't she blocked him after their last conversation? Because she was too polite, that's why. She'd acknowledge his greeting then get rid of him quickly.

Q

Hey.

NICO

Coffee tonight. 8 pm.

Old habits were apparently hard for him to break. He was still bossy, even though he'd given up the right to be. A cold anger formed and she pushed it down. It was just his way, she couldn't hold it against him.

Q

Can't. Have a date.

NICO

You do? With?

Q

A new Dom.

His end became quiet and she drifted over to her closet, wondering if he was mulling over what to say or if he'd gotten sidetracked. Lately she'd had the impression he wasn't very happy with his little slave anymore. He'd been hinting at wanting her back, but she was deliberately playing dumb. She wasn't sure what to do. She wanted to keep exploring things with Jude and Sabrina, even if they were ending after the summer. Was a Dom in the hand worth more than something intensely interesting, yet very temporary?

She grabbed an old concert t-shirt off of the floor, out of the clean pile, and a black bra and panty set out of her dresser. In the middle of getting dressed, she heard the bleep of the message alert. While yanking the t-shirt over her head, she walked to the computer.

NICO

Do I know him?

She sighed and typed a message. Why was she bothering with this guy again?

Q

No, hence the word “new”. He’s not from around here.

NICO

Are you fucking him tonight?

Q

I’m going to his place. But that’s none of your fucking business.

There was another lull and she cast around the room for shorts before remembering she didn’t own any. She grabbed scissors out of her desk drawer and looked for the jeans she’d decided were too short the other day. Was she really going to wear shorts? She never wore them out of the house and had thrown out the last pair about a year ago. Laughing at her own painful modesty, she hacked the jeans off at the knee. She slid them on, the pale skin of her lower leg making her feel more than naked.

She wandered back to her laptop, grabbing her makeup and a mirror on the way. Waterproof mascara in case it was as hot as the weatherman said it would be. Was the old house even air conditioned?

NICO

As a friend I’m just worried about you playing with a stranger. Do you need someone to safe call? Give me his address and call me every hour so I know you’re okay.

Um... was “fuck, no” too harsh a response?

Q

We have someone playing with us that I know well. Thanks for the concern.

NICO

Good. Who's the third? I really miss playing with you sometimes.

The brush banged against the wall before she realized she'd thrown it. Seriously?

Q

None of your business. You have an obedient little toy to play with, what do you want me for?

NICO

Sometimes a man likes a challenge. A girl with a little spirit.

Q

You thought I was too much work, remember?

NICO

Maybe I was wrong to be so lazy.

Q

Don't fuck with me.

She slammed the laptop closed, growling. There was a time she'd have done anything to please him, but his betrayal still stung too much for her to disregard.

Catching her reflection in the mirror, she stopped herself. Today wasn't the day to worry about Nico being a jackass. She pushed thoughts of him away. Jude's strong hands and pretty mouth quickly came to mind. She glanced down and wished she'd made the shorts shorter.

***

How they were supposed to concentrate on painting with Sabrina dressed like this was beyond Q. As Sabrina knocked, Q's gaze slid over her curves, all very distracting in the spaghetti-strapped navy blue sundress. Her hair was up in its customary messy bun, with tendrils of it brushing the back of her neck and shoulders. Looking that mouth-watering and seeming so oblivious about it was just cruel. She'd give it no more than an hour before she pinned her down somewhere and did an underwear check. It was only fair.

After a moment, the ornate door swung open and Jude was there in all of his shirtless, muscled glory. His chest and abs were amazing, but it was his arms that made her drool. It wouldn't take much effort for him to overpower her. She forced herself to look him in the eye, but she'd already been caught checking him out.

"See something you like?" he mocked.

"The washboard just reminded me I have some laundry to get done."

"Yes, I wondered about that. You're wearing shorts instead of long pants today. Your knees are mostly showing. Very risqué. It's a laundry issue? And here I thought you were just trying to distract me from painting."

"No, if I was trying to distract you, you'd know it." She smirked. "And I got the memo on the way over, that my shorts are too long. I just cut them off this morning. Apparently I should have looked up how to make cut-offs online, because Sabrina thinks I did a piss poor job."

Jude smiled and winked then turned his attention to Sabrina. "You also look delicious, as usual, Jersey girl. I'll have to make sure to give you all of the high parts to paint."

She laughed and eyed him coyly. "I'm the shortest. Why on earth would you have me paint the stuff that's higher up?"

The look he gave her left little mystery to his intentions. "Because that little dress will look even sweeter when you're up the ladder."

"You'd better not try peeking up my skirt!" Her mock glare was flirty, but she slapped his chest all the same. Her hand lingered there and she gazed up into his eyes. A moment later, the spell broke and she shrugged. "It's an old dress so I don't care if it gets covered in paint. Unlike our goth friend here, I don't see any point in owning clothes that aren't pretty." She turned to give Q a bratty look then asked Jude, "Do you have scissors handy? I'm going to fix Q's shorts for her, so she looks like a normal person."

Q rolled her eyes and shook her head in feigned disbelief. Her roommate had made snarky comments about her old concert t-shirt on the car ride over too. Apparently she should have consulted her before selecting a painting ensemble.

"I'm all for that," he answered. "There are scissors with the painting tape." Chuckling, he led them through to the back of the house, to a large room with cathedral ceilings. A big bay window with a vast and comfy-looking seat drew her attention. The view was of the spacious backyard that ended at a distance in greenbelt. The shed where he'd scared them the first night they met was in view.

"The scissors are there." Jude pointed to sturdy-looking wooden scaffolding that stood against a side wall. "This is the color I'm doing," he announced. Q turned as he opened a paint can and revealed a rich cream color. "With ochre accents."

As she stood in the middle of the room with her arms folded, Q watched Sabrina fiddle with various painting implements. She chose a roller. "Are you going to keep fucking around, or are you going to cut my shorts?" If they looked dumb she wanted them fixed now.

Grinning, Jude reached up and grabbed the scissors then held them out to Sabrina. He leaned casually against the wall beside the scaffolding.

Sabrina's blush reached her hairline. She met Q's gaze contritely. "I was joking. You do look like a normal person. I like you even if you *do* dress like a freak. It's part of your charm. I wouldn't actually want you to change who you are. Even for me."

A warm fluttering in Q's chest started as she looked into Sabrina's eyes. The temptation to tell her again that she loved her was strong, but she resisted. Repeating it would just make her look pathetic, since Sabrina obviously wasn't ready to reciprocate. The silence was getting too long to be comfortable. Time for a distraction.

With a glance at Jude, Q shrugged. "Put the scissors down before your arm gets tired. She's too chicken to follow through with her threats most of the time. She'd have to touch me and that scares her." She swallowed a grin and hoped Jude was watching Sabrina, because this was going to be fantastic.

"Chicken?" Sabrina growled. "I'll show you chicken." She stomped over to Jude and grabbed the scissors out of his hand. "I try to tell you that I accept you as you are, and you mock me. Do you think I'm just some cutesy doll that you can play with? I'm just as tough as you are, you know. Just because you can get me to kneel at your feet doesn't mean I'm a doormat."

"I appreciate the fact that you don't expect me to change who I am for you, Sabrina. And I know you're not a doormat. But the fact remains that You. Are. Chicken."

"We'll see about that." She stalked over to Q. Crouching beside her, she opened the scissors and slid them up the outside of Q's thigh until the denim was caught between the blades. She paused and looked up at her uncertainly, as though waiting for her to object.

"Do it." Jude's voice was low.

The feel of the cool metal against her skin made Q's breathing uneven and sent thrilling shivers through her. Maybe she shouldn't have marked no next to knife play. But having Sabrina do this was a bad idea. Making an excuse to have her close was one thing, but she was dizzy from the mix of dominant and submissive feelings rushing through her.

Scissors running along her bare skin. Sabrina kneeling shyly at her feet. Carefully, Sabrina cut upward until most of her thigh was visible. She cut around the front of her leg next, leaving the white pocket hanging out the bottom of the leg hole. As the scissors approached her inseam, Q wished she had something to grab onto, to steady herself.

As though her thoughts were audible, Jude's big hands wrapped around her upper arms from behind, making her feel both safe and a bit trapped. She hadn't even noticed him move in their direction. Q licked her lips and exhaled, realizing she had been holding her breath for too long. Squeezing between them, Sabrina cut away the fabric from the back of her thigh, and then Q felt her plant a kiss there. She squeaked.

Sabrina moved back into view and frowned up at her. "Did you just squeak?"

"No, it must have been a floorboard." Sabrina kissed the back of her thigh? That was more than a little shocking.

Jude snorted. "That was Q. Whatever you just did, do it again. I liked that noise."

Sabrina cut the other pant leg faster. Had she had freaked herself out? When she was done, Sabrina stood back and admired her handiwork. As Jude let go of her arms, Q looked down at herself.

"Wow, Sabrina." Q grimaced. "Now they're much... sluttier. You like?" She turned a little to give her roommate the full effect.

"You started it." She smiled. "Besides, they're not really slutty. The back doesn't even show cheek."

The banging of her heart must have been heard by neighbors a block away. She fought to erase the kiss on the back of her thigh from her memory, but the tingling there still hadn't subsided. "Fine. Whatever. Are we going to get any painting done today? Poor Jude has had to suffer through our shenanigans enough."

"Don't worry about me," he drawled. "This is much more entertaining than painting."

Q chuckled and threw a roller to him.

With three of them working, getting the first coat on the walls didn't take long. The open window made for a cool breeze, and when they were done they sipped the sodas Jude had brought them while looking for spots they'd missed.

"How'd you get so good at renovating houses?" Sabrina asked. "I mean it's more than just painting you're doing here, isn't it?"

"Sure." He nodded. "I worked for a builder in Spain for a while, and another in Norway. I started out as a bricklayer. I can do electrical work, plumbing…the works. I'm multi-talented in many areas." His twisted smile had distinctly dirty undertones.

Q scoffed.

"And you have an enormous ego. Hey! Here's spot you missed," sang Sabrina, putting her soda can down on the window ledge. She pointed to a section Jude had painted.

Frowning, he walked to her. "Where? I don't see anything."

"Right here!" Q saw Sabrina's intention an instant before she rolled paint across the ass of Jude's jeans.

Mouth pressed into a hard line and eyebrows raised, Jude drew himself up to his full height and looked down at Sabrina. She dissolved into a fit of giggles and covered her mouth with a cupped hand, looking like she was trying to hold back more.

Apparently Jude's Dom Face didn't work on the mischievous little brat. Q snickered.

"Yes, very clever." His smile was dangerous. He walked to Q and took the soda can from her hand, putting it beside Sabrina's on the ledge. When he turned back, Q bit her lip and tried to look contrite.

"Kneel, Q," he ordered. "You too, Sabrina."

He really wasn't wasting any time, was he? Part of her objected loudly. Did she respect him enough to kneel to him already? She decided to give it a shot. If this sucked, he'd have to earn it next time. As Q sank to her knees, Sabrina grabbed her hand and did the same. She looked up at Jude, who was damned tall from this vantage point, then quickly averted her eyes. She couldn't believe she'd forgotten to ask about eye contact rules.

"You may look at me unless I tell you otherwise." Jude walked to the painting supplies, set his roller in the tray and put the lid back on the paint can.

As soon as his back was turned, Sabrina moved to get up. Q rolled her eyes and lunged, pulling her back down.

"Seriously?" Sabrina hissed.

"So what kind of punishment do you think you've earned?" He swaggered toward them, a gleam in his eye. With a slow nod, he drew Q to her feet and led her to the scaffolding. From up under the lip of the platform, he pulled down a set of leather cuffs that trailed a length of rope.

"Really? That's not even fair!" Q glowered. "You planned this out ahead of time and were just looking for a reason."

"No." He grinned wryly. "With two naughty girls around I need to try to stay a step ahead." Without warning, his eyes turned to flint. "Now are you going to cooperate with the cuffs, or are we doing this the hard way?"

Q weighed her options, and decided to play along. After all, she'd been hoping today wasn't just going to be about home improvement. She shoved her wrists out to him.

He shook his head. "Not so fast. Lose the clothes."

She furrowed her brow. "What? All of them? I just laughed because she was laughing! I couldn't help it." Q tugged at the bottom of her t-shirt – she was thankful she'd had the foresight to wear one of her nicer sets of under things. But she still didn't want to part with her clothes. Not yet.

He arched a brow. "Keep bra and panties on for now. I can always cut them off if they get in the way." His steely gaze made her want to obey. At least for now.

Blushing, she pulled off her shirt and peeled off her shorts then kicked them both to the side. She offered her wrists more politely this time, and Jude fastened the cuffs on her while making no secret of perusing her body. He traced gentle fingers down the side of her tattoo, from her ribcage, over her hip, down her leg, to where the design pooled at the top of her foot. His investigation had brought him to a crouch, and his lips and tongue brushed briefly over her hipbone. A trickle of moisture dampened her underwear as he stood. With the rope he tied her arms above her head to an O-ring hidden under the scaffolding platform. A few feet to her right he pulled out an already paint-splattered chair and sat down.

"Come here, Sabrina." He held out a hand. Q hoped this wasn't freaking her out. "Ah, ah," he corrected. "Did I say you could get up? Crawl."

Q winced and waited for Sabrina to tell him off. There was a sound of indignation, but after that there was nothing but the slide of skin on hardwood. Sabrina's expression read half angry, half aroused. The sight of her smooth tanned thighs – more exposed when the dress was rucked up for crawling – made Q squirm where she stood. She wished she could follow behind her and watch her move.

When she arrived and knelt beside him, Jude patted his lap expectantly.

"You...you want me to sit on your lap?" Sabrina asked. Q could hear the hope in her voice.

"Over my lap, little one. Face down, to be more precise." He watched her carefully, as if he was waiting for her to balk or bolt.

Her forehead creased and she rocked from knee to knee. Looking like she was trying to touch him as little as possible, she rose to her feet and draped herself across his legs with a little whine.

Because of the way Jude had angled his chair, Q had a pervert's row view of the action.

He stroked her back and murmured, "Shh. Good girl. Pull up the hem of your dress until it reaches your hips and make sure it stays there. Understood?"

A sob escaped her, but she complied. "My safeword is ghost, right?"

"Yes," he replied. He chuckled as he stroked the gold lettering across the back of Sabrina's purple panties. "Naughty? A bit late for a warning. It should say that on the front of your dress just to give a guy a fighting chance. Like a name tag."

Another wave of heat hit Q. She'd bought those for Sabrina as a joke last Christmas. She'd never guessed the girl would actually wear them, let alone that she'd get to see them on... or ever so slowly sliding down. Jude slipped them to the tops of Sabrina's thighs and left them there. Clenching her legs together didn't relieve the throbbing of Q's clit – it only made things worse.

Jude raised his hand and brought it down in a resounding smack. "Should little subs play tricks on Doms?"

Other than a slight squirm, Sabrina was silent. Two more slaps landed in quick succession, making her screech. Her gaze flew to Q, and she looked indignant. She was totally going to tell him off in three, two…

"I'm sorry, Sabrina," Jude said when the first syllable left her mouth. "Did you say something?"

Seething, she threw a dirty look over her shoulder at him. "No."

"You didn't answer my question, little one. Don't you have something you want to say to me?"

Q could see that the answers racing around in her friend's head weren't at all polite or mollifying. Her imminent backtalk was cut off by Jude applying his hand to her backside. Would this spanking finally get Sabrina to watch her mouth? She doubted it. He swatted her so many times her ass turned a delicious shade of pink.

"Ow, ow, ow! Stop! I'm sorry! I shouldn't have pranked you," Sabrina conceded finally, trying to shimmy sideways off of Jude's lap. He held her in place with the hand that was still in the small of her back.

"I'm not done with you yet." He grinned, pressing the fingertips of his spanking hand to one rosy cheek. Her muscles jumped under his touch and a quiet moan escaped her. His gaze settled on a hardware store bag beside the chair. He leaned sideways a little, fished around in the bag and pulled out an old-fashioned style wooden paintbrush.

"No, Jude!" Q blurted. Sabrina's head whipped around and she paled.

"You're not in charge right now, Q. I'm not going to push her farther than I should."

She had no idea what his intentions were but it was difficult for her to not intervene on Sabrina's behalf – especially when wooden implements made an appearance. She watched in apprehension as he pulled the store plastic off of it.

"You color up very nicely, Sabrina." He stroked the blotches he'd made. With a wicked smile, he switched to caressing her with the soft bristles of the paint brush. She twisted around on his lap, breathing hard then whining when he wouldn't release her.

"Oh... Oh stop! It... tickles!" She gasped.

He ignored her, spreading her legs apart and dragging the brush lower. She panted and squirmed. "Tickle" didn't seem to be the right word. As she pulled ineffectively at the cuffs, Q inched forward, needing to be closer – wishing she could help touch her.

"I should get Q to take some pictures of you like this sometime." Jude looked up at Q. "What do you think?"

The tableau of the two of them together made her wish desperately for her camera. Not that she could use it while she was tied up like this. Her smile to Jude was feral. "If you untie me, I'll go get it now."

Sabrina renewed her struggle to slide off his lap. "No, Q!"

Jude gave her a sweet smile. "Oh, but I can't untie you now, Q. You might run away, and it's your turn next."

"Fuck you," she threw back. "I don't like spanking."

"Oh, but I do. And you didn't mark it as a hard limit. The only way you're getting out of an over-the-knee spanking today is if you safeword."

Q sputtered for a minute. There had to be a way out of this without safewording. She didn't want to be a wuss.

With hands on Sabrina's waist, Jude set her on her feet, steadying her as she wobbled. She mewled and pressed against him, wrapping her arms around his torso as he stood. No porn girl had ever looked as erotic as Sabrina did right then, with her tousled hair, hard nipples and pouty lips. Jude kissed her deeply, then crouched and slid her panties the rest of the way down, helping her step out of them. He peeled off her dress and unclasped her bra.

Sabrina. Naked. Pressure built higher in Q's groin. She wanted the cuffs off so she could run her hands over Sabrina's body. It was the ultimate cruelty that now she was allowed to, but couldn't.

With a hand on her back, Jude led Sabrina toward Q and the scaffolding. The possibilities raced through Q's mind. He pulled a second set of cuffs out from under the lip of the platform. Seriously? How prepared was he? As Jude buckled the cuffs on Sabrina's wrists, the girl pressed against him, kissing his chest. Impassively, he grabbed her hands and pulled her over to Q, fastening her to the ring that Q was attached to, so that they almost stood on top of each other.

Q groaned as Sabrina's silky skin skimmed along hers. Jude slid between them and unhooked Q's bra then lowered his head. He rumbled appreciatively as he discovered and toyed with her nipple piercings. The warmth of his mouth enveloped one of Q's nipples while his fingers toyed with the other. Sabrina edged closer leaning over Jude's head to brush her lips along Q's cheek. Their mouths met in a bone-melting kiss, tongues exploring. Sandwiched by them, Jude shared the attention of his mouth and hands between their breasts. Q wondered foggily if she was going to come by accident. She hoped she wouldn't get in trouble for it.

The tickle of Jude's hair on Q's belly as he moved down Sabrina's was exquisite. Sabrina shifted and whimpered. A glance down gave Q a glimpse of Jude kissing his way up the girl's thigh, toward her core. When she cried out, Q took her mouth, muffling her noises. Jude slipped out from between them and rose to his feet. The girls' bodies met, and Sabrina tried to grind her hips against her without having any leverage. Eyes glossy and skin hot, she rubbed up against Q like she'd die without attention.

Jude pushed Q's knee forward, sliding it between Sabrina's legs until it pressed against her groin. With a mumbled objection, Sabrina tried to pull away, but he was persistent and pushed them together until she stopped fighting it. They ground against each other but the position was more frustrating than satisfying. Jude cursed under his breath, like it was the hottest thing he'd ever seen.

"Behave, you two," he growled. He pulled them apart. Jude gripped the back of Q's hair and crushed her lips under his. She could taste Sabrina on him. Fuck, it was erotic. "Now for your spanking, little brat."

No! Not happening! He untied her wrists, leaving the rope dangling from the ring. She twisted away from him and ran for the door, planning to lock herself in the bathroom until she could negotiate her way out of this. Jude wrapped his huge arms around her, and he brought her down, shielding her from the floor with his own body. His chest was as hard as the wooden flooring.

Sabrina screamed.

Before Q could blink, he'd rolled her off of him and leaned down to grab her arms. She kicked out and struggled, pushing him away as he tried to keep her pinned to the floor. He put some of his weight on her and she bit his shoulder hard.

"Stop!" he boomed. She recoiled, releasing his flesh from her teeth.

Panting, she looked up at him repentantly. "Sorry. I got carried away."

"Oh, Q! Are you okay?" Sabrina yelled.

Q sent her friend a small, reassuring smile.

Jude looked down at her lazily, not even a little out of breath. Bastard. "I know you like to play rough, Q. Do you remember your safeword?"

She nodded.

"Okay, then. Game on."

She tried to scrabble out from under him, but he pinned her to the floor and kissed her. Her will to fight drained as she felt his hard cock pressing at her through his jeans. She wrapped her legs around him, returning his kiss.

"That's it?" he said. "No more fight out of you? You were easier to tame than I thought." He pushed himself up, sitting back on his heels. "Now I'm going to tan your backside for biting me."

Easy to tame? Fuck you, sunshine.

When he grabbed for her arm, he closed his hand on air. She spun away from him, trying to rise. He caught her then pulled her back down and she landed hard on her hands and knees. In a heartbeat he covered her body with his, pressing his cock against her from behind. With a buck, she tried to throw him off, but the feeling of him over the top of her – dominating her – was mind-blowing. It would be so easy to give in. She felt him fumble with his clothing, then he yanked on the flimsy fabric of her panties and they slid to her knees. She pressed back against him, wiggling her hips.

He growled and bit the back of her neck.

Fuck. Heat shot straight to her clit, and her eyes rolled back.

"If we didn't need a condom, my cock would be inside you right now." The snarl in her ear was made of frustration.

She bit her lip before she dared him to do it. Q's nipples were so hard she could cut glass.

Please, yes. Her body begged for his, but her brain wasn't such an easy sell. *Shut up! Quit being such a whore…and no more being nice.* Against all of her baser desires, Q flattened herself to the floor and rolled away from him. She gained her feet and made it a few steps before he grabbed her elbow. Instinct took over and she raised a knee, catching him in the thigh as he twisted aside.

"That's it. I think *I* need a fucking safeword." Jude dragged her to the scaffolding with an iron grip on her arm, ignoring her scratching and kicking. He brought her to the end of the structure and tied her facing it with some suspiciously handy lengths of rope. With her arms spread wide, her bare skin scraped against the roughness of the wood. "You want to play hard? Fine. But next time use your manners. No kneeing me in the junk." He swatted her once on the ass and backed a step.

She tingled where he had smacked her. The sound of a belt being slowly drawn from belt loops put her entire body on hot alert. She quivered in anticipation – she loved bite of a belt into her flesh.

"Understood?" he asked.

"Yes."

"Yes, Sir," he commanded.

"It'll be a cold day in hell before I call you Sir, sunshine." Q had a moment of re-evaluating her sanity. The man was holding a belt, but something inside her never let her give in so easily.

"Oh, really?"

Something whistled through the air. She tensed. When nothing happened she giggled crazily. "Shit, you never said you were a bad shot."

Sabrina gasped and shook her head frantically. Apparently her temporary insanity had become obvious to others.

"I was just getting a feel for this belt," Jude explained. "Don't worry, *you'll* be getting a feel for it soon enough."

With a lick of fire, the belt made its acquaintance with Q's ass. She rose up on her toes and hissed. His initial shot wasn't that hard, but she had little tolerance for being hit there. The next couple of blows left stinging pathways on her upper back. Her eyes rolled up as goose bumps rose all over her body. Her nipples hardened and brushed against the wood. She was glad she'd lost her bra somewhere in their scuffle so it didn't interfere with his work. Sabrina's face was a few feet away, and Q focused long enough to see she looked scared.

"It's good... I'm okay," she reassured. The tension in her friend's face eased.

The belt started to land in rhythmic patterns, with Jude pausing sometimes to drag his fingertips over the fire or pinch harder and harder at her aching nipples. The haze took her and she hung from her wrists, floating adrift in sensation, her breath loud in her ears.

Then everything just stopped. A whine rose in her chest. More, more, more! She heard arguing.

"She's not okay!" Sabrina shouted. "She doesn't look good. Check on her."

Jude sighed and something touched her face. Reluctantly, she opened her eyes.

"You alright, little brat?" he rumbled. His palm held her firmly under the jaw, his fingers stroking her cheek.

She tried to press against him, but her limbs weren't entirely under her command. Legs cooperated enough to take her weight. He breathed gently in her ear then bit the lobe. She cried out in pleasure.

Speech was dragged from her only by sheer power of will. "He knows what he's doing, Sabrina. My safeword is 'mercy'. I don't want him to stop, okay?"

Eyes wide, Sabrina nodded, and bit her lip.

Jude squeezed each of her hands in turn then grunted. "Your hands are fine. But you know what? I think we should stop now. I've already gone farther than I planned to today."

She exhaled. Was she disappointed or relieved to hear that? The secrets of her body were an open book to Jude, and she was afraid she would say something she regretted later if he kept hitting her. Titles he hadn't earned yet threatened to roll off of her tongue and she'd had to bite them back a few times. The fact that he hadn't needed any direction to help her find subspace awed her. He'd already gotten too much just right. It didn't bode well for her ability to think straight in his presence.

With swift efficiency, he unbuckled her cuffs and led her to the wide window seat, a supporting hand under her elbow. After she was settled, he went back and untied Sabrina then tossed her over his shoulder like a barbarian and carried her giggling and shrieking to the seat. He threw her down beside Q.

The girls snuggled into each other and he ran his hands over the pair of them, a look of affection in his very blue eyes. Q snuck peeks as he petted them, and felt her heart expand to include him. There was a possibility that he was gaining admittance to her affections too easily, but weeks of talking and texting about every subject that crossed their minds made her feel like she knew him more than she'd ever known anyone, other than Sabrina. It was too late to turn back now – she'd have to accept the feeling for what it was. If he betrayed her, she'd dust herself off.

After stroking their hair and backs for a long while, Jude's touches became more intimate – brushing their breasts and across their bottoms.

"So, is that it?" Q quipped, as she felt her arousal resurging. "No cock again today? Are you sure you're straight? 'Cause if you're not, it would be a damn shame for us."

Sabrina agreed, pretending to swoon – the back of her hand pressed dramatically to her forehead.

"Don't worry. I'm nowhere near done with you." He sat beside Sabrina's head, his leg against her side and his back against one of the side panes of the bay window. With an imperious wave of his hand he said, "Entertain me."

Sabrina stared at him blankly, and Q wrapped her arms around her, drawing her into a long kiss. "He wants us to touch each other," she murmured when she surfaced for breath.

"But I don't know what to do!" Sabrina groused.

"Do what you'd do with a man," Jude encouraged, with a nod.

"You want me to lie here and wait until it's over?" she said slyly. "*That* I can do."

Q snorted, but Jude was undeterred. He slid behind her, spooning her tiny form, mouth at her ear. Both of them lay on their sides, facing Q, who suddenly felt self-conscious.

"Look at her, little one," Jude ordered softly. "I know how you feel about her, even if you don't say it. I've seen how you look at her. You want to try this, don't you?"

"Can I take a rain check?" she asked, looking dismayed.

"Probably, but what would be the fun in that? She's naked, she's hot, and I just scrambled her brain with my belt. She probably won't even remember this tomorrow," he persuaded. "You've gone this far. You might as well see if you like it, right?"

She blushed. "Okay."

In her chest, Q's heart started one hell of a drum solo. Without preamble, he took Sabrina's hand and guided it to Q, using her fingers to draw patterns on her skin. Sabrina's gaze flicked back and forth between watching what Jude was making her hand do, and Q's eyes.

"She looks pissed," Sabrina mumbled uncertainly.

"That's Q's turned on face," he whispered in her ear. "Whenever she looks like she wants to kick your ass, she actually wants you."

Dreadfully embarrassed, Q bit her lip and tried to look less intense. Nico had told her the same thing.

When Jude slid Sabrina's fingers toward Q's nipple, he let go and her hand kept going of its own accord. He watched with rapt attention – as did Q – while her fingers trailed over the tip of her breast, toying with the piercing. On the second pass she squeezed it between her fingers and thumb, pulling and stroking.

Q's breath came faster. Shit. Was she hyperventilating? When Sabrina switched her attention to Q's other breast, she found some self-control and started reciprocating.

Jude backed off and sat up to watch the action. Anytime Sabrina stalled, he'd coax her back into motion.

When Sabrina's hand started meandering down her belly, Q held her breath. It stopped just below her navel and her uncertainty was palpable. Jude tried to slide it lower, but she jerked it back like she'd burnt it. She wasn't that bi yet, apparently. Q twisted her mouth to keep from looking amused.

"Do you think he's ever going to take his pants off?" Sabrina whispered in Q's ear. "Maybe he shares his penis with another guy and today wasn't his day to use it."

"I kept the jeans on so I wouldn't rush things," Jude replied, slapping Sabrina's ass.

"Well it's not exactly rushing anymore. Both of us are naked, so how is this fair?" she retorted, gesturing at the offending article of clothing.

"I'm the Dominant, so I get to make the rules." His head tilted in a look of smug amusement.

"Fuck that!" Q knelt up on the window seat, leaned over Sabrina and pulled at the button of his jeans. "This is a mutiny, Captain!"

After wriggling free, Sabrina tried to hold him still while he batted away Q's hands. They had just managed to get the button untied, when he dragged both of them over to sit on his lap. They didn't quite fit, but he didn't give them the option of getting up.

"Hold your hair up, both of you," he ordered.

Looking askance at each other, they complied. The sensation of his breath rippling over Q's neck sent shivers up into her hair. His mouth latched onto the place where her neck and shoulder met, and Q sighed in contentment. Sucking and nibbling on their necks and shoulders, he held them still for his enjoyment. Eventually he let them go so they could participate.

Sabrina sucked on Q's bottom lip then trailed tiny kisses down to her chin, past her neck, to her breast. She paused as though she was having an internal debate. Slowly, she backed off Jude's lap onto the cushion. She shifted onto her hands and knees, grazing Q's nipple with her lips and making her groan. Her pink tongue darted out, licking the very tip. She looked up at Q mischievously, her ass wiggling.

Both she and Jude eyed Sabrina's backside with interest, smiling at each other when they realized they were doing it simultaneously. Q's smile became a gasp as something warm and wet engulfed her nipple. She watched in fascination as Sabrina's sucking and nipping mouth alternated between her breasts. Her tongue investigated Q's piercings. Enraptured, Q ran her fingers though Sabrina's silky hair, the slide of it through her hands sensuous. The elastic that had been holding it when they were painting hung tenuously onto the bottom of a lock of hair, and she tossed it aside.

Jude slid out from between them, stood then pulled off his jeans.

When Q could steady her voice she said, "Lookee here, Sabrina. He decided to stop being bashful." Her friend looked up and sat back on her heels.

"Come here," he said, pointing at the floor before him.

Automatically starting to comply was a little shocking to Q, but she went with it. How was she going to retain any of her self-respect if she turned into an obedient sex toy? Maybe it was because things were new with him? She'd re-evaluate if it went on too long. No self-respecting brat would ever kneel so agreeably at a man's feet without the proper incentive.

Out of the corner of her eye, she watched as Sabrina knelt hesitantly beside her. Again she hoped that her friend was enjoying this, though Sabrina wasn't one to go along with something she didn't want to do without complaint. If she wasn't having fun she would've bailed by now.

"Mmm. Two gorgeous women on their knees. What is a man to do?" Jude drawled. His camouflage boxer shorts did nothing to hide his arousal.

"FYI." Sabrina chuckled. "The camo isn't working."

He raised a brow at her. "Hands behind your back," he ordered. They both complied without argument. He walked around them, inspecting. "Very nice."

Inspections always made Q feel crazy. Nico had insisted on them several times a day, without warning. They made her feel like a thing instead of a person. She shouldn't love it like she did – she was sure her reaction made suffragettes roll over in their graves. Waves of heat washed over her as he looked at them proprietarily. She craved a slap to the face, but doubted he'd be that rough so early in their relationship. His feather-light touch stroked over her breasts. Tented boxers so close to her mouth. But she knew better than to be presumptuous.

“May we touch you, S – ” Q barely caught herself in time. There was no doubt that Jude noticed her slip, from the smug look on his face.

He paused, waiting for her to say it. It wasn’t happening today, if she could help it.

“You may,” he finally conceded. Q hooked her fingers in the waistband of his boxers. Before she could slowly slide them down, Sabrina grabbed the bottoms of the pant legs and yanked – effectively pantsing him. Such a patient girl, their Sabrina.

He kicked the shorts away. With permission they both stood, pressing up against him and trying to entice him into kissing. He hugged them both, and then released them – kissing first Sabrina, then Q. Sliding their hands over his chest, they kissed and licked along his hard body. He tasted mildly of soap and smelled heavenly. Q circled behind him to kiss his back. When she leaned down bit his ass cheek, he jumped.

“Hey!” He grabbed her arm and swatted her ass playfully. “You behave, little brat.”

The slap stung. She rubbed her backside and frowned at him.

He was much more patient than most Doms. Amazingly so. Maybe he really meant it when he said he could handle her. She paused in front of him and then dropped to her knees, pulling Sabrina down with her.

“We can’t do this at the same time,” Sabrina hissed. “There’s not enough room for both of us down here.”

“Uh... there’s plenty. Just do what you can and remember to share. I’ll try not to get in your way too much.”

Together, they kissed their way down from the tip of his cock to the base, then licked their way back to the head – Sabrina somewhat hesitantly, but copying Q and following just a fraction behind. Q mouthed the tip, her lips unexpectedly meeting Sabrina’s as she mirrored her on the other side. They kissed fiercely, their tongues dueling around him.

Jude made a strangled sound and wrapped both hands in their hair. His grip directed them as they played with each other – his member their toy that was sometimes shared and sometimes fought over. With her nails, Q raked down his belly and up his thighs. He pulled them away, gasping for breath. Q looked up. Jude's eyes were squeezed shut, his jaw clenched. There was nothing quite as powerful as using your mouth to make a Dom your bitch.

Exhaling, Jude opened his eyes and sought Q's gaze. "Get her ready for me." As though he was in no great rush, he walked out of the room.

A growl of frustration rumbled in Q's chest. She had a love/hate relationship with being made to wait. Knowing she'd have to watch them together before she got any relief made the fire in her burn higher. She hoped he wouldn't make her watch and not touch. She couldn't be held accountable for her actions if he did.

She rose then took Sabrina's hand and pulled her up, too.

"What did he mean?" Sabrina asked, wide-eyed. "What does he want you to do?"

Q just smiled before leading her friend back to the large window seat. She took Sabrina's naked form in her arms, and kissed her deeply. Sabrina molded against her. Under the stroke of Q's hands over her back and bottom she became docile. Her sighs and moans made Q ache with need. With gentle guiding hands, Q sat her on the window seat and urged her to lie down.

"What are you doing?" Sabrina whispered in a small voice.

"You know what I'm doing, little girl," she replied, coaxing her knees apart and kneeling between them. "Do you want me to stop?"

Her breath came fast and she whispered. "No, please don't stop."

A flash of heat burned through Q. Sabrina wanted this – wanted *her*.

When she lightly dragged her nails over the sensitive skin of her inner thighs Sabrina squealed. Q followed the path of her hands with her mouth. By the time her lips reached Sabrina's mound, her friend was quietly sobbing.

"Shhh," she whispered, blowing softly on her bare skin. Q wrapped her arms around Sabrina's legs and spread apart her nether lips with gentle fingers. "I'll make sure you like this."

With the tip of her tongue, she brushed the sensitive skin she'd exposed at the top of Sabrina's slit, just above her clit. She screamed and bucked in Q's arms. As she held Sabrina in place and waiting for her to settle, Q heard Jude's bare feet scuff behind her. He moved around her and grabbed Sabrina's wrists, pinning them above her head, to the seat. Between the two of them, she was helpless.

She shared an evil grin with Jude then lowered her mouth, licking up one side of her slit and down the other, completely avoiding her clit. Sabrina wriggled, trying to maneuver it directly under Q's teasing tongue. She ignored her efforts, dipping it into her and tasting her instead. The scent and taste of Sabrina's arousal, paired with her cries of pleasure and the writhing of her hips was like a drug.

After teasing her for several minutes, Q flicked her tongue across Sabrina's clit. The girl's legs tensed, her breath hitched, and she let out a tortured moan. Q brushed her tongue over Sabrina's sensitive nub again and again, pausing between. As she convulsed in their grasp, the pitch of Sabrina's cries became progressively higher until the stiffening of her body heralded her imminent orgasm. Q's body tensed – Sabrina's reactions bringing her to the brink.

Without warning, Jude picked up Q and put her on the window seat beside Sabrina. Both girls whined in protest, but Jude leaned over Sabrina, captured her mouth with his, and thrust roughly into her. Under him, Sabrina's back arched and she shrieked in pleasure. After a barrage of hard strokes, he straightened up and ran his hands over her body with an appreciative rumble.

Q joined him, caressing Sabrina's silky skin and leaning down to latch onto a nipple. The hand that tangled in her hair turned out to be Jude's and he guided her lower until her mouth was over Sabrina's clit. He released her, lifting Sabrina's ass slightly to make her hips angle upward so Q could reach her more easily with her tongue. It was too awkward to do for long, so Q licked back up her sweat-sheened body to her breasts, while her fingers tortured Sabrina's clit.

When she found release, Q continued to stroke her, forcing her to climax several more times. Q lost count before Jude gave a shout, his neck muscles bulging as he emptied into their girl.

They all collapsed in a panting heap, although for Q it was more a matter of sexual frustration. Jude pulled out and removed the condom she hadn't even seen him put on. He cleaned himself off with a towel he'd thrown nearby. Q shifted Sabrina into her arms. Her eyes were glassy and half-mast and her limbs were limp.

"You okay?" Q asked.

"Mmmm. I think he broke my vagina," she mumbled blearily. "Can we do it again?"

Laughing softly, Q brushed her lips across Sabrina's forehead. "He might need a minute."

"You wish," Jude growled. "Your turn Q. Face down, ass up."

The ache in Q's groin became a painful lead weight and she cursed herself for blushing so evidently. Sliding Sabrina out of her arms, she glowered at Jude. "I think we've established I'm not that biddable, sunshine."

"Last warning." He glared down at her, giving her an internal frisson of adrenaline.

She scrambled to her feet and backed away, toward the door. "You pop a little blue friend earlier, or something?"

"I may not be ready now," he growled, stalking to her. "But it won't take me long. You two are... inspirational. Now, do as you're told."

"Fuck you!" she growled back, shoving his chest with both hands.

He grabbed her arms so fast she didn't even see him move. "No, actually. The plan is that *I* fuck *you*. Now are you going to be a good girl, or are we doing this the hard way?"

In response, she broke his hold and made a run for it. She was caught before she made it two paces. He wrapped her tightly in his arms, her back to his chest and groin. Turning into a limp doll, she tried to slip out of his grasp and drop to the ground, but he was ready for her. She hung bonelessly from his arms for a moment, her mind racing through possible escape options. A big part of her just wanted to give in, but she couldn't make it that easy for him. He had to know now – for real – how much trouble she was.

"You're scaring Sabrina," he said in her ear. "Tell her you're okay."

"I'm okay." She tried to keep her tone light, but she hated being dragged out of the moment. It wasn't Sabrina's fault. It must look awful from her perspective.

In their conversations, Jude had assured Q that he could handle her. But Nico had said the same thing. Then he'd ditched her for someone more obedient. The thought of Nico drove her on. Nico had made her his, collared and dependent on him, then he'd cut her loose because the extra girl she'd agreed to allow into their relationship decided she didn't like to share. Abandoned – like a puppy left in a box on a freeway. If Jude managed to win her submission, she hoped he would remember to leave her some independence.

He crushed her face down, flat to the floor, pressing her there with his whole body. Wriggling beneath him only resulted in his hard cock pressing against her ass. She stopped. Maybe he would think she was done fighting and let her up.

"Sabrina," he barked. "Get those cuffs for me. And one of the collars I threw on the chair."

Collar? She went wild beneath him, managing to dislodge him in her panic. Before she could gain her feet, he caught her wrists and held them together behind her, a knee in her lower back. She kicked but couldn't reach him with anything that was strong enough to do damage or knock him off of her. Grit from the floor ground into her skin and she panted hard. Sweat rolled into her eyes. Escape was starting to seem impossible.

"Shh," he said. "Just a play collar. Safeword if you can't handle it."

Fuck him and his safewords. She fought hard as he secured one wrist then the other, clipping them together in front of her. A leather collar was buckled on, and she could feel her free will slipping.

His.

He tied a short rope connecting the collar to her cuffs then let her go. She managed to pull her knees up underneath her, but as she tensed her stomach muscles to rise into a kneeling position, a hand pushed her back down. Her forehead pressed against her splayed hands and she realized she was exactly as he'd wanted her. Ass up. It was too late.

As she tried to slide her knees closer to her chin so she could sit back on her feet, he grabbed her hips and held her in place. A leg insinuated itself between hers, and she was wide open to him and completely helpless. She whimpered, shivering in his steely grip.

"Now stay!" he boomed in her ear and slapped her hard on the ass for emphasis. The throbbing print he'd left pulled the stopper on her anger and it drained away. "Condom please, Sabrina."

Sabrina's bare feet padded across the floor. "Are you okay, Q?"

Q caught a glimpse of her friend's frightened face. Poor thing. She nodded, gritting her teeth. "I need this."

"Roll it on me," Jude ordered. "If I let go, she might start fighting again."

A hiss of breath and some fumbling and then he was sliding the tip of his cock up and down her slit. One hand had disappeared from her hip. She mewled, pressing back into the stroke. He slapped her again. "No moving until I give you permission."

Toying between her legs, he sank down to kiss away the sting of the handprints he'd left. He nipped at her skin and she moaned. The firm caress of his tongue on her clit and at her entrance drove her mad.

"Please, please, please!" she begged. Fresh sweat of desperation sprung out on her skin.

"Please what?" he whispered against her tender flesh.

"Please cock!" The words tumbled out desperate and pathetic, but she no longer cared.

She felt him shift until the head of his member slid lazily back and forth across her pussy. So close! The effort of staying still made her quiver expectantly.

"Who's in charge right now, Q?"

"You, Sir. You're in charge." It came out in a babble. "I'm sorry I'm bad. Please fuck me. Please *choose* to fuck me!"

"You're a good girl, Q. You just need to be shown who's boss."

Without warning he thrust the head of his cock into her, grabbing her hips so she couldn't move. He pulled back until he was almost out, and then pushed a little further in, entering her so gradually and frustratingly that she struggled and screeched. He hit bottom before he was all the way in. She squeezed her eyes shut – he felt huge.

He groaned. "Fuck, you two are tight." It sounded like he was gritting his teeth.

"... he says like it's a bad thing." Sabrina snorted. Sabrina. She'd forgotten she had a front row seat.

Jude's rhythm sped up and Q shuddered as the tickle of a soft hand trailed over her back. She opened her eyes. Sabrina was lying beside her, staring at her face. Sabrina bit her lip and drew her fingers over Q's ribcage, stroking to where her nipples were almost brushing the floor.

Jude pounded into her, holding her by the back of the hair. Floor grit dug into her knees and forearms. The dichotomy of violence and gentleness twisted her arousal tighter. Her heartbeat accelerated. She sobbed, writhing beneath him and trying desperately not to orgasm.

"She's fighting it," Jude snarled, his voice animalistic. "Lower, Sabrina. Make her come for me."

Tentative fingers spread apart her folds, finding her swollen clit and tapping it. Her breath caught, and she wriggled back against Jude, trying to avoid the sensation. The tapping repeated, becoming rhythmic. She couldn't hold out much longer. God. Sabrina was...

Jude swore. Fire exploded between her neck and shoulder as he bit down.

Q screamed, the pain throwing her over the edge. Her body seized up, trying to crush him within her. With eyes squeezed shut, tears leaked from them like blood. The pressure on her clit intensified and she came again, her own hoarse cry deafening her. Muscles contracted over and over. Her voice gave out and she could do nothing but whimper and accept the waves of pleasure. She wondered if it would ever stop.

Their stroking gentled as her orgasm slowed. Her heart was stuttering in her chest and her legs felt wobbly. Fainting was not entirely out of the question.

Jude slid out and pulled her into his lap, cradling her against his chest. Something brushed her leg and Q cracked open an eyelid to see Sabrina sitting down beside them, leaning into Jude's embrace. Q shifted a bit and buried her face blissfully in Sabrina's hair.

When her heart finally slowed back to its usual speed, Jude removed the cuffs and collar. Freed, she rose, drawing her lovers up with her and dragging them to the window seat. Even with the three of them stretched out, there was still plenty of room.

The sky beyond the window blazed with hot purples and cool blues, but Q discarded the idea of grabbing her camera in favor of staying exactly where she was – pressed as tightly along Jude's right side as Sabrina was on his left. Jude's arms wrapped around them both and Q's fingers laced with Sabrina's on his chest. Lethargy swept over her and her eyelids drooped.

"So did you pick something, Jude?" Sabrina said. Apparently she wasn't sleepy.

"Hmmm?" His tone suggested he had started to drift off, himself.

"For your safeword?" she explained. "After seeing Q's disturbing need for violence, I think you might need one."

"Passports," he mumbled. "You'll need one to make a run for it if either of you tries to knee me again."

Sabrina was laughing as sleep stole Q away.

Chapter 9

Sabrina

Nestled in the warmth of two bodies, limbs tangled with hers, Sabrina woke slowly. Q's soft breath on her skin made goose bumps rise on her arms. Her face was nuzzled against Jude's chest, his manly scent made her insides clench with the memory of the afternoon. The strange surroundings triggered more memories. This was Jude's bedroom, not the sitting room.

Mmm. She wanted to throw her arms around both of them and hold them tight while drifting off into a sweet dreamland. But unfortunately her bladder had other plans. She opened her eyes then blinked a few times. Pitch black. It was still the middle of the night.

She groaned quietly then began the process of untangling herself from the duo, careful not to disturb Q and Jude. How did she get stuck sandwiched between the two? She should've warned them about her impatient bladder.

She swung one leg over Jude's hip and gracefully lifted herself over his body. Then not-so-gracefully lost balance and flopped to the floor with a loud thud.

"Ow." She shifted to her knees and checked that the two were still asleep. Their soft snores were the only sound in the room. She needed light. Her phone was on the side table. She fumbled around for it, knocking into other objects. Jude and Q didn't even stir.

Finally, she felt the solid rectangular shape in her hand. She turned it on and used it like a flashlight to tip-toe her way through the room. Third door on the right, third door on the right, she chanted. Jude had made her memorize the layout for this very reason. She flipped on the bathroom light, shielding her eyes from the brightness.

On her way back from the bathroom, a blinking light in the hallway caught her eye. Red, green, and yellow lights flashed on the floor in the corner. The EMF detector! She rushed for her equipment bag. She must've left it on yesterday when she packed up.

After she pulled it out, she studied the readings. Disbelieving, she checked it over and over. Then she dug through the bag and took out her infrared air thermometer and turned it on. They all said the same thing.

"Holy shit," she mumbled. There was an active spirit in the house right at this moment! She grabbed the small pouch at the bottom of the bag labeled *Emergency* – a competent investigator was always prepared – and set off to find her ghost.

It crossed her mind to wake Jude and Q but she didn't want to risk their irritation if this was a false alarm. She'd feel guilty if they lost sleep because of another dead end. Besides, ghosts couldn't hurt her. It helped to chant that in her head as she crept through the dark hallways.

Ghosts can't hurt me, ghosts can't hurt me. The floorboards creaked with each step. Her PIN pointed down. She peered down the pitch black stairwell toward the first floor.

The *Ghostbusters* theme song popped in her head and she rolled her eyes.

Then, steeling her courage, she flew down the stairs as fast as her bare feet could take her. At the bottom, she cursed herself for not throwing on a pair of shorts before she went so far from the bedroom. Hopefully, any ghosts she ran into weren't literate. Otherwise they'd know she was a "naughty girl." And how embarrassing would that be?

At least her t-shirt was decent – a black v-neck borrowed from Q. Shoving back the hair from her face, she followed the signal onward. From her emergency pouch, she pulled out the cheap digital camera and a flashlight. She held the flashlight between her teeth while she fiddled with the camera, turning it on and putting it on the nighttime setting.

Then she felt it. A cold spot. Right in the middle of the rundown dining room where they'd done the séance. A shiver rocked her. Early July on the New Jersey coast was muggy and warm. But the dining room was at least ten degrees cooler than the rest of the house. There was an active spirit here. Her equipment agreed with a series of soft beeps.

Trying not to tremble – from excitement and fear – she held the camera up and spun in a circle, snapping pictures as she went. Sometimes spirits invisible to the human eye, showed up on film.

A low moan came from behind her. She jumped and the flashlight clattered to the wood floor. She spun in a circle, but it was almost impossible to see without the light. Silence encompassed the dark room. The air grew colder, making her teeth chatter. That and her heavy breathing were the only sounds.

But there had been someone, only a moment ago. She was positive she'd heard a human voice. As if someone was right behind her.

She squinted into the dark. If Q was playing a trick on her, she was so dead. "Q," she whispered. "I'm gonna kick your ass if that's you."

The moan came again, from her left. Her chest tightened and a small squeak escaped her. Fuck! She dropped to all fours, reaching frantically for her flashlight. The groans got louder – a woman's voice.

Fuck, fuck, fuck! It'd never seemed this scary in the books. Her fingers grasped the hard plastic of her flashlight and she shot to her feet, whirling the light around. Big fucking mistake.

Something floated by the light. So briefly, she almost didn't catch it. Her heart leapt in her throat. It crossed the light again – gaunt, translucent figure – then disappeared.

She squeezed her eyes shut. *Ghosts can't hurt me, ghosts can't hurt me.* What the fuck was she thinking looking for ghosts? And why the hell didn't she carry one of those ghost-sucking backpacks from *Ghostbusters*?

Wails of pain bounced off the walls. She could barely breathe. Stumbling back, she put her arms out behind her, searching for the wall to steady her. Finally, she found the hard surface. She pushed her back up against it, dragging air into her lungs in big mouthfuls.

The wall moved. It fell away behind her, gravity taking her with it. She tumbled backward into a small tunnel, a yelp her last noise before the wall swung shut in front of her.

No! She jumped up and felt around the door. No handle. She pushed, straining with all her might. It didn't budge. She tried to find purchase for her fingers between the door and the wall, but she couldn't get a firm enough grip.

With a whimper, she stepped back and covered her eyes with her hands. *Get yourself together, Sabrina. Don't be a helpless victim.*

Think. This must be the other side of the secret passageway Jude had showed her upstairs. So if she followed it, she should come out in his closet. Yes. That was a good plan.

Carefully, she made her way down the narrow passage, tripping a bit on the uneven floor. Only a few yards along, she hit a dead end. Pushing at the wall blocking the passage over and over did nothing. Hopeless.

Tired and sweaty, she banged on the hard surface. "Q! Help me!" While she paused to listen for footsteps, she caught her breath but all she heard was the harsh sound of her own panting. "Jude! Heeeelp!"

No one answered. No one came. Alone in here. Unless the ghost returned.

Beating the wall and screaming exhausted her, made her throat ache, and her fists throb with small pains. She slumped to the floor, tears streaming down her face. The ground was grimy under her bare legs. She hugged her knees and cried.

When they found her – *if* they found her – she was turning in her paranormal investigating badge for good.

Chapter 10

Jude

The shift of the bed woke him. Jude blinked open his eyes to see Q sitting on the edge, her white back standing out in the darkness. The moonlight cast in through the gap in the curtains bathed her in creams and subtle grays, enticing his eye with curves and shadows and the fall of raven hair tumbling down her back – her tattoo barely visible. Q, the voluptuous siren. Where had his wrestling champion gone? Or the mouthy woman who'd twisted and moaned in his ropes a few hours ago?

"Fuck." she said, so softly it might not have woken him if he wasn't already yawning.

Ah. A grin pulled at his mouth. There it was – Miss Attitude.

Q turned her head, her hair swishing across her back. "Jude, you awake?"

"Yes." He reached out to her and smoothed his palm over her hip. "What is it?"

"Sabrina's been gone a few minutes, and I think I heard a weird noise. My heart's still pounding."

If anything could upset Q it would be something happening to Sabrina. Funny, but he felt a twinge of envy. He sat up next to her. "Come on. Let's take a look. She probably got lost on the way to the bathroom."

"Yeah, maybe. Or she's pranking us."

"She'd better not be or I'll make her stand in the corner for the rest of the night." He tweaked a curl of Q's hair then slipped from the bed.

The night had cooled but not enough to make Q pull on more clothes. He adjusted the waistband of his boxers. The timber underfoot echoed a little as they walked. This house was big enough to feel like an empty world at night.

This was so distracting – following along behind her when she only wore her black underwear. Like all her clothes, Q's underwear was functional. Maybe he could get her into something a bit prettier, or sluttier? He smiled at the thought of Q in a breast-baring corset and stiletto heels.

"Sabrina, you in there?" No answer. He pushed open the bathroom door and switched on the light. The room was empty. He stepped back out into the hallway and listened, but heard only crickets and creaking timber as the house settled with the change of temperature. "Where'd you hear this noise?"

"I don't know. It woke me. But it wasn't that loud, I think."

"If she was pranking, she'd be making more noises."

Q shrugged. "Maybe."

Then he heard something. A sob? "Shh. You hear that?"

She paused then shook her head. "Uh-uh."

He filled his lungs. "Sabrina! Where are you, sweetheart?"

The yells were distant but definitely from Sabrina. The desperation in her voice chilled him. For some reason, the poor girl was terrified. "Did you get what she said?"

"Not really. I think she said something like stuck, maybe? Sabrina! I'm coming!" Q turned to him, her eyes wide and dark. "How do we find her? Where is she?"

"Tell us, Sabrina! Where exactly are you?"

Loud bangs rattled timber somewhere, and kept going, punctuated by more sobs and cries. Was she doing that, or… No.

He wrenched his thoughts together, ran back to the bedroom with Q following, grabbed the flashlight from the drawer and thrust it into Q's hand.

"Okay. If she's stuck, there are three places I can think of. The passage up here dead ends after a few feet. Can't be that. There's another passage on the first floor. I'll take that. The attic – the door sticks sometimes. Go all the way to the end here." He pointed. "Door at the end opens onto the stairs. There's heaps of junk up there, and you need to lift the attic door up a bit to open it. Don't let it slam shut on you. Go!"

Though why in hell would she have gone up there, or downstairs?

Didn't matter. From the continued banging, he could tell she was hysterical. Despite calling to her, she didn't reply in any coherent way. The sobbing tore at his heart.

He found his way downstairs by moonlight and memory. He switched on the room light. After turning the hidden switch, the passage entrance opened with a faint creak. The loud shriek from up ahead told him he'd found her.

"It's me, Sabrina. It's me." Very little light penetrated to the end but he shuffled along until he found her, his foot bumping into her shuddering flesh.

"Shh. Shh. It's me. Jude. Come here."

"Jude?" Her voice quavered. "I'm sorry, I'm sorry. I got lost." Her small hands patted at him and he pressed them then crouched and took her face in his palms. The wetness of tears made him ache so much to comfort her.

"Yeah, we figured that. But I'm here now."

"There was a ghost…or, or something, in here with me! Please. Get me out! Did you leave the door open? It didn't close?"

"It's open. Nothing here. Just me. Come on." He carefully tugged her upright and led her back to the entrance.

"Let's sit a while." But when he went to pull out a chair from the dining table to sit and comfort her, she hissed at him.

"No!" He felt a shudder run through her. "Not here, Jude. I'm too scared."

"Okay. Come back to bed then."

When he stepped on her camera with his bare foot and swore, Sabrina didn't even make a single snarky comment. Not once. Damn, she needed some TLC. He picked it up and put it in Sabrina's hand. She absentmindedly clutched the camera as if barely aware she held anything. Before they went up the stairs he was careful to show her the emptiness of the room.

"Nothing. Right? You just got panicked in there. It's not hard to do. I understand." He swept her tousled hair from before her eyes and kissed her softly on the lips. "Come on. We have to tell Q. She's looking for you in the attic."

When he turned off the room light, they plunged into darkness. Carefully, they made their way to the bottom of the stairs. He hadn't fixed the blown stairway chandelier light yet – hard to get to way up on the ceiling without a super long ladder.

"Oh." In the dark he saw her hand go to her mouth. "She'll be worried." She inhaled deeply. "Q! It's okay! I'm okay. Come back to bed!"

He added his own, much louder, shout, then felt more tremors rock Sabrina's body. So he crouched and lifted her into his arms. "I'll carry you. Snuggle in."

"Can you see?" she asked tentatively, as he took the first step. "Can you carry me that far?"

"Sure. You're light as a feather and I've got excellent night vision, my little ghost hunter. I'm not that old."

That made her giggle and he felt her stroke his back. "That's good. I wouldn't want to have to negotiate a trade-in."

He mock growled at her. "I think I already proved I don't need senior vitamins." More giggles made him grin. She was recovering. The fragrance of her hair and the soft feel of her body in his arms seemed to flow in and fill a hollowness inside him. This was so good. He'd not been this *right*, despite the scare, for ages, maybe even forever.

"How'd you get in there anyway? There's a secret switch."

"It just opened. I fell in, sort of."

He grunted. The catch must not be clicking back in place. Half this house was falling apart in some way.

"But there was a ghost," she whispered. "A real one. Like a floating lady type apparition thingy. I swear it." Sabrina trembled. "Where were you both? I frickin yelled and yelled and yelled! I could've built the pyramids waiting! There I was with a genuine apparition and you two were snoring! Freaked me out."

He frowned, took a few more steps. "Harsh, and a little ungrateful, brat."

"I *am* grateful. I am." She kissed his chest. "But… Oh! And I have pictures! I took some with this." Her hand waved the thing madly and faint light reflected off the screen. "Put me down. I have to look."

"Not now."

"Please? Please, please, please?"

He ignored her and took the last steps with big strides.

Q met them at the bedroom. The lights were on and the relief on her face was clear. "Are you okay, beautiful?" Her gaze met his. "Is she?"

"Sure." He walked to the bed and dropped Sabrina onto the sheets from a foot above, so she bounced a little, then rolled her over into the center. "Pile in everyone. We're cuddling."

To his delight, that drew a chuckle from Sabrina.

By the time they'd gotten comfy, he had an armful of Sabrina on one side with Q on the other. The women's heads bumped his chin now and then as they whispered to each other. Seeing them care for each other like this, letting him be a part of it… He watched as Q played with Sabrina's hair. Damn if he didn't want to keep this going. Summer only? What a waste.

"You scared the fucking shit out of me, little girl." The sternness in Q's voice made him jiggle her.

"Hey. Q. Be nice. I just spent five minutes gluing her back together."

"Yeah. Shh, Miss Dommy Pants. Besides…" Sabrina shifted where she nestled and reached over to prod at Q's side. Only Q grabbed her hand first.

"Besides?" Q's tone made him feel like an emperor peering down at two sparring gladiators.

"Besides…I can't help that I had to pee. I didn't check bathroom control on my questionnaire so my bladder only works on my schedule."

He smiled. The return of the feistiness. Brat One versus Brat Two.

"You weren't just going to the bathroom, brat. You were off downstairs, doing something else."

"I was..." She cleared her throat, pulled her hand out of Q's hold. "I was looking for a ghost. My detectors went off. I thought I saw something, and then I got trapped..." Her breath hitched and he wondered if she was about to cry. "I'm sorry I worried you both. But look..."

She squirmed a bit and he felt her fiddle at his side before her hand popped back up with the damn camera, again. "This! I took pictures of the ghost."

"Uh-huh." Q sounded skeptical. "So you went off gallivanting and got yourself in trouble. In all the time you've been ghost hunting, what have I said? Go with a chaperone or not at all. You get hyper focused on your gadgets and don't look at your surroundings, Sabrina. You could have fallen down some hole in this house." Q's hands stroked over Sabrina, as though to reassure herself that she was okay.

"A hole? Like a bottomless pit to hell?" She snorted. "Let me guess, Jude is Satan's evil demon sidekick? Seriously, Q? I have a fucking picture of a fucking ghost! And you're talking about home repairs?"

"Enough with the pictures. Put the camera away. Check in the morning." Jude squeezed them both to him for a second. The ache in his chest had just multiplied by a thousand. "What am I going to do? You two are going to give me several heart attacks before this summer is over."

Sabrina stiffened and sucked in a breath. "I'm sorry. So...I was bad? You want us to go then? I don't want to go," she said wistfully.

"Hell! No." He lifted his head off the pillow and peered down at her. "I never said that."

"Jude," Q murmured, toying with his chest hair.

"Yes?"

"Thank you for not bitching out Sabrina. Some guys would have lost their shit instead of being nice."

He couldn't help frowning. "I didn't do anything special. Besides, it was a pleasure. I got to carry Sabrina up the stairs."

Q, seemingly without realizing it, had wound her fingers into some of his hair so tightly she was tweaking it at the roots. He resisted protesting. Something bothered her. He waited.

"I've met some men who'd have been pissed."

"Assholes then. There's no reason for a man to be like that. Boyfriend?"

Her shoulder moved as if she shrugged. "Yes."

"Well, forget him. I've got you both now."

She stayed quiet but exhaled slowly then her muscles relaxed and Q snuggled closer.

"Her last boyfriend was awful. But you're good, so far." The smugness in Sabrina's voice made him wonder where she was going.

"I'm okay, so far? Be careful, Brat Two." He pinched her ass and smiled as she jerked.

"Ow! *You* be careful. Both of you were so slow coming to rescue me I think I should take away your Dom cards." Then she lifted the camera and turned it on.

"What are you doing?"

"Checking my photos."

"No. Put that on the side table. I'm going to turn off the light."

Sabrina whined and looked up at him while doing little squirms in place and tapping the screen with her thumb. "I can't wait! I can't! I have to know. Oh my god! Look! Isn't that a ghost?" She shoved the bright screen up at him.

"It's too blurry." The woman was like a squirrel on crack. He frowned. Another sub he'd had needed punishment or she regularly chewed her fingernails to the quick and worried herself into a frazzled mess.

"Then your laptop! We can zoom in. I can clean it up with a sharpening filter." She tried to sit up. "I'll never sleep like this. I need to know. You're being mean."

Q snorted. "Asking for trouble."

He held Sabrina tighter, stared as she kept trying to wriggle away.

"I said, no." He looked at Q as she lifted her head. "Q? Wanna help me?"

"Sure."

He sat up, rolled over to Sabrina's other side then grabbed her and flipped her onto her stomach. Though she wriggled, he and Q pinned her there with her hands at the small of her back. Her shriek of delight was cut short when he whipped her panties down below her butt.

"Oh, that looks good." Q grinned and slapped Sabrina's ass once.

Sabrina yelped. "Noooo. I'll wait! I'll wait till morning. I'll be good!"

"Promise?" He placed the camera on the side table then raised his hand, palm ready to connect. The pink from Q's slap already showed and he admired the mark.

Sabrina turned her head and looked up at him with big eyes.

"I promise! Just no hitting!" Her voice dropped and she muttered, "Mean fuckers."

At that Q chuckled so hard she almost choked. "Mean fuckers?"

"That is *not* the right form of address. Q, want to take turns? Seven each?"

She nodded.

Despite her squeals and squirming they managed to deliver the fourteen spanks. He noted to his satisfaction, that Q toned down the force when Sabrina quieted. The last few were delivered to a very submissive Sabrina. Curious, he put his hand to her slit and gently slid a finger along. She was very wet. Her ass arched upward and she wiggled.

"Well. I can see spanking like that isn't much punishment for you. Next time I may try a crop."

Sabrina whined.

"Shh." He pulled her panties back up. "Now, everyone back to sleep. It's damn late."

"But…" Sabrina whispered.

Q glanced down, smiled. "But what?"

Again Sabrina wriggled her ass and peeked at him. "You can't leave me like this. Now I'm horny." She pouted.

"And you'll stay that way until morning, at least. Maybe then, if you beg, I might relent."

"Fuc –" She cut the word off then sighed. "Sorry."

"Sorry, *Sir.*"

She blinked. "Sorry, Sir."

"Good."

When the lights went out and he again had his two girls cuddled up to him it took at least a half an hour before he could stop smiling and go to sleep. He'd found a slice of heaven for the summer, at least.

***

Something woke him – was it the morning sun, the warm woman on one side, who must be Q, or maybe it was the toes wiggling before his face and the delighted humming. He blinked again and focused on those toes, let his eyes follow the flow of the leg muscles – shapely calves, thighs, wiggling butt. The word "naughty" emblazoned across the underwear on that butt.

Why was Sabrina facing the wrong way?

He leaned on his elbow. Q sprawled on her stomach, taking up half of the bed. He was surprised at how vulnerable she looked as she slept.

But Sabrina.

He sat up and moved carefully about until he too faced the end of the bed, to look over her shoulder. Sabrina grinned back at him. Of course, she had his laptop out and was starting up his camera app.

"Sabrina." He made it a growl. What was this? Six in the morning?

"Yes?"

Ah. At least she had the decency to look guilty. By feel, he sneaked his hand over the roundness of her butt until he encountered the edge of her panties.

"Were you supposed to start up my laptop this early?"

"Umm." She sucked in her lower lip. Cute, girly, and guaranteed to raise his testosterone level. "You never said a specific time. It is technically morning. Some people get up this early for work even."

"You woke me. You got yourself up way too early. Shut it off."

"Nooo." She screwed up her mouth. "Please?"

"Close it. We'll have a little talk then maybe if you beg nicely, we'll both look." He rested his chin on her shoulder and inhaled through his nose. Woman. *Mmm.*

She could do with a shower, but his dick stirred, hardened. It obviously didn't mind. He put his arm across her back so she'd feel his weight, that a man had hold of her. "Sabrina."

The softening of her back, her one slow deep breath, and her stillness, told him he'd done the right thing.

"Okay," she whispered as she inched the lid shut.

"Thank you, sweetheart. Now, the talk." When she went to turn over he stopped her. "No. Stay there. Tell me." Beneath the T-shirt he stroked up her backbone then paid attention to the rest of her back, massaging all her delightful curves. As he spoke she subsided more and more, until she lay prone, with her head to one side, watching him.

"I know what you wrote on the questionnaire, but I'd like to hear it from your mouth too. Especially now you've tried some of the things out. What do you know you like? What do you really want to try?"

Despite his massage, her forehead wrinkled and she did a little squirm. "Do I have to? It's," she closed her eyes for a second, "not something I like saying."

"Yes, you have to." He raised an eyebrow. "Go."

She huffed but when pleading with her eyes did nothing, she began to speak. To his amusement she squirmed her lower body on the bed with each announcement. "Getting tied up, that I liked. More of that…ropes and stuff." Small squirm. "And spanking." Squirm. "Especially when you had me on your lap." She met his eyes, looked down. Big squirm. "I liked…I liked what Q did to me, with her mouth." Swallow and lick of her lips. "Didn't know for sure before, but I did."

"And when we both spanked you?" He tugged on her hair.

"Hot! Fuck, that was so hot. Just thinking about it."

He looked down and saw her spread her legs a little and do the biggest wriggle yet.

"Hmm. My guess is that was more than just the spanking. I'll try you out with other impact play, like a crop and floggers, maybe a belt?" He focused on her as she parted her lips and stared. "Like that idea?"

"Yes," she said quietly.

"And looking at how much you liked both of us controlling you, especially since you checked begging and following orders on that form, I think you love Dominance and submission an awful lot, Jersey Girl. I might try you with a play collar and leash."

Her eyes widened. "God. No! I don't think so. Uh-uh." She shook her head violently. "I'm not your pet!" Her words came out in a harsh whisper.

He waited a moment. Then he traced his hand across her nape. "I think you are. I think you like being a little sex toy."

"I'm…I'm still me. I don't want you controlling me like that. No. I didn't check collars." But she pouted and stared at the bed as he let his palm drift down her back.

"You didn't say they were a hard limit either. What would Q say?"

The bed moved. As he'd thought, Q was awake and listening. She crawled across and flopped down on Sabrina's other side. "Q thinks Sabrina would look hot in a purple collar and almost bought one a few days ago. She also thinks Sabrina makes an excellent sex toy, and that the naughty girl secretly loves it."

She arched a brow and gave Q a bratty glare. "Well, Sabrina thinks it's silly when people talk about themselves in the third person."

Q chuckled and shook her head.

"And, you two…" Sabrina looked grumpily from one of them to the other. "Stop ganging up on me."

"You're new to this. Sabrina, you don't always know what you want without trying it sometimes." Jude turned over on his back and peered sideways at her. If she still said no he'd honor it. They didn't have enough history for him to push this. "Let's try the collar sometime. You can safeword from the first moment if you don't like it, but at least give it a try."

For a little while she stared and just chewed on her lip, until Q put her hand across Sabrina's neck and held her a little. "Please, beautiful girl. Try it for me."

Submission melted into Sabrina's eyes, her eyelids drifted lower and she swallowed. "I guess I can try."

"Thank you." Q kissed the top of Sabrina's head

Sometimes Q figured her out before he did. But they'd been friends for a long time. "Good. Now if you want to see those photos, ask nicely."

She barely hesitated. "Please, can we look at them? Pretty please, Mr. Jude, Dom of the Universe?" Then she batted her eyelashes furiously.

He couldn't help guffawing. "Damn, girl, you ask for it. You can look, but there are consequences. If you protest even one of them, no photos." This could be a fun game. Would she play along?

"Um. Okay." She looked uneasy, but she shrugged, hauled herself up on her elbows, and popped open the laptop.

He stopped her with a hand on her arm. "You get to do it naked. Q, take off her t-shirt."

"I like this idea." Q grinned.

Sabrina let out an aggravated sigh. "Okay, okay. I'll look at ghosts naked while you two stare at my butt." She sat up to let them strip her.

Finally, naked, she lay down again and he and Q lay beside her. "The card's loaded the pics. Now to find the album. What's this stupid program? Nothing's where it should be."

She muttered to herself until he slid his hand over her bare ass and down into her crevice.

"Jude!"

"Keep looking. I'm going to play with you here." Very wet and her labia felt swollen and ready for sex. For all her nay-saying, she'd probably been aroused by the idea of a collar and leash. He thrust his forefinger inside her an inch and started to pump.

"Jude!" she said in a hushed tone. "Unfair." Her bottom tilted. "I can't not get all –"

"Is that a protest?"

Her mouth snapped shut. "No. It's not."

"Q play with her breasts. If I don't hear lots of moans and see some leg spreading and humping of this bed, I will be disappointed and crop you both. But Sabrina, you are not to come."

Her whine and incredulous look made both he and Q laugh.

"You won't have to crop *me*, Sir. But you may have to crop our toy when she comes."

"Oh shit! Not protesting, Sir, but…fuck." As Q reached beneath and pinched her nipple, Sabrina gasped. He pumped into her harder. "Ohh…" She writhed a bit, moaned, and slumped on her elbows, but to her credit stayed at the laptop. He pulled his fingers out and found her clit. Circling around and around on top of it rewarded him with a shudder from Sabrina.

Even so, she said huskily, "Look! Told you. Ummm. Told you. Oh god." She collapsed entirely onto the bed with her head in her arms.

"Up!" Q bit her shoulder. "How can I play with your nipples if you lie…Oh my!"

The change in Q's voice made him look at the screen. What the hell was that? He stared.

"See?" Sabrina whispered. "A ghost. I told you both."

The pale white face of a woman peered out of the laptop screen. Through her misty shape, beyond her, he recognized the dining table. Fuck. He stared at Sabrina.

"See?"

"Fuck." Q leaned in closer, her hand planted on Sabrina's back. "What *is* that?"

Either someone was playing a joke, or…he had ghosts.

"CGI," he muttered. "Must be."

"CGI, my ass," Sabrina said.

"Hmm." He gave that ass a slap. "We'll sort this out later. Turn over so Q and I can get at your body properly. And do not come. Keep your hands above your head and stay still."

Though her eyes were wide, she did as he asked. He sat up on his heels and observed her. Already her nipples were tight little buttons and her mouth was parted. "Now. Where will I start?"

Sabrina whimpered.

***

For all his misgivings, the photo looked to be that of a ghost. From where he sat on the stool at the kitchen bench, the sun bounced in through the window and off the screen and made everything damn glary. Jude took another bite of the French toast and stared at the laptop screen.

"See!" Sabrina put her hand to his shoulder and leaned in to poke at the screen.

He caught her hand. "No. No, strawberry jelly flavored fingers on my laptop, thank you." His father's favorite saying came to mind. "If you hear hoof beats, think horses not zebras."

On the other side of this island bench, with a fork halfway to her mouth, Q paused. "What the fuck? Zebras?"

"It's a medical aphorism. A saying. It means that common things happen commonly. That is, don't think up weird reasons for things to happen."

"Uh-huh." She lowered the fork, and frowned. "Meaning what, exactly, in this case?"

Good question. The photo Sabrina had taken looked like a ghost. How could anyone have fiddled with it if she took it last night? He glanced at her eager face. "Would Jersey Girl here do some sneaky switch with a photo just to scare us?"

"No." Q's answer was matter-of-fact, and Sabrina looked miffed.

"Good. Then, I guess I mean that if it looks like a ghost, maybe it is one?"

"See?" Sabrina crowed. "Knew it! Yes!" As if he'd delivered the Ten Commandments on a tablet, to her doorstep, Sabrina did a war whoop.

Not smiling was impossible. Crazy woman. "Why are you so happy? I thought that ghost last night scared the hell out of you?"

She leaned an elbow on the counter next to Q, and seemed to ponder his question while stealing bits of Q's food. "It did. It was fucking scary. But…" A grin spread across her face and she locked her gaze on him. "I got a real photo! You don't understand. That's every ghost hunter's dream!"

The doorbell rang. "I'll get it," Q volunteered.

At least she and Sabrina were decent. Earlier on, upstairs, Sabrina had been prancing around naked while brushing her teeth with a borrowed toothbrush.

Tuesday…Tuesday morning. He remembered who was coming and leaned back on the stool to shout more effectively down the hallway. "Hey, Q, it's probably Cross delivering that wood. Tell him I'll be out in a minute to help unload it in the front yard."

Cross was a godsend with his truck. It seemed like almost everyone he knew here he'd met through the club.

He'd bought the timber at auction. Salvaged from an old house, the oak planks should be a close match for the treads on the staircase.

Q came through the doorway followed by Cross. A big man with bristly black hair and multiple tats, Cross looked like he was used to working out, and like he could swallow Q and spit out her bones.

"Brought your lumber." Cross nodded at Sabrina where she'd perched herself on a stool before a plate stacked with pancakes. Then he cocked his head. "Aren't you Q's friend, from the shop?"

She sucked maple syrup off her finger and waved vaguely. Red washed over her cheeks. "Umm. Yeah, I am. Hi."

"Did you wear the outfit Q got you?"

She nodded and said quietly, "To a concert."

He glanced at Q then winked.

All Sabrina's energy seemed to have drained away to be replaced by a quiet embarrassment while her face grew ever redder. Jude studied her. Of course – she'd said she didn't want this relationship known in public, and here she was sitting in his kitchen in PJs. He looked at Q and she looked back, a small frown of anxiety marring her forehead. Guess she hadn't thought Sabrina would count Cross as public.

"Cross. Let's get that wood off your truck. I really appreciate your help." After swallowing the last chunk of toast and some coffee, he slipped from his stool. "The girls are staying with me for a couple of days." Inspired, he thought of a distraction, "Sabrina is a bit of a ghost hunter so she's investigating a ghost I might have."

"Here?" Cross's eyebrows arched upward.

"Yes. Here." Maybe ghosts weren't his thing?

"I got a picture." She grinned like a Cheshire cat on crack. "I can't wait to do it again. But not alone. And with a better camera."

All of them stared at her.

Looking bemused, Cross headed for the door. "Finish your coffee, Jude. I'll go back the truck in. Let me know if you need a hand with anything else, while I'm here."

"I will. Thanks." When he got up to put his mug in the sink, something smacked against his backside. He swung around, expecting to find Sabrina smiling with her hands behind her back. It surprised him when Q smirked then leaned against the opposite counter.

With a head shake and a chuckle, he told her, "I'll take care of you later."

Cross looked back and forth between the two then rumbled as he passed, "You'd better keep a firm hand, man. They've got you outnumbered." They'd had this discussion at the club awhile back. Cross hadn't been sure what he thought about bratty subs.

Luckily, Jude liked them just fine.

Chapter 11

Q

The girls giggled as they slid out of the backseat of Jude's car and straightened their clothes. Q tugged surreptitiously at her short skirt, wishing he'd let her wear jeans. She felt more naked than naked. Fortunately, he had parked on the side of the building away from the door and windows, and no one was in view.

"You *really* never wear dresses, do you, Q?" Jude asked. "If you stopped pulling at it, it would be much prettier."

"No, she doesn't wear them anymore." Sabrina laughed. "She used to wear skirts and dresses all the time when I first met her."

"Nico forced me to wear dresses. I hated it. I gave them all away not long after I moved in with Sabrina."

"Well, they look beautiful on you." Jude smiled. "You shouldn't stop wearing them out of spite." He adjusted his jeans. "It's a good thing you two decided to wear the same shade of lipstick," he grumbled. "It would have been less distracting if you had put it on directly, instead of Sabrina putting it on you, Q, and you kissing it back onto her."

"We had to touch it up anyway," Sabrina smiled slyly. "Besides, you shouldn't have been spying on us in the rear view mirror. And don't even *think* of complaining about us switching shirts."

"I wouldn't dream of complaining about that, Sabrina girl."

The other two walked off through the parking lot arm-in-arm, then paused as they realized that Q was lagging behind.

"Coming?" With the sun having sunken below the building already, Jude's face was partially in shadow.

She stayed where she was, by the side of the car. Dressed like this, she felt like a complete idiot. She scratched at the gravel with the pointy toe of her knee-high boots. "I think I'll stay out here for a while. I've always wanted to take up smoking. It seems like a good time to start."

"Come on! It'll be fun," Sabrina encouraged.

"Remind me why we have to go out again?"

Jude walked to her and looked down with his blue, blue eyes. "I thought it would be fun for all of us to go out somewhere together."

"To avoid the inevitable likelihood of having to fuck us all evening?" she asked, arching a brow.

"Take pity on me, Q. I'm only one man."

"I'm sure we'd have no problem finding volunteers to stand in for you," Q quipped. She turned to look self-consciously at her reflection in the car window. How did she manage to attract men anyway? Nico used to say it was because she oozed sexuality, even though she wasn't feminine enough to be beautiful. Other people had told her she was gorgeous, but Nico had heartily disagreed. He believed in Painful Truths, but only as they pertained to other people.

A tight fist in her hair startled her. Jude pressed her forehead to the car and leaned in close to her ear. She gasped and mewled as a hard throbbing began in her groin. Fuck, fuck, fuck.

"You plan on replacing me, do you?" he growled. "Do other men give you what you need?"

"No!" she squeaked. Her voice had gone up several octaves.

"No what, little brat?"

"No, your Majesty?" The words were out of her mouth before she could swallow them. She had only just managed not to add "purple" before "majesty".

He shook her a little by the back of the hair. She thought of him yanking down her panties and fucking her against the car and she squirmed.

"Do you seriously think I'd be that easy to replace?" He didn't sound like he was playing anymore.

"No, Sir," she whispered. "Sorry, Sir."

"Good girl," he rumbled, kissing the top of her head. He released her and looked down into her eyes when she turned to face him.

The sight of his satisfied smirk made Q squirm inside. Ever since they'd gone to Jude's to paint, it was hard for her not to kneel at his feet whenever he walked into a room. The protocols she'd learned with Nico were far more ingrained than she'd thought. Jude had dommed her ass good, and now she couldn't help acting all goofy schoolgirl around him. Temporary. Temporary. She had to keep reminding herself. She was going to be crushed when he left, no matter how hard she tried to stay emotionally distant. They clicked way too well for comfort.

He walked away and rejoined Sabrina. Q looked back at her reflection in the car window, trying to regain her composure. She smoothed her hair and walked after them, worried that at some point this evening – before they got somewhere private – he was going to magically transform her skirt into a belt.

The unpromising exterior of The Rig was nondescript stucco that was looking the worse for wear. As they rounded the corner, they saw that, despite the building's disrepair, a crowd had formed itself into a line. Trance music drifted out the door and the heavy bass throbbing through Q's body made her think of fucking even more.

"Why would someone drive all the way outside of town to go to a dive bar?" Q whispered, hoping that no one overheard.

She held her arms at her sides, hoping a stray breeze wouldn't flip her skirt. Jude had insisted they wear sexy panties. Hers and Sabrina's matched – wispy blue thongs that were more mockery than undergarment. Tonight, when he'd picked clothes for them out of Sabrina's closet, it felt like he was dressing up his new toys.

Sabrina grinned. "They didn't use to card girls that were a little underage so I used to party here a lot."

The idea of Sabrina in a dive bar seemed incongruous to Q. "I've never been. I did most of my underage drinking at pit parties."

Jude shook his head at them in mock exasperation. "Underage drinking? I hope you both got spanked for being so naughty."

They glared at him. He hadn't been whispering and two guys in line turned to check them out with appreciative leers. Q reddened.

Jude cleared his throat. "Anyway, the new owners have rebranded the place and it's kind of artsy and edgy now."

When they reached the door, Jude was allowed in directly, but the girls both got carded. "I guess you look like you're robbing the cradle," Sabrina said. He swatted her ass and she squeaked.

After settling them on a funky, zebra-print couch, the padded back of which extended several feet up the wall, Jude went off in search of drinks. The room was cavernous and dark. The trance music and throbbing lights made the figures on the dance floor sinuous and erotic. Q shifted in discomfort, trying to get enough skirt under her to shield her bare ass from the couch. She reassured herself that even if there were people in the room that she and Sabrina knew, they'd never recognize them. Although she felt like she was dressed like a whore, most of the young women dancing wore even less.

When Jude didn't come back right away, Sabrina shifted closer to Q, their bare legs pressing together from knee to upper thigh. "You okay? You looked a little rattled after the smack-down you got in the parking lot."

"I'm fine. Probably just a little too horny and naked to be in public. I'm glad it's dark." She brushed Sabrina's knee with her fingertips, then dragged her nails up the side of her bare leg. Sabrina shivered. Even in the dim light she could see the hardened points of Sabrina's breasts bumping the fabric of her thin top. "So what are your rules for PDA with me?"

Sabrina gave a short laugh. "Here? It's dark and people are getting drunk. If we get caught by someone we know, I'll just say I was drunk."

The words hurt a little, but she understood. Sabrina had family close by and Q knew she didn't want to be out about their relationship. Despite that, she couldn't help but feel like Sabrina was a little ashamed of her.

A moment later, Jude was back with a fancy girly drink for Sabrina and a whisky and soda for Q. It was disturbing how he knew their preferences, even though they'd never told him. "Only two each then you're switching to something non-alcoholic."

Q glared and Sabrina pouted.

"Hey, I'm not drinking at all. If we're going to play later, I don't want anyone drunk."

"You wouldn't screw two drunk girls?" Sabrina snorted. "As if."

"Oh, I'd fuck you both. But I won't play with a drunk girl. Your body won't respond right and I might not get the messages I need from you. I don't want to damage either of you." He winked, sliding in between them as Sabrina shifted back over to make room.

With one of Jude's arms around each of them, they watched the dancing crowd and commented on people who caught their eye. Jude and Q were amused to discover they had the same taste in women, even beyond Sabrina.

The latter became indignant – jealous girl that she was – and Jude pulled her into his lap. Lowering his head, he kissed her. Q casually ran her fingers under Sabrina's legs and up toward her panties. She stroked her pussy through the delicate fabric. Sabrina made a small noise that even Q could barely hear over the music then settled against Jude's chest. Staying still must have been a struggle, knowing Sabrina. She was already damp. Q hoped no one else could see anything, and she watched the crowd to make sure. Jude might have been oblivious except for the brush of Q's hand over his thigh.

When he lifted his mouth from Sabrina's and sat back against the couch, Q withdrew her hand and let it rest innocently on her own lap.

Jude's amused gaze met hers. "Were you being mean, Q?"

She arched a brow. "She's my toy, too. I'll play with her when I want to."

"I'm not a toy." Sabrina frowned somewhat convincingly. If Q didn't know her so well, she might have been fooled. The sparkle in her eye suggested she wanted to be told that she was, indeed, a plaything.

"Really?" he looked displeased.

"Well, as long as you don't tell me I can't. Sir," she amended swiftly. Being both a sub and a Domme in the same relationship was confusing – like being two people with two personalities simultaneously. Prior to this summer, she'd been one or the other. With Nico, she'd been submissive, even allowing him to push boundaries toward making her a slave. Before him she'd thought she was all Dom – not Domme, since she didn't identify with being that female – and had a short and tumultuous relationship with a girl who had introduced her to being both bi and dominant. Although it had been fun before Q had gone away to college, the girl hadn't been nice or very bright. They hadn't even bothered staying in touch after the first couple of months.

"I can't foresee myself limiting you there, unless there's a very good reason." He looked down at her and stroked a hand through her hair.

Damn, he was gorgeous. She took the last sip of her drink and felt the alcohol making her mellow. Not as good as the afterglow from a beating, but there was time for that later. The Rig's spastic lighting was on the verge of giving her a headache, but it emphasized Jude's strong cheekbones and sensual lips. She arched up and gently bit his jawbone. Before she drew back, he caught her to him with his free arm and kissed her deeply. For a moment she forgot to breathe.

"Go on now, my little brats," he drawled. "Entertain me."

Q's gaze snapped to him in alarm. He looked back and forth between her and Sabrina – who was also goggling at him – then started to shake with mirth. "Not like that! Go dance for me."

She groaned aloud. "But I *hate* dancing!"

"It's true. She never dances. And I'm no good at it," Sabrina said.

"Hmm. I don't recall asking for opinions or excuses from either of you. Do as you're told or suffer the consequences when we get back to your place." His jaw muscle popped as he set his face in the stony expression they were becoming very familiar with.

"Come on, Q." Sabrina slid off Jude's lap and pulled Q up by the hand. "I think I'd prefer sex to whatever he's threatening. Let's give the man what he wants."

They walked arm in arm to the dance floor, staying as close to Jude as it allowed. Q leaned in. "Interested in putting on the kind of show that will make him uncomfortable?"

Sabrina's gaze swept the other dancers. Couples all around them danced suggestively, grinding together to the heavy beat. "Okay. But your hands have to stay over my clothes for this. And nothing too rude."

Q aimed an evil look over her shoulder at Jude and started dancing. She grabbed Sabrina's hand and pulled her in close. Sabrina's half-nude body and the memory of her damp arousal spurred Q on and she circled her as they danced, sliding her hands over the bare skin of her neck and collar bone. She kept casting looks at Jude to make sure he watched them. Sabrina caught on and joined in. Q ground against her and grabbed her around the waist, holding her close. One song flowed into another, then another without pause, becoming a long series of thuds in her head – a shared heartbeat of the writhing horde.

Sabrina lost her inhibition and rubbed against her, their faces inches apart. The smaller girl's arms slid up around her neck and pulled Q's lips down to hers. They stopped moving though the chaos continued around them. Their lips brushed and Q groaned. Her heart accelerated and throbbed roughly in her chest. Sabrina deepened the kiss, her tongue probing Q's mouth. Anxious yet unable to help herself, Q let her, hoping her friend wouldn't regret this later. When their lips finally parted, Q's head spun. Sabrina no longer needed kissing lessons.

Looking incredibly smug, Sabrina grabbed Q's hand and led her off the dance floor toward Jude. His eyes were riveted to them in the gloom and a lazy smirk played across his lips. His approving look made Q's already hard nipples ache for attention.

Sabrina's steps slowed. A man was sitting with him. As they got to the couch, the baby-faced man grinned up at them hugely, ridiculous in his enthusiasm. The stranger hopped to his feet and zoomed off toward the bar.

"Friend of yours?" Q asked.

He nodded. "My brand new best buddy, as a matter of fact. I think he said his name was Jon. He realized we're all together and he had a fanboy moment. Wanted to know what my secret was. I think he's coming back." He chuckled. "He asked if he could buy you two a drink, but I told him it wasn't safe for you to accept drinks from strangers. He tried to buy me one first." Jude drew them down to the couch and they draped around him like concubines.

Moments later Jon returned with a drink in one hand, his phone in the other. "This is so awesome! Can I take your picture?" Jude shook his head, but the man's eagerness was undeterred. "I guess that's kind of creepy. Right. Well, can I get a picture with you Jude? I want to remember this. Maybe someday I'll figure out your secret, but for now this will remind me that it *can* happen!"

He held the phone out to Sabrina who laughed but accepted it. When she and Q rose from the couch, he sat beside Jude. As Sabrina raised the phone, Jon grinned and put an arm around Jude's shoulder, pointing at him with the hand that held his drink. Apparently Jude was the shit.

The girls' peals of laughter seemed lost on Jon and he chattered to Jude. Sabrina tossed his phone back and the girls headed toward the restroom together.

The line extended almost into the hallway, of course. Sabrina waved Q off. "You go. I'll find my way back on my own."

After Q gave her lipstick a quick check, she grabbed her phone out of Sabrina's handbag. "I'll wait in the hall."

She was reading status updates when a hand stroked up the back of her bare thigh. "Sabrina!" She jumped and turned, about to give her shit for scaring her. It wasn't Sabrina.

"Nico," she breathed, fighting to maintain eye contact. She trembled a little but tried to not to betray her surprise and anxiety. It was always like this, since they'd split. "What the fuck are you doing here? It's not really your kind of place."

He was still a vision of the gothest kind. Arching a black brow, he looked down at her disdainfully. "Not exactly your kind of place, either, Q. Ivy told me you were coming here tonight. You didn't answer my text this morning so I decided to come by and check out your new play partner. You waiting for him here, like a good girl?"

Not much had changed in six months. He still knew how to press her buttons. She glowered at him. "I'm busy having a life. We're friends and all, but stalking me isn't very friendly. I'm having fun. Don't ruin it for me." Two girls strolled out of the restroom, leaning on each other for support and went past, oblivious to the drama.

His dark eyes narrowed and he leaned in, his hand on the wall beside her head. They were so close that his smooth black hair brushed her forehead. "It's temporary. You said he's leaving at the end of the summer. Why not make a clean break of it now before you get too attached? He doesn't know you like I do. You have trouble letting people go. He's not going to keep you, long-distance. I'm willing to take you back right now, but don't bank on the offer still being good when he's done with you."

Tears welled up in her eyes, but she managed to blink them back. She knew no other Dom would put up with her shit. Not long term. Not even Jude. She hadn't answered Nico's text today, because she hadn't known how to respond. He'd claimed he alone could handle her. Nico was a complete ass sometimes compared to Jude, but he was offering permanence – and a convenient source of pain.

He leaned forward, growling quietly in her ear, "I kicked Isabelle out this morning, like I told you I was going to. I expect you home by next weekend at the latest. Understood?"

Her hackles rose. She was not a slave for him to bark commands at. He'd dumped her – he didn't get to run her life. "Fuck you, Nico! You can't boss me around anymore. I never made you any promises – and I'm free." Her vehemence surprised her.

Nico recoiled, and after a quick glance up and down the hall he slapped her hard across the face. Fire bloomed. She clutched her cheek. The blow hadn't been that hard, but it was unexpected.

"In your deepest, darkest heart you know you're a slave, Q," he hissed. "You're my slave. Being free doesn't make you happy. How many times have we discussed this? Just because I set you aside for awhile doesn't make you normal. You're not like everyone else."

It was true, she was a freak. She craved so much physical dominance and pain. Jude didn't want a freak. Did anyone? Nico's eyes softened and he traced gentle fingers over the heat of where he'd hit. He stared into her eyes and she could feel herself falling under his spell. Q knew he didn't really love her. No matter what she did, Nico was always angry with her. She burned the food, stayed up too late, showed too much skin. There was always something. But was it because he was mean or because she was a fuck-up? Q wasn't stupid. Part of her knew he was an abusive asshat, but at least he understood her. And still wanted her.

What a confusing mess. She ducked her head, averting her gaze. "You have to give me time to think please, Sir. I'm... I don't know yet."

He chuckled, stroking her hair behind her ear then tracing her jaw. "No 'Master' from you tonight? I'll accept it for now. But you know what you call me in your head."

Asshat? She giggled but covered it with a little cough.

"Q? Is everything okay?" Sabrina appeared nearby, looking uncertain. "Hi, Nico. I never thought we'd see you here."

Q watched as his face transformed from sneering mega-Dom to pleasant acquaintance. "Hello, Sabrina. I dropped by to talk to Q for a minute. We had something to discuss." His gaze snapped back to Q and his lips pressed together in displeasure. "Now I see who your third is. Congratulations. I know how long you've been waiting to get at the straight girl's cunt."

She flinched and glanced at Sabrina. That was harsh, even for him. Impressive that Sabrina held back. Q didn't miss Sabrina's hand clenching at her side, ready to deck him.

"I'll talk to you tomorrow." Then he was gone, stalking away in a swirl of black clothes and silver buckles.

She watched until he turned the corner, admiring the way he moved in spite of herself. Her body begged to follow.

Fingers snapping in her face brought her back to reality. "Q. Q, honey. Listen to me." Sabrina was staring at her intently. "He is such an asshole! What the hell did he say to you before I came out? And why the fuck is your cheek red? Did he hit you? I'm going to kick his ass!"

She took a step to chase after him, but Q caught her by the arm.

"Leave it be, Sabrina. I made him angry. I know he has a short fuse, I shouldn't have been so rude."

"You do realize you sound like an abused woman, right? You need to get some counseling for that shit. Jude's going to kill him."

"Oh, Sabrina. Please don't tell him!" she pleaded, clutching her hand. "I was having fun before Nico showed up and I don't want it all to be ruined."

Though she looked uncertain, Sabrina nodded. "I don't think Jude will be happy if he finds out we've kept things from him. Especially something like this."

"Well, maybe we'll just wait until tomorrow or something? Come on! Don't ruin it."

She sighed. "Fine. But you owe me."

"Do you take payment in orgasms?" she asked with a smirk. The words left her mouth just as a young woman rounded the corner from the bathroom. The girl's eyes went huge and she hurried off toward the common area.

Sabrina and Q both howled with laughter, leaning on each other and the wall for support. When they'd calmed down they walked back to Jude, checking each other's make-up and giggling intermittently.

His friend Jon was nowhere to be seen. Jude grinned at them. "That took forever! Was the line long or did you two make out in the bathroom?"

"Line, unfortunately," Sabrina replied. "Where'd Jon go?"

"His mousy little girlfriend just came running up to us and dragged him out the door. Said something about this place being full of sex-crazed perverts." He caught their expressions and raised his eyebrows.

"I'll explain later," Q said, holding back more giggles.

He handed them their fresh drinks and they took up their harem girl poses again. "So did we entertain you with our dancing, oh Domly one?" Sabrina batted her eyelashes at him.

"If by 'entertain' you mean have to work diligently to hide my hard-on from a roomful of people, then yes, I was entertained. Lucky for me every other guy in here was having the same problem, so no one came by to tease me about it. I have the feeling that Jon's girlfriend isn't going to make it all the way home before they pull over somewhere. Poor girl." He paused, and with a wink he grabbed Q's whiskey and took a sip. "Watching you dance together was very enlightening."

"How so?" asked Sabrina.

He handed Q's drink back and took his time answering. "Well… you, for instance," he looked at Sabrina "show yourself off to Q constantly."

"I do?" Her big eyes were the picture of innocence.

Grinning, Jude nodded. "Watching the body language between the two of you is like watching the Discovery Channel. You walk into a room, acting completely oblivious to Q but making sure she notices you. She pretends not to watch you, but is patiently waiting for the chance to take down her prey."

Q arched a brow at him as Sabrina sputtered in indignation. "So I'm a predator?"

"A very patient one, apparently. The most dangerous kind."

"I'm not some sort of innocent little bunny here!" Sabrina snapped. "I'm not Q's level of badassian, but I do okay for myself."

"You're like a little fluffy bunny with fangs," Q said, trying her best not to smirk.

Jude grabbed Sabrina and pulled her into his lap, pinning her arms behind her back and presenting her to Q. The little t-shirt pulled tightly across Sabrina's full breasts made Q lick her lips.

"See that face?" Jude pointed at Q. "Only you do that to her, Sabrina. That's a powerful thing, and you know it."

"Shut up!" Sabrina laughed. Jude let her arms go and she smacked his chest, but she didn't deny it. "You were supposed to be entertained, not sit here analyzing us."

"Watching you and analyzing you were both quite entertaining," he reassured. "I'm a good multi-tasker."

"A good multi-tasker, are you?" Q questioned. She forced dark thoughts of Nico and servitude out of her head and focused her attention on the two people who made her feel like things were right in the world. With them she felt fun, pretty, and smart – more so than she ever had in her life. With them, she felt like a person instead of a freak.

"Yes," replied Jude cheerfully. "Finish your drinks and I'll take you home and show you what I can do, my sweet girls. And, in case I forget to untie you, what would you like for breakfast?"

Chapter 12

Sabrina

The rush of waves hitting the shore was like a flashback to Sabrina's childhood. Long hours spent digging trenches in the sand and filling them with crabs and shells. She smiled, watching the water glisten in the last couple hours of sunshine.

It was just about dinnertime so most of the beach-goers were packing up and heading home. Flip flops in one hand, her bare feet sinking in the sand, she made her way toward the line of rocks jutting out in the water.

"There's an art to walking in sand, isn't there?" Jude said from behind her.

She spun to face him and laughed. Poor Jude – born and raised inland, away from the beauty of the coastline. He was struggling to keep up, trudging through the sand with his sneakers on. "Take your shoes off, silly."

He sighed. "Is the sand hot?"

"A little. You get used to it." She watched him balance on one foot while taking one shoe off then switching. "Hurry up. I know of a little spot just beyond those rocks that should be less crowded."

"How will Q find us?"

"I've taken her there before and I texted her on my way here. She shouldn't be long. The bride she was shooting turned out to be a Bridezilla and had a tantrum about the flowers so the wedding ran late."

Jude chuckled then made his way toward her, smoother without the cumbersome shoes. "Poor Q. She must be out of her mind dealing with that."

"Yeah. She hates that kind of drama. But maybe she'll have a funny story for us when she gets here." Sabrina grabbed his hand and walked him toward her spot. "Come on. It's easier without shoes, right?"

"Yes. Thanks for the tip."

"I don't know why you'd wear sneakers to the beach anyway. Beaches are for flip flops. You're just like Q. I don't think I've ever seen her in a bathing suit. Jeans. Who wears jeans to the beach?"

Jude laughed. "She's one of a kind."

"Yes," she said on a sigh then kicked herself for sounding so damn wistful. Like a love-sick puppy. How silly. It was just Q – her best friend for the past five years.

"I'm surprised you're not prancing around in a little bikini, Sabrina girl." He gave her body an appreciative glance.

She scoffed. "I'm not a show-off!" Not in the mood for a swim, she'd opted for a flowy spaghetti strap dress with a blue-and-purple pattern that afternoon.

"No, but you enjoy teasing Q." One side of his mouth curved up into a smile. "Naughty girl. No one would guess you were straight."

He was the one teasing but it struck a little too close to home. She flushed then stared down at the sand. She *was* straight, wasn't she? It wasn't as if she lusted after other women. Only Q. Could someone be bi for one person only? What a ridiculous notion. A squeeze of her hand pulled her attention back to Jude.

"Hey," he said. "I'm kidding. Don't worry so much. Not everyone fits into a box, you know."

She mumbled an agreement but felt her mood dampen. They made it to the small peninsula of rocks. "Be careful climbing. It can be slippery on the mossy parts." Low tide used to be her favorite time at the beach. Good for hunting crabs and poking jellyfish.

They climbed carefully over the boulders. "Now this would've been easier with sneakers," he said.

She giggled. "Wuss."

"Did you just call your Dom a wuss?" he asked in mock disapproval. "Not smart. You'll pay for that later."

"It's alright. I'm banking on your poor memory. You forgot Q's smartass comment the other day when we played. And you swore earlier she'd pay for that too."

She paused at the top of the rock pile and looked back. Jude looked puzzled. "What smartass comment?"

Should she remind him and get Q in trouble? The writing assignment Q made her do last week came to mind. Writing out her fantasies in detail? So embarrassing! "She said you needed to get on an aerobics program and the little blue pill to keep up with us."

He thought for a moment. "Oh yeah. Well, now I owe you both. Remind me if I forget."

"Yeah." She snorted. "Cause that's in my best interest."

Suddenly, he jumped toward her and landed on her rock, crowding her until she slipped backward with a yelp. Strong arms caught her before she fell, but he didn't set her right. He held her suspended, just a little off balance so she had to depend on him to stay upright. Frantically, she grasped his shoulders and held them hard.

"You better make sure your mouth doesn't write checks your ass doesn't want to cash," he growled. He narrowed his eyes and added, "Or maybe I should spank you right here. Is that what you're asking for?"

She shook her head, terrified at the idea. In front of Q was one thing, but there were still stragglers on the beach that could see them. "No."

"No, what?"

Her throat closed up. She swallowed hard. "No, Sir."

A smile then he kissed her lips. Hard and panty-melting, but he stopped too soon. "That's my good girl."

Setting her right again, he steadied her 'til she got her bearings. "Now be nice," he said and gave her ass a swat.

She slowed her heavy breaths. God he could make her hot so fast. Maybe she could entice them back to the house to play earlier. Her insides already felt warm and her clit throbbed in time with her pounding heart.

"Hey!" Q called from behind them. "Wait for me."

Sabrina turned to see Q jogging toward them across the beach. Oh great. Now she had to try to suppress her sexual appetite with *two* Doms. Q was just as adept at getting her turned on as Jude was. And, despite Jude having called Sabrina a tease, Q was as bad, or worse.

"It's Brat one," Jude said with a smile at Q. "Come on up, sweetheart." He held out a hand to help Q up the rocks but she ignored it, quickly making her way up on her own.

"Sorry I'm late," she said, a little out of breath.

"No problem." Jude gestured to the other side of the rocks. "Sabrina was just taking me to a secluded part of the beach. Can we really trust her though? She's small but has a vicious look about her in a scrappy kitten sort of way." He flashed a dimple. "Is it a good idea to follow her to a mysterious place away from any witnesses?"

Sabrina rolled her eyes. "Ha, ha. If I wanted to murder you, I'd have done it while you were sleeping. I often sit up at night and watch you." She pointed to Jude. "You snore. And you," she motioned to Q, "you talk in your sleep."

Q's eyes widened. "What do I say?"

She bit back a grin then raised her voice an octave in a silly girly voice. "Oh, Jude. Sex me up, baby! Oh yes, feed my disturbing need for violence!"

Jude chuckled. "Nice."

"Sex me up?" Q arched a brow. "Who even says that?"

"Nineties pop songs. Can we go?" She gestured impatiently down the rocks.

"Go on," Jude said. "Lead us to your beach sex cave."

Q and Sabrina laughed then the three carefully made their way down the rocks. Back on the sand, Sabrina walked closer to the water, enjoying the cool wetness on the bottom of her feet. Despite the beach breeze, it still felt muggy. Her dress clung to her body and she fought the urge to strip it off and go for a swim. Maybe she should have put on her bikini instead of the fancy bra and underwear set.

She looked back at Jude and Q, walking arm in arm and smiled. So cute. She didn't even feel a twinge of jealousy. She'd always been the jealous type so it surprised her. But with Jude and Q…she didn't know exactly…the three of them just fit. Though the Nico thing was getting on her nerves. It terrified her to think that Q might give in and go back to him. For some reason, Q seemed to need a man in her life frequently. What would happen when Jude left after the summer? Her heart ached for a moment but she pushed it away. Enjoy their time now. That was all she could do. What future did she have with two lovers anyway?

Ugh. She wished it wasn't so hot. And Q was wearing jeans again! She stopped and waited for them to catch up. "I can't even look at you in those jeans," she said to Q when they came close. "Aren't you hot? What happened to the shorts I made you?"

"They got paint on them. And I'm used to wearing jeans. It's not a big deal."

A thought came to mind. "What do you have underneath them?"

"Underwear, of course."

"What kind? They might look like bikini bottoms."

"They don't," she answered too quickly.

Sabrina sidled up to her with a sly smile. "Let me see." She placed her hands in the waistband of her pants and undid the button.

A soft grunt left Q's lips and she grabbed Sabrina's hands. "What do you think you're doing, little girl?"

Jude stepped in. "Not a bad idea. Take them off Q."

Q let go of Sabrina and faced Jude. "You take them off."

Oh boy.

A fleeting look of amusement crossed Jude's face before he traded it for a stern glare. "Brat."

A second later, Q fled. Jude followed her. Sabrina watched with an equal sense of humor and trepidation for her friend's fate – though she'd asked for it. Typical Q.

It didn't take long for Jude to catch her. He wrestled her to the ground. Pinned face down, he yanked down her jeans, Q kicking and fighting the whole time. He managed to get them all the way off then gave her a smack on the ass before helping her to stand. With a glare, she brushed the dry sand off her face and neck.

He traded a grip on her hand for one in her hair then growled something in her ear. It must've been good because she watched her friend's eyes glaze over and her body melt into him.

"You're lucky I'm letting you keep the underwear on after that," he said louder, walking toward Sabrina with Q's jeans in his hand. "What did I get myself into?" he mumbled to himself. "Brats. The both of you."

Sabrina smiled at Q, taking in her long, lean legs and black boy shorts. "Cute Q. And totally passes for bikini bottoms."

Q stalked toward her, wearing a determined and somewhat frightening expression – her turned on face. Sabrina gulped and took a half a step back. Without a word, Q grabbed the front of her dress and yanked her in for a kiss.

Though Q was often gentle, this time, as she crushed her mouth onto Sabrina's, she thrust a hand into her hair and dragged her head back. The *take*, the dominance, blew away Sabrina's last fragment of resistance. She shut her eyes. For what seemed like forever, Q kissed her, hard and without mercy.

When Q pulled away, Sabrina caught her breath. "Fuck," she whispered, staring into Q's lustful eyes.

"Mmm," she murmured. "I plan to."

"Hey." Jude placed himself between them, looking from one to the other. "You starting without me? That's not very nice."

"No," Sabrina jumped in quickly. She took a quick survey of the beach to make sure no one had wandered over. "No more. Not here."

Jude frowned. "I thought you said this spot would be empty."

"I said *maybe*. Anyone can wander over." She touched her fingers to her lips, the taste of Q still lingering. "It's just...I have family close by. And friends..." The hurt in Q's eyes made her trail off. Guilt rose up in her belly. It killed her to cause her friend even a touch of pain. But she just wasn't ready to reveal this situation to people. Even she didn't understand what fucked up thing they had going on.

"It's just a kiss, Sabrina," Jude said.

"No, she's right." Q inhaled a breath then let it out slowly. "It's not fair to force her to come out."

Jude nodded. "Okay. Then let's find somewhere truly private and quick. That kiss was fucking hot."

Q and Sabrina laughed. "Come on, tough guy," Sabrina teased. "We just got here. Suck it up."

"I want some sucking alright," he mumbled, hissing in a breath.

Q gave him a sideways glance. "Later. If you're nice."

He arched a brow. "Or maybe I'll string you up again and keep you on edge for so long you forget your own name." With a twinkle in his eye and an evil grin he added, "Or maybe until you tell me your real one."

Q shook her head hard. "No way, sunshine. You're getting nothing from these lips."

"Except them wrapped around his cock," Sabrina added. They both looked at her in shock. She shrugged. "What?"

"I think that's the dirtiest thing I've ever heard you say," Q answered.

She shrugged. "You must be rubbing off on me."

"Hey, there's a nice flat spot up there." Jude pointed up the beach to where an outcropping of rocks made a ledge over the sand, shielding it from view unless you stood right in front. "I'm gonna run back to the car. I think I have a blanket in the trunk."

Sabrina and Q nodded and watched him walk away.

"So," Sabrina turned her attention to Q, "you had the bride from hell, huh?"

Q grimaced. "You have no idea. She freaked out the flowers were the wrong color of white and stomped all over them. Who knew there were different colors of white?"

Chuckling, Sabrina took her hand and squeezed it. "We must have the same client. I had a diva today too." When she tried to pull her hand away, Q gripped it tighter.

"Let's walk."

She looked down at their hands then swept her gaze over the beach. It was empty. "Okay." Two girls holding hands wasn't a dead giveaway like it used to be. Lots of platonic friends did that nowadays.

"So what happened with your client?" Q asked as they strolled down the beach. "Is this the author who wanted a book cover?"

"Yes. She kept going on and on about wanting a masculine font. What the fuck is a masculine font?"

Q laughed and swung their hands between them. She liked this – walking on the beach, holding hands. It seemed so very…normal.

"I gave her several versions with different fonts I thought were masculine. But then she said they were too thin. She wanted something thick, but not cartoony. All thick fonts are cartoony!" She growled. "I could have thrown a book at her head."

"But you didn't. You were calm and professional."

"Yes, though it almost killed me."

"You're so dramatic." Q chuckled then looked behind them. "Jude's back. Come on."

"In a sec." She dropped Q's hand and looked out at the white crests dotting along the water. "Go spend a minute alone with Jude. He missed you."

Q gave her a small smile. "He missed you too."

"I had him all to myself before you showed up."

She nodded. "Okay. Don't be long." Then she walked to help Jude set up the blanket.

Sabrina stayed by the water, dipping her feet into the small pools, searching for hermit crabs like she had as a child. There was something peaceful about spending the afternoon here at the beach. Even though she was hiding them from her family, having Q and Jude in her favorite childhood spot just felt…right. Like they did belong despite logic steering them away.

A piece of green, rubbery seaweed wrapped around her ankle. She untangled it and a nefarious plan came to mind. With an evil smirk she turned around, looking for Jude. He was up by the blanket, his back facing her. Perfect.

She crept up behind him quietly, keeping the long, slippery seaweed behind her back. From the corner of her eye, she spotted Q watching her. She put her fingers to her lips in a silent gesture. Q shook her head with a sigh but didn't shout a warning.

At the last few feet, she sprinted, grabbed the back of his shorts and pulled. She stuffed the seaweed down his pants then backed away, almost falling down in a fit of laughter.

He grabbed his ass and spun around. The look on his face was priceless. Equal parts shock, anger, and disgust. It took him a minute to reach down and find the seaweed, grimacing the whole time.

Her stomach hurt from laughing so hard. Even Q chuckled. Finally, after throwing the seaweed on the ground, Jude looked at her. His eyes narrowed.

Oh shit. She spun on her heel and got about four steps before she felt her body lifted into the air. Jude scooped her up in his arms and jogged toward the open water.

She clung to his neck when he padded into the waves, not slowing down for a second. "No!" she screamed, trying to climb up him, away from the rising water. "No! I'm sorry. I'll be good."

Jude was undeterred. He went farther in – the waves hit the bottom of his shorts. Finally, he stopped then made like he was going to toss her in.

She held him tighter. How could he even breathe with her arms wrapped so tight around his neck? "No, Jude! Please!"

Just when she thought he was going to drop her, Q came to her rescue. "Don't do it, Jude. She'll be all sticky and salty and totally unlickable."

That gave him pause. "Are you going to behave?" he asked her.

"Yes! Yes. I promise I'll behave."

He sighed and adjusted his hold before walking back to the shore. When they reached Q, he let her down and walked toward the blanket. "Come on, brats. Let's sit and relax."

Q looked at Sabrina and shook her head. "Sometimes I don't know which of us is worse."

She laughed. "Me neither."

Jude was already sitting, legs stretched out in front of him, when they reached the blanket. Q sat down on one side of him. Sabrina bent to take the other side, but before she could make it all the way down, an arm wrapped around her waist and toppled her over. She shouted as she fell onto Jude's lap, stomach down, ass in the air.

"Oh shit," she grumbled.

When her dress went up, she was glad for the full panty coverage instead of a thong that day. Jude gave her a quick dozen or so slaps, making her grip the blanket in her fists and squeal. A moment later, he pulled her up and maneuvered her to sit between his legs.

Ouch! Her ass stung as she perched there gingerly.

"That was for the seaweed," he growled in her ear.

Her stomach *thunked* and warmth fused with the cool dampness in her panties. She caught her breath.

"Fuck that was hot," Q rasped.

Sabrina gasped. She'd forgotten they were in public! Frantically, she scanned for an audience.

"Relax," Jude said and kissed her neck. "There's nobody here. I checked."

She exhaled a breath. Thank god. Her face must've been flaming red. And her ass! Damn he had a hard hand. Ugh. As if the kiss weren't enough to get her going. How long until play time? Last weekend Jude had cut Q off, telling her she wasn't allowed to come until they played again this weekend. Five whole days. Q loved that sort of thing. But then Q had given Sabrina the same order. Orgasm denial was *not* one of Sabrina's kinks. She was ready to combust.

Q scooted up close to Jude. In a spontaneous moment of affection, Sabrina grabbed onto Q's shirt and pulled her down across Jude's leg. Q arched her brow but let Sabrina lead her head onto her lap. Gently, she played with Q's long black hair, taking small pieces and braiding them. Jude ran his fingers up and down Sabrina's arm, making goose bumps rise on her skin. Q kept one hand resting on Sabrina's leg and her other hand under Jude's. The three of them, each one touching the other, completed a circle.

She sighed contentedly, watching the water darken in the twilight. Q rubbed soft circles on her thigh. Jude kissed her shoulder then shifted slightly to hold Q's hand. Everything felt so…right.

"We're good together," she blurted.

"Hm?" Q asked drowsily.

She shrugged, struggling to come up with a way to express her happiness without sounding like an idiot. "I'm just saying, we're good together. The three of us."

"Mm," Jude mumbled in agreement then kissed her hair.

Something nagged at her, threatening her perfect moment. Maybe she was being insecure but she had to clear it up. "It's time consuming, being in two relationships. Even if they are temporary."

"That's true" Jude rumbled.

Q turned her head and gazed up at her. "Would you give one of us up?"

Sabrina caught the slight panic in her voice though she tried to cover it with nonchalance. "That's not what I said," she answered and tugged on one of the braids she'd made in Q's hair. Q glared but Sabrina continued. "I just mean I can't see how any of us could have another relationship outside of this…kind of, sort of one." She chuckled nervously.

"Are you trying to say you want to be exclusive, Sabrina?" Q asked with a smirk.

She stared down at Jude's hand, now resting on her belly, feeling her cheeks heat. She'd always been brave about certain types of feelings and shy about others. Rejection was damn scary. She swallowed hard then answered, "Only if that's what you want."

"Well, I think I can agree to that," Jude said confidently as he kissed her hair again. A warm fuzzy feeling started in her chest and a smile crept up on her lips.

One down, one to go. "Q?"

She quirked a brow. "Yes?"

"No Nico."

Q chuckled. "No Nico."

She choked back the last of her insecurity and asked, "And no other girls?"

Q turned to give her a stark look of sincerity. "You're the only girl I need."

Joy bubbled up deep inside her and she grinned. How novel to be wanted. And not for her body – well, not *only* for her body. But Q knew her like no one else did – all of her insecurities, her annoying habits, her deepest secrets – and wanted her anyway. Her heart felt like it swelled up, making room to fit two people she could possibly grow to love. The summer was too short for an experiment like this. The kinky part had been successful. She liked it alright. Loved it. But how could she decide her sexual orientation in only three months time? Especially when it had so many complicated implications.

Chapter 13

Jude

Jude counted the days. For Q it had been five days of being turned on with no orgasms. And today at the beach, there'd been spanking and a little kissing. That Q had forbidden Sabrina the same was an exquisite touch. He would've loved to have been inside the girls' heads. Jude flopped back on the mock-Georgian couch and dialed Q's phone.

"Q? Hi. Where are you both?"

"Home. Sabrina's in the kitchen. Why?"

"I think our little sex toy needs to suffer." He couldn't stop an evil chuckle. Time to test Q's dominance over their pet.

"Mmm. What did you have in mind, Sir?"

He was sure Q could think of her own torturous plans but it was too much fun to resist being a part of it. "First, is she wearing underwear?" He'd found out recently, Sabrina was notorious for walking around the apartment without it, just to tease Q.

"Sabrina!" Q's sing-songy voice would make anyone suspicious. "Hey! No running away." Her voice turned stern. "Stay right there, little girl."

Bratting already? He heard a bit of scuffling then a startled squeal.

"Nope. No underwear," she said to Jude. "Hang on. Putting it on speaker." A moment later, he heard Sabrina's voice too.

"No, Q." She giggled but it sounded nervous. "Stay back! I'm trying to cook our dinner."

"You know what I said I'd do if I caught you without underwear," Q said.

He pictured Q circling the little brat in their kitchen like a hunter focused on its prey. This was too much fun. He'd have to remember to do it again.

"Stay back!" Sabrina yelled. "I have a spatula and I know how to use it."

Another scuffle with a few grunts thrown in then three loud smacks.

"Ow!" Sabrina howled.

"I'll show you how to use a spatula." Q's voice rose above Sabrina's protests.

There were three more slaps then quiet.

"Ack!" Sabrina yelped. "Did you just bite my ass?"

Q chuckled. "That was for prancing around without underwear. Again."

Silence.

"Q?" he called into the receiver.

"Yes?"

"Bend her over the counter."

"Already there."

Mmm. Delicious. He contemplated grabbing his keys and rushing over except that he'd promised his mom a call. "Is she wet?"

A second went by and Sabrina groaned.

"Soaked," Q answered.

"Stop talking about me like I'm not here!"

Q snapped, "Hush!"

"Good girls," Jude said. "Q, tease her as long as you'd like but don't let her come." In his mind, Q grinned wickedly and Sabrina stomped her foot.

"Yes, Sir," Q answered, sounding a little out of breath.

Sabrina whined. "But…but…I can't hold back!"

"Sabrina," he said sternly. "It will please me if you try. It's just one day. I'll make it worth your while."

In a smaller voice, she answered, "Okay."

"That's my girl. Q?"

"Yes?"

"You being a good girl and waiting for me too?"

"Yes, Sir," she answered shakily.

He wished he could be there – kissing them, holding them. His girls. His perfect subs. "Good. I'll reward you both tomorrow. See you then."

He shut the phone off and lay back. His smile lasted a while.

***

The last thing Jude expected to see when he pulled around the corner to Q and Sabrina's apartment was Sabrina taking to a black Chevy with a can of spray paint. A goth type was at the top of the porch staircase with his hand in Q's hair and a devastated expression on his face. And yet Sabrina kept on spraying. Orange did not go well on a windshield, or with black body paint…or over the top of the hubcaps.

This must be Nico. Bastard.

Fuck. He was going to kill him for doing that to Q. The pain on her face…

A pile of ruptured bags on the ground spewing clothes, spoke of them being tossed overboard from the top of the stairs.

And Sabrina was a demoness with claws when riled. He grinned.

No parking spot except a handicapped one presented itself.

He drove in at an angle and stopped with a small screech about the same time as Nico did a double-take, let go of Q, and sprinted down the steps.

The door of his pickup squeaked plaintively as he thrust it open. The stack of ladders in the back wasn't likely to impress on Nico the heights of his badassery. Couldn't be helped.

What were the principles of fighting? Never go to a gun fight with a sword, or start a land war in Asia? Well, he didn't have a gun or a sword, or a land war. The crowbar on the floor on the passenger side would have to be his last resort.

By the time he'd run up to Sabrina, Nico had reached bottom of the steps and was striding toward them, drawn up to full height, and so angry that it was a wonder steam wasn't coming out his nostrils.

"How dare you, you little cunt!"

"You're lucky I only fucked up your car, dickhead!" Sabrina spat the words. "He just slapped Q around and wrecked our apartment! Call the cops. No, fuck that. I'm going to kill him!" She stared at the can in her hand. "If this were a gun… I'd ram it down his fucking throat."

"Take it easy." He stepped in front of Sabrina. Cute and spunky in cut-off denim shorts only got you so far against an enraged guy with a thing for snarling and trying to rip women's hair out.

Her reply made him think of a cat spitting. "I want to do something horribly fatal to him!" Then her hand touched his elbow. "Be careful, Jude. Nico is batshit crazy."

"Got it." He flicked his gaze upward. At least Q was out of the way, even if her face was dead white. Except, now she was heading down the stairs too. Trying to control this guy without anyone getting hurt would be damn near impossible with two women close by.

Get this over fast.

"You!" Nico jabbed a finger as he stalked. "This is between me and Q and this little cunt. Step back." He stopped a few feet away and seethed. His jaw worked and his eyes stared madly as if at any minute they'd pop. The collar of his black shirt was askew and one button hung on a thread.

Q had reached the bottom few steps. Jude opened the car door and prayed the man had some sense. While herding Sabrina back behind him, he stepped away to give Nico room. "Go. Get in, and leave. You do not own Q."

"Get your hands off my car, you fucker!"

The lunge and lash of Nico's fist was expected. He grabbed the wrist, then yanked Nico forward as he kicked at the man's ankle and swept it out backward. Momentum, gravity, and luck agreed with what he wanted, for once. A second later Nico was on his knees, screaming with his arm wrenched behind his back.

"Fuck! Let go!" Though he was yelling, Nico's lack of resistance, after one futile jerk to try free himself, made it clear he'd got the armlock right.

Jude leaned in and growled. "You will get in your car and leave. You won't come back. You will stay away from the girls. If I catch you near them again, I'll beat the living fuck out of you. I have many, many friends who will be keeping an eye on you. Got that?" He screwed the arm a little higher.

Nico gasped and bowed forward. "Fuck! Yes! Got it!"

"Up!" He maneuvered Nico to his feet and shoved him into the driver seat then with his hand twisted in the man's conveniently long hair, he gave a last command while staring down into Nico's fear-widened eyes. "I know people in the community. Don't try showing your face at any clubs. The word will be out that you're a fool who can't control his temper and assaults women." He slammed the door shut.

When Nico started the engine and drove off, smoking the tires, but without more fuss than a string of shouted expletives and a finger out the window, the tension drained from Jude. He heaved in a breath and turned to the women.

Red-faced, hair plastered to her forehead, and paint can dangling from her fingers, Sabrina stood there, stunned. Then she whipped her head around. "Q!" She dropped the can to the pavement and sprinted away.

The collision of her body with Q's was a small hurricane arriving – all noise and flailing arms, then she quieted. Her arms wrapped around Q and she did the same to her while patting Sabrina's back. All he could hear were whispers.

When he reached them, Q was still saying it. "I'm okay. I am. Sabrina, I'm okay."

"You're sure?" After one last sniff and hug, Sabrina let her go, though they still held hands.

"Q?" At his voice, Q raised her gaze. *Fear.* There was fear in her eyes, of him?

She straightened and the familiar self-assured look took over. "Thank you, Jude. I'm sorry you had to see that." As if the episode were done with, she straightened her t-shirt. "I'm going to get my stuff back upstairs."

"No." He frowned. There it was again – that twitch as if he'd scared her. Was it his voice, or just that he was a man, a Dom? "Come here."

At the shake of her head, he stepped up and gathered both of them to him. Her protests could go to hell.

"Jude. No," she croaked. "I'm –"

"Q!" Sabrina piped up. "Give the man a hug. He just saved our lives. Well, mine, anyway. I'm pretty sure Nico was about to strangle me." She laughed nervously.

Her struggles lessened and, when he kissed her forehead, Q let out a sharp exhale.

Though she didn't cry, tears lined her eyelids. Q blinked them away. They hugged for a while in silence. When he had both their heads resting on his chest, and their soft breaths warming him, he felt at last that he had everything going the right way.

Maybe now was a good time to shore up the foundations of trust again.

"I'm glad I was here. If I hadn't been – if Nico had hurt either of you – I don't know what I would have done. You can't be alone forever Q. Sometimes you have to let someone else take the load. As your Dom, I consider it my duty, and as a friend and a man too. If you refuse my help, you hurt me."

Then he turned her face up to him. He brushed a strand of hair from her eye, and kissed her softly on her trembling lips. "Okay?"

"Yes. I'm sorry."

"Wasn't your fault. Forget him. You two are coming to my place. We'll pack some clothes and stuff, and you can stay until I've done all I can to make sure he won't bother you again."

Q nodded. Determination surfaced in her eyes. "And Jude. Just so you know, you've shown me there's a difference between being a Dom and being an abusive asshat. I don't think I really understood that before."

He grinned. "Thanks. I think."

Sabrina pursed her lips and examined them both. "You two were so cute kissing." She stepped toward Q and stroked her hair, the sweetest look on her face. "See, Q? It's not true, what Nico said – that no one will ever love you."

Nico said that? The guy couldn't really feel that way about Q, even if he was a psychopath. Who wouldn't love her?

Shit. Love. Uh oh. But, there was a truth there that rocked him. Falling in love with these two was not on his agenda. Or not on his father's agenda anyway. And med school was not compatible with moving in with Q and Sabrina.

Or with anything else I want from life.

Q put her hands around Sabrina's shoulders and tugged her closer. "Thank you for trying to distract Nico." She lowered her head and kissed Sabrina. Not hard and sexual, just the kiss of a woman appreciating the one who held her heart. As quietly as the sun rising at dawn, he felt peace drift down on them. Magic.

Q cupped Sabrina's face. "But that was the stupidest thing you could've done."

Sabrina flinched at the sudden change of tone.

"Seriously. He could've really hurt you. Or pressed charges. If Jude hadn't arrived, what would you have done when he reached you?"

"Ran like hell." Sabrina shrugged.

Q nodded. "That's the right answer. Don't you ever, ever, endanger yourself for me again."

"I can't promise that. I care about you too much."

Q opened her mouth to say more but Jude cut her off. "Enough." They turned to him. "Let's pack. We'll forget him and have fun all morning. I'll take you shopping, swimming at the beach, out to lunch, whatever you want. Then back to my place. That's an order. Snap to it and run your little asses off getting everything you need."

With an evil glint in her eye, Sabrina nodded then did an exaggerated salute, with her hand doing a huge circle before she touched her forehead. "Yes, Sir!"

Q dragged Sabrina's hand down. "My turn to rescue you. Let's get to it."

He looked up at the heavens. "God, give me patience."

Well, he had sort of asked for it. The day was going to be interesting.

Chapter 14

Jude

Jude pushed open the door, smiling inside at the silence of the new hinges. He liked a job done well, and the whole room had turned out the way he wanted. The last of the afternoon sun coming in through the bay window didn't do the room justice, so he switched on the two head-high lamps, and the muted ceiling lights. A rich color scheme of creams and ochre, with a hint of oxblood red – but it was the broad sweep of arching stems and delicate leaves of the potted plants that impacted on him first. The greenery made it *live.*

A little sadness crept in. He was going to miss this, fixing up houses – there'd be no time for this sort of frivolity, as his father used to call it, while studying medicine. Surgeons paid someone else to fix their houses.

This wasn't the time for moping.

"What do you think, girls? You helped paint this."

Everything clicked together in his brain. He'd known he'd miss Q and Sabrina for a while, he just hadn't admitted it to himself. And it wasn't just that he loved having two gorgeous young women who'd give him a blowjob if he told them to. Part of it, but not all. This was something…more.

"Wow." Sabrina paced forward, and her short little pink dress sucked him into looking at the woman's thighs. Thank god her light tan didn't extend to her ass – marks always showed well. "I love these." She ran her hand over the red upholstery of the closest of the two Chippendale couches then picked up a pillow and hugged it. "And these. Mmm. I adore big pillows. Makes me want to sleep on them on a rainy day."

He raised his eyebrows, but shut the door, and followed in behind the more subdued Q. When she stared at the cleared area between the couches and the two ropes dangling down from his O rings, he smoothed his hand down her back. "They're temporary. I'll have to take them down soon."

"I guess they do advertise your kinkiness." Q put her hand over his where it rested on the lower curve of her back. He stepped in close, trapping her hand there, then wrapped his arm around her waist, and settled her against him. For once she wore a dress, even if it was plain black. Beneath the light fabric, his palm registered the solid warmth and movement of her flesh.

"They do, but it's not that. The owner of this place is a local Dom. But I don't think he plans to sell this as the House of Fetishes." Then he nuzzled her neck while Sabrina looked on, bright of eye and with her bottom lip sucked onto her teeth. "We're going to play now."

"Oh, really?" Her voice was already husky and her hips swayed. Leaning her back into his shoulder was easy. Those clear blue pupils of hers broadcast wariness. Her focus darted here and there, and she studied him. Never a dull moment with Q. "Presumptuous of you."

"I don't need an appointment. You're staying with me. It's Monday night. I've seduced you both with my chef-quality food and sat on the beach and fed enough seagulls. Time to pay for your keep."

"Is that how it is?" Sabrina chuckled.

"Yep. Kneel where you are." He released Q, and slapped her on the butt. Her yelp and indignant look, he ignored. "Q, strip to your underwear and come here next to me." This must be a mellow night. Q began to obey without question and Sabrina slipped to her knees. He perched on the couch that held three shopping bags and the crop, and waited as Q pulled the dress over her head. "Good. Come here."

With his hands lightly holding Q's hips, he examined her slowly despite her blush. The things bras did to women's breasts were the eighth wonder of the world…or was that ninth? Matching electric blue bra and panties…and on her curves they were mouthwatering. "Turn." When her ass was under his hands, he squeezed. "Much better."

"My doing." Sabrina smirked and folded her arms. "Told you he'd like them. We found them at a store in…" Then she went on and on.

He stayed silent and waited for her to wind down. Finally, she stopped and sat back on her heels. "What? What are you looking at?"

"You talk too much, Sabrina." How long would that cheeky attitude hold up with what he had in store? "Q." He patted the couch next to him and pulled her in close when she sat. Then he turned his full attention on Sabrina, who'd been shifting nervously on her knees.

"Stand up, strip, then kneel again at our feet."

"Yes, oh Royal One." When she pouted and rolled her eyes, he hardened his smile. One little submissive had a surprise coming.

"Use this." He tossed a pillow to the floor for her to kneel on.

The double distractions of Sabrina undressing and a half-naked Q right next to him made his cock stir but he waited patiently.

After folding her sundress and underwear and putting them to one side, Sabrina knelt again. Ample breasts. Plump pink nipples. Cute, with big brown eyes, and she looked as interested as a puppy waiting for breakfast. He was going to enjoy this.

"Comfortable?"

"Yes, Sir." She nodded.

"Look appetizing, Q?"

"Yes, Sir."

"I think I hear you drooling." He drew a little circle on her thigh and blew softly in her ear, then smiled at Q's flinch.

"That's more than likely." Her swallow was audible.

"I figured." He switched back to Sabrina. "You have only been playing at submission. And I've been bad. I've let you get away with too much."

"What?" Seemingly dumbstruck, she kept both palms on her thighs, wiggled a little, then stopped. "Um? What do you mean?"

"I've allowed you to put off several things, though they're not in your hard limits. That's not happening anymore. Tonight, you are going to be my pet, and Q's pet." He rummaged in one of the shopping bags and took out a purple collar and leash, a few other things, and picked up the crop.

The crop swished nicely. He stood and circled around behind her. All the while Q watched him as if he'd sprouted horns.

"Pet?" she squeaked. "Umm. No ears. And none of those…ew, butt plug tails." Sabrina craned her neck back and stared anxiously.

"Shush. Eyes front."

"I've seen those. Yuck. No way. And a collar and leash is not really –"

"I said, *quiet*! Head on the floor. Now!" And he smacked the couch with the crop.

Startled, she bowed until her head touched the rug and her pretty ass was presented high.

"Five." Without other warning, he cropped her ass five times, hard enough to make her squeal. Hard enough to make brilliant red stripes on her skin.

"Sit up again. I know anal's a hard limit of yours and Q's. Ears aren't." Then he bent down and gripped her neck. Slowly, with her tracking him out the side of her widened eyes, he pulled her upper body to him, as if he were a fisherman hauling in a catch. "But this isn't a pair of ears." He lifted his other hand and showed her the pink ball gag. A training one only – he didn't want to freak her out.

"No!" she whispered.

Though his hand was on her neck, he could feel her straining to get away. But no safeword. He waited another moment to be sure. "I need you quieter." Then he put the ball between her lips and did up the buckle at the back. Though Sabrina shuddered, she let him. "Good girl." He kissed her cheek. "I know you can still talk, if with less sass. Say 'ghost.'"

When she gargled it out, he nodded.

With her mouth out of action, she seemed to have dropped straight into submissive mode and only whimpered a little as he put on the collar, then the wrist and ankle cuffs.

"Tonight," he murmured in her ear, "You will address me as Sir, always. Mistakes will be corrected with the crop. Understood?"

Sabrina nodded quickly.

He clipped her ankle cuffs together and her wrist cuffs with her hands at her back then held her chin. "I might take it off now and then, when I want to. But," he traced her lips where they formed an O around the ball, "I love the look of it in your mouth. It makes you look…mine." An urge took him, to push this farther. "Do you like being mine? Do you like me doing what I want to you?"

Though she shut her eyes, she opened them again a moment later, swallowed, and nodded. And that, alone, sent a thrill all the way to his balls.

"Good." He placed his hands on her breasts and caressed them until she was breathing fast, then slid one hand down to her pussy and played with her clit and her entrance. "Don't drip too much on the carpet, pet. Though watching you squirm is the most fun I've had all day."

Her whine made him chuckle. "I should have gagged you earlier," he rumbled.

A few leisurely pumps of his finger, all the way up inside, had her trying to spread her legs. He slapped her pussy once and she whined again.

He climbed to his feet. Though his pants were uncomfortable with his erection straining against them, he'd leave his clothes on for a while. Both of them had a thing for submitting to a man in a suit who kept them naked. A suit though, was a bitch in summer. Pants and shirt would have to do. He adjusted his boxers to let his cock have some relief. God, already he was quivering. Sabrina on her knees, like this, pressed all his buttons. Making her ass redder would up things to nuclear level, and getting Q doing things to her…the sun might explode. He looked at Q, where she still sat on the couch, mouth slightly open.

"See something you want?"

"Yes, Sir. Very much so. She looks…hot enough to lick all over. To eat."

"Women do, when on their knees, waiting for their Dom to instruct them."

"May I touch her?"

Sabrina gargled indignantly and shook her head. He snorted. The woman protested about everything even when gagged. The crop…he found it where he'd left it propped against the arm of the couch, picked it up, and gave Sabrina a slap on the side of each breast.

She silenced.

"Not yet, Q. First…"

Tearing his gaze away from Sabrina was difficult, but he managed. He searched in the bags again and took out the leather body harness, then held it by the collar for Q to see. "Like this?"

Knowing Q, he went closer, stroked her head then slid his hand up to lightly grab a handful of hair at the roots. Gripping her hair tighter would happen in a flash, if he needed to.

After one deep breath, a dreamy look pooled in her eyes.

As if he didn't already have that checked on his mind list of things that made Q melt.

"Is it a slave harness?" Q smiled. "I like it. She'll look even sexier in that."

"Call it a body harness. But it's not for her, it's for you." Smirking, he scrunched his fingers in the roots of her hair.

Her frown arrived a millisecond later. Now, her attempt at escape. She jerked, and took hold of his wrist. Nothing budged, of course.

"Not a chance, Q. I'm stronger." By sheer force, he manhandled her into a facedown position on the couch, held her there with a knee parked on her back, and his hand still controlling her head, while he growled to her. "Be careful. If you do anything wild you might knock our pet over, since she's cuffed. And I know you don't want that. Behave." He shook her head, turned it so he could watch her mouth.

With her hands like claws, she gripped the upholstery, as if what he did pained her. Well, he was doing it wrong if it didn't. She choked in few heavy breaths, then gasped out, "Yes, Sir."

"I have no tolerance for over-the-top bratting tonight. Do it and I'll put you in a corner for an hour with a vibe strapped to your clit and a dildo inside you. Got that?"

"Yes," she added softly. He yanked her hair for emphasis. "Yes!"

He hauled her upright and took off her underwear himself – making sure to keep contact while he did it – dominating her with his presence. While bra clasps were undone, and straps slipped half off her shoulders, he pressed up against her, and bit from her collarbone to the upper curve of her breast, to her nipple and its piercing. Pulling the bra all the way off, gave him the opportunity to drag his nails up her back, through the fall of her raven black hair then down her arms with the descent of the straps.

The quiver of her body and pitiful whimpers made him smile. But she was grinding against him by then, or trying to. He had Q marked in every way. Once he got her like this, she was his.

"Hands at your back. Grab your elbows."

As her shoulders went back, her breasts thrust out in a delicious way. Fuck. Tempting. So he went around behind her, grated out, "Stay still," and took each nipple between finger and thumb, then squeezed and tugged until she whimpered some more.

And taking down her panties, well, he'd need his brain transplanted if he didn't curve his palm into her pussy and feel between her legs.

With his fingers molded into the warm wetness of her slit, he crouched and bit her ass cheek. She trembled like a leaf torn at by wind. "You like being fucking crushed, being dominated. Don't you? Answer."

"Yes, Sir."

He could swear his hand got wetter at that.

Slowly he rose, sliding up the length of her body. He touched her everywhere, keeping close to her skin, smelling her femaleness. Reveling.

When he reasserted the grip in her hair, she bowed her head, lips parted. Without letting her go, he picked up the harness. The collar went on first then he unkinked the strap leading downward. Next came the straps around her body – one buckled above her breasts, a middle one went below them, and another went around her, across her stomach. From that strap the removable heavy silver chain travelled down between her legs and up again to fasten at the back of the same strap. He fished the wrist cuffs from the couch, buckled them on, and pulled her hands to her back where he clipped them to a D ring on the middle strap.

"I didn't leash our pet, yet, but you…you need it." He clipped the leash onto the collar, played his fingers lightly over her face. "Now," he said softly, "You're both mine. There are enough D rings on this harness to fasten you to anything. So be very, *very* good."

Q gulped.

What to do next? With Sabrina looking up at them all watery-eyed and wet chinned, and Q subdued with her hands behind her, there was one last hurdle he wanted to send Sabrina over before…before he left them.

"Stay here." The couch was a foot behind Q. "If you overbalance, the couch is here to sit on. Now." He squatted, undid Sabrina's ankle cuffs, and using the pillow she kneeled on, pulled her in close. Then he sat on the couch. Both women were in easy reach. He cupped Sabrina's face while he took off the gag. Licking her lips, she waited for him to go on.

"In the last few weeks, I've let you two play and let Q have a say in what happens. And she's respected your wish not to go down on her. But" – he tapped Sabrina's nose –"you suck my cock. You've let Q go down on you many, many times. Tonight, I'm going to watch you do her. Uh-uh. No frowning." Her eyes dilated when she saw him lift the crop. "This is for the frown."

Q wasn't going anywhere. With a grip on Sabrina's hair he stretched her forward and placed a few good swats on her butt, paused, and did a few more, even harder, making her wince.

"Ow!" She hissed in through her teeth.

He stopped and watched her pained wince transform into an angry glare.

"I didn't frown!"

"Do you want more?" He raised the crop menacingly.

Q jumped in to rescue her friend. "I don't recommend arguing with your Dom, little girl."

Eyes downcast, she stared at nothing. "No."

He planted a light warning slap on her thigh.

"No, Sir!" she amended quickly.

"Good. Start thinking more or I'll be using this a lot. Now." He edged her chin up with the business end of the crop. "Any real, serious problems with doing this?" She strained with her arms as if she tested the inescapability of the wrist cuffs. "None?"

"I don't wanna." Her pout almost made him laugh. With that he pulled the pillow forward another few inches. The pillow she knelt on matched them up almost perfectly – Sabrina's dark pink lips were four inches from Q's pussy. Q's expression was rapt.

"'I don't wanna' is not your safeword, pet. You breathing, Q?"

She sucked in a ragged breath. "Mmm."

This time he did laugh. "Up higher on your knees, pet." Slowly Sabrina raised herself, The tip of her tongue came out then zipped back in. "Begin. Make it good."

Her eyes flared. "You can't rate my performance! You'll make me nervous." He tapped the crop. "Sir."

"Make Q happy. That's all I ask. I'm not rating you. And pet, you really think that's going to be hard to do? As soon as you put your tongue on her, she'll be close to coming."

"Sir," Q muttered. "Please don't. I'm having enough trouble."

"I noticed." He grinned, laid down the crop, put his hand on Q's ass, the other in Sabrina's tumbled mess of beach-blonde hair, and gently urged them together.

"Sir?" The anxious look in Sabrina's eyes made him stop.

"Yes?"

"I don't know what to do." She sucked in her bottom lip. "I've never –"

Q awoke at that. "Don't make her, Sir. She doesn't want to."

If he asked Sabrina directly if she wanted to do this, he had a feeling she'd never say it.

"Are you safewording, pet?" He waited.

She ducked her head. Her answer was so subdued, he had to strain to hear.

"No, Sir."

He'd bet his last dime she wanted to do this. He considered, checking them both. Quiet instruction seemed the way.

"Then I'll guide you. Okay?" He stirred her hair with his fingers, and let her have some time to think.

"Yes," Sabrina said quietly before she looked up at Q's face then at him. "Okay. Thank you."

"Good. Try a kiss first."

She shut her eyes, slowly leaned in, and kissed Q on the clit. At Q's drawn-out groan, she glanced upward again.

"Now use your tongue on her. Alternate. Soft at first. Then harder then soft again. Try that."

"Okay." She took a big breath then bent forward again. She gave one lick then her mouth sucked and worked at Q, in little spurts. Every so often he saw her little tongue dart out and lick again.

Never had he had a front row seat to a girl testing out the limits of her bisexuality. Never like this. His dick seemed so hard it might just pop off and whizz around the room. He nearly laughed out loud at that picture, then sighed and zeroed back in on what Sabrina did to Q. She became bolder – curling out her tongue and swiping from the slit up across Q's clit then swirling around and around it.

Under his palm, the muscles in Q's ass tensed and relaxed and her groans grew louder. She stiffened, pulled at the cuffs so the strap below her breasts tightened. About to come? With both of them cuffed he had some control.

"Rest, pet." He pulled Sabrina back, smiling at how she licked her lips, seemingly enraptured with what she'd done to poor Q who was now catching her breath.

"Oh, fuck. Please, Sir." She gasped a few times. "Please, Sabrina?"

"Wait. Both of you."

When he judged it right, he pushed Sabrina back onto her. The little sounds of sucking, the gorgeous females right here in front of his nose…in front of his poor dick. Ugh. There was no way he'd come in his pants but this was the closest he'd been to that since he was a teenager. And Sabrina was enjoying this too. Every now and then she'd pause, look up at Q, then reapply her tongue and lips.

And yes, Q was quivering with tension again. Her breaths came fast and staccato. Her torso stretched and her thighs went rock-hard. He pushed Sabrina in closer, jamming her mouth onto Q as the orgasm hit her. She screamed and writhed and Jude gritted his teeth as he watched her pleasure.

When the undulations of Q's body stopped and she was standing there swaying and panting and coming down from the high of the orgasm, he stood.

"Good girl," he said to Sabrina. "Stay on your knees a bit longer. I'll be back."

He took Q by the leash and, with one hand on her bound arms, guiding her, led her to below one of the dangling ropes. Unlike on other days, she gave him no trouble as he linked her wrist cuffs to the rope above.

His hand on the angle of neck and shoulder, he bent till his lips were on her ear. "Was that good?"

"Yes. Thank you, Sir."

"Excellent. Now though, I'm going to make you pay for it."

Her head turned and he saw the fire in her eyes.

"You're so transparent, Q. Don't hope too much. I may get you dripping wet, but this will hurt."

She watched carefully as he backed away.

"We need Sabrina, though." He turned-on his heel and stalked back to her.

A few minutes after, she too was secured with her hands above. From the bags he took out her little costume and the broad leather belt then he collected the crop and a few other things, and walked back with his attention completely on her. "I feel like dressing you up."

"Is it pretty, Sir?" She wrapped her hands in the rope, and raised a skeptical eyebrow.

When he shook out the little black lace skirt and let the bra dangle she barely caught her frown before it spread.

Sabrina sighed. "Sir. I have a thing about only wearing what suits my complexion. And that's like slutty vampire slut gear. I'm really not feeling all that undead today."

He swallowed the laughter, let the ball gag uncurl from his hand. "Whatever made me think I'd need this?"

"Nooo."

"Yes."

Though she ducked away as far as the rope would let her, he caught her and popped in the gag.

The little skirt when he wriggled it up her legs sat on her hips, so short it revealed her ass. He loved it. The matching see-through bra was strapless and he did up the clasp then made sure her breasts sat with her nipples framed in the openings. He kissed each, once.

"Beautiful. Watch while I do things to Q. But, come to think of it…now I have you all tied up…" Like he had before, he played with her breasts and her pussy, even put his mouth to each nipple and sucked a while. When he had her screwing her toes into the floor, he stopped. "There. Now you know how you make Q feel, most days. Tease."

He circled her, cruised his palm over her ass. "I can't pass this up. If I put one hand here…" He cupped her pussy with the heel of his hand on her clit. This would do it for her. He spanked her hard, six times on one cheek, then ten on the other.

Her muffled groans came out past the gag. He started spanking her again, alternating ass cheeks, and kept going until she pressed herself rhythmically onto his hand. "There you go, pet. Now you're extra hot."

That made her growl indignantly.

He grinned. "You can learn how to wait. Waiting builds character."

He stripped off his shirt and tossed it aside, did the same with his shoes. Then he admired his two captives, walking around them with crop and belt in hand. Sabrina and Q in ropes – two women he'd be happy just to watch if they passed him in the street, and here they were naked and bound, and with Sabrina's little ass still bright red. Fucking gorgeous.

Today was a good day to be a Dom.

He ended his tour of them behind Q. The crop was first. He used it on Q's thighs, where she loved it most – first the very end, and then the whippy shaft after she warmed up and could take more. Then the belt, hard and methodical. Then more of the crop. Every gasp, every tremble, every whimper, and every mark that appeared, he drank in with his eyes.

To give her a rest, and let her feel the change in sensations, he'd stop now and then to trace the damage with his fingertips, or draw a finger along her swollen pussy.

A final *thwack* with the crop made her clutch the rope with her fingers. Done. He smiled. His latest work of art.

Red welts from the belt stood out on her back. A few lines from the crop crossed her ass but most were lower. Lines of pink, and bright red, as well as few early bruises, marked her thighs where he'd hit. Too bad he didn't have a cane to try on her. She'd probably love it. He'd never had a sub that liked this kind of pain. He wiped away sweat with his forearm then went to her and ran his thumb over her lower lip. Her whimpers and moans had again succeeded in making his cock hard as steel. She was standing, but swaying. Blue balls? Ha. His were probably purple.

"You ready to be fucked, little brat?"

He had to lean in close to hear her reply.

"Fuck, yes." Though hazed with the delicious pain, her eyes pleaded softly. "Please, please, fuck me."

He checked on Sabrina…who looked as turned on as he was. The gag, maybe he should remove it? Just in case he lost concentration. After taking off his pants and throwing them over near his shoes, he went and removed the gag.

As he walked away, she called to him. He spun around and noticed her gaze on his cock.

"Can I be first Sir? I'm going to die if you don't fuck me now."

"Not yet. Be good, pet."

"Sir. Please," she asked quietly. "I'll do anything."

"Really?" He studied her. If she bratted more, he'd put the gag back in, but for once she didn't say a word. Her glum resigned expression almost made him choke with laughter. Talk about fishing for attention. But, he looked at the two of them. Q was desperate, as she always was after being beaten. But one of Q's kinks was a love for being frustrated.

He stalked to Q, freed her then pulled loose the leash from where he'd tucked it under a strap. "Come."

When they reached Sabrina, he made her wait while he retrieved a condom and a pillow then had her kneel in front of Sabrina. She hadn't complained, but he explained anyway.

"You're going to lick her," he told Q, gesturing at Sabrina, "while I fuck her."

Despite her own needs Q looked pleased. "Yes, Sir." Her voice was a rasp. She'd screamed a lot.

A curl of hair dangled over Sabrina's ear and he rolled it onto his finger "Do whatever you like to her. Afterward, she's going to pleasure you again."

Q nodded, and slid her hands up the front of Sabrina's thighs.

His cock jerked a little when he brushed against Sabrina's ass but he paused to watch Q. Though she clearly loved Sabrina, Q had no qualms about making the submissive dance to her tune.

"Let's see how much I can heat you up, little girl," she said in a sultry voice, low and sexy enough to make his balls take notice. "You're making him fuck you first, so I'm going to make you squeal. Especially since Jude has you all tied up."

At first she deliberately kept well away from Sabrina's most sensitive erogenous zones, but instead climbed up her body, kissing and nipping. Once she reached Sabrina's breasts, she put a hand beneath each then suckled on one while her thumb circled the other. After a few gasps, Sabrina arched forward, dancing on her tiptoes and groaning.

His cock throbbed, reminding him it wanted something too.

He pulled Sabrina's butt back even more, so she had to lean into the wrist cuffs and overhead rope. Her ass played peekaboo under the tiny skirt and moisture shone on her inner thighs. The tip of his cock breached her opening. The squeeze on him was exquisite after playing with them both for so long.

"Christ. I'm not gonna last long. Get her off, Q." He thrust all the way in then kept up a slow steady rhythm, feeling her inner muscles clamp and release.

Sabrina's noises became more and more primitive, more desperate, but then so was he. He barely made it. When she orgasmed and collapsed into the ropes, he gasped and started to fuck her in earnest. Each thrust jarred her body. He vaguely registered Q sitting back. He kicked Sabrina's feet apart at the ankles, hoisted her up onto him so she was off the ground, and exploded into a flurry of hard, fast thrusts that hit up inside as deep as he could go.

Her squeals spurred him on. Faster, deeper, and harder.

"Ah!" As he came, the pressure and pleasure held him in that rapt eternal moment, squeezing his balls down tight.

"Fuck," he said, awestruck. "Holy hell." He bit her neck, once, twice, sinking his teeth in and not releasing her for a few seconds, though she whimpered. Then he pulled out and unglued his fingers from her hips.

The view down below, as he withdrew, made him admire Sabrina's curves.

"Your ass would sink a thousand ships, girl." The quiet giggle from Q and shake of Sabrina's shoulders made him rethink. "And launch them too."

After he'd released the rope from the wrist cuffs, they were still giggling.

"You're both on probation." The burst of more giggling just left him shaking his head. He swept Sabrina into his arms.

Coyly, she shook out her hair and hung onto his shoulders. "Where are you taking me, fair prince? To the shower?"

"No." He hefted her higher, and paced toward the couch. "Over here. You haven't forgotten your promise?"

"Umm. No. But I'm all sweaty and icky though. We both are. We want a shower, don't we, Q?"

"Uh-uh. No shower. Not yet. I like you all sweaty. You're tastier." He paused to kiss her deeply, before setting her down at the front of the couch. A blanket he'd put next to the couch went over it. When he pointed to the floor, Q followed suit and kneeled next to Sabrina. "I want to see what my pet can do to my switch."

Q eyed him a little suspiciously.

The bag on the couch yielded what he wanted – ankle cuffs and his hogtie straps. Without asking her, he flipped Q over, gathered her wrists in one hand, and sat on her with enough weight to keep her still while he put on the ankle cuffs, then secured both them and her wrist cuffs to the ends of the X of straps.

Sabrina moved back with a fingernail stuck in her mouth. "You're in trouble, Q."

Jude flopped down on the couch.

She glowered at them both and wriggled from her stomach down position onto her side but facing Sabrina. "Hey! Sir, I thought I was –"

"You thought wrong. I'm exhausted, for a while at least. Pet, show me how many times you can make Q come. I'm going to be lord and master here on the couch." He grinned and set his feet on Q's waist so he trapped her on her side. "She's all yours."

Truly, he hadn't thought Sabrina had it in her, but after perusing his poor switch's trapped body for a minute, Sabrina shuffled up on her knees and began her assault.

Using her mouth, tongue, lips, nails and even her breasts, the little minx teased Q endlessly without actually touching her clit or pussy. Soon Q was panting and attempting to squirm both away and toward Sabrina. At first he sat back, watching, but everything ramped up, and as Q became intensely aroused, his cock stirred. He sat forward, smiling.

Sabrina gave Q's breasts one last nibble and lick. Then she studied her like a cat watching an upturned beetle with its legs wriggling. "Let me guess what you want. Umm." She tapped her teeth. "You want me to put my mouth down there? Ask nicely and I'll do it."

"Sir?" Q begged him. "Make her do it."

Jude rubbed his chin. Should he stop her? No. This was way too entertaining. He merely raised his eyebrows.

Q glared. "Listen, evil brat, go down on me or I'll hide your vibrator and tease you for a week."

When Sabrina still hesitated, he snorted. "Enough. Do it."

The sight of Sabrina with her mouth buried in Q's pussy, pleasuring her, made his cock rise to attention. Within seconds, Q gasped and stiffened and came. When Sabrina kept sucking she writhed again, and squealed. Clearly she was still coming. He ripped open a condom and put it on. Reaching down, he worked a finger into Q's slit from behind, before sliding the finger in and out a few times. Fuck. He growled, then crouched and picked Q up, leaned her over the side of the couch and plunged into her.

Her screams of ecstasy as he worked inside her…god, if that didn't do it…the second time he usually took longer. Not this time. Wet, hot and so ready – Q might have been a little volcano. His last thrust as he came shoved her face first into the couch. From her cry, and panting moans, she didn't mind.

Exhausted, it took him a minute to recover. This time all the cuffs and straps came off. Q rested on the couch on wobbly hands and knees. Her muscles trembled. He sat beside her and pulled her a little nearer.

"That was awesome," Sabrina whispered. Eyes bright as a robin's, with her elbows on the couch's edge, she brushed Q's hair back and kissed her cheek. "Did I do it right?"

"Yes." Q weakly patted Sabrina. "You did."

Why did his chest ache whenever he saw them like this? Surely this was just BDSM and sex? Because he wondered if they felt the same about him? Get a grip. Fantasy – pure fantasyland. "You two may kill me if this keeps up."

"Yeah?" Palm outward, Sabrina pretended to swipe something across in the air. "Wild girls kill old man with kinky sex. I can see the headlines now."

The smack as his hand cracked on her ass echoed. So did her squeal.

"Ow!" She massaged her butt.

"You never learn." He shook his head. "Naughty girl."

She kissed his knee then smirked. "You like it."

"Just wait, little girl." Q groaned and shifted to cuddle up next to him. "After you teasing me, I plan to personally deliver more smacks later. Since our Dom is too old to."

He rolled his eyes, and pinched Q. It was impossible not to smile though.

Funny, but he did love the two of them and their antics. Who'd have predicted that? For a moment he imagined what it would be like if they could stay together. If he could live here, find some way of making money. If they really loved him back. If he didn't have the weight of his father's lifetime expectations on his shoulders. So many fucking ifs.

Such a mess. He stared at nothing while he tried to sort it out in a way that made sense. For starters, he didn't know for sure if they loved him back, and he wasn't totally sure this "love" wasn't just some cranked-up outcome from getting laid too often. He almost laughed at that. But…if he wanted to give it a try, he'd risk it and ask them, wouldn't he? Then what? Get them to move in at medical school? No. Not happening. Maybe they could visit each other and keep in touch?

He couldn't pull out of school. His father's wishes made him clog up inside with a gutful of sadness when he thought of going against them. Betrayal was the word that came to him – a terrible betrayal of his father's love to back out now. Medicine was a wonderful career. Tuition covered by his parents, the fast track to a good job that made a shitload of money…his path was laid out before him and all he had to do was reach out and take it. Only an idiot would walk away from that. Only a coward would toss in his dad's dreams when the man couldn't speak up anymore… When he couldn't get Jude to sit down for that heart to heart talk.

The image of the hospital bed sprang into his mind, of all that waiting they'd done…weeks of it.

Fuck.

And the other side of it – how many polyamorous triads did he know in the kink community? Two, maybe, that were stable? Jealousy and time and human frailty tore apart most threesomes. It was an eternal juggling act. Sabrina, for one, was already struggling with her sexuality. He'd never thought himself a cruel man and subjecting the girls to all the guaranteed uncertainty only to end in tears and broken hearts – he couldn't do that to them.

He sighed and pulled them closer. When they both rested their heads in his lap, he stroked their hair, watching Sabrina's blonde locks overlay the black of Q's. Fredrick had assured him that Nico was blacklisted unless he behaved. It was the best he could do without involving the police. Tomorrow, they'd be going back to their apartment. Damn, he was going to be sad when this ended.

Chapter 15

Sabrina

"Do I look okay?" Sabrina turned a circle in front of Q. She'd selected the nearly sheer peach-colored knee-length dress for the way it blended into her suntanned skin, making her look almost nude. Showing off to Q like this might have been asking for trouble, but she smirked and did it anyway.

Q's eyes darkened as her gaze slid over Sabrina's curves slowly, head to toe then back up again. "Mmmm," she murmured. "Jude's going to have a hard time keeping his hands off of you." She reached out and tucked a tendril of hair back in Sabrina's up-do. "I know I am."

Then Q slid her hand down over Sabrina's collarbone while her other hand touched Sabrina's thigh. The hand on her thigh moved higher and slipped under her skirt. Sabrina moaned.

"Q." It was a soft plea, though she didn't know for what.

A hard knock at the door startled both of them. "That'll be Jude," Sabrina said, a hint of disappointment in her voice. She'd missed Jude the last work week but part of her wanted to finish what Q had just started.

Sabrina opened the door to reveal a dapper six-foot-something specimen of manliness, in a gray suit and blue tie. She'd picked the tie out last weekend to match his eyes. She looked him over and licked her lips. Damn she had some sexy arm candy for her cousin's wedding.

"Hey, sweetheart," Jude said with a wide smile. He leaned in and kissed her cheek while wrapping an arm around her waist for a hug.

She pried his hands off of her. "Down boy! You're gonna ruin my hair. It took me more than an hour to make it look this good."

He stepped back and appraised her. "You can't expect me to keep my hands of you looking like that, sexy girl."

"That's what I said," Q chimed in from behind.

Jude's smile widened and he walked to her, grabbed her around the waist and pulled her in for a deep kiss. Sabrina watched with a grin. Too bad she'd just applied a heavy dose of lipstick or she'd demand they share.

When Jude released Q, she was gasping for air. "Missed you," he said with a wink.

"Me too." She smiled with freshly kissed lips. Sexy as hell. "When will you guys be back?"

Sabrina's heart sank. Her cousin – who'd been like a sister to Sabrina – was getting married today and she had to leave Q at home. She'd picked Jude as her plus one, ashamed to acknowledge Q as anything but a friend. Though she could've gone dateless or even brought Q as a platonic friend, part of her wanted to show off Jude. For the last few years, she'd been the pathetic one who couldn't get a date for any family function. So she'd ditched Q for Jude just for a few *take that* moments in front of her sisters and aunts. She was the suckiest temporary girlfriend ever.

"Probably late," she answered. "My family's weddings are notorious for being long." She sighed then gave her a regretful look. "Q…I –" She started to apologize, again.

"Stop," Q said softly. "You don't have to explain and you don't have to apologize. I get it. Go. Have fun and stop worrying."

Sabrina nodded sadly.

"Oh!" Q's eyes lit up. "Make sure you put your phone on vibrate though."

Q and Jude exchanged a sneaky glance. What were they planning? Suspicion crept up in her mind, and a sense of excitement. They made her uncomfortable at times, but it always ended with pleasure.

"Come on," Jude said, opening the door. "I don't like being late."

"A man who likes to be prompt," Sabrina gushed. "Amazing!"

Q laughed. "And what bad luck he's paired with two girls who are always late."

Sabrina gave her a look. "*Fashionably* late." She waved at Q and walked through the door Jude held open and followed him down the stairs to his car.

Late afternoon in early August was some of the worst humidity in the year. But luckily a cool breeze came in from the ocean, making it bearable and even pleasant. Jude opened the passenger side door and she slipped in with a smile.

When he slid into the driver's seat and shut the door, she turned to him. "I'm sorry to drag you along. But this will get my mother off my back for a few months at least. So you're doing me a huge favor even though I know you're leaving..." She trailed off with a frown.

Though she'd said it matter-of-factly – which was how she'd been forcing herself to think of it – she felt her face droop. It was too depressing to think of him leaving, to worry about the summer ending and life going back to the way it had been, so she'd just ignored it. But that was getting harder. Besides the sex – which was out of this fucking world – she enjoyed his company. When she wasn't texting or spending time with him in person, she found herself daydreaming about him. Sometimes about what he and Q would do to her next, but she always imagined it ending in cuddles and whispers of affection.

"Why would I turn down the opportunity to take one of my pretty girls out?" Jude asked in his smooth-talking way.

She arched a brow. "Cause weddings are lame."

"Free food."

"Open bar too."

He held his hand up for a high-five. "Score!"

She giggled and slapped him five. Butterflies took flight in her stomach. He was so fun – almost constantly making her laugh. When he wasn't making her laugh, he was turning her on. A soft threat in her ear could bring her to her knees in an instant – and often did. When he gave her that commanding look, she felt her insides melt into a pile of goo.

He's leaving, she told herself, for the millionth time. Maybe she needed one of those rubber band programs to break her addiction. "Just don't let me get drunk and give a slurred toast while sobbing uncontrollably," she muttered. She felt herself going down that road already.

The ceremony was beautiful. Gina looked like one of Q's models in her off-white tiered gown and big spiral curls down her back. In their seats, Jude had survived round one of her family. Her sister Mindy had not only tried hitting on him, but she'd even told humiliating stories about Sabrina's teenage years. Just when she'd thought Mindy would pull out a picture of the awkward, slightly overweight, braces-wearing Sabrina, Jude had distracted her with questions about her new job.

Sabrina was beaming as they entered the reception venue. Glowing lanterns sat on each table surrounded by several shades of blue and purple flowers. She smiled at one of the baby blue ones that reminded her of Jude's eyes.

"You were adorable trying not to cry during the ceremony," Jude whispered in her ear as they took their seats.

She glared at him. "You were looking a little choked up yourself."

He chuckled and placed his hand on her knee under the table. Already she felt a shiver run up her spine. At just one touch? Damn she had it bad. Suddenly, she longed for Q's touch on her other side. She felt almost empty not having her there.

Family and friends poured into the room, chatting and gushing about the groom. Her aunts' shrieking rose up over the crowd. Apparently Gina had selected an acceptable match. Any minute now, her family would start interrogating Jude.

When the seats began to fill at their table, she leaned into Jude and cautioned, "My family is like a school of piranhas. Be careful."

He nodded coolly, but she didn't miss his slight shift of discomfort.

Guilt flooded her for dragging him into this mess. It wasn't fair, given their current agreement. But how she wished this was for real. Not just because it would please her family, but, well, he just fit. With her, with Q, in her life, in her heart. If her meddling and judgmental family hadn't been involved, she could picture living happily with one on each side of her.

Not gonna happen, girly.

"If it's too much trouble, it's okay to tell them you're not really my boyfriend," she said to Jude.

"And desert you in your time of need?" He squeezed her knee. "Never. Besides, aren't I your boyfriend?"

"Yes but –"

"Hush," he ordered softly. Her heart *thunked* at the command. He leaned in and brushed his lips against her ear. "I'm your boyfriend tonight and that's all that matters. But don't forget I'm also your Dom."

She let out a soft groan, her insides clenching in need. "I'm turned on already. Can we leave early?" As a second thought, she added, "Sir." Maybe that would catch his attention.

He grinned. "Nice try, little girl." He pulled something out of his pocket and handed it to her. "Here. Q has a message for you."

She'd given him her phone to hold since she wouldn't know if it vibrated in her purse or not. She looked down at the text.

Is Jude behaving himself?

She sighed and typed back. *Yes but I wish he wouldn't.* She wished he'd agree to a quick dinner then home for a long fuck. Knowing him, he wanted to drag out the torture as long as possible.

She waited for Q's reply, getting anxious as family started greetings around the table. She'd recognized a few distant relatives, but so far they only smiled at her. At least her mother hadn't found her yet.

Finally, Q's text came through.

You really shouldn't have said that.

Huh? Another came up before she could reply.

Hand the phone to Jude.

She started typing a protest. As if Q could read her mind, the next text interrupted hers.

Do it, little girl!

Fuck. With an eye roll she handed it to Jude. “Apparently she’s done with me.”

He looked down at the text and grinned. “That girl is diabolical.” His wicked gaze met hers. “I like it.”

A shiver of fear kicked her heart beat up a notch. “What did she say?”

“That,” he stuffed the phone into his pocket and leaned in to whisper, “is for your Doms to know. And you to find out later.” He chuckled at her expression then tapped her nose. “Don’t pout. I may spank you right here in front of your family.”

She gasped. “You wouldn’t!”

He laughed out loud. “No. But you certainly tempt me.” Stealthily, he peered around the room. “I’m sure there’s somewhere private around here.”

Unsure whether he was joking, she made a mental note to behave. Though the idea of it didn’t ease the ache between her legs. Was she blushing?

“Sabrina Romano?” a red-haired lady with too much eyeliner said from across the table. “I haven’t seen you since you were a little girl. How are you?”

“Uhh,” she replied brilliantly. God she hated these situations. “Good.”

“I’m your mother’s cousin, Dina,” she exclaimed.

Good for you, she wanted to say. “Nice to meet you,” she said instead.

Jude’s hand perched on its spot on her knee. “Introduce me,” he whispered covertly.

“Oh!” She sucked at formalities. “This is –”

"There you are!" Her mother's distinctive high-pitched voice sang from behind her. "I've been looking everywhere for you, dear." She appeared at her side and stood over her. Though not much taller than Sabrina, her curvy mother, dressed all in scarlet, took over the room with her presence. She could probably dom Jude if she tried. "Why didn't you come say hello when I waved at you from the ceremony? I had a seat saved for you right in front. Your second cousin, Jamie, flew in from Washington and I wanted to introduce you." She perused Sabrina's body while chattering. "What are you wearing, Sabrina?" she asked. "You look like a slut."

"Mother!" Sabrina peered around them to see who'd heard. Thankfully, the background noise drowned her out.

Her mother ignored her outrage and pushed back a piece of hair falling in Sabrina's face. "Roots, dear. Haven't you made enough money with your little art business to keep up with your hair highlights?"

She flushed and shrank back, ashamed though she should be used to the criticism. But it was different in front of Jude.

"Hi." He jumped in to rescue her. "I'm Sabrina's boyfriend, Jude."

Her mother's mask of confidence dropped for a fraction of a second before reappearing again. She was stunned speechless for the first time Sabrina could remember.

Sabrina grinned.

"A boyfriend?" her mother questioned, as if it didn't seem possible. "I didn't know she…" She trailed off, giving Sabrina a stern look. "Why didn't you tell me you were dating somebody, Sabrina? Honestly! You should call me more often."

She rolled her eyes. Was it any surprise why she didn't?

Jude came to her defense again. "It's fairly new, Mrs. Romano."

"Oh, call me Leonora." She giggled.

Giggled? Well, Jude did affect every woman he encountered.

"Leonora." He grinned charmingly. "Sabrina wanted to keep things quiet while we got to know each other. But it's nice to finally meet some of her family."

"Likewise." She turned to the right and yelled, "Marcella! Silvia! Come meet Sabrina's new boyfriend!"

Sabrina winced.

"I know, it's about time!" her mother shouted, furthering her embarrassment.

Jude patted her knee reassuringly then whispered in her ear, "You're beautiful. Never forget that."

Her heart melted. Tears pricked her eyes and she didn't have to force a smile when her two aunts made their way to the table.

Sabrina stood to greet her aunts, giving kisses on each cheek. Jude rose too, and shook their hands. He answered the barrage of questions beautifully, artfully dodging some, but still revealing important things that gave him status. The women swooned like high school girls talking to the school heartthrob. She almost rolled her eyes. But every time she and Jude made eye contact, something sparked. He was hers. He wanted her. Well, temporarily. But still, it made her feel confident, worthy.

"Do I get to meet your dad?" Jude whispered in her ear during a short break of questions.

She scanned the room for him. "He must be having cigars with the other men."

Jude grinned.

"Yes, I know we're one big stereotype. Deal with it." Though she knew it wasn't important, part of her wanted Jude to meet her dad. She and her father had a special bond. His approval meant everything to her. Almost the exact opposite of her mother, her dad was warm and accepting, didn't pass judgment until he knew someone on a personal level. That's not to say he wouldn't give Jude – or any other potential match – the runaround. Her mother used to say, "God help the man that tries to steal Sabrina from her daddy."

Dinner was served and they all sat down. Her mother and one aunt stayed at their table. They lost interest in interrogating Jude eventually and moved onto family gossip. After dinner, Jude shoved the phone in her lap with a silent command to read it.

I hope you're behaving, little girl, Q's text read.

She looked to see if anyone was paying attention. Her mother was going on about the latest family scandal. *She typed back, of course I am. I'm always a good girl for my Doms.*

A message came through right away. *Mmhm. Remember when Jude held you down the other night when we played? Picture that and my tongue on your clit.*

She hissed in a breath and felt her face heat. Instinctively, her gaze shot to her mother sitting beside her. Her heart raced with the familiar feeling of being in trouble. It was ridiculous. Her mother couldn't see what she'd just read. But it still felt naughty. Just then, Jude's hand moved up her thigh a few inches. She gulped.

Q! she texted. *That's not nice!*

The reply was immediate. *Shh! Pay attention to your family!*

Her family? She looked up. They all gazed at her expectantly. "Huh?"

"They asked what you thought of the food, sweetheart," Jude said sounding amused. "Did you fall asleep?"

She gave her head a little shake. "Just a little foggy today. I was up late with a work project. The food was excellent." She looked down at her mostly full plate. "Uhh… especially the roasted potatoes." They were completely uneaten. She cursed under her breath. She could almost feel Jude's mocking amusement beside her. Such a bratty Dom. He'd need a safeword when she got her hands on him later. And Q too!

They stared at her a moment longer then Dina declared, "At my wedding, we had apricot salmon." Then they burst into a busy chatter again, each competing for the best food title at their wedding.

Sabrina texted to Q. *I'm trying! You're distracting me.*

Stop looking!

Stop texting! She grinned.

Lol. Go talk to your mother.

Sabrina chuckled. Sometimes she thought she might be falling in love with Q. But as more than a friend? It was hard to know. Was loving a woman the same as loving a man? Just before she tucked the phone back into Jude's pocket, one last text came through.

Naughty girl ;)

Naughty? She hadn't seen naughty yet. "Mom, did you know Jude comes from a family of doctors?" Let him deal with that while she showed Q just how naughty this little sub could be.

She pushed the phone further under the table and snapped several pictures of her bare legs. Growing braver, she aimed for her thighs next. Then, in an uncharacteristic move, she took a picture underneath her skirt. A thrill swept through her at the thought of sending the dirty photos to Q. Could she do it?

Jude adjusted his hold on her leg, digging his short nails into her skin gently but sharply. Was that a warning or encouragement? With an evil smirk, she decided to take it as encouragement.

She brought the phone to her lap and quickly sent all of them to Q, including the one of her lacy underwear. With a stifled giggle she shoved the phone to Jude, ignoring Q's reply. Jude gave her a puzzled glare then, after distracting her family with questions of weddings, he gazed down at the phone.

It was satisfying watching his eyes widen as he browsed the pictures. Did she surprise her Dom? How fun!

Finally, he leaned over and hissed in her ear, "Tell your family you need to use the restroom." At her hesitation, he added sharply, "Now."

"Uhh," she stuttered. "Where's the bathroom?"

Her mother gave her directions and she rose from the table and straightened her dress. Jude stood and took her elbow and said loudly enough for her family to hear, "I'll come too. Knowing her, she'll get lost."

By the stern set of his jaw and the narrowing of his eyes, she knew she was in for it. Walking through the maze of tables, it felt like her knees were turning to jelly with each step. Jude held her hand tightly, like he was preventing her from escaping as he marched her toward the firing squad.

Firing squad. She couldn't stop a silly giggle.

Jude looked back at her. "Something funny?"

"No, Sir." She bit her lip to keep back a smile.

He quirked a brow then stopped just in front of the reception hall exit. After shuffling in his pocket for a moment, he withdrew the phone then handed it to Sabrina with a smirk.

Oh boy. She looked down at Q's message.

Nice panties. I think they should come off now.

Jude tugged her hand and she followed mindlessly down the hallway. Another text popped up.

If he finds them wet, I get to spank your naughty ass when you get home.

She barely stifled a moan. Her knees threatened to buckle. It was far too late to avoid that fate. Fuck, why couldn't they leave now?

She lost track of how many turns they'd made before Jude stopped them in a deserted hallway near what looked like a utility closet. He checked around the corner then yanked her into a little alcove in front of a closed door.

She yelped when he pressed her up against the wall, none too gently then crushed her mouth with his. He tasted like wine.

"Mmm," she murmured, melting against him.

He ran his hands up her thighs, over her ass. She felt her body slide down the wall, but he slammed a knee between her legs and his hips against hers and pinned her there. Though she tried to avoid him capturing her wrists, he collected them in his fist and pushed them over her head against the wall.

Her whimper turned into a moan when he lifted her skirt with the other hand. Warm fingers slid up her thigh, finding her center.

He grinned. "You're soaked, little girl."

Ugh. She squirmed. *Just move your hand!*

"Q will be happy," he said. Gently, he ran his fingers over her underwear. She wanted to kick and swear and demand he fuck her. But she knew better. Still, she didn't need to be his plaything. This was her date after all. Frustration burned a small storm in her chest.

"If you're not man enough to take me home and fuck me," she snapped. "At least have the decency to leave me to enjoy my family in peace." Yeah, maybe she could've said it nicer. So it didn't surprise her when he stepped away and gave her The Look. She whimpered, regretting her words already.

"Kneel," he commanded.

Remorseful, she sunk to her knees.

"Head down."

It was already down. Her throat tightened and tears formed in her eyes. If she was just playing at submission, like he'd said, why did she feel so awful about disappointing him?

He didn't say anything for a moment. Should she apologize for losing her temper? She didn't know the rules for this situation.

"You know you're in trouble, don't you?" he finally asked.

She nodded.

"Do you have something to say?"

She nodded again, afraid to even open her mouth without permission.

"Speak, girl."

After a deep breath, she said shakily, "I'm sorry, Sir. I just lost my temper. I was…frustrated."

He kept her waiting for too long and the tears spilled over. Finally, he stroked her hair. "You're forgiven. But you'll pay. Since you have trouble with your mouth, I have something to keep it busy." She heard the sound of his zipper. "Head up."

Raising her head, she took in size of his shaft just in front of her mouth then shifted her eyes to his face. Gazing into those deep blue eyes – the ones that lit up when he laughed – started fresh tears in hers. She opened her mouth to apologize again but a small shake of his head stopped her.

"This is for me, not for you. Be a good girl and I won't have to ruin your pretty hair."

She nodded eagerly. Yes, she would. She wanted to be his good girl again.

His fingers stroked her jaw lightly. Then he tapped once, twice, with his fingertips. "Open."

***

Dessert was a heavenly blend of chocolate and cheesecake. Jude and Sabrina took turns feeding each other forkfuls, looking an awful lot like the newly married bride and groom. Her mother *tsked* at the public show of affection, but right now, she couldn't care less what her judgmental family thought of her. And if Q were there, she'd have fed her too.

After the forced blow job, Jude had held her in the hallway, using a tissue to wipe her tears. He'd even helped reapply her make-up. When she'd blubbered about him being mad at her, he'd assured her the slate was clean – that she was his good girl again. The box she'd put him in – the one that kept her emotionally detached – had just been blown to pieces. He'd stolen her heart. And now she was good and screwed.

Laughing, she teased him with a bite, pulling it out of reach every time he tried to bite it. Amusement danced in his eyes when he grabbed her wrist to hold her steady.

"Brat," he mumbled so only she could hear.

"You like it," she sassed back then quickly added, "Sir."

He leaned in like he was going to kiss her. At the last second, he moved his lips to her ear. "I do like it. Know why? It gives me a reason to funish you."

"Funish? Don't you mean punish?"

"It's not exactly punishment if it's fun for you, is it?" He smirked. "Or maybe it's only fun for me. Do you like being told what to do by two Doms? Tied up so you're helpless then receiving pain and pleasure, but only when we want to give it?"

She squirmed on the seat. He'd been enjoying keeping her on edge since they'd returned from the "bathroom break." Whispering threats in her ear, relaying the plans Q had for her when they got home. Wasn't it bad enough he had her underwear in his pocket? During the slow dance, it had been all she could focus on. The cool breeze on her flesh and the naughty feeling of being so bold at a family function. It had felt like all eyes were on her, though no one could possibly know other than Jude. Oh but he made sure to rub it in, the evil bastard.

"Did you see who Anthony brought as a date?" Her mother's elbow knocked into Sabrina, startling her back to attention. "He brought a man!" she whispered too loudly to be a true secret.

"Oh. My. God," Dina said. "His mother must be mortified!"

A pit formed in her stomach. She placed her fork gently on the table. "Mother, Anthony's been out to his family for three years now."

Her mother blinked then smiled sweetly. "Well, yes, but that's different than bringing a…" She gestured with her hand as if searching for the right word. "What do they call it? Life partner?"

"Yes, a life partner," Dina chimed, knowingly.

"That's what I thought. You know I used to watch that show…what was it called? *Will and Grace*! Yes, the gays have a good sense of humor. Anyway…" She turned to Sabrina. "Bringing a life partner to a family event is different." When she stared, dumbfounded, her mother explained. "I've kept you sheltered all these years, thank god, because you don't need to understand these things, Sabrina. You were raised straight. That's all that matters." She turned back to Dina and the other guests. "You know I'm not prejudiced, but I'm just glad it's not one of my kids."

Their words of agreement muffled together and sounded distant in her ears. Her stomach dropped. Bile rose in her throat. Her family would never accept Q. Who did she think she was anyway? She alone couldn't be the gay rights warrior against her family. They'd crush her like a bug – like they had about everything else.

Daddy adored her, spoiled her, but it was a stretch even for him to accept two people stealing away his precious daughter – and one a woman. If Sabrina wanted to be in a non-traditional relationship, she might as well move across the country with Jude. She froze. Where the hell had that thought come from? She was sure he liked her and Q, enjoyed spending time with them, definitely loved dominating them, but he didn't seem anywhere near ready for a long-term commitment. The only person she could depend on for absolute unconditional love and acceptance was Q. And yet Sabrina couldn't even hold her hand in public.

"*Mia Bella*!" A familiar voice boomed behind her.

She shot up from her chair and spun around. "Daddy!"

Her father, dressed up in a suit, was as handsome as a movie star. She threw her arms around his neck. He returned her hug and kissed her cheek.

"Is your mother giving you a hard time?" he asked, when she pulled away.

"Just about my hair. And my job. And, well, you know how she is."

He touched her cheek. "Don't pay any attention to her. You're gorgeous."

She smiled. "Thank you, Daddy." Now for introductions. "I have someone for you to meet. This is Jude." She motioned him up from where he sat watching at the table.

Her mom saw the exchange and chimed in. "It's her boyfriend, Anton. Can you believe she didn't tell me? And he's studying to be a doctor!"

Her father chuckled when Sabrina rolled her eyes. He shook Jude's hand, looking him over with an appraising glare. "Nice to meet you, Jude."

"You too, Sir."

Sabrina held back a laugh at the formal greeting. Just last night she'd been calling Jude, Sir as he ordered her around the bedroom. He caught her giggle and raised a brow.

"I hope you're taking very good care of my princess," her father said, wrapping an arm around her shoulders.

But Jude wasn't easily intimidated. "Of course. Sabrina is…" He paused and stared at her, a mysterious look in his eyes – almost sad. "A very special girl. Every moment I get with her feels like a gift." Though he spoke to her father, his gaze remained on her.

I'll miss you too.

She cleared her throat and shook away the sudden sorrow. "Come on, Jude. Let's dance. I'll catch up with you later, Daddy. Tell Mom to stop blabbing about everybody."

He chuckled. "You know that won't work. Then she'll just blab about me. Go have fun, *tesora*."

The rest of the evening went by in a blur. Jude made an excellent dance partner. His mother would've been proud the six years of ballroom classes she'd made him take as a child had paid off. Sabrina laughed all the way home at his stories of being made to practice the waltz with women from his mother's bridge club.

"How was the wedding?" Q asked when Jude and Sabrina entered the apartment.

Sabrina kicked off her stilettos with a loud sigh. "Son of a bitch, these were killing me!"

Q shook her head. "I don't know why you bother."

"Beauty is pain," she answered, grimacing as she reached around behind her and unclasped her bra.

"And apparently a lot of money," Jude added, flopping onto the couch. "I learned that tonight. As well as the best bras at Victoria's Secret, who baby Talia's real father is, and how to make a strapless dress stay up." He furrowed his brow. "Apparently they make tape for that."

Q laughed and pushed the ottoman under his feet. "Poor guy."

"Hey!" Sabrina cut in, tossing her bra into the laundry room across the hall. "Uh-uh. Don't 'poor guy' him." She pointed to Jude with a scowl. "He got a blow job in the hallway. What do I get? Nothing!"

Q gave her a sly smile. "Oh, but that's not true, Sabrina." She turned to Jude. "Were her panties wet when you checked?"

He nodded.

"Then I owe you something." She stalked toward Sabrina. Her gaze swept up her barefoot, nearly naked body. The sly smile she wore earlier disappeared. "Come here," she ordered.

Q's turned on face. Oh boy. She looked to Jude – for help or encouragement, she wasn't sure. But he gave neither.

He laughed and put his feet up on the ottoman. "Good idea, Q. Take over for me. I'm beat and could use some entertainment."

Sabrina glared. "I'm not your toy!"

Q's brow arched. "Aren't you?"

Well... She averted her gaze and held her hands behind her back – an open gesture that could be interpreted as affirmative without saying so. She was an expert at dodging uncomfortable questions.

"That's what I thought." Q chuckled. "Do you have the collar we used the other day, Jude?"

"Oh! Left the toy bag in the car." He stood and traipsed to the door. "I didn't think we'd be playing so soon. I'll be right back."

When he disappeared, Q stepped in and kissed Sabrina quickly on the lips. They wrapped their arms around each other, squeezing tight. Sabrina inhaled the scent of Q's hair – earthy shampoo with a hint of delicious mint. She'd been chewing gum. How could she miss her in only the span of a few hours?

Keeping Sabrina close with one hand on her back and the other stroking her hair, Q asked softly, "Did you have fun, beautiful? Was your family good to Jude?"

Sabrina smiled. "It was mostly fun. And they loved Jude, of course. One of my aunts called him a hunk of burning love. I almost died laughing."

Q chuckled. "That's good. I bet he fit in well."

"He did." She nodded, staring dreamily at the floor. "He did fit in." Too well. But that acknowledgement brought heartache. She pushed it away. Looking back up at Q, she giggled. "The best part was when I asked the DJ to play *Hey, Jude* and made him slow dance to it. I never thought a guy could glare so hard. I might be in for it later."

They both laughed and when their chuckles faded, Q blurted, "I wish I could've been there." She flushed immediately and tried to pull away, but Sabrina held her still with arms wrapped tight around her waist.

"Me too," Sabrina admitted. She felt Q relax against her again and she pressed her face into her neck. Summer was almost over. *This*...was almost over. Soft, minty kisses, snuggling up on the couch to watch a movie, kneeling at Q's feet with her fist in her hair.

She inhaled a deep breath, locking the scent, the memories, deep in her heart. "I missed you," she muttered into Q's soft skin.

Chapter 16

Q

"Are you *sure* we've never met?" the future Mrs. Julie Eagleton asked for the umpteenth time.

Q shook her head again with the same pleasant smile. "Oh, I'm sure I would have remembered. I'm very good with faces."

From over Julie's shoulder her fiancé grinned like an idiot. Smallish cities sometimes sucked. At least Jon was being discreet and not letting on that his fiancée had, indeed, run out of a bar on Q's account only a few weeks before. Q didn't often get last-minute wedding bookings, but of course this awkward situation would be one.

The bride and groom paid the amount they owed and Q's mind switched to auto-pilot. She drifted through the memory of the conversation with Nico at the bar a few weeks ago. Had she really been stupid enough to consider taking him back? Even knowing how things had eventually fallen spectacularly apart, not having him as a fallback made her anxious. How fucked up was that?

Things with Jude and Sabrina had shown her how wonderful a real relationship could be. But what would she do at the end of the summer? Deep down she wondered if Jude was really leaving – he was starting to drop subtle hints that he didn't want their relationship to end. But how would it work with him living across the country? Would getting together a few times a year, the whole time he was in med school work? Sabrina didn't want to move that far away from her family, and Q's business was established here. She shook her head. Now she was getting ahead of herself. Did he even like them enough for that to be an issue right now? But if and when he did move – what would happen between her and Sabrina?

The Eagletons left the building, excited to be seeing Q again in a few days for their engagement pictures. Jon was a little too enthusiastic for Q's comfort, but business was business.

When the front door jingled, she left the rest of the wedding contract paperwork on the back counter. With her professional smile plastered on her face, she walked into the front room... The grin turned real when she saw who it was.

Jude and Sabrina strolled around the small lobby, checking out some of her latest display pictures. "Wow, Q. I didn't realize you were so talented," Jude said thoughtfully.

People always said things like that to photographers. It was normally about as sincere as being told to "have a nice day" at a shop. His tone convinced her that he meant it though.

"Thanks! You two are an unexpected surprise. What brings you by?" Sabrina visited once in awhile, but Jude never had.

"We thought we'd take you out for lunch, since we were just sitting around waiting for you to get home." Jude walked closer, stopping only when he was standing well within her personal space. His expression went from friendly to molten. Her body responded without hesitation – her heart sped up and her knees tried to buckle. Fight or flight took over and she backed into the reception counter.

Without losing a beat, he followed. His big hands rose to grip the granite countertop on either side of her, boxing her in. With alarm she saw Sabrina flip the jocular *Out to Lunch* sign then slide the deadbolt.

"Behave, you two," she said "Don't turn my studio into a den of iniquity." Q's intended grumble came out more like a plea.

The press of Jude's groin against hers made her groan and he caught the sound with a deep kiss. When it ended, she was pretty sure her knees had rubberized. He steadied her. "Shh! You're going to disturb the people at the pet shop next door. Really, Q, control yourself." He looked smug.

She gazed up at him, slowing her gasping breaths. "Let's go for lunch before I figure out how to rape a man twice my size."

His hand closed tightly in the back of her hair and she melted. "You can't rape the willing, little brat."

"You two are such pervs." Sabrina chuckled and shook her head. "Did your new background come in, Q?"

Regrettably, Jude released his grip on her.

"Yes, I haven't had a chance to unpack it yet though. Unexpected wedding booking this morning. You'll never guess who."

They looked at her blankly.

"Jude's best buddy Jon, from the bar."

"Nooooo!" Sabrina yelled in mock dismay. "How awkward was that? Did they remember you?" She strolled over.

Without warning, Jude grabbed the smaller girl and perched her on the counter. Sabrina squeaked.

Q's gaze was drawn to the girl's shapely legs. Bare, and so very close to her face. Was she wearing underwear?

"Jon remembered me. He grinned like a tool through the whole process. His fiancée, Julie, kept thinking she knew me from somewhere." She shrugged. "One of the hazards of being a photographer in such a small city. At least I didn't grow up here. Having people tell me all the time that they remembered me from grade school would be a pain in the ass. Want to help me set up for my next shoot? It's not until five."

When she struggled to lift the shipping box with the new background in it, and Jude grabbed it out of her hands, she was secretly pleased. Fuck women's lib. The damn thing was heavy. She led the way into the studio.

Showing Jude how to hook it up was almost unnecessary. He unrolled it and hung it in place in record time. The rich, deep red reminded Q of the painted walls in Hollywood whorehouse scenes.

"Sexy!" Sabrina said approvingly. "You said this was for boudoir shots, right?"

"Yup. I did boudoir pictures for Ivy as a gift to her newest Dom a few months ago, and I've had a steady flow of kinksters through here ever since. Just don't tell the brides or the moms who come in to get their baby pics done, or my entire vanilla career will be ruined."

They all laughed. Q asked Jude to help her slide the brown leather chaise lounge into the centre of the room. They all stood back to look.

"Nice!" Jude nodded.

Grimacing, Q gestured at the set up. "I should be able to visualize it in my head more than I do, but without the subject I have trouble imagining good poses. Um. Sabrinaaaaaa...?"

Her friend rolled her eyes. "Where do you want me?"

She'd helped out before so Sabrina knew the drill.

"Go sit on the couch while I adjust my tripod. I'll be there in a minute." Q fiddled with her equipment for awhile then turned on the lights and adjusted the lighting umbrellas.

"Okay, could you lean on your side with your head on your hand? Propped up on an elbow." After Sabrina maneuvered into position, Q zoomed in closer. "Now give me a sexy smile."

Her subject froze, a pained expression on her face.

"No, Sabrina. Sexy. Give me the expression you would use if you were trying to give a guy a come hither look." The girl looked like a deer in headlights.

"I don't know how to be sexy, Q. Maybe that's why I've only had three boyfriends before." She giggled uncomfortably.

"You *are* sexy, Sabrina." Q came out from behind the camera and adjusted her friend's pose a little. "I've seen you with a lot of sexy expressions. Maybe it was subconscious. Give it a try or I'm going to do things to make you uncomfortable." She schooled her expression into something sinister.

Sabrina wriggled in place a bit before settling down.

Q ducked behind the camera again and had to stifle a laugh. Her subject now looked as though a poor, unsuspecting Christmas nutcracker had been lured into doing boudoir shots. Sabrina's open-mouthed grin would terrify a walnut at thirty paces.

She sighed. "A little help, Jude?"

Rubbing his hands, Jude approached Sabrina with an evil glint in his eyes. All he needed was a top hat, a handlebar mustache, and some train tracks.

Mouth half-open, Sabrina watched them approach. She curled up into a ball and squealed. "No, no! I don't know what you want. I'm sorry!"

"Give me your dress," Q ordered.

Sabrina glared, but knelt on the couch and pulled it over her head. The white bra she wore was only a demi-cup and her hardened pink nipples were held up and out on display. A matching thong left little to the imagination. Together, the color said innocent, while the cut said otherwise. Perfect for Sabrina.

Jude groaned. He traced his finger along the string that went across her hip then followed it down to the cleft of her ass. She quivered and gasped, lips parting. Her expression was breathtaking.

"Jude, you stay with her. Touch her until I tell you to back away, okay?" Q licked her lips, wishing she was using a video camera instead of a still. She pressed a hand between her own legs for a second, trying to relieve the ache.

"I saw that," Jude growled.

"Shut up, Sir."

"You watch yourself, girl."

His vague threat barely registered. Her hand-held camera seemed more appropriate for this job. Grabbing it out of the open case on the table only took a second. When Q turned back, Jude was standing behind Sabrina, rolling her nipples between his fingers. Her head was thrown back against his chest. The little whining noise that came from Sabrina's lips shot straight to Q's clit.

She nodded at Jude when she caught his attention, and he slipped out of the picture. She barked Sabrina's name and her subject's eyes opened, but her wanton expression suggested she wasn't paying much attention to what Q was doing. She snapped a few pictures in rapid succession – the flashes seemed to bring Sabrina back to herself.

"Stop," she complained feebly. "I look like an idiot."

"No, you don't," Q and Jude replied in unison.

"Stand up for a second." She got Jude to help her turn the chaise lounge so that the back of it was facing the camera. Q took Sabrina by the arm, led her to the couch and placed her hands on the top near the higher end. She moved Sabrina's feet back until her ass was practically sending the camera love letters.

"What? No," Sabrina complained. Her shifting feet only served to draw more attention to her luscious ass. But she didn't move or cover herself. Or safeword. Q took several shots with Sabrina's ass forefront, her expression pouty as she looked at Q over her shoulder. At Q's side, Jude sighed blissfully, sounding like he'd found heaven.

"She's so spankable," Jude said admiringly. "A Dom's wet dream."

Q nodded in agreement. "She walks around the apartment in these tiny little towels, the bottom of her cheeks hanging out. Like she doesn't know what she's doing to me. At least now if she does it, she knows I'll bite her."

A whimper from Sabrina got their attention. "You bite it too hard, Q. And quit talking about me as if I can't hear you!" She tried to get up.

"Stay!" they both growled.

"You know what this shot is missing?" Q asked.

"It needs a little color, I think," he replied.

They smiled at each other and he stalked back to Sabrina. He raised his hand high then brought it down hard – the slap echoing loudly in the large room. Sabrina screeched, and stomped her foot. The glare she gave Jude was priceless. Q could almost see the red print throbbing on Sabrina's ass – Jude's fingers and thumb all in bright scarlet relief on her pretty white backside. Q's camera had started clicking as the blow descended, so she'd captured images of the hulking man menacing the dainty girl. In the final frames, Sabrina's marked ass was the focal point, the pain and pleasure on her face its accent. She flipped back through the shots and was caught between wishing she was Jude and wishing she was Sabrina.

"Good?" asked Jude.

"Yes, several. We could easily sell these as cover photos." She smirked.

"Ghost!" Sabrina squeaked.

Q chuckled. "I would never sell these, little girl. Jeez, next thing you know you'll safeword for having to do dishes. Safewords are for emergencies."

She rolled her eyes. "Not funny. Can I move now? I'm getting tired of standing like this."

"Sure," said Q. "Kneel on the floor and put your hands behind your head."

Sabrina balked.

"Now!"

Looking startled, she knelt on the floor. Q strolled over, unhooked Sabrina's bra and slid it down her arms, then pulled the girl's hands into position. Her breasts thrust up and out. Q crouched beside her. She bit firmly at one nipple then the other, and then sucked them until Sabrina mewled.

She stood back with Jude and looked down at her. Sabrina squirmed in place, looking up miserably at the pair of them. Poor kitten. It must have been hard having two Doms.

"Are you wet, Sabrina?" Jude asked.

"Why don't you check and find out?" she snapped. "Sir."

He tapped Sabrina's face lightly with his fingers – a mockery of a slap. She blinked furiously then her eyes widened in shock. She gulped.

"What did I tell you about sassing us?" he demanded.

Her skin reddened. She squirmed. "Sorry, Sir."

Jude nodded and got down in front of her while Q went behind. They ran their hands over her body, exploring with gentle fingers. As Q nudged aside her tiny thong and probed the wetness between Sabrina's thighs, her fingers bumped into Jude's where he toyed with her clit. Q coaxed a finger into her, stroking with a slowness she knew Sabrina would find frustrating. She fastened her mouth onto the back of her neck, biting and sucking hard. Jude's head lowered and he latched onto Sabrina's nipple.

Her breathing was erratic and labored, her moans getting progressively higher pitched as she got to the precipice. Before she went over the edge, both of them stopped and stood, looking down at her again. The scream of frustration was pure desperation. A couple of tears streaked down her face.

"Please, let me come?" she begged, brown eyes round and pitiful. She had managed not to lower her arms, and her tits still thrust forward, nipples shiny from Jude's attentions.

Q fought the urge to lay her back on the couch and suck her clit into her mouth. Hearing and feeling Sabrina come was even better than having an orgasm herself. Instead, she caught Sabrina's gaze and smirked then suggestively licked her bottom lip. Sabrina eyed her mouth as though just watching it in action might be enough to give her relief.

She snapped a few pictures before Sabrina came to her senses.

They posed her in a few more positions, alternating between staring at her and touching her. Jude stripped her of her panties at one point. Eventually she'd had enough.

Q had used a wide white ribbon to tie her wrists behind her and she was standing, looking over her shoulder at them. "How come you don't have to be in any of these, Q?" she grumbled, not that she'd budged from where they'd put her.

"Because I'm the photographer," she replied sardonically. "I'm also barely a sub, if you hadn't noticed."

Jude's gaze swung to Q, and his brow arched. In two strides he was looming over her, making her feel little. Hard blue eyes stared down into hers. She could almost feel her internal controls shift to him, as though he'd just eaten part of her soul. Knees buckled and she sank to her place at his feet, head down. A gentle hand on the back of her head spoke his approval. With a shudder, she pressed her face to his pant leg. He stroked her hair and everything was right in her world. Tears welled, but she blinked them back before they ruined everything. A sniffle escaped her.

"You are a sub, Q. A good girl." He pulled her back to her feet, grabbed the camera from around her neck and put it on the couch. In a moment, she was stripped naked. Jude pointed at the floor and she dropped back to her knees. With a crook of his finger, he summoned Sabrina then pointed to indicate she should kneel beside Q. He walked behind them, and Q felt her wrists being tied to Sabrina's. Her friend grabbed her hand and squeezed it then relaxed her grip but didn't let go.

The camera's flash startled her, but she didn't look up. He took several more pictures, moving around them and murmuring his appreciation. With her eyes lowered, she got a close-up view of the way his hard cock pressed against the inside of his jeans.

Q groaned and leaned toward him, hoping he'd cooperate and fuck her mouth. Instead, his hand snaked down and he pinched her nipple deliciously hard. He switched the torture to the other one and kept increasing and decreasing pressure until she screamed into her closed mouth.

"Do you get to choose when to suck my cock?" he corrected, his words gentle but dangerous.

"No, Sir!" she panted.

"As long as you remember that, little brat."

She bobbed her head in a nod. Beside her, Sabrina wriggled, rubbing her thighs together.

"Look at me," he commanded. He knelt in front of them and ran a hand down each of their bellies, then between their legs. Thick fingers toyed with Q, and she moaned. Sabrina did too. He teased them simultaneously and their breathy cries filled the room. Both the sensations and Sabrina's panting, made Q grit her teeth. Jude's thumb gently circled her clit and soon she was lost to the feeling – the consuming need for release. He brought them both to the brink then stopped.

"No! Please Sir," Q choked out.

Sabrina whined.

"Who decides when you can come?"

"You, Sir." Q knew she sounded pitiful, but she didn't care.

Jude untied them and led them to the couch, laying Q back first and spreading her legs. What was he up to? He made Sabrina straddle her. The silken glide of Sabrina's thighs on hers… Mmm. She squirmed and Sabrina ground against her.

A stinging slap to her inner thigh stopped her. Another loud smack and Sabrina howled.

"No moving until I give you permission, naughty girls."

The camera flashed again and Q did her best to stay still, feeling her muscles protest. She needed to move. Sabrina looked like she was going to explode. Q heard a zipper and caught a glimpse of muscled shoulder as Jude shed his clothes.

His hands gripped her thighs as he sank between her knees. Tongue swept deftly over her clit. With her breath unsteady, she opened her knees wider, a silent plea for him to take pity and finish her. After far too long, his teasing stopped and a moment later Sabrina was whining and writhing on top of her, the brush of her skin on Q's electric.

Jude's hard cock pushed roughly into Q and she gasped. Although she couldn't see Jude thrusting into her, Q had a good view of him spreading Sabrina's slit and catching her swollen clit between two fingers. He pressed Sabrina down toward her, making the girl's breasts brush Q's face.

So tempting – having those pretty pink nipples in reach. The scent of Sabrina intoxicated her. She caught one nipple with her mouth, and sucked, brushing her tongue over it in broad strokes. Moaning, Sabrina rubbed against her, and Q felt Jude's hand pinned between them. His knuckles rubbed her pussy as he stroked at Sabrina's clit.

The slow rhythm of his thrusts gradually and frustratingly wound the coil inside Q. Something pinched her clit hard. The unexpected pain made her buck beneath Sabrina. Her mouth opened in shock as the wave of pleasure swept her up and tumbled her, helpless. Sabrina shuddered above her shrieking out a series of high-pitched cries before a long groan from Jude drowned her out.

Everyone collapsed on top of her. Warm, protected, and maybe even loved. She smiled. When had she ever felt like this before?

Moments later, Jude leaned over Sabrina's shoulder to brush his lips against hers. He nuzzled Sabrina's ear, then pulled out and rose to his feet. A small whine escaped Q as half of her happy feeling went away.

With a sigh, Q shifted herself and Sabrina into a better position onto the couch. They lay on their sides, facing each other, trading little kisses and dragging their fingertips over each other's skin. Sometimes Q's body quivered with the aftershocks of her orgasm. She never wanted to let Sabrina go.

Just as she started to wonder where Jude had wandered off to, she heard the click of the camera. He'd been watching them. Sabrina ignored their photographer for awhile, and continued kissing her. Not sexy, lust-addled kisses. These were sweet – caring. Q's throat tightened and she held back tears that pricked her eyes. Was it possible that Sabrina loved her? Really loved her? For the first time, she let herself hope.

Q was drifting off when Sabrina gave her a gentle shake.

"Don't go to sleep, Q. I'm starving!"

She wriggled out from under Q's arm and slid over her to get off the lounge. The softness of Sabrina's skin against hers was heaven. She turned over to watch her friend's lovely body while she moved around the room, collecting her strewn articles of clothing. Jude sat beside her, pulled her head into his lap, and petted her hair.

Once dressed, Sabrina collected Q's clothing and threw them at her. "Really, I'm seriously starving. I haven't eaten all day. I'm going to die of starvation and you're both going to just sloth there and let it happen?"

"Slave driver," Q muttered, but she rolled to her feet and began pulling her clothes on.

"That's usually my job, but I'm too lazy today." Jude smiled.

"Lazy Dom," Q teased.

"I don't deny it. Your shirt is inside out, by the way." He stood, yanked it off over her head then redressed her properly. After grabbing the client loaner brush off a shelf, he insisted on brushing both girls' hair, in turn. Q smiled as he did hers, gently unsnarling her hair with the brush and smoothing it with the palm of his hand. Bliss.

***

The day was sunny and warm without being too hot. A cool breeze swept in from the ocean from time to time, like the foreshadowing of autumn. Only a couple more weeks until September. The summer had blurred past so quickly that Q felt both like she'd missed it, and had intensely lived every moment of it.

They walked to a small restaurant down the street. Both girls linked an arm with Jude. Q wondered if other people saw what she could see – three people that knew each other too well to just be friends. When they went out to eat, she could predict what the others would order, they picked off of each other's plates, and there were so many inside jokes it was like they had their own language. It made her feel important, valued, loved.

The place wasn't busy, but they'd missed the noon rush by a couple of hours. They chose a table on the outdoor patio with a view of the ocean in the distance. Watching her two blond, tanned lovers as they ordered, she wondered what people thought of the three of them sitting together. *Baywatch* meets *The Addams Family*. Predictably, Jude ordered the special and Sabrina ordered seafood. Q didn't care what the main dish was because the place had awesome fries.

As the server left to get their drinks, Sabrina leaned toward Q. "I feel like people can smell the sex coming off of us," she whispered.

Q laughed, and when Jude raised a brow, she put her mouth to his ear and said, "Sabrina is worried we smell like fuck."

Jude barked a laugh just as the waitress plunked his drink down in front of him and she eyed him appreciatively.

Nice! Q had been so wrapped up in her own thoughts she hadn't seen their server. It wasn't often she was oblivious to an attractive redhead. Jude hadn't noticed her either. And he wasn't just being polite to them by pretending not to. The girl moved off, looking disappointed she hadn't caught his attention.

"Hey, Jude, if you collect her, you'll have the whole set," Q said.

Sabrina looked annoyed and muttered something under her breath about not liking to share.

He stared at her blankly then gave a lopsided grin. He'd missed the joke. They both laughed, and he shrugged and settled back, sipping at his beer.

Lunch came and they fell ravenously on their meals.

Jude groaned. "I feel like you two haven't let me eat in days."

"Yes, you've been too busy getting laid. You poor bastard." Q arched a brow at him, daring him to complain. She'd lost momentum and already felt full. Sabrina was so hungry Q wasn't sure she bothered to chew.

Jude's dazzling blue eyes narrowed to sexy slits. His expression was damned smug. "I know, Q. If I had any buddies around here I wouldn't get much sympathy. Maybe Fredrick would understand."

"He won't be very understanding if you don't take those O-rings out of the sitting room ceiling soon," Sabrina mumbled. Her eyes darted around to make sure no one else had heard her.

His expression changed to a pained smile. "Yeah. I'd better get on that. It's hard to believe I'm leaving in a week. You two want to help me pack?"

The fries settled like a lump of lead in Q's stomach. "A week? But there's two more weeks until September."

Compassion flashed in his eyes. Too close to sympathy for Q's comfort. "I need time to settle in and visit my family before school starts, Q. I thought you knew that." He paused, looking uncomfortable. "I'm sorry."

They had never actually discussed when exactly he was going. And that, by itself, had seemed to mean maybe he wasn't.

As if this were an everyday conversation, Sabrina poked at the remains of her meal. But as she placed the fork next to the knife, her hand shook and metal tinkled against metal. Her knuckles were white. Q felt like a rug had been jerked out from under her feet. Was this such a non-event that Jude could drop it into trivial conversation?

The silence stretched but no one seemed to want to break it. Jude looked from Sabrina to her and back. She'd always adored the hint of humor in his eyes and his mouth that turned into a grin at unexpected moments. It made him a man and not just her Dom. It wasn't there now. His eyes seemed…dead.

"I wouldn't have given this summer up for anything in the world," he explained. "But it had to end. I have no choice. I never had." He dropped the balled-up napkin from his hand and batted it into the middle of table.

He sighed and looked up at the sky. "I think I owe you an explanation." Then he spoke very clearly though softly, enunciating words like they might explode if he handled them wrong. "I care for you both, a lot."

Q swallowed.

"I didn't mean to get emotionally involved, but it just kind of happened. Having two girlfriends was fun while I had the summer off but... You can't leave your careers to follow me halfway across the country. And I can't let my family down and stay here. Though I'd love to keep this going longer, I can't see it working out. We could try for long distance I guess." He shrugged.

That suggestion was out of pity. He didn't really want to try to make things work long-distance – he was just trying to soften the blow. And that made things worse.

"But it'll be hard for me to give you the attention you deserve. I'll be swamped. I remember my brother going through it. We barely heard from him for two years. Sabrina…" he looked at her, "you have something to lose here too. Do you think you could keep this up indefinitely?"

This time the silence seemed so solid the air might be glass. Q's heart stopped.

Sabrina avoided eye contact, her lips turned down in a frown. "No."

And so easily, the glass shattered.

"No. I can't," she added, frowning. "I'm sorry."

"Hey." He reached and patted her hand. "It's okay. I thought so. This just makes it simpler, for all of us."

Except me.

As if shaking herself from some heavy thought, Sabrina cleared her throat. "It'll be weird to go back to just dating vanilla guys after this. Though, I guess it's time to look for a real partner."

"A real partner?" A ringing started in Q's ears. She didn't feel well. They were done with her. Simple as that.

"Yes." Sabrina still didn't look her in the eye. "It's not that this wasn't *real* but it couldn't last, you know? We can still be just…friends. I mean, we have for five years, right? We can do that, can't we? You promised." Her final wistful tone might have given Q hope if this was the start of a relationship, but now it said precisely nothing to her numb heart.

"Sure." She nodded. In her head she worked fast, trying to build the wall back up. But it was too late. There was nothing left to protect herself with. She stayed in her seat, trying to look as blasé as they did. They glanced at her intermittently, but she knew she couldn't trust herself to speak. When the topic changed she excused herself, grabbed her bag, and escaped to the bathroom.

She bit her lip hard all the way there, trying not to cry before she was somewhere safe. With a gasp, she rushed into the room. It was empty. A flood of tears erupted, her hands unable to hold them back. Her heart fractured, grinding down into dust. She locked a stall door behind her. The sobs were too loud and she tried to quiet herself – she didn't want to be the girl that made scenes in public restrooms.

It's okay, it's okay, she kept telling herself, frantic to calm down before Sabrina came looking for her.

Her default fix popped into her mind but she pushed it away. There had been therapy for this, when she was younger. After her parents died. Unbidden, the thought came back again. The knife in her bag was sharp. It would only take a couple of minutes. She could go somewhere quiet.

Shut up. She'd promised Sabrina they could still be friends no matter what. And Jude? Neither of them deserved the guilt she'd leave them with. This is what they'd agreed on. She could do this. Splashing water on her face helped a little, but she still looked red and blotchy. She'd tell them she'd had an allergic reaction and sneezed a lot. A little sob escaped her, and she bit the next one down. Her stomach knotted and she felt nauseous. Breathing slowly, she calmed.

She started to reframe. What had she learned from this? When she walked out of the restroom, the girl who cared too much would stay behind. The old Q would be back. Trying to be loving had been a mistake. First Nico, now this. Getting attached to people was for idiots – no more making a fool of herself. Her inner cyborg shut off the part of her that craved love. Violence, and how it made her feel, would have to be enough. She left the room awhile later, the last of her tender feelings ground beneath the soles of her boots.

Chapter 17

Jude

One of his lecturers had mentioned his father's favorite saying today and it had hit home. The old medical saying that was supposed to help with diagnosis: *If you hear hoofbeats, expect horses not zebras.* He hadn't been to see his dad yet.

Study and hospital rounds absorbed his time. Shit. Jude slammed shut the laptop and beat a short drum solo on the lid with his hands. The words in his head pattered in time with the beat.

An-atomy, an-atomy, path-ology and zebras. Fuck-ing zebras.

He slumped back in the chair and scrubbed his fingers through his hair. Fact was, he hadn't done much at all for two months except try to settle into studies, and he was still a fish out of water…or was that a zebra?

And he still missed the girls – missed them so much his gut ached. Just yesterday, he'd come across a photo of the three of them Sabrina had emailed him a month ago.

Every night he shut his eyes and went to sleep remembering the feel of their hair in his hands. The feel of their bodies too, but mostly he pictured their hair gliding across his fingers. Sabrina's tousled blonde. Q's dead-of-night black. His beach bunny and his goth. The sexiest chicks ever and he was obsessed with their hair…and the way they talked. And what they'd said. How good they'd made him feel just by being there. Sometimes he wafted into dreamland, thinking of them both lying with their heads on his chest, snuggling.

Snuggling for chrissakes. He was destined to study medicine, to be a doctor, not to be a playboy Dom with girlfriends left and right.

Fuck. He set both elbows on the desk and leaned his forehead on his palms. Fuck fantasies. Fuck swearing when there was no reason. Fuck everything.

He sat up and shoved back the chair then went in search of his jacket and a pair of pants suitable for visiting his father. Far as he knew, all that was clean was a blue T-shirt and a pair of faded brown pants. Maybe he should start just buying black, like Q. At the sudden ache, he froze, halfway to the closet, and put his hand to his chest. Heart attacks didn't happen to men this young, did they? Not commonly. Think horses, not zebras. He squeezed his eyes shut.

Fuck horses too.

As soon as he pulled into the parking lot at the nursing home, he felt queasy. He hated visiting this place. In fact, he hated all places with the sick. The accumulation of illness and sadness overwhelmed him every time. Blood, he could handle. Puke, wet diapers, kids vomiting on him…all those were okay. Just not this. Not places where death poked its scythe in way too often.

He stared at his hands on the steering wheel. Some doctor he'd be. The smell of fresh-cut timber excited him, and the firm feel of a hammer in his hand. Making things. Building. That was him. Sick people made him sick.

The nurses smiled as he went past. The entertainment room was packed with elderly men and women in wheelchairs watching TV, playing cards and gossiping. IV drip stands stood like strange metal trees. His march down the corridor was as lonely as that of a soldier coming home from war without his buddies. His soles squeaked on the floor. He took the right turn to the door, and pushed it open.

The room itself was clean and smelled fresh. A vase of beautiful roses sat on the table – his mother must have been here recently. She still came most weeks. The view out the opened French door was stunning – trees, an expanse of green lawn, flower beds overflowing with bright blossoms. A few birds flitted past, chirping.

He took a breath and went to the bed. He stood a while, flexing and clenching his fists. Looking at the man in the bed made him feel so empty. This wasn't his dad, not anymore. Not since six years ago, soon after he'd started pre-med.

He looked around and found a chair then pulled it up next to the bed. The noise at last attracted the attention of the skeletal figure in the bed. Drool hung from his chin and his eyes were rheumy and sightless. Though the nurses must clean his face each morning, crusts had already collected on his eyelids and lips.

His father. His world, until that day. The stroke had taken his father's mind if not his body. The family, him included, had waited in turns for weeks, praying at first that he'd survive, then praying the brain damage might not be as bad as the tests indicated. All for nothing.

No matter the positive spin people tried to put on this, he'd never been able to see the point in life if you didn't even know it was passing you by. This was the man who used to carry him on his shoulders, and who gave him bear hugs when he needed comfort. If he'd so much as nicked his finger, his mother had sent him to Dad. As if she couldn't put on a Band-aid.

Jude smiled weakly. He saw through it now – her plan had been to let his father be involved in his son's world. As a surgeon, his days had been filled with work. The good memories still crowded in though – waking at night to a gentle kiss on his forehead and a smile, sitting on the floor with him laughing as his armies of toy soldiers got flattened by their basset hounds galloping through, buying popsicles at the beach.

But the brilliant surgeon had become a husk.

The ache in his stomach intensified but he reached over and took his father's thin hand. What to say? He always went through the news when he visited…no matter how gruesome or strange or how bland. His years in Europe had meant telling some hair-raising tales of traffic on the autobahns as well as sexy stories of the European girlfriend who'd dumped him for a German accountant, of all things.

When he'd begun this story-telling routine it had been in the hope that somewhere inside, his father understood. He knew better now but the habit remained. He took a breath and began to speak.

The start of his story went fast – the early days of summer at the beach and how his friend, Fredrick, had given him the mansion to renovate. When he reached the time when he'd found Sabrina and Q in the yard that night, hunting ghosts, his throat tightened. But he went on, describing Sabrina's antics and smart-ass replies, and Q's quiet, no-nonsense, yet amused, way of handling her. He stopped talking. Was feeling like throwing up when you thought of a girl, or girls, a good or a bad sign? He shifted on the chair.

Diagnostically, he was doing a shit job. This was not the result of a stomach ulcer. When you hear hoofbeats, think horses. He'd been avoiding his true emotions all along. But what could he do? He was trapped in limbo – in the land of not knowing which way to turn without disappointing himself, his father, his mother, and wrecking his life in general.

In the quiet, the flick of a book's pages and crack of its spine carried from somewhere outside.

The wind gusted and a swirl of bright fabric curled across the door opening. The perfume was familiar. His mother? The toe of a red shoe, a woman's shoe, made its appearance in the doorway. Yes, his mother. Ever the polite one who held you and listened to your grievances without criticizing – she was saying, *hey, I'm here*, without intruding too much.

He bent his head and held his father's hand tighter. He couldn't tell her, not face to face. Every time he'd gone home to say hello, or had met her for lunch, he'd stayed silent about the girls. This big bad Dom was a chicken.

He'd never shied away from telling his mother of past girlfriends, but he'd kept his kinkier activities to himself. This time though, the risk was there. Two girlfriends…two lovers, was not average, not acceptable in polite society. Maybe it wasn't even normal but he wasn't going to broadcast it to all and sundry. Somehow though, he needed to tell her. Would she be disgusted? He desperately hoped not. His mother was his bedrock – the one he'd relied on when the world went nuts.

He cleared his throat and went on.

The summer rolled past in his head, given life by his words, made all bright and shiny and wonderful. Though the reconstruction of the mansion played a part, it was the women who came to life as he spoke.

His voice strengthened as he told of the days on the beach, of Q's nasty boyfriend sent packing, of the way the girls' hair shone in the sunlight and their legs… No, not that. He stopped and began again with the time of the séance and how Sabrina had fooled him and Q, but then she'd laughed and they'd figured it out, and she'd made a run for it…

He stopped again. Damn. They'd had a lot of sex. Kinky sex. And a lot of crazy fun too. He'd just censor things. So he told of Sabrina painting him, but not of tying the girls up and beating Q until she nearly orgasmed from that alone, or of making rough love afterward. The ghost episode got a mention, but not the spanking. All in all, he found himself telling of how he'd slowly and inexorably fallen in love with Sabrina and Q.

By the end, his eyes were wet. He wiped them, squeezed his father's hand and walked to the door. She was there, of course. In a pretty floral dress with her blonde hair in a chignon. Though her hair was streaked with grey, it was clear from which side of the family he'd gotten his hair and eye color.

He sat on the bench beside her and kissed her cheek. "Hi, Mom." Then he waited. If she hadn't heard him…hell, could he say all that again?

"Oh, Jude." She brushed back a straying lock of hair from his forehead. "Why didn't you tell me? You love them, don't you?"

He dipped his head then looked her in the eye. "Yes. I do. But they both live in New Jersey."

"And so?" She waited, fingering the book on her lap.

Though he searched there seemed no anger or criticism in her tone or expression. "You don't mind?"

She sighed. "Well, it would have been nice if you'd found some girl next door to fall in love with, but you've never fit in any mold, Jude. You were always the one who stole the cookies before they were cool, or fell out of the tree and broke your arm. And playing cops and robbers, you were the one who forgot to untie the girls, but…I suppose that prepared me."

"Um…" Trust mom to bring that up.

"So." She patted his leg. "No, I don't mind if you have an extra girlfriend. It's unusual, but really dear, you'd have to be a serial killer to get me worried…or want to run for president. When are you going back to speak to them?" She raised her eyebrows.

"I may not have said this before, but Mom, you must be the most awesome mother ever." It didn't help him much though, not with his career to keep in mind. "Going back though, I don't know. How can I? There are other difficulties and by now they may have forgotten me."

"Hush! Never. No girl could ever forget my boy. And other difficulties? Jude, for the last two months, whenever I've met with you, I've seen your pain and I've been meaning to speak to you." She sat up straighter, and took his hand. "Be honest with me, please. Do you wish to continue with this medical career?" When he opened his mouth to reply, she held up a finger. "Because, it's clear that you hate it."

"Uh. How the hell…how did you know?"

"I'm your mother. And don't swear. It looks bad. Why then, are you continuing to torture yourself?"

What a question. But, freed of all expectations from her, he saw it. "Dad. He always wanted this."

When she shook her head, shock hit him. "No. He did not. Do you think your father an ogre?"

An ogre? "No. Of course not."

"Good. Then why would you think he would want you to study medicine when your heart lies elsewhere?"

That floored him. The world stood still while he unscrambled his thoughts. His only words seemed inadequate. "I don't know."

"Now we're getting somewhere," she said brightly. "I will not have you this unhappy. Go say goodbye to your father, then I am taking you home, and we are going to talk and figure this out, even if it takes all night."

If only it were that simple. No matter what she thought, the chances were that Sabrina and Q would toss him out on the street if he tried to ease his way back into a relationship.

"Stop frowning at me!" She slapped his thigh then rose to her feet. "Be positive. We will sort this out. Come."

He stared after her. And maybe it wasn't just hair color that he'd inherited. He stood. If freed from this medical career that had been dragging at his soul, he wasn't giving up. If she or Q gave him the slightest chink of an opening, he'd use it. If there was one thing he was good at, it was persuading women.

Chapter 18

Q

The throbbing of the dungeon's music seemed to control the swish of the flogger against her back. Stretched tight against the St. Andrew's cross, Q wondered if this asshole was ever going to get on with things. Enough fucking warm up, already. It wasn't the rye she'd downed before she left the house either. This idiot was just clueless. She tossed her head in annoyance, forgetting there was no longer a sweep of hair to work with. At least it didn't get in the way. Neither did her tiny boy-shorts or the X's of black tape over her nipples.

He came to check on her again. With a disdainful flick of her eyes, she met his dark gaze. The uncertainty she saw there completed the mood-kill.

"Are you okay? Was it too hard?"

Never send a boy to do a man's job. She glared at him. "Sorry, I hadn't realized you started yet."

There was a chuckle from someone just out of her field of vision. "You're new at this." An unfamiliar man's voice.

The young man smiled wanly and nodded. "My submissive likes sensual play, but not pain. I'm not even quite sure how to get a flick out of this thing. Q volunteered to be my guinea pig."

She'd been playing at the club a lot lately. Tonight it was hard to decide if it was helping her forget or forcing her to remember.

"May I?" The flogger changed hands, and a man walked into her line of sight. Not much taller than her, he was stocky and well-muscled. He looked a little rough around the edges, but it might have just been in comparison to the kid. He raised his brows at her.

"You're a pretty little thing. What's your name?"

The look she gave him would have turned a lesser man to stone. "Like he said, it's Q. Just the letter. And no, it doesn't stand for anything."

He didn't even blink. "I'm Lee, in case you care. Do you want me to take over?"

"If you know one end of that thing from the other, it will be an improvement," she growled, low enough that her words didn't carry to the young man. He might be useless but even in her nastiest mood, she didn't feel the need to knife innocents with insults.

Lee backed up a few paces and shook out the falls of the flogger. "How much can you take?"

"Whatever you can manage to deliver... Lee." The sarcasm with which she delivered his name made it an insult.

He smiled pleasantly and proceeded to beat her.

***

The screams he drew from her won him Q's grudging respect. They talked a bit and Lee told her he had a single-tail back at his place, and a selection of canes. Q wanted to check them out and figured tonight was as good a night as any. When he took her down, she tucked her cold, numb hands under her arms. The changing rooms first then she could have more pain.

"O-M-G! Q!" The riot of red curls and buxom figure made Ivy easy to pick out, even in the club's gloom. "Honey, what did you do with your hair? New piercings too?"

She nodded to Ivy as she brushed past. Her friend followed. Even hammered, Q couldn't bring herself to be rude. Ivy had helped her hold it together when Nico had disposed of her. At the time, she hadn't had anyone else in her life who'd have understood it all. She turned, and concentrated on not slurring.

"Hey, Ivy. Yeah. Just the bridge of my nose, the bull ring and my tongue. I'm trying to decide what to do next. I'm looking to get a brand or some cutting done."

Her friend smiled and squeezed her arm. The kindness set Q's teeth on edge. "I love the blue hair. Where'd you get it done?"

“I did it myself.” She’d hacked it off with a knife about five minutes before she left the house, but that sounded crazy even to her drunk self so she didn’t add that bit. Was that enough? Was this little tete-a-tete done yet? Her body started to rock a little to the beat of the metal blasting from the sound system.

The aggressive feeling was coming back. She needed to get out of there. “I gotta go, Ivy. I’ve got a guy waiting.”

“Yeah, about that, Q...” She walked her to the changing room and sat on a bench while Q found her clothes and struggled into them.

Tight leather pants were a bad idea when one was drunk. She hissed as she drew them up her thighs, feeling every welt individually.

“That Lee guy is new. You hadn’t met him before tonight, right?”

“You the morality police all of a sudden, Ivy? Don’t judge me. I have no intentions of fucking him yet. I just want to see what he can do.” Internally she was grumbling. This conversation and the entire situation was pissing her off and she was losing her endorphin buzz.

“Q. No, no,” she backpedaled. “Play with him if you want to. I just wanted to warn you that he’s getting a reputation for playing too hard. For pushing limits to scary places. A few subs I’ve talked to lately have said he ignored their safewords the first few times. Maybe leaving with him now isn’t the best idea?”

“Why is now an issue?”

“Just a friendly warning, Q. I’m worried about you. This isn’t the Q I know. The fact that he’s new to the scene here means there’s no one to vouch that he’s safe, and early reports about him aren’t good.”

She’d rattled that off fast, like she had to get it off her chest in case she was stopped. Ivy hated confrontation.

Q exchanged stares with her. “Thanks for the concern, Ivy, but I need this tonight. If he lands me in the hospital, feel free to tell me ‘I told you so.’”

Ivy bit her lip. The Rubanesque submissive looked disconcerted. “At least let me be your safe call then.”

“Fuck! You just don’t give up, do you?” Q grumbled.

“Or call Sabrina if you don’t want to use me. Is she home?”

It was like being stabbed in the chest. She caught her breath. A string of profanity escaped, actually making Ivy recoil. "Leave Sabrina the fuck out of this."

Big brown eyes came to mind – sad ones. Sabrina was always sad when she talked to Q lately, perhaps because Q had a hard time talking back to her. Her throat felt swollen and she fought down tears. She'd promised Sabrina their experiment wouldn't fuck up their friendship, but seeing her and not being able to hold her was hell on earth. Sabrina didn't want her like that. She wanted a vague, happy, shopping-buddy love. The type of love Q felt was tearing her heart out.

It had been two months but, if anything, it was getting worse instead of better. At first, she thought living almost on top of each other in the small apartment would get them back together – that maybe Sabrina would come to her senses. But Sabrina didn't want her. Eventually even Q had to admit all the things she'd thought she'd seen there, between them, had been pathetic delusions on her part. It was impossible to move on and forget her when they even shared toothpaste.

Lee didn't look pleased about giving Ivy his full name and address, but her friend stood her ground under his intimidating glare. When the exchange was complete, he turned away from Ivy without wasting breath on pleasantries.

As Q grabbed her jacket at the coat check, she avoided making eye contact with several regulars she knew. She hoped no one else would talk to her. Cross walked in. He was so quiet, she always forgot how huge and dangerous he used to seem – like a Titan dropped into the mortal world.

Cross nodded at her, unsmiling.

She nodded back as he checked the coats of the two new girls he'd brought along. He was in the zone – which, for Cross, meant even less talking. Not that he was the type of guy to prattle. The girls were hot and cowered behind him a little. Fresh meat.

"Yours?" Q asked as she passed him.

"I wish," Cross murmured back.

She stifled a laugh until she remembered that the last time they'd been talking about... She blocked memories of Sabrina and focused on the low level of pain her body was feeding her.

Lee gestured Q out the door ahead of him. It felt more like a prison guard keeping an eye on an inmate, rather than something gallant or gentlemanly. It was a continual struggle not to compare Lee to Jude. Jude would have opened the car door for her. Jude would have teased her, flirted, and made jokes on the ride. But Jude had cast her off. How had she ever believed that he'd had feelings for her? Easy. She'd wanted to be fooled. Happy in her own little delusion, she had probably missed any number of hints that she was temporary in his life. Like the fact that he'd actually said so.

By the time they pulled into the driveway of the farmhouse where Lee lived, it was starting to feel more like a business transaction than a date. She wanted pain – he wanted to hurt her. Q had negotiated there would be no touching and no sex, and he said he was fine with that, for now. He'd mentioned that he didn't believe in fucking brats he hadn't mastered – whatever the hell that meant. The flask he'd had in the glove compartment mellowed her out. He didn't look at her much. Some Doms she'd played with were like that though. They thought paying too much attention to a sub gave them too much power. She missed the way Jude looked at her – like she was eye candy.

The decor was Spartan. There was no pretence of normalcy once you passed the kitchen. In the living room, a huge double St. Andrew's cross was bolted to the wall. The coffee table had built-in restraints. Cuffs dangled from ropes that were O-ringed to the ceiling, along with some other things Q couldn't identify. With no neighbors close by, there was no one to hear her scream. A loud instinct screamed to get out while she still could. Lee went to the kitchen and made that pesky instinct another drink. It was quiet after that.

She wobbled a bit as he hooked her into some O-ring cuffs and adjusted the rope length so she could stand flatfooted. More cuffs went around her ankles, and were clipped to another ring recessed into the floor. She hadn't noticed the floor rings at first. Even with the booze-goggles on, she was happy she didn't have to have sex with him. He wasn't bad, but compared to Jude's angelic countenance, Lee was a bit of a troll.

They had a short conversation about what toys she was willing to try. It was about as intimate as telling the guy at the pizza place what toppings she wanted. Lee seemed to care about as much.

He began. A beating from someone who didn't care about her wasn't the same – like masturbation versus sex. He slid needles under her skin. She had to remind herself that she'd agreed to try it. Maybe it was different with someone you trusted? Subspace found her eventually, despite their lack of connection, and the relationship became all about her and the flogger, with Lee becoming incidental. She lost all sense of time, only vaguely aware when he switched to the crop. It pulled scream after scream from her, until she felt empty.

Pain changed and ramped up. The cane and single-tail vied for her attention. Her comfortable haze abandoned her. She hung from her wrists, hands numb. Shoulders ached. He was saying cruel things to her. Skin was fire. *Whore*. Blows stopped waiting for her, and she couldn't process the pain. *You deserve to suffer*. Agony rained down. "Red! Red! Red!" she screamed. Did the words come? It didn't stop. Red ran through her head, but she didn't know if it came out of her mouth. *You're a waste of flesh*. Did only she hear red? But red was universal. Red worked everywhere. He didn't understand her? He didn't care. She was going to die here. She stopped screaming. She didn't care either.

Chapter 19

Sabrina

Sabrina grinned, staring at the email message on the computer screen. The photo of the apparition from Jude's house was a finalist in a photo contest. A professional paranormal investigating organization wanted to buy her photo. Two hundred dollars! She couldn't hold back a little squeal. Q would be psyched. And Jude would –

Her grin faded. It'd been two months. Why was she still thinking of him as if he was still here? Even Q – who was technically living with her, wasn't really here.

Her gaze fell to the photo in the cheap colorful frame on the desk. She'd left it next to the computer despite Q's protests. She'd hoped it would make her smile – the three of them making goofy faces at the camera – but more often than not, it made her cry. Especially when Q had started pulling away in earnest.

And Jude…he didn't answer her emails. Yeah, the experiment was over but she'd hoped they could at least remain friends. He hadn't replied to a single one, even when she'd attached photos that he asked for before he left. She wanted to hate him, to yell at him, but she dissolved into tears before the words became clear in her head.

Every little thing reminded her of him. Half the time his fucking song was stuck in her head. The alert sound on online chat reminded her of conversations between him and Q. Even her solace, her special place at the beach wasn't safe. All she saw was Jude carrying her over his shoulder into the waves and feeding strawberries to Q on a blanket. Small moments – snippets of a different time and place. People who'd changed, drifted in and out of her life.

But Q. She was supposed to stay. Forever. She hadn't been eating much, despite Sabrina cooking her favorites and bugging her every night. She'd barely even been home this past week.

She'd randomly dyed her hair blue – not so unusual for Q. But then she'd gone out and pierced almost every spot on her face – and who knew where else. She shuddered. When Sabrina tried to engage her, she pulled away. She ignored her texts. She acted gruff and uninterested when they were in the same room. But then, when she thought Sabrina wasn't looking, she'd gaze at her with a longing expression. It broke her heart and made her angry all at once.

Q had promised they'd stay friends after the experiment, no matter what happened. Damn her for going back on her word. But then, Sabrina was having a hard time with that herself. She had to fight the impulse to wrap her arms around Q from behind when she made her coffee in the morning, kiss her pouty lips when she looked sad, ask her to cuddle on the couch and watch a favorite movie. But nobody did those kinds of things with platonic friends. Were they even that anymore? One thing was for sure – her best friend and favorite person in the world was slowly slipping away. And the only person she might have turned to for help was gone. Jude.

Not for the first time in the last few days, tears ran down her cheeks. Ridiculous! She'd just gotten great news and she was crying!

"Look what you've done to me, Q." She cursed her out loud.

If things were different…if her family were more accepting…they'd probably be sitting on the couch, giggling and cuddling right now. If life were simpler, she'd follow her heart. She'd happily live in her own little world with Q, oblivious to the judgment and scathing looks around her.

The summer had been the best time of her life. Was it worth it – giving that up to do what was proper according to her family? Even if it meant she suffered? Where was the trade off? She'd sacrificed Q, now where was her prince charming and house and 2.5 kids and perfect, normal life?

Normal, suddenly seemed highly overrated.

What she really wanted was her unconventional, odd, sometimes stubborn, often sweet, sexy girlfriend. What she really wanted was Q – in her arms, laughing at her silly jokes, kissing her after a bad day, standing over her with a crop in her hand. And her prince charming? Well, he came in the form of a good-humored, blond Dom with a thing for turning old houses into kinky, well-decorated dungeons. She craved his hand in her hair when giving gruff commands, the gleam in his eye when he'd caught her being naughty, his beer-flavored kisses, his laughter booming off the empty walls of the house.

More tears fell. The best time of her life had passed in only a summer. It wasn't fair.

But neither was famine or slavery or war or way worse predicaments than hers. Nobody got what they wanted in life without big sacrifices.

Her phone rang. The name Ivy flashed across the screen. Q's kinky goth friend? What did she want?

"Hello?"

"Sabrina? This is Q's friend, Ivy." They had talked a few times just after Nico had kicked Q to the curb. She seemed to know more about how Q was feeling then than Sabrina had. More recently she'd learned it was because Q had been keeping her kink life in the closet. "Is Q home yet? She was supposed to call me and she hasn't been answering her phone."

"No." She glanced at the time. Midnight wasn't late for Q, but Ivy sounded alarmed. "Why? What's wrong?"

She hesitated then blurted, "I knew I should've have let her go with him. I'm so sorry. God, if anything happens to her I'll just die!"

"Whoa! Slow down." Her heart started to race. "Where is she?"

After an audible breath, she told her Q had gone to play at a private residence with a stranger who had a bad reputation.

"I'm sorry." The girl sobbed. "She assured me she was fine. And, well, you know Q. She doesn't back down easy."

"Okay. It's okay. Just tell me where she is." Shaking with nerves and anger and…fucking desperation, she grabbed her purse and keys and headed to the car while Ivy rambled off an address. "You're at the club right now?" At her affirmation she took control. "I'm swinging by to pick you up. I'll need help getting Q out. You may be a sub but I've heard you can put a wayward Dom in his place."

Tires screeched as she peeled out of the parking lot and let her inner bitch take over. If Q went and died because she was too hung up on a guy to use common sense, Sabrina was going to kill her.

After collecting Ivy, she followed the GPS out of town and into a sparsely occupied wooded area. The long driveway led to a house up on a hill. The outside lights were on but it still looked sinister. Or maybe it was all in her head.

She jumped out of the car and stared at the old farmhouse. "Come on. We have to make sure Q is okay." Damn her for not listening to her uncle and getting a handgun permit. That'd be helpful right about now. She looked back at Ivy, who seemed to have swallowed her guilt and replaced it with determination. Good. She needed the back-up. "Call the police if this guy threatens us or Q at all, okay?"

She nodded.

They walked to the door and stopped. "Should we knock?" Sabrina asked.

Ivy shrugged.

The sound of Q's voice answered her question. "Red… red…pleeease." It was little more than a whimper, but she could hear it clearly through the door. There was a loud crack and Q sobbed.

Oh hell. She burst through the door and followed the heart-wrenching sounds through a kitchen and straight into a nightmare of kinky proportions. She barely registered the man standing to the side, whip in hand. The only thing on her mind was Q, hanging limply from her wrists…and bleeding.

"Hey!" The man yelled. "Who the fuck are you?"

Ignoring him, she choked back a sob and rushed to Q's side. "Q! Are you okay?"

She stared at the wall, moaning. Needles had been slid under her skin, making a line down her un-tattooed side. Blood oozed to the surface on the back of one thigh where it looked like a cane had hit too hard and split the skin. Bruises marred her back and breasts.

Anger welled up in Sabrina's chest. She grabbed Q's face. "Wake up, honey. Tell me you're okay." More moaning that tore at Sabrina's heart. "We're gonna get you out of here. Just hang on."

The man placed himself in her line of sight. "I said, who the fuck are you?"

Sabrina whirled on him. "Her fucking girlfriend. I'd suggest you stay the hell out of my way before I decide to call the state deputy. Also known as my cousin." It was a lie but he didn't need to know that. Sometimes bullshitting was the best way out of a situation.

"You just trespassed on private property. And as far as I'm concerned, you're stealing something of mine." He took a step forward, tapping the whip handle on his leg.

Ivy moved to Sabrina's side, looking between them nervously. "Don't antagonize him, Sabrina," she whispered. "He looks like he might have a few screws loose."

She was beyond caring. Anger outweighed any sense. "Start taking out the needles," she told Ivy before addressing the fuck that hurt her Q. "You have a girl strung up in your torture chamber, barely conscious. And she's bleeding. Do you really want to invite law enforcement in here?"

He looked at Q, still dangling from the ceiling then shrugged. "Fine. Take the bitch. I'm finished with her anyway."

Fucking asshole. She released a breath. Good that she wouldn't have any trouble, but how she wished she could pound the living daylights out of him. She turned to Q, who barely registered that Ivy was carefully pulling needles out of her skin.

She searched the room for her clothes. At least she had underwear on. A t-shirt would be fine for the car ride home. She grabbed the black shirt off the floor. Ivy placed each needle on the coffee table. Sabrina did a double-take. Not a coffee table – a restraint system.

She shuddered. When the needles were out, she handed Ivy the t-shirt and unbuckled the cuffs. She barely caught Q when her knees buckled.

"Stand up, Q," she gritted out, crushed under the weight of her taller friend. "You have to stand so we can help you." Sabrina gave her a shake and Ivy patted her face.

Q seemed to come to a bit. She nodded and straightened, on wobbly legs but at least standing. Sabrina helped support her with an arm under hers as Ivy tugged on her shirt.

"Grab her jeans," she told Ivy, guessing Q had stashed her wallet and keys in her pockets. Headed for the door, she spared a glance at the bastard who dared call himself a Dom. He'd just sat down on the couch with a beer and was about to turn on the TV – as if it were an ordinary Saturday night and nothing had happened.

"Asshole," she muttered. "Let's get you home, Q."

Ivy and Sabrina shuffled Q out to the car barefoot, not wanting to stop long enough to buckle her knee-high boots. Sabrina motioned for Ivy to drive but she was already one step ahead and opened the back door for them. The shout of pain when Q sat down in the car was like a knife to Sabrina's heart.

"Fuck. What were you thinking, Q?" Sabrina grumbled to herself. She pulled Q sideways so her upper body lay in her lap. Her shoulders trembled and at first she thought Q was crying, but when she rolled her face up, her teeth chattered. "Shit. She's gonna go into shock. Ivy, there's a blanket in the trunk, can you get it?"

A moment later, Ivy draped the blanket she used for beach trips on Q's body, then she slid in the driver's side and blasted the heat. "To the hospital?" Ivy asked.

"No!" Q tried to sit up but Sabrina held her down – or tried to. The girl was fucking strong, even when barely conscious. "No hospitals. I just need to sleep."

"Q, you're –"

"Sabrina, please?" The sorrow in her voice tugged at her. "Please don't make me answer questions about what happened."

Nosy doctors would be all over her ass, demanding answers, calling in social workers. Q would be mortified. Now that they'd covered her body, she stopped shivering. Her eyes looked clearer. The wounds were superficial – they could bandage them at home.

She sighed. "Alright. To the apartment." Gently, she tugged Q back into her lap. Stroking her hair, she scolded, "Why on earth would you do this to yourself, Q? You scared the shit out of me. I get that you're upset about Jude. Piercings are one thing, but my god, you could've been murdered! Do you have any sense at all?" Then her brain processed what her fingers already had. "Your hair!" It looked like someone had taken a blunt machete to it. "What did you do to your beautiful hair?"

Q remained quiet, but her breathing had steadied and her muscles relaxed.

"I should have never broken things off," she whispered, more to herself. It was her fault Q had almost just died – hers and Jude's. She wished she could kick his sorry ass for leaving her. And if Sabrina had been brave enough to stand up for what she believed in instead of hiding – like a coward – this never would've happened. Thank god she'd made it in time. If something worse than this had happened to Q…tears welled up in her eyes.

"I'm so sorry." Sabrina leaned down and kissed her hair.

"I don't want your pity," she slurred.

"It's not pity. I mean it. I love you. It just took me a while to…realize it." Denial was a powerful trap.

"No." She shifted as if trying to get away then seemed to think better of it and gave up with a sigh. "I definitely don't want your pity love. I'm pathetic enough without it."

Sabrina's patience snapped. "It's not pity, dumbass! I busted down the door of a stranger's house for you. If he had tried to keep me from taking you, I probably would've gotten myself killed protecting you. If that's not love, I don't know what is. Now lie still and shut up!"

There was a pause long enough to make Sabrina think she'd fallen asleep, then, "When did you get so bossy?"

She chuckled and kissed her temple. "When I thought I'd lost you."

Ivy dropped them at the apartment, promising to get her car back to her in the morning. Q seemed stronger and pushed Sabrina away when she tried to help her into the house. But Sabrina managed to bully her into her bedroom and lie down on the bed while she bandaged her wounds.

The dim lamp on the side table didn't provide much light but Sabrina didn't want to disturb Q, who seemed to be resting soundly. She only winced a few times when Sabrina dabbed on the antiseptic cream. The wounds would probably heal without scarring. Luckily, it did seem like Fuckface knew what he was doing – for that part of things anyway. There wasn't much Sabrina could do for the bruising though. Q would feel that for at least a week. But she bandaged up the gashes on her thighs then tucked her under the covers.

She considered her options from here. This was Q's room and they hadn't been the closest of roommates lately. Should she sit beside her or leave right away or –

"Fuck it," she mumbled, unzipping her jeans then letting them fall to the floor. She kicked off her flip flops then freed herself from her bra before approaching the bed.

"What are you doing, little girl?" Q's voice sounded too small to be in big, bad Domme mode.

"Oh, I'm 'little girl' again, huh?" She made a scooting motion with her hands. "I'm getting in bed with you, and you know I only wear underwear and a tee to bed. Move over."

Q chuckled softly as she made room for Sabrina. It was good to hear her laugh, even if it was weak. Sabrina slid in under the covers and lay down on her side, facing away from Q.

She could feel Q's breath warming the back of her neck but Q didn't touch her. After a few moments of scrambling for something to say and coming up empty, she reached back and grabbed Q's wrist then tugged it around her waist. Q chuckled again and tightened her hold while Sabrina ran her fingers up and down her arm.

"You don't act like a straight girl," Q whispered, nuzzling into her hair.

She smiled into the pillow. "You don't make me feel like one."

Another moment of silence then, "So this is it, Sabrina? One night I was in danger and suddenly you're bi?"

She inhaled slowly then exhaled, thinking through the right words. It was more complicated than what Q boiled it down to. And it would be hard for Q to believe her no matter what she said. So she did her best to explain.

"You know that song, *Big Yellow Taxi* by Joni Mitchell? Counting Crows did a cover of it in the early two thousands, I think. It was a good cover. I almost like it better than the…"

Q's soft laughter made her trail off. "A serious conversation and you talk about pop songs. Figures."

Sabrina squeezed her arm. "I have a point. Anyway, the idea of the song is that you don't always know what you have until it's gone. And I…"

Her voice cracked and she had to stop.

"I…I didn't know." Tears flowed down her cheeks, forming a wet pool on the pillow. "I don't know if I'm bi or straight or lesbian or asexual…" She snorted a silly, tearful laugh. "And I don't really care. I just…I want to go back to the way things were. Before Jude left." She couldn't stand facing away anymore – she needed to see Q, to see her face. Carefully, so she didn't shake the bed too much, she rolled to her other side.

Q was there, with big watery blue eyes. Sabrina smiled and placed her forehead against hers. "I want to be your girlfriend again. And I want to be your sub. Your little girl."

Q's hand came up and wiped the falling tears from her cheeks.

"I'm sorry, Q." Her tears came faster. "I'm sorry I didn't say something sooner. I didn't know. I thought I knew what I wanted but…" She had to pause because she was sobbing so hard. "Please say you forgive me."

"Shh." Q petted her head. "Of course I forgive you."

"And…and…" Dear god she was blubbering like a baby. "And you'll be my girlfriend again?"

She frowned and dropped her gaze. "Sabrina, I…" Her expression told of a war going on inside her head. "I know you say you love me, but…"

"You don't love me back?"

Q shook her head. "No. Never that. I always loved you, Sabrina. It was just hard living with you when I couldn't show it."

She slowed down her sobs and took a few deep breaths. "It was awful!"

"Yes. So you know it's hard for me to believe you love me. To take that risk again."

Sabrina nodded and bit down on her lip. "I know. But I'll do anything to prove it to you. You'll see."

"You've done a lot tonight. I'm sorry I dragged you into that. I didn't mean for my –"

"Stupid act of recklessness," she filled in for her.

Q gave her a small smile. "Yes. That. I didn't mean for it to affect you. I didn't mean to scare you."

"Well, you did." She looked over her best friend's face – which used to be familiar but now seemed so strange. "And so does all this…punk, goth, whatever you call it stuff." She pointed to her hair then the piercings.

"You don't like my new look? And here I thought you were tired of black."

"It's fine if you're going to wear blue shirts from now on. But if you keep wearing black, you'll always clash."

Q laughed. "Funny girl. I'll dye it back if you want me to. But there's still one thing I have to know before we go any further."

"What?" Sabrina froze. She really couldn't take much more tonight.

Q smirked. "You really think you might be asexual?"

A big snort escaped her and they both giggled. Then they held each other, runny noses, tears and all, until the sun came up the next morning.

Chapter 20

Sabrina

The smell of sautéed onions filled the small kitchen, bringing a smile to Sabrina's face. Q stood in front of the sizzling pan, stirring the onions with a wooden spoon. Sabrina was giving her a cooking lesson. And so far, it wasn't going too badly.

"That's good for now, Q. Slice the peppers and we'll add those next."

Sabrina moved to the other counter and unwrapped the sausage then started to cut it into round pieces. "So I made a lunch date with my mom. I'm going to start dropping hints about us." She glanced at Q, trying to gauge her reaction. "No, no, no!" She took the knife out of Q's hand with a sigh. "Lengthwise. Like this." She flipped the pepper around and cut a few pieces to show her.

Q rolled her eyes but copied her instructions.

Sabrina smirked. "You need lessons on being a girl."

"I thought you liked me the way I am."

She walked behind her and pressed a kiss to the back of Q's neck. "I *love* you the way you are."

Q's shoulders tensed and the knife froze in place, hovering over the vegetable. It'd been a week since Q's bad night with that jerk Dom. Sabrina had used the L-word dozens of times since then yet she still acted as if she didn't believe it. She'd known it would be hard to prove to her friend after what she'd put her through. All she could do now was keep at it, until she finally gave in and accepted her love.

A long sigh then Q said, "I know, beautiful."

Sabrina paused halfway to the fridge. She knew? A big grin stretched across her face. It was about time! Though they'd been acting like girlfriends, something was still missing. The last week had been the best they'd had since Jude left, but it wasn't perfect. Things were tense between them. They hadn't done anything kinky and she was beginning to crave it. She'd even bratted a bit last night, hoping Q's inner Domme would rise to the surface and deliver a smack-down. But it hadn't. Though moping less than before, Q was still unhappy. What would it take to get the old Q back?

Sabrina felt it too. An emptiness. Like a piece of them was missing. She had Q on her right but her left was gone. Jude. She still got choked up when she thought of him. His song had been on the radio a couple days ago and she'd had to pull over the car to cry.

She sighed and wiped her eyes. Damn onions. They had to force themselves to move on. At least now they had each other.

She threw some ingredients on the table then grabbed her mp3 player and docked it. Picking some quiet background music only took a few minutes, but she kept checking on Q anyway. The girl was next to helpless in the kitchen. It was both amusing and sad. Funny because Q needed adult supervision to attempt an omelet. Sad because Q's older brothers raised her through her teens – meaning that beer in her morning cereal had been common, whereas real food hadn't.

A knock at the door startled her. She turned to Q. "You expecting someone?"

Q shook her head. "It might be the neighbor looking for his cat again."

"Hmm. I'll get it. Keep stirring the onions." She left the kitchen but called over her shoulder, "Take them off in a minute though if I'm not back." At the door, she wiped her hands on her jeans then gripped the doorknob, swung it open, and gasped.

Six plus feet of masculine beauty stood in her doorway. He hooked his thumbs in his pockets and rocked back on his heels, his expression pained.

"Jude," she breathed. She couldn't move. Never in a million years had she expected him to show up on her doorstep.

"Hi." When she just stared, he pressed his lips together and gave her a tiny smile that spoke more of discomfort than humor.

Sabrina gave her head a little shake. Swallowing down the words that were dying to spill out was almost impossible. Her jaw worked. Saying, you bastard, where the fuck have you been, would not endear her to him.

He's here. But why?

"Um… come in. We're cooking." She backed out of the way. Then she couldn't resist it anymore. "If you left a toothbrush behind, it's long gone."

Those eyes of his, focused down on her. Had he even registered what she'd said?

He stepped closer, then tentatively reached out and took a lock of her hair between his fingers. The nearness, the scent of him – it sent some indefinable emotion spiraling down inside her. She should speak, slap him, do something.

When she didn't pull away, he played with her hair then released it. "God, I missed this," he whispered.

She blinked, opened her mouth then closed it again. "Look, whatever it is you want…" Tears brimmed in her eyes but she tensed, blinking to make them go away. "You can't just…"

So damn confusing…showing up like this. The possibilities confounded her. Was he truly back? Or just visiting? If she asked him bluntly if he was staying and he said no again, she would break. If she let him in, Q would think it too. And twice might shatter her friend. She couldn't let that happen.

"I can't just what?" He searched her face then straightened a little and took a breath. "I missed you. Both of you."

"Who is it, Sabrina?" Q asked from the kitchen.

But when he raised his head to reply, she put the flat of her hand on his chest. She looked directly at him, blinking back more stupid tears. She wanted to wrap her arms around his waist, lay her head against his chest, inhale his familiar scent, feel his heavy hands on her back…she wanted to stay like that forever. But she had to protect Q.

"Don't… Don't you hurt her. Please. Go away now if you're not staying. You don't know what this did. I won't have her hurt again –"

"Shh." For a second, he gently laid his finger across her lips. "I won't. I promise, Sabrina. I'm sorry." Regret surfaced in his eyes.

"Okay," she said softly then raised her voice. "Q. It's Jude."

A moment of silence then, "Ha, ha. Very funny."

Jude smiled. "You're not going to come say hi, brat?"

A loud clatter in the kitchen made Sabrina run in to check on Q. She stood, eyes wide, cooked onions around her on the floor. If she'd burned her bare feet she hadn't noticed. Sabrina went to the counter for a towel, when she turned around, Q was gone.

"What are you doing here?" she heard Q demand from the living room.

Sabrina dropped to the floor to clean up the mess.

"I need to talk to both of you," Jude answered.

After scooping the onions into the towel and tossing them in the garbage, she placed the pan into the sink then rushed back to Q and Jude. She came to a decision. No matter what Jude had said, she couldn't put her hands back in his – couldn't trust him that easily.

World War Three was about to break loose. She stood between them, but closer to Q – she knew her allegiance.

"Jude." Q sighed and pinched the bridge of her nose. "You can't just pop in like this. You don't know what it does to…" She paused. "Sabrina."

Sabrina tossed her an irritated look.

"I'm not just popping in," he said. He inhaled deeply then exhaled. "I want to take you two home."

"Home?" Sabrina snorted.

Q tilted her head, looking skeptical. "Home? What do you mean?"

He shrugged then stared at the floor. "Well. When I have one. Which I'm working on. And some contracting jobs." Lifting his head, he gave both of them a long look, his eyes pools of hope. "But none of that matters right now." His brow furrowed as he zeroed in on Q's neck.

Sabrina followed his gaze and saw it. A bruise, leftover from jerk face Dom, right next to her collarbone. Q's face turned pink as she placed her hand over it.

"Is there someone else?" he asked, his voice husky.

Q shook her head. "No. There's no one else, but…" She swallowed hard.

Sabrina jumped in to help. "I agree with Q," she said, stepping toward Jude, placing herself between him and Q. "I just got her put back together. It's been…difficult." She felt her voice start to choke up too. Oh god, and here she was trying to be strong for Q!

"I messed up," he blurted, frowning. "I've been miserable without my girls." He took a step toward them. "I missed you so much. I didn't realize how much you meant to me until…" His voice trailed off with a funny sound. And were his eyes watering?

Sabrina looked at Q. "If he starts singing *Big Yellow Taxi*, I'm gonna faint."

But Q only had eyes for Jude. Not googly ones – guarded but hopeful. Maybe…maybe, could she hope too?

"I quit school," he said. "I made Fredrick an offer on the house."

Kerthunk. That statement hit home. He meant this then? He quit school. Can't go back after that, right? She felt her body lean a little, toward Jude.

Q said nothing. She wished she was telepathic and could know what she was thinking. Taking her lead, she just stared.

Jude shifted. He lunged and captured Q's hand, ignoring her gasp. Then he grabbed Sabrina's. Oh fuck. She closed her eyes, enjoying the rough feel of his skin against hers. She felt the sting of rising tears.

His grip tightened, like he didn't want to give them a chance to get away. Like he was desperate.

Like I am.

"I know I've been an ass, but I just couldn't respond to your emails. I knew if I did, I wouldn't be able to let go like I needed to. Or thought I needed to. It was supposed to be just for the summer, but I can't get the two of you out of my head. Could we try again? See if we can make things long-term?"

Sabrina couldn't hold back big sobbing tears. "I missed you so much." Her lip trembled.

He beamed at her, then turned, bent his head as if to meet Q's downcast gaze. "Q? Will you give us a chance?"

"You quit med school because of us? Are you an idiot?" When Q's eyes came back up, an angry storm brewed. "And you might have won Sabrina back fast, but I'm a harder sell."

"I never wanted to go to med school, Q. Quitting was about me, not about you two. If anything, you made me realize that being happy and being successful don't have to be mutually exclusive. The fact that I've been miserable without you both – that I realized I made a huge mistake by leaving like I did – well, I guess that's about me too. Would you even think of taking me back? How can I prove to you that I'm a mess without you two? I think about you day and night. I can't eat. I feel like there's a hole where my heart was."

Q's jaw clenched and she wiped tears away with a gesture of annoyance. Sabrina waited. Jude sucked in a breath. Finally, she nodded. "If you break Sabrina's heart again, I'll do worse than knee you in the balls."

His joyful grin made Sabrina laugh, even while tears rolled down her cheeks. He was back! In a startling move, he yanked them both closer then dipped, pushed forward, and threw each of them over a shoulder. Sabrina screeched.

"Jude!" Q yelled and smacked his back.

He lumbered into the first bedroom on the right – Q's room though they'd both been sleeping there since she had the queen-size bed. He lowered them onto the mattress then followed them down, landing half on top of them.

"Ow!" Sabrina rubbed her arm where someone's knee had landed. They settled, wriggling, untangling their bodies. "That was not so graceful," she said with a scowl.

Jude maneuvered them, one on each side, until they were tucked under his arms. "Quiet, brat two. I'm in my happy place." He closed his eyes, inhaled a breath of each of their hair then did a double take at Q. "What on earth did you do to your hair?"

She glanced up at him then mumbled, "Long story."

"She left in the tongue piercing." Sabrina sighed happily. "I bugged her to take out the other rings in her face, though." She rested her head against his warm chest, smiling blissfully at his rumbling laugh.

"Mm," he purred, kissing Q's head. "I want to hear every detail of your lives while I was gone. But first…"

He kissed each of them long and deep, reminding Sabrina exactly why things hadn't been the same without him.

Now she had her right and her left – and she was whole again.

"We're going to make this work." She sat up and wrapped her arms around him, just below the shoulder. Then she laid her cheek on his shirt sleeve and said softly, but with determination, "We will. Or I'll send my ghost after you."

Epilogue

3 months later

Q officially loved February. Not that she liked winter – snow was the mortal enemy of a woman who was perpetually cold. But this one was the best. It had proven so cold that none of them strayed far from home unless they had to. Instead of dragging Q out skating and skiing, they spent time goofing around in bed – not just having mind-blowing sex, but cuddling, talking, and watching old movies. There was nothing worse than company showing up, because everyone had to get decent. However, their landlord, Fredrick, had told Jude that he was welcome to keep the girls as naked as he liked when he was over to collect the rent. Jude had yet to take him up on the offer.

They'd been lucky to get the house back. Fredrick had managed to rent it out to a young couple the week Jude had moved out, but their friendly neighborhood ghost had shown up one night. The couple had not only moved out, they'd demanded all of their money back.

By the time Jude had asked to rent it again, Fred was just happy to have it taken off of his hands. He'd set up a rent-to-own agreement with Jude then added Sabrina and Q when they'd moved in at the end of December. With recommendations from Fredrick, Jude had started a small home renovation company, and had a few contracts already. Between the three of them, they were doing well for themselves.

The worst, though, was waiting for him to get home from work. He'd been at their disposal over the summer, and they weren't used to sharing him with a j-o-b. Juggling schedules around the three of them working full-time was tricky, but they were getting the hang of it.

In bed, they waited for him with a monster movie cued up and a bowl of popcorn at the ready. For now they were snuggling. Q was having trouble warming up – grocery shopping in the slush today had been the worst. Her only hope was that cuddling under the duvet with her best girl might thaw her out before spring.

They'd showered together when they'd gotten home, and had played a little, but they were under orders that things weren't to get too involved in Jude's absence. He'd also ordered them to dress in matching lingerie. Since it was freezing in the old, still mostly empty house, she was hoping he meant the matching flannel PJ bottoms they'd gotten from him for Christmas. She'd bossed Sabrina into going along with the idea. If she was wrong, they'd be in for it when Jude got home.

Her chest was currently Sabrina's pillow. The faint floral scent of her girlfriend's freshly-washed hair drifted up to her. Running her fingers through her blonde mane was heavenly. Sabrina didn't seem to mind either – but her sighs of enjoyment were making Q think of more naughty pursuits. She snaked her hand down and stroked Sabrina's collar bone, pleased when the simple act made her lover's breath hitch. As she slid her hand farther toward her breast, Sabrina stayed very still.

"Do you want me to stop?" Which would she choose? Sabrina hated being frustrated, and she was probably still horny after their shower activities.

"Mmm... no. But when's Jude getting home? I can't handle this much longer."

Q chuckled. "Such a spoiled girl! Do you think Jude would like it if he knew you were just waiting for him to get home so you could have some cock?"

A sulky whine escaped Sabrina as Q tugged gently at her hardened nipple. She looked up at Q, giving her the pitiful big brown eyes. "Nooooo, Q. I'm ready enough. Please?"

Q ignored her pleas, eventually succeeding in making her writhe under her hands. "What's the matter, my girl? Do you want something?"

"Yes, but Jude told us no."

"I won't tell if you don't." Q flashed her a wicked smile.

Her forehead wrinkled in consternation.

"Hmm, sounds like my little brat needs a spanking," Jude drawled from the doorway.

She gasped and yanked her hands from Sabrina as if she'd burst into flames. "I was just messing with her. I wouldn't have done it."

"Mm-hm." He sauntered into the room, and arched a brow at them. "That doesn't look like what I told you to wear, either."

"You don't think we look sexy in tank tops? We're braless and everything." She'd guessed wrong and scrambled for more excuses but came up with nothing.

"You did buy us these pajamas, Sir. It's a waste of money if we never wear them. And poor Q! I thought she was going to die from hypothermia. She was blue and everything! Sir." Sabrina – the girl thought up escape routes faster than a ninja did back flips. "Oh, and she made me do it."

Jude pinched the bridge of his nose, as if he was battling a two-brat-sized headache. "Passport."

They both gaped at him for a moment, and then burst into peals of laughter.

Sabrina scoffed. "You can't safeword flannel! That's ridiculous!"

"No. My two naughty little subs are ridiculous," he growled, trying to keep the amusement out of his voice. His shoulders started to shake, then Sabrina giggled and all was lost. Laughing, Jude toppled onto the bed and gathered them to him. After an evil chuckle he leaped on them – one, then the other, tickling them until they were screeching and shaking, and batting away his hands.

When they'd finally all calmed, he slipped off the bed and folded his arms. "Kneel where you are."

The two women knelt, being at least that well-trained – or at least faking it for the moment. Q hoped he didn't have any intention of following through with the spanking threat, because if he did she'd need to make a run for it with legs that were quickly falling asleep.

Jude cleared his throat, and stared at the ground. Was big bad Dom nervous? "We've been living together for awhile now, and I've been thinking."

In her chest, Q's heart tripped over itself. Oh, bad. No, no, no... things had been going so well!

"Sabrina," he looked at her as she eyed him curiously, "Q and I have discussed this." Her heart slowed to an even beat as she let out a breath in relief. "As much as it could have been confusing to all of us to share you as a submissive, it seems to be working really well." He stopped, and drew Q to her feet to stand with him. "Are you enjoying having two Doms?"

She lowered her eyes shyly, and Q admired the line of her body and the submission in her posture. Lately she'd had the overwhelming desire to mark this woman as hers. Although she and Jude had talked about this, they hadn't decided when to do it. It seemed Jude had made that decision. Being the uber Dom in this relationship was definitely making him cockier.

He went on. "You've told us that you weren't against the idea of being collared. Do you still feel that way?"

Sabrina's gaze flashed up to them then back down. Her face turned a lovely pink. "Yes," she breathed.

"To Q and me, collaring is as serious a commitment as marriage. We don't want you to make this decision lightly. If you need time to think, we understand completely."

Q glanced at Jude – from the tension in his stance, he seemed to be anxious too.

Sabrina worried at her lip, looking uncertain but adorable.

"You need some time?" Q smiled.

She smiled. "No. I love you both. I want this as much as you do. But…" Q's chest tightened – she hated the word but. "I just wish you would have told me ahead of time. I feel terribly underdressed."

They grinned at her.

"Do you want to get changed first?" Jude asked.

"No, I suppose pajama bottoms with bunnies on them will do."

"I told Q that both of you were supposed to be in something sexy, so don't blame me."

"It's easy enough to fix." Q tackled Sabrina to the bed and the girl protested as she stripped off her pajamas. As the line of the waistband slid past her hips, she soaked up the lovely image. Stripping Sabrina was one of her favorite hobbies – it didn't matter whether it was PJs or fancy lingerie. Her naked girl. *Mmm.* "There. Now she's perfect."

"Not exactly what I had in mind," Sabrina grumbled, but she knelt on the bed again.

Jude smiled at Q then fished in his jeans pocket, pulling out a shiny palm full of gold. He picked up the necklace and untangled it. "It came in a box, but that didn't fit in my pocket."

It was the collar they'd picked out together at the jeweler's – with a heart-shaped lock that held the ends of a pretty chain together. Each half of the heart lock was a different tone of gold.

Jude let Sabrina see the lock. "The two colors are to remind you that you have more responsibility than most submissives, Sabrina. Think you can handle us?"

"Yes, Sir. Yes, Q. It's beautiful. I'll try to be good, but you'll have to keep being patient with me. Sometimes my mouth runs off on me, and I don't mean to be bratty, it just kind of happens." She trailed off, tears forming in her eyes. "I just can't believe you both still want me."

When she paused for a breath, as if lining up more words to say, Jude silenced her with a look. His expression warmed. "I love you, Sabrina. Just as you are."

Sabrina's mouth fell open a little and she blushed a deep red. She dropped her gaze and stared at her knees.

He loved Sabrina! Q wanted to clap her hands and jump around the room, but that'd be kind of a mood-kill. After Jude handed her one end of the chain, they looped it around Sabrina's neck and clicked the lock shut at the front. The necklace looked elegant against the bare skin of her neck. Q grinned, almost dizzy with satisfaction. A portion of her inner caveman escaped. This was *her* woman. Well... hers and Jude's.

"And you know I love you, little girl." Q's voice quavered a little, and she leaned in to place a chaste kiss on her Sabrina's lips. "I have for a long time, even when you weren't ready to hear it."

Sabrina squealed and threw her arms around Q's neck then dragged her down onto the bed in an enthusiastic hug. She kissed Q hard, only releasing her when they were both sniffling. As they wiped the tears from their eyes, Jude stroked their hair, running his fingers gently through the tangles.

After giving them both a last pat, Jude caught Sabrina's eye. "I'm now going to give you your first order as my collared submissive, Sabrina. You up for it?"

Her eyes narrowed. "If your first order is to tell me to make you a sammich, I'm going to make Dom-fondue out of you."

"Strip Q." He crossed his arms, waiting.

The girls stared at each other, and an evil grin spread across Sabrina's face. Q didn't argue. As her girl slid her pajama bottoms down, Q caught her by the hair. "Don't forget what end of the crop you're on, beautiful." Sabrina gave her doe eyes, and Q had to fight off going into predator mode. What a pity it was sub-time and not Dom-time. She released her grip on her hair.

When she was naked, Sabrina's hands hovered over her skin, only alighting when she reached Q's nipple rings. She toyed with them for a minute and Q was gasping for breath before Jude stopped her.

"Sabrina, bed. Q, floor."

They eyed him curiously, but followed orders. The kneel that Sir preferred them to use was different from the one Nico had taught her, so she was still working on making it smooth. At least it was starting to feel familiar – even comforting. She loved knowing how to please him. Waiting, she wondered what his devious plans might be.

Jude walked back to the doorway and picked up a bag that had been on the floor around the corner. He put it on the antique dresser they used for both their lingerie and his t-shirts. The pliers he pulled from the bag shocked her. Q shot a glance at Sabrina, who looked like she too was on the verge of safewording.

Her stomach dropped as a second pair of pliers joined the first, followed by something metal. He walked slowly to her, his expression ominous.

"I've been thinking, Q." One of the pairs of pliers opened and clicked closed in his hand, like a tiny snapping alligator.

"Y-yes, Sir?" Why was she worrying? Jude wouldn't really hurt her. Not more than she could handle. If he wanted to play with pliers, she'd be brave. She felt the soles of her feet break out in a sweat. Now *that* was attractive.

"Are you more of a sub or a Domme?" He raised a brow.

The change of subject startled her but she made herself think. Did he want the truth, or a comforting lie? She opted for truth. "I'm not sure, Sir. I used to think I was a Domme. Eventually, I realized that I'm also a high-maintenance submissive. It seems to depend on the person I'm with, more than anything. Like I love being Sabrina's Domme, but I don't think I could be yours."

His eyebrows shot up. He barked a laugh. "Yes, I doubt very much that you could dom me, Q. Which do you prefer?"

She shrugged. "I love both. I know I'm too much work for most Doms, but there's this guy I met that gets it just right." Would he accept that answer? She glanced at the pliers, then away, trying to ignore them. In her mouth she played with her tongue ring, trying to distract herself.

"Every time you play with that piercing it makes me want to fuck your mouth." He groaned.

"She always had that kind of mouth, Sir. The tongue ring just makes it worse," Sabrina pointed out.

"Fair enough. I'm sure men on the street fantasize about that mouth. But I'm trying to have a serious conversation here, beautiful."

Trying to hide her blush, Q ducked her head.

"As I was saying," Jude continued. "Do you consider me your Dom, Q, or just a Dom that you play with?"

"My Dom, Sir." She was shocked that he had to ask. Had he honestly wondered about her answer, or was he just making her say it aloud?

"Good." From his closed hand he pulled a thick metal chain that looked like a stylized dog choker. "I'm not giving you a choice Q. You're mine. You will wear this mark of my ownership because it pleases me." He put the chain around her neck. Ice cold metal against her skin stiffened her nipples. Maybe it wasn't just the cold. Pliers fiddled at her throat, metal scraped on metal, and it was done.

Hooking a finger through the small O-ring at the front, he pulled her to her feet. He lowered his face until it was inches from hers. "Mine," he growled. "Do you understand?"

"Yes," she whispered. Hot and cold, she shivered, stroking his collar with trembling fingers. She loved this man. The last of her internal defenses collapsed. A quiet peace stole over her, and she felt both safe and free. "I'm yours."

He took her mouth in a fierce kiss. Her legs trembled. Just as her knees buckled, he caught her around the waist. "What's your real first name, Q?"

"It's Q?" she said hopefully. Sabrina snickered and she shot her a dirty look.

He laughed, brushing his lips against hers. "No. What did your parents call you?"

She paused, looking pained. "I suppose it's about time I told you." She sighed. "It's my mother's maiden name."

"Yes?" prompted Jude.

"It's... Quimby."

He paused, looking thoughtful. "That's not so bad. I don't know what the big deal is."

"Think of possible short forms."

The last penny dropped into place and he winced. "Yeah... I hadn't thought of that."

She rolled her eyes. "So you understand why I don't make fun of your name. But why ask now?"

He gazed down at her. "Because I wanted to say this right. I love you, Quimby."

Did he just…? She lit up inside, as though someone had detonated a fireworks factory. He loved her? She grinned at him like a silly idiot, all pretense of reserve dropped.

"I love you, Sir. But please, just Q?"

"Okay. I love you, Q."

"Woooo-hoooo!" Sabrina crowed, jumping around on the mattress in her enthusiasm. Q had the urge to join her.

***

"So, now that's done, I have two sweet women to warm me in bed." Jude gathered the pillows up and threw himself down on the bed, then beckoned, grinning. "Come warm me."

"How romantic. So I'm a hot water bottle?" Sabrina seemed to be trying for pouting angriness but to Jude it came off as annoyed sex doll. "Have I just sold my soul to the Devil?"

"Probably." He patted the right hand side next to him. "Here."

Sighing, she slid in close. He almost sighed, himself, when she snuggled up and rested her head on his chest. His palm found the upper curve of her ass.

Yes, this was his dream. On hands and knees, Q crawled in close. Her hair had regrown quickly, and it swayed across – long enough to block his view of her cleavage under her tank top.

"Room for me?" she asked.

"Always." He reached and ran his hand along the front edge of the collar, watching the change in her eyes. For Q it meant something just a little deeper than it did for Sabrina. He didn't mind. It was their differences that drew him to them, that made this relationship work. "Come on, beautiful, lay down with us."

"Beautiful?" Smiling, she leaned in to kiss him. "Thank you."

"I've figured it out." Sabrina popped her head up. "You want us to help pay the rent."

He snorted. "Yes, that too. It's not for the hot sex. You've barely scratched the surface, Jersey girl. Don't you know all the perks Doms get from collared subs?"

Her eyes went wide. "What?"

To his surprise and amusement, Q followed his lead. "He's right. Maybe I should have told you all the details."

In mock astonishment he went on, "You didn't know? I get to tattoo my name on your asses, get you both pregnant and then take you behind the woodshed on Fridays to beat you."

Before Sabrina could blurt out some smartass reply, there was a crash that sounded like something breaking downstairs.

"Oh my god!" As if she were on springs, Sabrina shot upright into a sitting position. "Maybe Grace is back!"

He grabbed for her but his hand met emptiness – she'd hopped off the bed already.

In her fleecy pajamas and skimpy top, she did a fast tiptoe to the door then listened with her head cocked to one side. "I think it's in the kinky sitting room."

"Sabrina!" he and Q cried in unison.

"Shh! Quiet, you'll scare her," she answered then she went through the door.

By the time they had caught up, Sabrina was poised outside the sitting room door. Reflections of streetlight revealed her warrior stance – umbrella raised in one hand and her camera in the other.

"Sweetheart, you're joking." Jude smiled indulgently. "An umbrella? Is it a patented anti-ghost umbrella?" Nothing said Sabrina more than a ridiculous weapon on a ghost hunt. He wrapped his arms around her and held her back. More noises from within made it clear something was moving inside.

He whispered in her ear. "You will wait here. If it's not a ghost it may be an intruder."

Though she scowled, she offered him the umbrella. It was all he could do not to laugh. But he took the umbrella and stealthily opened the door. It swung in silently.

Just as he was about to take a step, they both grabbed an arm. "What?" he hissed.

Q glanced at Sabrina then at him. "You should let us come as back-up."

"No. You're staying here. I'm going in." That they cared gave him a warm and glowy feeling. But he wasn't caving on this one.

Sabrina scowled. "Keep the umbrella, at least, if you're gonna be so stupid to go alone."

He growled quietly. "Stay, both of you."

Despite mutinous glares, both of them waited. He sneaked through the door, and after listening a while and only hearing the flap of cloth, he switched on the light. A freezing cold breeze wafted past. By the window, the curtain snapped and curled out as the wind gusted in and caught hold of it. A vase lay smashed nearby, fractured pieces strewn on the floor. Nothing else moved.

"It's okay, you can come in. Someone left the window open." He stepped aside and laid the umbrella on the floor. When Sabrina tentatively came up and grasped his hand, he added, "I've cleared the room of hostiles with my automatic rocket-launching umbrella."

She whacked his stomach with the flat of her other hand. "Very funny." It only made him grin more.

"It might have been a ghost."

"Sure." Q grabbed her attacking hand then looked at him. "Did the curtain knock a vase over?"

"I think so."

"Supposition and circumstantial evidence," Sabrina muttered. "I should go get my equipment. Just because you see a curtain, doesn't mean a thing. Who opened the window?" Though he saw Q open her mouth to reply, Sabrina rambled on regardless. "Not me. Maybe we need another a séance even? I mean just because the last one –"

He put his hand over her mouth. "Shh. No more."

When she poked her tongue at his hand then closed her teeth over a fold of skin on his palm he addressed Q. "Get the ball gag please and wrist cuffs."

Sabrina's muffled shriek of protest made him smile and hug her to him as Q ran to the toy chest. "Naughty little sub."

By the time Q had returned with ball gag and wrist cuffs in hand, he'd wrestled Sabrina to the floor into a kneeling position and had both her wrists in one hand and her nose to the carpet. Though he'd freed her mouth she did nothing except pant and strain at his grip.

He knelt beside her. "Do I have a second sub who likes wrestling?"

She whined and squirmed.

"Ah. I see I do. Do we need the gag?"

"I'll be good, Sir." Then she peeked out the corner of her eye. "No séance?"

"Let me think." He ran his hand over her body while he did so. He didn't really want to suppress Sabrina's crazy way of looking at the world. "Here's what we'll do. Every time you have a séance or any other ghost-related activity, we get you as a pet for the night. Understood?"

By now she was squirming at his touch, but he kept her wrists tight under his hand. "Understood?"

She looked up at Q. "Help me?"

Q only laughed softly. "I don't think so. The more séances the better, little girl, if we get a pet Sabrina as the result."

Sabrina's whimper was pitiful enough to make his balls tighten. There was something excruciatingly arousing about a woman giving in to the inevitable, to submitting.

Then she added, with her nose still an inch from the carpet, "This Tuesday, eight PM…and then three AM too if we get no spirits contacting us." She swallowed. "And no butt plug tails."

He found himself trembling, holding it in, his face contorted, but no use, he cracked up. He let her go and rolled onto the rug laughing in half-choked guffaws before he broke out howling. "Oh, god, Sabrina… That's…"

They stared at him, shocked. Between Sabrina's matter-of-fact negotiation, and their expressions, he fell apart laughing again.

"What?" she asked, completely dumbfounded.

He shook his head. "Nothing." Gazing at them in awe, he wondered how he got so lucky. "I just love you. Both of you."

A naughty smirk his only warning, they tackled him, knocking him down on his back. Warm bodies. Laughter. For once, he let them have it their way and they tumbled over him and pretended to hold him down with their weight. When they stopped wrestling, they lay with their heads on his chest, their hair spread across, tickling and soft on his skin. He patted their backsides and sighed. Luxurious. Feeling a woman's ass must be the cure for all ills.

Sabrina shifted to look up at him, and waggled her eyebrows. "I thought you were tying me up and having your wicked way with me."

"Uh-uh. Right now, I'm lying here staring at the ceiling."

Q snorted derisively. "Lazy Dom."

He smiled and squeezed them close. "Shh. As long as I'm with my two girls, I'm happy."

As they snuggled into him, he sighed with contentment. No one had told him that sometimes in fairy tales the guy gets two princesses and the princesses are in love with each other and him. But if anyone came by to repossess their happily ever after, he hoped they had a safeword. Because no one should fuck with true love.

Acknowledgements

Cari, Sorcha, and Leia would like to give a special shout-out to their fabulous beta readers; MJ, Bianca Sarble, Casea Major, and Nerine Dorman.

Also, thank you to our fans who keep us going even on the hardest days. We couldn't do this without you guys.

About the Authors

Sorcha Black

Sorcha writes fantasy about women who are too busy fighting, suffering, loving, and generally getting shit done to think of themselves as heroes.

In her real life, she is married to a lazy but well-loved man and has a shoe full of children. She does her best writing on scraps of paper at red lights.

Find her at: www.sorchablack.blogspot.com

Leia Shaw

Leia Shaw is the bestselling author of the paranormal romance series, *Shadows of Destiny*. Thinking up fae politics, plotting dragon power games, and calculating how fast werewolves can change forms has given her a way to express those dark places in her mind. More recently, she's branched out into the erotic world and has written two humorous but heartwarming contemporary BDSM romances, 31 Flavors and The Dom with a Safeword.

Leia lives in New England with her husband and two kids. Though she will go to her grave denying it, her husband insists she would be thrilled if he suddenly sprouted fangs.

Find her at:
www.leiashaw.com
www.facebook.com/leiashaw
Twitter @LeiaShaw

Cari Silverwood

Cari Silverwood writes the way the world should be - dangerous and sexy with bullets piercing the darkness and lovers wrenched close by ropes. When you need escape, when you need that rough lover to bring you to your knees, here you will find stories to singe your fingers. The taste of adventure, the tang of BDSM, the burn of fantasy run wild. Brace yourselves, if you dare to read.

And...in this real world, she has a lovely family in Australia, with the prerequisite teenager who dwells in the dark bedroom catacombs…a husband who raises eyebrows when he catches glimpses of what she writes, and a furry menagerie of other animals barking, meowing, and swimming about the place.

Find her at: carisilverwood.com

Also by Leia Shaw and Cari Silverwood...

31 Flavors of Kink (a true BDSM story)

There are some things in life you have to try before you know how they will affect you. After five years of awful sex, I was ready. Bondage and spanking had always featured in my fantasies, and one day, I convinced my husband to try them. That day was a turning point.

Ice cream comes in many flavors and that's us too -- not vanilla, maybe not Rocky Road either. We can be a combination or make up our own and no one has the right to judge us. But there will always be one question that tears at my soul: Will my husband, Nick, ever be happy with what I crave?

"Come here."

His voice, low and full of authority, slides through me like a cold shiver. My breath hitches as I glide silently over our office carpet.

"On your knees."

I immediately drop. Acutely conscious of my nudity, I sit with my ass resting on my heels and my hands on the curve of my upper thighs.

"Do you know why you are being punished?"

A lump of anticipation lodges in my throat. I keep my eyes downcast and nod.

"Good. Now, I'm going to tie you to the desk, spank you, and stuff you with the vibrator. And you're not to come without my permission, do you understand?"

My stomach lurches, and I'm soaked with arousal. I can't trust my voice, so I nod again.

"Answer me."

I clear my throat and croak a shaky, "Y-yes, sir."

"Stand up and bend over the desk."

My knees tremble. I can barely hold my weight as I walk to the desk. A thin rope dangles from his hands. I dare to look in his eyes. They remain impassive, foreboding. I'm a prisoner in the shadow of my executioner. Can I do this?

His brows rise a fraction of an inch. "Go on."

I steel myself and bend over the desk. The glass top is like ice on my naked breasts. My breath quickens as he coolly and effectively ties my ankles to the desk legs, then my wrists behind my back. I twist my hands, checking the tightness. No give, at all. Suddenly I feel vulnerable. Too open, too exposed.

I notice the wooden paddle on the desk only when he reaches for it. I gasp. From fear or anticipation, I'm not sure. He moves away so I can no longer see him.

From behind me, I hear, "Count, Sidney."

I squeeze my eyes shut, and the paddle whistles through the air –

Beep. Beep. Beep.

I wake with a start, flushed and wet. A dream. I exhale a deep breath, then slam my hand on the Snooze button. Nick stirs beside me, his body heating me through the blankets. My dream comes back full force, an assault on my already overeager libido.

Nick. His eyes stern, his lips turned down in a disapproving frown. The rope, the paddle… *Oh*. I can't stop a sharp inhalation.

The idea is laughable. Nick wielding a paddle? He's more likely to cross-dress and pierce his nipples than mercilessly paddle my ass. Nick is the nicest man I've ever met. It's why I married him.

I sigh in frustration and push my fantasies away. The dog jumps at the door. Nick rolls over. His voice is groggy. "Honey. The dog wants to go out."

"I know."

Welcome to real life.

11452332R00168

Printed in Germany
by Amazon Distribution
GmbH, Leipzig